TRAIL *of the* BRAVE

Books by Susan May Warren

Montana Rescue

Wild Montana Skies

Rescue Me

A Matter of Trust

Troubled Waters

Storm Front

Wait for Me

Global Search and Rescue

The Way of the Brave

The Heart of a Hero

The Price of Valor

Sky King Ranch

Sunrise

Sunburst

Sundown

Alaska Air One Rescue

One Last Shot

One Last Chance

One Last Promise

One Last Stand

Call of the Wild

Track of Courage

Scent of Hope

Trail of the Brave

CALL OF THE WILD • 3

TRAIL *of the* BRAVE

SUSAN MAY WARREN

Revell
a division of Baker Publishing Group
Grand Rapids, Michigan

Published by Revell
a division of Baker Publishing Group
Grand Rapids, Michigan
RevellBooks.com

Printed in the United States of America

Library of Congress Cataloging-in-Publication Data
Names: Warren, Susan May, 1966– author
Title: Trail of the brave / Susan May Warren.
Description: Grand Rapids, Michigan : Revell, a division of Baker Publishing Group, 2026. | Series: Call of the wild ; 3
Identifiers: LCCN 2026004057 | ISBN 9780800746070 paperback | ISBN 9781493455645 ebook
Subjects: LCGFT: Christian fiction | Thrillers (Fiction) | Romance fiction | Novels
Classification: LCC PS3623.A865 T73 2026
LC record available at https://lccn.loc.gov/2026004057

Cover design by Mumtaz Mustafa

Baker Publishing Group publications use paper produced from sustainable forestry practices and postconsumer waste whenever possible.

26 27 28 29 30 31 32 7 6 5 4 3 2 1

Soli Deo Gloria

1

SO, THIS WAS a disaster.

Stormi White watched her Malamute-Labrador mix run his third circle around the bloody trail from the raw steak she'd dragged across the snow in the backyard of her veterinarian compound. Her chest tightened. When the local SAR team leader, pilot Moose Mulligan, called for that progress report—and he *would* call—she'd have nothing but another failed training session. Her hopes of joining the team were dwindling with every useless steak.

Because clearly she had no clue what she was doing.

"It's not going well, is it?"

And of course her famous life-coach sister Aspen read her mind, all the way through the cell phone airwaves to her cute bungalow in Brainerd, Minnesota. Aspen's daily "Are you sure living in remote Alaska is a good idea?" phone call.

Yes. Usually.

Aspen breathed hard as she power walked on her treadmill in her DIY remodeled house.

"Not great, no." Stormi turned to her dog. "Come on, Rome."

She tugged the rope, dragging the steak in a wide arc around black spruce trees. "It's right there."

Rome stood in the snow, his ears perked. Moose had once said the dog reminded him of Balto. Maybe, but the famous sled dog had been a nearly all-black Siberian husky. Rome's fur scattered hints of gold around his ears and snout, and he had plenty of white from his Malamute sire. So, sure, Rome had the heart of a sled dog, but the Labrador in him also made him funny, distractible, and currently, a disaster.

"I think you need to give up and admit he's just a lap dog, Storm," Aspen said. "I mean, c'mon—you tried to make him a sled dog. Now, you're trying to resurrect his sense of smell?"

"Alaska Air One rescue needs a tracking dog. Rome used to be a K9. And it's been three years since he's had COVID. Certainly his sense of smell has come back."

"I dunno. One of my clients had COVID a few years back and she still can't smell anything. I can't believe dogs can get COVID."

"Well, they can, and he did, but . . . aw, poor guy doesn't know what his purpose is."

Case in point—instead of following the obvious scent trail, Rome bounded toward the tree line where ptarmigan tracks crisscrossed the snow. He held his nose high yet was completely confused.

Behind her, her misfit group of wannabe sled dogs erupted in noise, barking, braying, jumping in the fence of their enclosure.

"What's going on?" A beep on Aspen's end, and then her voice came easier, so maybe she finished her five-mile workout.

"The kids are probably jealous of the raw beef trail I left in the snow. And, of course, because I'm brilliant, I might even attract a bear out of hibernation for a stroll by White Vet Services." She dragged the meat toward the big barn that housed her vet clinic. "So, that'll be exciting."

"Don't make me come out there. You know you could always come back and work with Dad—"

"Not a lot of mushers in Brainerd."

Stormi sat on the stoop of her clinic, watching the sun set against the far Alaska Range, a blaze of fire on the horizon. If she waited, maybe the northern lights would ribbon across the sky.

"What you should be doing is packing up and heading back to Anchorage. You had a good gig going there."

"As an assistant to the vet. I'm good at what I do, and I specialize in sled dogs. I like having my own practice—"

"At the far end of the earth!"

"I like it here. It's quiet." Sort of. She glanced at her dogs.

Silence pulsed on the other end of the phone.

"Listen," Stormi said, "it's only ten miles from Copper Mountain. I'm not going to get buried in a snowdrift."

"Is that a joke? Because you know people get buried in avalanches up there."

"Yes, it's a joke. Calm down, Aspen."

"Maybe Ridge should come up—"

"Sheesh. I'm fine. I don't need Mr. Awesome coming up here to babysit me, although if he does, tell him to bring me a pie from the Skylight Diner."

"You're hilarious."

"Besides, this is where I need to be if I want to really learn how to mush. I need the practice if I want to run the Iditarod."

More silence.

"What?"

"I just think . . . Stormi, I read the news. Wilder Frost is missing. Probably dead."

Her mouth opened, closed, her eyes burning just a little. "You don't pull your punches, do you?"

"I'm sorry—it's a tragedy for sure. But maybe it's a sign. I mean, just because Dad dreamed of running the Iditarod doesn't mean you have to."

Rome had turned and started barking as if to say, *Why are we out here if we're not going to play?*

Good question. "I gotta run. Listen, I know what the news says, but . . . Wilder's a survivor. I don't believe he's dead."

"You barely know the man."

"I know him enough."

"An autographed picture on your wall and a collection of news articles does not mean you know him."

Ouch. "I *do* know him, Pen. I've helped him with his dogs for over a year now. He's . . ."

"Not invincible. And, if he is still alive, probably grieving his wife, and not to mention he's eight years older than you."

"This is so fun. I'm hanging up now."

"Stormi!"

"I'll try not to get mauled or buried in a snowpack or, I dunno, trampled by reindeer before our next oh so encouraging call."

"I'm just trying to help—"

"Love you too." Stormi ended the call and looked at Rome. "Training is over." She trudged through knee-deep snow back to her home, carrying the meat. She'd stew it for the dogs' dinner. Rome ran after her, still barking.

"I know, buddy. But if you can't smell a juicy ribeye, I don't see how you're going to figure out how to track down lost hikers." She opened the door, set the meat inside, then closed it and knelt in front of the dog.

Fine, more than once when the wind rattled through her cabin door, she considered throwing in the towel on her current wild idea. *Ideas.* Plural. Move to Copper Mountain, train her dogs to run in a straight line, take over Anuk Swenson's vet clinic, join the local SAR team . . . Okay, maybe she was spreading herself a little thin, but sheesh. Everybody could calm down. She knew what she was doing.

Mostly.

Poor Rome. She should probably face it. Despite her efforts, he would never be a sled dog. His personality was too wild to fit in with the rest of the ragtag team. And, apparently, she wasn't a great vet, either, because she hadn't been able to restore his sense of smell.

Which left him as . . . well, what Aspen said. An oversized lap dog?

Rome leaned his head into her hand as she rubbed his ear. Made a small whining sound. "I love you too, pal," she said and got up.

Her breath formed white puffs in air so cold, it burned her lungs. The wind carried the scent of an upcoming blizzard. The third blizzard in as many weeks.

Which meant that anyone out there probably wasn't coming home . . .

No. Wilder Frost, legendary musher, Iditarod finisher, and local hero, had to be alive . . .

Her radio crackled against her hip. "Stormi, you copy?" Deke Starr, local sheriff.

She fumbled for the handset with mittened fingers. "This is Stormi. Go ahead, Deke."

"Winter flew over your area earlier and reported a car in the ditch on Copper Creek Road. Sedan, dark color. Can you check it out while we send the emergency team?"

"Where exactly?"

"Mile marker forty-seven. Probably tourists who got stuck trying to get up to the ski hill."

She knew the type—city folks who ignored weather warnings and drove rental cars into, as Aspen would call it, the far end of the earth. "I'm on it. ETA about fifteen minutes."

"Copy that. Be careful out there. Weather's turning ugly fast."

As if in warning, wind whistled through the boughs overhead. She glanced at Rome. "Wanna go for a ride?"

Rome barked and ran beside her as she headed toward her truck. He clambered into the front seat, wagging his tail. The engine turned over with a reluctant groan, fuel thick in the cold. Frigid air blasted from vents until the motor warmed.

Too long out in these elements and a person without the right gear could freeze to death.

She turned her defrost on high to clear the ice crystals from her windshield as she pulled out of her clinic area.

Her truck barely fit down the snowy path to Copper Creek Road, but once she turned onto the main road, it opened up. Copper Creek Valley spread below—a white expanse broken by dark lines of cottonwood and willow along the half-frozen streambed.

Her studded tires bit into the surface of the icy pavement, four-wheel drive engaged for the steeper sections. Mile marker forty-seven sat at the bottom of a long curve where the road followed the creek.

She almost missed the car—just the dark outline of a roof above a snowbank where the vehicle had plowed nose-first into a cluster of young birch trees.

She left her emergency kit in the back while she got out and grabbed her shovel. Rome jumped out after her, barking.

"Yeah, I see it." The passenger side of the sedan was buried to its windows, but tracks surrounded the car—boot prints leading away from the driver's side.

She followed the prints with her flashlight beam. They led about fifty yards down the road, then cut off into the forest to the north. Maybe the driver had gone hunting for help.

A sound made her freeze.

Thin. High-pitched. Barely audible over the wind moaning through bare aspen branches.

Crying.

Her pulse hammered in her throat. She plunged through snow toward the car, fighting drifts that swallowed her feet. Wind-driven snow stung her exposed cheeks as she went back to the driver's side and wrenched the front door open with a shriek of cold metal and a shower of ice crystals.

The smell hit first. Blood. The sweet, cloying odor of death in an enclosed space.

A woman slumped against the far window. A tree branch had stabbed through the glass and plunged into her body. A face, eyes lifeless. Just to make sure, Stormi leaned in and pressed two fingers against the woman's carotid artery.

Nothing.

Looked like the tree branch had found her heart, ended her almost immediately. More branches cluttered the back seat.

But that's where the crying was coming from.

Stormi scrambled to the back door and wrenched it open.

A car seat was strapped behind the passenger seat, expensive-looking, with thick padding. A baby in a snowsuit lay nestled under layers of blankets, pinned under the assault of a tree branch. Maybe eight months old, eyes red, nose dripping with snot. And screaming with the desperate fury of someone who'd been cold and scared and alone.

Hang in there, little one.

No wonder the driver had gone for help—and maybe he thought the baby would be safer here. Or . . . she tried to move the branch, but it wouldn't budge, the baby stuck under it.

Maybe they simply couldn't get the child free.

"I'll be right back, sweetheart." Stormi climbed out and ran to her truck, opened the back. Her emergency supplies included, of course, a small saw, for moments just like this. She also had a small generator, an overnight survival kit, and extra food.

Because, you know, *Alaska*. So maybe Aspen's worrying had paid off.

She returned to the car, Rome circling her, barking. "I know, I know, buddy. I'll get her."

The branch that pinned the car seat seemed about the width of her wrist, and she set her saw against it, trying to deafen herself to the baby's wailing.

The tree fought her, the bark stiff with cold, but she braced herself and the saw bit in, chips sparking off. She managed to saw through it, but the angle kept her from releasing the car seat fully. She was able to move it enough to reach the buckles.

Inside, the child lay seemingly unhurt, despite her shrieks. Stormi reached for her, pulling off her own thick mittens, fingers already stinging in the frigid air. The baby's lips showed the telltale blue tinge of mild hypothermia.

She checked the baby's pulse—fast but strong under her fingertips. She felt cold skin through the pink snowsuit but not the deadly coldness of severe hypothermia.

She'd found the child in time.

"Okay, we're getting you warm." She lifted the baby out of the seat, tucking her inside her own winter jacket, against her warmth. The child gulped, still screaming.

"That's right. You're okay." The wailing quieted to exhausted whimpers.

The sedan's engine was dead, and cold had leeched out any remaining heat. She'd been here for hours, easily. Stormi reached into the front seat and picked up the woman's purse. Then she headed back to her truck and cranked the heat to maximum.

The baby settled, sniffing hard, hiccupping in residual panic. Stormi set her down on the seat, then pulled emergency blankets from her kit, the mylar crinkling as she wrapped them around the baby while keeping her close to her own body heat.

Her radio crackled. "Stormi, what's your status?"

She keyed the handset with her free hand, careful not to jostle the baby. "Two victims. One adult female, deceased. One child, alive but hypothermic. Treating on scene, then transporting to Copper Mountain Medical."

"Copy. Emergency services en route."

"How long?"

"Thirty minutes, maybe."

"Negative. Don't send them up here. Weather's deteriorating rapidly, and we can't wait. I'll transport to the clinic myself."

Static, then, "Understood. Drive safe."

The baby had stopped crying, snuffing hard. Stormi kept her hand on her.

She needed that car seat. But the branch still wedged it in.

And the baby needed to get to help. Stormi reached over and belted the baby into the regular seat.

Please God, keep us on the road.

Outside, Rome barked, alerted, maybe by the wind. She opened her door. "C'mon, buddy, we need to go." The dog turned to her, his eyes bright, head tilted in that way that meant he was listening to something she couldn't hear.

Then he bolted down the road.

What? "Rome! Come back!"

Not a hope. The dog was a bullet, running after . . . well, who knew? "Get back here!"

But he was already disappearing into the forest, his dark form vanishing between snow-heavy boughs.

Fine. Shoot. She glanced at the baby, then the car. No good choices here.

She called for Rome one last time, but the wind ate her voice. At least he was chipped. But . . .

Shoot.

She put her hand on the baby. "Stay with me, little one."

Thank the Lord for her studded tires, for four-wheel drive. The blizzard hit with full force as she reached the highway, transforming the world into a swirling chaos of white. Her headlights barely penetrated five feet ahead. She leaned forward over the steering wheel, hunting for the yellow center line that marked the lane's edge.

The baby had gone quiet. *Please let her just be sleeping.* "Almost there. Stay with me, sweetie."

The Copper Mountain clinic was lit up like Christmas, the ER entrance lights a beacon of red and white. She pulled up and the automatic doors opened, spilling warm yellow light onto the snow.

Dr. Mitch Hutchins appeared at her door before she could turn off the engine. Two EMTs flanked him, their breath steaming in the frigid air.

"How is she?"

She unclipped the baby, pulled her into her arms. Still breathing—*thank you, Jesus.* "Mild to moderate hypothermia. Pulse is strong but core temperature's low. I don't know how much longer she had."

"No car seat?" one of the EMTs asked as Stormi passed the baby into his arms, making sure the warming blankets stayed in place.

"She's been alone in that car for hours. The woman was impaled by a branch. I had to cut her out of the car seat."

Dr. Hutchins nodded grimly as they moved toward the clinic. "We'll get her warmed up. Good work getting her here in these conditions."

Right.

She followed him into the ER.

"Any idea who she is?" an EMT asked. Already, someone had set up warming equipment—heated blankets, temperature monitors, IV supplies.

"Oh, I grabbed the woman's purse." Stormi turned around and nearly ran into Deke, who'd appeared from somewhere. Snow melted off his uniform jacket.

"Hey," he said. "Good job. The volunteer crew was having a hard time assembling in the storm."

"Which is why we need a full-time SAR team stationed in Copper Mountain."

"Tell it to the county budget committee." He'd followed her out into the snow. "Moose is working on establishing a private team here beyond Dodge Kingston and his chopper."

She opened up her car door and grabbed the purse. Handed it to Deke. He took it and she followed him back inside.

Dr. Hutchins had peeled off the baby's clothing and wrapped her in new warming blankets. His stethoscope moved across her tiny chest. "Temperature's coming up nicely. Good work, Stormi. Another hour in that car and we'd be looking at organ failure."

A nurse was changing her diaper. "Sweet girl. All this diaper rash too."

Stormi walked away, back to the nurses' station where Deke had put on gloves and started to go through the contents of the woman's purse.

But the praise couldn't chase away the worry gnawing at her stomach. She checked her phone—Rome's GPS signal was still moving. He was almost two miles from her property now, heading deeper into the wilderness area where avalanche danger ran high during storm season.

Deke pulled out a driver's license. "Abigail Walker."

She walked over. "I think she was with a man. I saw boot prints leading away from the car, through the forest. Maybe he thought it was the closest route to help."

Deke nodded, sighed. "They're only a few miles from the ski resort, but . . ." He shook his head. Glanced at her. "People don't survive an Alaskan blizzard if they're not in shelter."

He held her gaze and, shoot, probably saw the ongoing question there. And why not? She'd only called the sheriff's office a dozen times over the past month. She dropped her voice. "Any sign of him?"

Deke shook his head. "Sorry, Stormi. We've been out to the crash site a couple times, even with Jericho's search dog—Wilder's vanished."

She shoved her hands into her pockets, nodded, looked away. Aw, her sister was right. It wasn't her business, anyway. It's not like Wilder Frost had her on his personal radar. Sure, she'd helped his sled dogs whelp for the past year, but the man probably had no room in his life beyond his seven-year-old daughter and his sled team and, well, trying to stay alive.

Which, apparently, took a sudden, disastrous slide to tragedy three weeks ago when the plane he was on had crashed just south of town. And worse, with a fugitive on board. Not to mention that said fugitive left the pilot dead and the other two passengers on the run and . . .

Well, it just figured that the man she loved died before she had a chance to tell him. And okay, the word *love* might be a little overcommitted, and declarations of the heart hadn't been on her immediate to-do list, but she might have liked the chance. Someday.

Maybe.

Aw. See, this was her problem. She was a dreamer—always living the life of someday, following big dreams that got her in over her head and only led to failure.

Case in point—moving to Copper Mountain with a ragtag bunch of dogs, hoping Wilder would teach her how to mush, and along the way, maybe he'd fall in love with her too.

So, what? They could live their happily ever after ending under the aurora borealis?

Good grief. She turned to Deke. "I need to get back to the

clinic. My dog took off." She shrugged into her jacket, already dreading the drive through worsening conditions.

"Stormi." The voice brought her around. Kennedy Bowie stood in the lobby, wearing her parka. "You okay?"

She frowned, and Kennedy pointed to her jacket. Oh, blood, maybe from when she touched the victim. "It's not mine. I responded to a car wreck—found a baby still alive and brought her in."

Kennedy glanced in the ER. "Is she okay?"

"Yeah, but her mother's dead." Stormi made a face. "What are you doing here?"

Kennedy's husband, Sully, worked as a bush guide in the area. The Bowie outpost was not terribly far from her place, as the crow flew. And the town of Copper Mountain wasn't so big that she hadn't heard about Kennedy's nearly lethal ectopic pregnancy a few weeks ago.

"Checkup. Sully wants to head back out to the outpost, but . . ." She lifted a shoulder, her gaze a little haunted. "I need more time."

More time before she trekked out into the remote bush with a husband who often took off for days? Yeah, Stormi got that. "I could always use help at the clinic," she said. "You know, feeding the animals, assisting with general care."

But Kennedy had turned, her gaze on the ER. On the baby.

Oh, right.

Kennedy sighed, then turned back to Stormi. "How's it going? You still traveling back and forth from Anchorage?"

"They found a replacement, so I'm here full-time now. Bought Anuk's clinic a few weeks ago." She glanced at her phone. Rome was still moving.

Silence. She looked up at Kennedy, who gave her a soft smile. "You're out there all by yourself. At least Anuk had her husband. You sure that's a good idea?"

Not even a little, but that was Stormi—jump first, look later. "I'll be fine. I need to get going."

Kennedy nodded, watching the ER, the expression on her face twisting inside Stormi.

Longing. Maybe Stormi understood that too well.

She headed out to her truck. Snow fell so heavily she could barely see the road.

If she didn't have Rome out there, she might stay in town. She checked her phone. The GPS signal showed Rome moving just southeast of her house.

"Come on, Rome." She spoke to the storm, to the darkness, to the night. "Come home."

Wind howled through spruce boughs around the parking lot. The wind shifted, and for a moment the snow cleared. Above her, the aurora borealis blazed, wild, across the Alaskan sky. Ribbons of green and silver pulsed and swayed against the backdrop of countless stars, nature's own light show playing out across the vast wilderness.

She stood transfixed. That's when she heard it.

A howl. Long and mournful, carried on the wind from somewhere deep in the forest. Raw, honest, and way too familiar.

The cry of the forlorn.

The sound latched onto her heart as she climbed into the driver's seat and headed for home.

WILDER FROST moved his knight across the chessboard, but his mind wasn't on Orion's inevitable checkmate—it was stuck on the fact that no matter which way he moved, he managed to find disaster.

"You're getting predictable." Orion Starr leaned back in his chair, his tall frame filling the wooden seat. Brown hair, and those green eyes—flecked with blue and gold—that held the patient assessment that came from years as an Air Force Pararescue Jumper. "You've repositioned that knight three times in a row."

"Maybe I like that knight."

"Maybe you're not paying attention." Orion's calm demeanor carried authority born from guiding climbers up Denali and talking panicked rookies through dangerous rescues. An artificial knee from Afghanistan gave him a slight limp, but nothing about him suggested weakness. "Something eating at you?"

Everything was eating at him. The infected wound in his upper thigh that still woke him in a teeth-gritted moan at night. Orion's wife, Jenny, watching him with those psychologist eyes, cataloging every wince and restless movement. Her long blond hair was pulled back in a practical ponytail, and she wore an oversized homemade wool sweater that made her look like a wilderness PTSD counselor—which she was. The scanner in the corner crackled with emergency chatter but never the voices he needed to hear.

Three weeks had passed since Orion found him bleeding out in a snowbank, delirious with fever and hypothermia. Three weeks of forced rest while his body healed and his mind fractured with worry.

Two weeks since he'd heard from his daughter, Luna—heard her voice, confirmed she was okay with Vic Dalton, their neighbor.

He needed to go home.

He needed to keep his daughter safe.

Felt like he couldn't have both.

"I'm fine." He moved his bishop, immediately regretted it when Orion's rook swept across the board.

"Check."

The rich scent of venison stew drifted from the kitchen, making his stomach growl despite the anxiety eating at his gut. The cabin smelled cozy—pine logs, woodsmoke, and Jenny's cooking.

Made him miss his house, just north of town, the home he shared with Luna and, once upon a time, his wife, Dawn. Oh, could she cook a venison pie.

And just like that, the old wounds opened, bled.

"You know what your problem is?" Orion captured Wilder's king with unnecessary enthusiasm. "You're thinking like a man on the run instead of a man playing chess."

"I *am* a man on the run." He folded his arms and leaned back on the sofa. "I should have kept Luna with me instead of asking Vic to watch her."

"Vic is a former cop. And you could hardly know that Conan Sorros would jump on your charter plane and try to kill you. It's a good thing Luna wasn't with you."

He sighed. "Yeah. It was hard enough keeping myself alive in that blizzard . . ." He met Orion's eyes. "What I should have done is found a way to end this without putting everyone I love in danger."

Orion glanced at Jenny, who was probably looking at Wilder with a sort of sad compassion. Or pity.

He gritted his jaw.

"Listen. According to Deke, Conan and Mars are locked up tighter than a tick on a dog. You could walk into Copper Mountain tomorrow and nobody would bat an eye."

Wilder stared at him. "Like a tick on a dog? What's that from, *Hee Haw*?"

"It was in the lyrics of a recent Oaken Fox song."

Wilder shook his head. "Conan and Mars aren't the only problem. Don't forget Sloan Sorros."

"Who?"

"Their cousin."

The emergency scanner crackled to life. Static filled the warm air, followed by a voice Wilder recognized—Sheriff Deke Starr, Orion's cousin.

". . . dark-colored sedan, mile marker forty-seven on Copper Creek Road. Appears to have been there several hours. Requesting civilian assistance to check it out while emergency services respond."

Ice water replaced the blood in his veins.

Vic drove a dark sedan.

"Stormi, what's your status?"

He stilled. *Stormi?* What was she doing here? Last he saw her, she was all nicely tucked into her place in Anchorage. And now she was drawn into this?

Oh, super swell.

"Two victims. One adult female, deceased. One child, alive but hypothermic." The chessboard blurred. *One adult female, deceased. One child, alive . . .*

Vic and Luna?

"Treating on scene, then transporting to Copper Mountain Medical."

"Copy. Emergency services en route."

"How long?"

"Thirty minutes, maybe."

He was on his feet before the transmission ended, his leg on fire, of course. The room spun, but he grabbed the back of his chair and stayed upright. He needed to get there first.

"Whoa there." Orion reached for him. "Sit down before you fall."

"Vic has an old model dark sedan. What if that's them?"

"We can't assume it's them." Jenny appeared in the room. "Dark sedans aren't exactly rare in Alaska."

"It's them." His hands shook as he reached for the winter gear Orion had loaned him. "I know it. I haven't heard from Luna in two weeks."

"Even if it is—and that's a big if—you can't help them by bleeding out in a snowbank," Orion said. He'd gotten up, walked over to the door. "Don't be stupid. You're not even a month out from getting shot. That infection nearly killed you. Still might if you're not smart."

"I can't just sit here playing games while they die." He looked at Jenny, back to Orion. "I appreciate all you've done for me, but the fact is, people want me dead. And if they can't find me, they'll find my daughter." He grabbed Orion's heavy parka from the hook by the door. "Can I borrow your snowmobile?"

"In this weather?" Orion glanced toward the windows where snow was starting to fall harder.

"Listen," Jenny said, "you called them—told them you were alive. They promised to stay hidden until this is over."

"Yeah, well, what if they were running? What if—" He reached for the snowmobile keys hanging by the door. "I'm going."

Orion's hand closed over his wrist. Not rough, but unmovable. "Look at yourself, bruh. You can barely stand up straight. How far do you think you'll get before that leg gives out?"

"Far enough."

"To do what? You don't even know where they are."

"Mile marker forty-seven. Copper Creek Road."

"That's fifteen miles through terrain that'll kill you in good weather. In this?" Orion nodded. "What if you end up in a snowdrift? You'll be dead before you're halfway there."

Jenny moved closer, her expression grim. "The emergency response team is already en route. Stormi knows what she's doing. If anyone can help them—"

"She's a veterinarian, not a paramedic."

"She'll know what to do."

"I'm still going." Wilder pulled free of Orion's grip. His wounded leg nearly buckled under him. "That's my daughter out there. I am not going to let her . . ." His throat thickened.

"This is about Dawn, isn't it?" Jenny asked softly.

He shot her a look. "Don't psychoanalyze me right now."

"I'm not." Her blue eyes were serious. "I'm trying to understand why a man who's spent years keeping his daughter hidden suddenly wants to expose himself."

Because hiding was what cowards did. Because seven years old was too young to lose everyone you loved.

"I should have never left her." His voice cracked on the words.

"Then going out there and getting yourself killed won't fix it," Orion said. "All it'll do is make sure she's an orphan instead of just scared."

"Wow, way to pull your punches."

"Just sayin'."

"Doesn't change the fact that my little girl might be bleeding out in a crashed sedan while I stand here arguing. Key." He held out his hand. "Please."

Orion glanced at Jenny, back at him. "All right." Orion pulled the keys off a hook by the door. "But take the radio."

"Orion—" Jenny's protest died when he held up a hand.

"Sometimes a man's got to choose between safe and right." He looked at Wilder. "Can't say I'd do different if it was my kid out there."

He dropped the keys into Wilder's palm. "Thank you."

"Don't thank me yet. That machine's got enough gas to get you there and back, but not if you get lost. Stick to the main trails, and for the love, don't try to be a hero."

Jenny had gone to the kitchen and now came back, a first aid kit in her hand. "If that wound starts bleeding again—"

"I'll be careful."

"No, you won't." Her smile was sad and knowing. "But you'll survive. You're too stubborn to die."

Probably.

The wind buffeted him like a punch when he stepped outside. Snow pelleted the air, fat flakes that stuck to everything and blurred the world into white and gray. The cold bit through the borrowed gear and went straight to his bones.

The snowmobile started on the second pull. Its engine roared against the gathering storm.

But he knew Alaska better than he knew himself.

He set off, the light plowing through the darkness. And yes, his wounded leg cramped every time he shifted position, vibration from the machine sending fire through healing tissue. But the pain kept him focused. Kept him from thinking too hard about what he might find at the crash site.

By the third mile, the storm stirred, angry, serious. He'd grown up in this country, knew every ridge and valley, but everything looked different in a whiteout.

His leg burned, the wound probably seeping blood that saturated his bandages. Jenny had been right—he was in no shape for this.

But if Luna was hurt . . .

Mile marker forty-seven materialized out of the snow and he spotted a dark shape in the ditch.

A sedan. Dark blue. The same color as Vic's.

His heart stopped.

But as he got closer, wait—Washington license plates. A rental.

Not Vic's sedan.

Okay, so he'd overreacted.

He was about to turn around when he spotted them—paw-prints in the snow around the crash site. Big ones. Familiar ones.

Rome?

Stormi's dog. The beautiful Malador who'd caught his attention during veterinary visits.

He seemed to be tracking boot prints.

And it occurred to Wilder, then, that maybe whoever trekked out into the white might be in trouble.

The tracks led deeper into the forest. Winding around fallen logs and through underbrush. Whatever Rome had been tracking, it had taken him well away from the main crash site.

Wilder gunned his snowmobile into the white, slowly, following the vanishing imprints in the snow.

And then he spotted him.

A man. Face down, wearing a ski jacket, jeans, and hiking boots that would have been inadequate for Alaska even in summer. He'd made it maybe a half mile from the road before the cold took him.

The father. Had to be. He'd tried to go for help on foot while his family waited in the car.

Wilder knelt beside the body and turned the man over to check for signs of life. Futile, really. The man's skin held the gray pallor of death, eyes open and staring at nothing.

This would have been Wilder's fate if Orion hadn't found him, and maybe that's why his leg gave out as he tried to stand, sending him to one knee in the snow. The wound was bleeding freely now, soaking through his pants and leaving dark spots in the white around him. Jenny's warnings echoed in his head. Aw, shoot—but he was too far to turn back.

The lights of the sled illuminated the deep indents. Rome had taken a different route back. One that bypassed the main road and headed cross-country toward a cluster of lights in the distance.

A building. Maybe a house. Definitely shelter. Shoot, he'd turned desperate again.

See, that's what happened when he let his emotions take over. And now he'd flung himself so far from common sense, from logic, that he hadn't a clue how to find his way home.

Maybe it was better for everyone if he just disappeared into the wind.

Maybe. But he couldn't tear his gaze off the lights in the distance, glowing through the storm.

It had to be a cabin. And a barn, or outbuilding—something

substantial enough to have generator power. Wait—he recognized Anuk's vet clinic.

Thank you, God. Although honestly, Wilder wasn't sure the Almighty listened to him anymore. Still.

By the time he reached the building, his vision blurred dark around the edges. From blood loss, hypothermia, or both. He pulled up in front of the cabin, the lights pushing out into the gloom. He fumbled for the radio with frozen fingers, keyed the mic. Static. He tried the next channel. Then the indicator light flickered out altogether. Dead battery.

He fell off the snow machine and stumbled toward the front porch, his wounded leg dragging behind him. "Anuk!"

The lights promised heat and safety and please, *please*, let Anuk and her husband be home.

Or at least someone who might find his body before any local wildlife did.

And wasn't that a happy thought.

He made it three steps up the porch before his leg gave out. The pain shot through him—a white-hot spike that drove him to his knees. He fell onto the snowy porch, the wind casting bullets over him.

This was how it ended. Not in a gunfight with the Sorros family or a plane crash into the wilderness, but alone in the snow.

Him ruing every decision he'd ever made.

He should be cold, but the numbness was spreading from his extremities inward, taking the pain with it.

Maybe this was better. Luna was safe. Vic was safe. He'd spent years running from death and dragging everyone he loved into danger. Maybe it was time to stop running.

Something warm pressed against his back. Fur. And then a huff as a large dog settled down beside him. Sharing body heat.

Wilder turned his head, expecting to see some stray or working dog seeking shelter. Instead, amber eyes looked back at him.

Rome. His thick coat was already dusted with white, but he showed no sign of moving.

"Good boy," Wilder whispered.

Rome's tail thumped once against the porch boards. Then he settled his head on his paws and kept watch while the snow fell and the wind howled and Wilder lay on the porch.

The dog's warmth might not be enough to save him, but it would make the end less lonely.

2

STORMI MIGHT BE LONELY, but at least the storm hadn't cut her power.

Her headlights sliced through the whiteout as she swung her truck off the snowy road, gravel crunching beneath the layer of snow.

The log cabin's amber glow spilled across wind-carved drifts, the aurora blotted out by the storm clouds.

The diesel engine's rumble died, leaving only the shriek of arctic wind through the evergreen trees that surrounded her compound. Pine scent mixed with the sharp bite of snow, and somewhere in the distance, a wolf howled—lonesome and wild.

Please, God, let Rome be okay.

The kennel had erupted before she'd even killed the engine. Six voices in frantic chorus, but not the usual welcome-home racket. This was urgent. Alarmed.

Cell service near her house wasn't great, so Rome's signal had dropped off radar.

Perfect.

She cut the lights, squinted through the windshield where condensation fogged the edges.

Something dark sprawled across her porch. And beside it, a snow machine—not hers—hunkered in the drift.

Her pulse hammered in her throat. The truck door creaked as she pushed it open, and bitter wind slapped her face as she stepped out. Porch light cast long shadows across the deck where something—*someone*—lay motionless.

The shape moved.

"I can see you." Her voice carried across the yard, steady despite adrenaline flooding her system.

A whine drifted toward her through the wind. Low. Familiar. *Rome.*

He lifted his massive head. Snow had collected on his dark fur. He barked once, and the breath in her chest released. But he wasn't alone. Someone lay beneath him, crumpled up on her porch.

The figure groaned, the sound barely audible over howling gusts.

Dark hair tangled with snow crystals that caught the porch light. Beard covered with frost. Winter gear soaked through—and not just with snowmelt. The copper scent of blood hit her even through the storm, metallic and sharp against the clean smell of snow.

Blue eyes cracked open. Piercing. *Impossible.*

She'd stared at those eyes on magazine covers. An autographed photo on her wall. And in her forbidden dreams.

What?

Wilder Frost was supposed to be dead.

"Wilder?" The name barely whispered past her lips, carried away by wind.

He stared at her, almost unseeing, and then closed his eyes again, nonplussed.

She scrambled up the porch, dropped beside him on deck

boards slick with ice, her knees hitting wood so cold it burned through her jeans.

Wilder Frost was bleeding on her porch.

She pulled off her mitten and pressed her palm to his head. Fever-hot, skin as dry as paper despite the storm raging around them.

"What happened? How are you—" She shook her head, breath puffing white in the frigid air. Questions later. "We're getting you inside. Now."

Rome whined, tail beating a worried rhythm against wooden planks as she worked her arms under Wilder's shoulders. Dead weight.

"Help me out here, hero." Grunting, she hauled him upright, his weight threatening to topple them both. "Unless you want to freeze to my porch."

He roused then—as if he heard her and startled.

"You're okay. I got you."

"Stormi?"

"Yeah, it's me. I have questions, but let's get you inside."

Rome ran in anxious circles around them, barking.

"I know, buddy. Good job." Her breath came in harsh puffs as she fumbled for her keys with fingers already stiffening from cold.

"What are you doing here?" His weight sagged against her as the lock finally turned with a metallic click.

"That's my line, tough guy." Her mind spun as she shouldered the heavy oak door open, blessed warmth rushing out to meet them. The scent of home hit her—woodsmoke from the fireplace, the lingering aroma of this morning's coffee.

He seemed to be trying to summon strength, then, and somehow he roused, gripping the doorframe. Wobbly at best. "This your place?"

She slipped her arm around him, supporting him. "Yep. Let's get you to the sofa."

She half carried him into the cabin, their boots leaving puddles of snow on hardwood floors that gleamed honey-gold in the lamplight. She wrestled him toward the one large room with a sofa and a couple overstuffed leather chairs.

Rome bolted ahead, as if saying, *Over here, Mom, over here.*

"I got him, Rome. I got him." She eased Wilder onto cushions that sighed under his weight.

"I followed Rome's tracks from the crash to your cabin," he said, his voice low and ending in a moan.

"You went to the crash?"

"Thought it might be . . . Luna." His eyes drifted closed, thick lashes dark against pale skin. "When I heard 'woman and child' on the scanner . . ."

Luna.

Seven years old. Green eyes. The little girl had visited the clinic once, her tiny hands clutching a stuffed husky while Wilder's racing dogs got their shots. She'd been quiet, polite, a sort of seriousness about her.

Oh wow. The punch of understanding nearly knocked her backward. "You thought your daughter was in that car."

"Haven't been able to reach her for two weeks." Each word seemed to cost him. "Had to know if she was okay."

"Yeah, well that's what happens when the world thinks you're dead."

Aw, that didn't come out at all like she meant it. But frankly, shoot, her panic emerged as anger, and her chest filled, seeing him in pain.

And not just physically. She'd pulled a baby from that wreckage—and he'd raced through a blizzard thinking it might be his child.

Clearly things were not all well in Wilder-land. She schooled her voice. "It wasn't Luna."

Relief flickered across his face before he tensed, clearly another wave of pain.

"What's going on? Where have you been?" Stormi reached for the wool throw blanket but stopped cold when she got her first clear look at his leg.

Blood had soaked through his pants in a dark stain that was still spreading, warm and wet against thick fabric.

Way too much blood.

The copper scent was stronger now, mixing with the woodsmoke and making her stomach clench. "Wilder. What happened to your leg?"

"Gunshot." He managed something that might have been a grin, though it didn't reach his eyes.

"*Gunshot?*" The word exploded out of her, echoing off the log walls.

"Long story."

"Give me the short version." She walked to her kitchen and grabbed a towel, then returned and settled on the coffee table, facing him.

"You know about the plane crash?"

"Everyone knows. They've been searching for you." The memory still made her stomach twist. She'd watched the news coverage, had seen the helicopters searching empty wilderness. "They gave up."

"Yeah, I had to disappear." He tried, with clumsy fingers, to work his jacket zipper, the metal teeth chattering with his trembling. "Sloan Sorros wants me dead. I needed to buy time."

Sloan Sorros? The name meant nothing to her, but the way he said it—like speaking poison—made ice crawl up her spine despite the fire crackling in the hearth.

"Time for what?"

"Get Luna safe." He shrugged out of his jacket with painful movements.

She, in the meantime, grabbed a pair of scissors.

"Don't you dare cut my pants." He worked the snow pants down, leaving only thermals stained crimson down his thigh. The wet fabric clung to his skin. He made a face. "Didn't exactly go as planned."

Her vet training kicked in automatically. Blood loss calculation. Infection risk. Time since injury. She could practically hear her professors' voices cataloging the danger signs.

All bad news.

"How long since you were shot?"

"Three weeks."

"What?" She cut away the thermals with her scissors. "Have you lost your mind?"

"Charming bedside manner, Doc."

"Wait until you see me crabby." She knelt beside the sofa, scissors cold in her hand. "This is going to hurt."

"More than it already does?"

"Significantly."

The thermal peeled away with a wet sound that made her teeth clench. Angry. Swollen. Ugly. The bullet hole had torn through his thigh muscle, and red streaks radiated outward, reaching toward his heart.

Infection, maybe even heading toward sepsis. The smell hit her—sweet and sour underneath the blood. Without treatment, he'd be dead in days.

"You've been hiding in the woods with this wound for three weeks?"

"Calm down. Orion Starr found me. He and Jenny hauled me back to their place. She dug out the bullet."

"With what, a bowie knife?"

"I dunno. I was out of it right about then."

She'd bet he'd passed out from the pain. Pus oozed out of the wound, still draining.

"You could lose this leg. I need to get you to Copper Mountain."

"I'm fine. It just needs to get cleaned out."

The fact that he was conscious defied everything she knew about trauma medicine.

"You magnificent idiot. That wound is infected six ways from Sunday."

She sat back on her heels, met his gaze straight on. No point sugarcoating. "You need surgery. Real surgery, not field surgery by a vet."

"How real?"

"Preferably under the bright lights of an Anchorage hospital."

He shook his head. "Nope."

"Or the Copper Mountain clinic."

"I mentioned that Sorros wants me dead, right?"

"Which brings me back to—who is Sloan Sorros?"

"Later. Right now, I need you to patch me up."

She stared at him. "You do know I'm a vet, right? I work on *animals*."

"Aw, Doc, I sorta smell like one. Close enough?"

And then he smiled.

Shoot, he *smiled*! And those magical blue eyes found her and latched on, and just like that, she lost her brains. Really lost them because she heard herself saying, "That means me digging bullet fragments out and pumping you full of canine antibiotics." She studied his face for shock signs—pupils, skin color, responsiveness.

He just nodded.

Not the response she was hoping for.

"You're saying you trust me not to kill you."

"Trust you?" Something shifted in his expression. "Stormi, back in Anchorage, I've watched you save animals other vets wrote off as hopeless. If anyone can patch me up, it's you. Yeah, I trust you."

Her breath caught in her throat.

He'd been watching her?

Stop! He didn't mean it that way!

"Besides"—that ghost-grin again, warmer this time—"Rome's tracks led me straight to you. Clearly he trusts you."

Ha. She didn't want to mention that she hadn't been able to fix him either. Rome appeared at her elbow, pressing his cold nose against her shoulder. He gave a soft woof.

She scratched behind Rome's ears, feeling snow crystals melt under her fingers. "He ran away at the crash site. Kept running into the trees. I thought he was being difficult."

"I found a dead body out there. So maybe . . . ?" Wilder's fingers found Rome's head, tangled in thick fur still damp with snow.

"A dead body?" She stilled. Wait. "Could be the driver of the car I found."

"Maybe your dog followed his scent?"

"Naw. He's lost his sense of smell. I doubt . . ." But she looked at Rome, who turned to her. Licked her chin. "Maybe he heard something."

At the very least, he'd led Wilder to her front step. She kissed his snout and then got up. "Come on. We're moving to the clinic."

"Clinic?"

"The barn. I've got proper surgical setup out there." She reached for Wilder. "Unless you'd rather I operate on my kitchen table."

"Barn works." He tried to push upright, but then there was a sharp intake of breath as he sank back, face going white. "Gimme a second here."

"No rush. Except, you know, you're bleeding out. But sure, take all the time you need."

"Again, I'm loving that bedside manner."

"What can I say? Want a dog biscuit?" She smiled at him but returned to his side and slipped her arm around shoulders that were broader than they looked. Even injured, he radiated strength, the kind of survival attitude that helped him run about a thousand miles in the dead of winter. She almost wanted to remind him of that as he grunted his way off the sofa and out of her house.

He must be all muscle, too, because the man was heavier than he looked. He managed to muscle up his snow pants over his destroyed thermals. But getting him to the barn required every ounce of strength she had. The wind tried to knock them sideways as they stepped outside, and fresh snow stung her cheeks. The path she'd shoveled this morning was already filling in, and their boots broke through the crust with each step, making progress slow and treacherous.

"Sorry," Wilder said on a tight breath as he tried to carry his weight, but his left leg buckled repeatedly. Each stumble sent him harder against her side, his breathing coming in puffs that steamed in the arctic air. By the time they reached the clinic doors, both of them were shaking—him from blood loss, her from effort and cold that bit through her jacket.

The barn had been remodeled long before her time in the clinic. There was a small waiting room up front and surgical rooms in the back. She came in the back entrance, then hit the lights, and fluorescents flickered to life, revealing stainless steel that gleamed.

Rome trotted ahead, settling into his spot near the exam table.

"Impressive setup." Wilder surveyed the clinic as she helped him over to the padded table, then turned on the warming pad. "Is that a flat-screen? What, for the dogs to watch dog TV?"

"Funny. Laparoscopic surgery, for one, and the occasional video chat with a colleague if need be. I did an update right after I bought the place."

"I didn't realize you were moving here." He grimaced as he moved his leg onto the table.

"Oops. Better drop those snow pants again, champ. I can't roll your pants up past your thigh."

"Is there a male doctor in the house?"

"Funny. And no." She moved to the supply cabinet, her hands automatically reaching for what she'd need—forceps, Novocain, gauze, cleaning solution. "Were you this shy with Jenny?"

"No. But Orion was there."

Behind her, she heard the swish of his snow pants, then a groan.

"Plus, I didn't have much choice. There wasn't exactly a drive-through-clinic-while-hiding-from-an-assassin option available."

Assassin.

The word hung between them, even as she turned, holding her stainless steel tray of utensils.

"Wilder." She set down the tray. "What kind of trouble are you in?"

"The kind that takes down planes and shoots their passengers." Another attempt at humor that fell flat in the sterile air.

She gave him a look. Shook her head.

"Fine. The kind that means I can't come home until Sloan Sorros is behind bars."

"Again with Sloan Sorros—"

"I promise, I'll tell you everything. But preferably not when you're holding that." He nodded toward the long needle, the syringe filled with Novocain.

"I just need to know . . . is my clinic in danger?"

He met her eyes, drew in a shaky breath.

And nodded.

She blinked at him, the silence loud in her ears, only the hammering of her heart filling her head.

"I'm sorry." His blue-eyed gaze locked with hers. Steady. Serious. No more jokes to hide behind. "I shouldn't have come, but I was . . . desperate, and frankly, I thought this was still Anuk's place, and that her husband might be here—"

"Stop." She stepped up to him, checking the Novocain dosage. "I get it. And I don't blame you." She swabbed around the wound with disinfectant. "This is the best I can do. It should numb the pain, or most of it."

"Most of it?"

"There's always the bear tranquilizer."

"Please tell me you're kidding."

"Completely kidding." She depressed the plunger, watching clear medication flow into the tissue around his wound. "I save that for really difficult patients."

"I'm not difficult."

"Whatever. Lay back and let me know if this hurts."

He eased himself back on the table. "I'd call that moderately cooperative."

She touched his wound. No response. Just to make sure, she used forceps. "Anything?"

He shook his head, breathed out as if uncoiling the tension in his chest. She put a hand on his shoulder. "Close your eyes. I got this."

He did as if, indeed, he did trust her. He caught his breath as she eased more Novocain just a little deeper, but in a moment, his face relaxed. She again tested the skin around the wound. No reaction.

Under the bright surgical lights, she could see exactly what the last three weeks had cost him. Hollow cheeks, lines etched around his eyes. The pallor of blood loss and constant stress made him look older than his years.

But he was alive.

Against all odds, Wilder Frost was alive and breathing on her table.

"All right." She snapped on surgical gloves, the latex warm from the heated dispenser. "Let's see what we're working with."

An hour passed in a bubble of sterile concentration. The familiar rhythm of surgery—cut, clean, irrigate, suture. Her hands moved with trained precision, Wilder's breathing the only sound besides the whisper of heated air through vents and Rome's occasional shift of position.

When Wilder's breathing evened out, she realized he'd fallen asleep. Huh.

She cleaned the wound with Betadine that stained everything orange, removed three angry bullet fragments that clinked into the metal pan, then irrigated infected tissue until the drainage ran clear. The smell of antiseptic overpowered everything else.

Wilder's fever broke halfway through, sweat beading on his forehead despite the barn's chill. By the time she finished the final suture, his color had improved from gray to merely pale.

She stepped back, stripping off gloves. Clean incision. Properly irrigated. She gave him a shot of antibiotics.

He'd have a scar, but he'd live.

"Not bad for a vet," she murmured to Rome, who'd maintained his vigil from the corner.

Outside, wind howled with renewed fury, rattling the clinic's metal siding and sending snow against windows in waves that sounded like thrown sand.

Wilder stirred, eyelids fluttering.

"How do you feel?" She moved to check his pulse, fingers finding the steady beat at his wrist.

"Like I got shot and had surgery in an old barn." Voice stronger. Clearer. The slur was gone, replaced by something closer to his normal rich baritone. "But better. Definitely better."

"Good. That means the antibiotics are working." She helped

him sit up. His coordination had improved dramatically. "Think you can make it back to the house if you lean on me?"

"Yep." But he reached out his arm, and she put it over her shoulder.

The wind had calmed by the time they stepped outside, though snow still fell in fat, frenzied flakes that caught the porch light. Their boots crunched through the fresh accumulation—maybe another six inches since they'd made the trip over. The storm had nearly blown itself out, and in the sky, aurora painted everything in impossible colors—emerald and sapphire and deep purple—that made the whole world look magical.

Her breath puffed white in air that smelled of more storms to come. But for now, the worst had passed.

Her quiet life had just taken a dramatic turn.

The great Wilder Frost was alive.

And she was going to make sure he stayed that way.

CONSCIOUSNESS DRIFTED back to Wilder, wrapped in the alluring scent of coffee perking and bacon frying and something else.

Safety.

Wilder's eyes cracked open to unfamiliar pine beams overhead, each knot and grain distinct in the gray tint of morning light. His mind launched straight to the one thought that haunted every waking moment for three years.

Luna.

Was she still safe? Or had his stupidity last night put his daughter in even more danger? She was probably just fine with Vic. But he was tired of the worry that knotted his chest. He needed to end this nightmare.

He tried sitting up. Groaned and then lay back. His leg burned, the surgical pain sharp enough to bring last night flooding back. Rome's tracks leading him through howling wind to salvation. Stormi. Surgery.

Alive.

Against all odds, he was alive.

"Easy." Stormi's voice drifted from across the room. "You've got about sixteen stitches holding you together."

He turned his head on the soft throw pillow. She stood at a granite kitchen counter at the far end of her great room. She wore faded jeans and a cream thermal shirt, her brown hair pulled back in a messy ponytail that escaped in soft tendrils around her face.

Oh, Stormi White was beautiful in a down-to-earth, doesn't-even-try sort of way. She had expressive lips that now held a slight smile, and there was an intelligence in her eyes that said she saw more than she let on.

Sure, he'd noticed her before—hard to miss during vet calls when she'd handled his racing dogs with that competent touch that never seemed flustered. But seeing her in her own space, humming under her breath while making breakfast . . .

Yeah, this was different. Personal, even intimate.

Beyond the window, snow fell in fat flakes. The storm's fury had gentled to a whisper.

"How long was I out?" His voice emerged rusty, his throat dry.

"About eight hours." She poured coffee from a glass carafe into two heavy ceramic mugs, steam rising in lazy spirals. "I checked every hour. No fever, good pulse, bandages staying clean."

The coffee's rich aroma reached him, and his mouth watered. "You didn't have to stay up—"

"Actually, I did." She moved toward him, and he caught something floral—lavender, maybe. "It's what I do for all my dogs in trouble. Standard postsurgical monitoring." She crossed the room and held out a mug. Grinned.

He pushed himself up, made a face but managed to hold in a groan. "Am I a dog in trouble?" He accepted the mug, ceramic warm against his palms. Her fingers brushed his for just a moment, and he registered soft skin, steady hands, the faint ridge of a scar across her knuckle.

And noted how the touch seemed to simmer through him, hot.

What*ever.* Maybe he was still running a fever.

"Let's do the math," she said as she sat in one of her overstuffed chairs. "You end up on my porch in the middle of the night, bleeding, curled up with your fellow pack dog. You smell like the outdoors and, frankly, you're about as hairy as one of my Malamutes, so . . ." She lifted a shoulder, still grinning.

And shoot—that felt warm inside him too. He took a sip of coffee. It hit his tongue, rich and bitter and perfect. "Thank you." His voice emerged rougher than intended. "For everything."

"Don't thank me yet." She settled back into the worn leather chair, cradling her own coffee in both hands. "We need to talk."

Rome appeared from the shadows, near a stone fireplace, pressing his cold nose against Wilder's free hand. The dog's tail wagged once—a quiet greeting—before settling beside the couch with a soft whuff.

"Good boy." He scratched behind Rome's ears, and the dog leaned into his touch. "You saved my life." He looked at Stormi. "Is he a working dog?"

"He used to be," she said, an odd note in her voice, coffee mug pausing halfway to her lips. "Worked as a K9 tracker. Now . . . I dunno. He lost his sense of smell and then ended up on an adoption list. I took him in, hoping to make him a sled dog." She made a face. "He's not a fan."

Something in Stormi's tone made him study her face. Dark circles under her eyes spoke of a sleepless night. There was a slight tightness around her mouth that he recognized from watching her work on difficult cases.

She was trying not to show it, but she looked scared. Or deeply worried.

Of course she was. He'd brought danger to her door.

The weight of that settled in his chest. "Stormi—"

"I called for backup." She made a face. "Last night, while you were under. I didn't know . . . I mean, you mentioned people wanting you dead, so . . ."

His chest tightened, breaths coming shallow. "Who did you call?"

"Sheriff Starr. I told him I found you, and he said to sit tight. He's bringing Jericho Bowie and Harley Tatum with him this morning. They should be here soon."

Jericho and Harley. He knew them, of course, from ages ago. Harley's dad had been sheriff once upon a time, and Jericho's dad a state senator. They'd both died in the same airplane accident over seven years ago.

"You know them?" he asked.

"I know Jericho. He has an avalanche rescue dog and works down in Anchorage at a local ski resort."

Great. More people who could get hurt because of him. He leaned back and the coffee turned bitter in his mouth. "You shouldn't have—"

"Yes, I should have." Steel edged her voice now—he recognized the vet he knew kicking in. "Because you haven't told me everything, have you? About why someone wants you dead badly enough to bring down a plane. And who is this Sloan guy?"

Right. He blew out a breath, glanced outside. Wind rattled the double-paned windows in their frames, and snow continued its relentless pelleting against glass. The storm hadn't ended—just paused to gather strength.

"It's complicated."

"Try me." Her gaze didn't waver. "I'm a veterinarian, Wilder. I deal with complicated diagnoses every day. Internal bleeding that presents as simple lethargy. Poisoning that looks like old age. And right now, my diagnosis is that you're in the kind of trouble that means you need help."

The accusation hung between them.

Yeah, he probably did. And she deserved the truth.

"You're right." His leg throbbed and he guessed he might need some pain meds, but clearly the surgery had been a success. He sighed. "Three years ago, I was working as an informant for the DEA, feeding them information about local drug activities I observed during mushing runs."

Her eyebrows rose but no interruption came. Just the steady tick of a mantel clock and Rome's quiet breathing.

"I witnessed something I shouldn't have." He looked away. "A guy named Conan Sorros executing a DEA agent named Darrin."

"Executing?" Stormi's voice grew quiet. "You mean murdered."

"Shot him in the back of the head, execution style, while the guy was on his knees." The memory made his gut clench, brought back the taste of fear.

He could still see Darrin, dead in the snow.

"Wait." She leaned forward, coffee forgotten. "Back up. How did you end up witnessing this? Where were you?"

Wilder closed his eyes, forcing himself back to that day three years ago. "I was training my lead dog about fifteen miles north of Copper Mountain. There's an old mining access road that cuts through federal land—good for conditioning runs. I heard snowmobiles and voices, so I pulled the team behind some trees."

"Smart."

"Should've been smarter and left immediately." He opened his eyes, met hers. "But I recognized the voices. The Sorros brothers had been using their construction vehicles for their drug runs, and I'd been reporting their movements to Darrin, the DEA agent, for months."

"You were already working as an informant?"

"Unofficially. It's a long story, one that starts back when I was working at the Copper Mountain FBO. I had a feeling that North Face Construction was doing something illegal, and I even thought . . ." He sighed. "I thought maybe they had something to do with the plane crash that killed Jericho's and Harley's parents."

Her eyes widened.

"I started to gather information and then I talked with Gabe Tatum, Harley's little brother, and he led me to Darrin. I started to just, you know, pay attention. I would see their trucks in areas that made no sense for construction work. Remote drop sites, abandoned cabins." His fingers tensed around the warm ceramic. "See, the Sorros family had been running drugs through Alaska for years. Brand Sorros, the father, got arrested years ago in a sting operation involving Gabe Tatum and his dad. But Brand's sons—Conan, Jago, and Mars—they kept the operation going."

"And Darrin was investigating them?"

Wilder nodded. "Building a case, yeah. The DEA knew they were using construction vehicles to move product, but they needed evidence. Locations. Times. That's where I came in."

Stormi nodded, processing. "So when you heard them that day—"

"I thought maybe I could get more intel. See what they were moving, where they were headed." His hands clenched around the coffee mug. "Instead, I watched them drag Darrin out of a black SUV."

The words came harder now, each one scraping against his throat.

"Hands zip-tied behind his back, blood streaming down his

face. They'd beaten him badly—broken nose, split lip, one eye swollen shut. Conan was furious, kept asking Darrin about 'the witness' and 'what the feds knew about the northern routes.'"

"They suspected there was an informant?"

"Darrin wouldn't talk. Even with a gun to his head, even when Conan started counting down from ten." Wilder's voice dropped to barely above a whisper. "He just kept saying he didn't know what they were talking about. Protecting me right up until the end."

"What exactly happened?"

Wilder stared at the hardwood floor, remembering. "Conan forced him to his knees in the snow. Darrin was shaking. From cold, from fear, I don't know. But he didn't beg. Didn't try to bargain. Just . . . accepted it."

The silence stretched between them, filled only by the wind outside.

"The sound . . ." Wilder swallowed hard. "Sound carries in the cold air. Echoes off the trees. My dogs heard it and wanted to run, but I held them steady. Had to. Any movement and they would've seen us."

"How close were you?"

"Maybe fifty yards. Close enough to see . . ." He took a breath. "Anyway, close."

Stormi's face had gone pale, but her voice stayed steady. "What did you do?"

"Nothing. Sat there and watched them dump his body in a mining shaft. Watched them pour accelerant over everything and light it up. The smell." He shook his head. "Then they drove away. I felt like a coward."

"You weren't a coward. You were smart. If they'd seen you—"

"I'd be dead too." He nodded. "But Darrin would still be alive if I hadn't been feeding him information. If I hadn't gotten him killed by being their informant."

"You didn't pull that trigger, Wilder."

"No, but my reports put him in their crosshairs." He set down his coffee with shaking hands. "The next day, I went to the FBI field office in Anchorage. Told them everything I'd seen. They arrested Conan and Jago within a week."

She stared at him. Because, yeah, she probably knew the other part. Who didn't, in this area.

"Somehow, my testimony got out," Wilder continued. "I don't know how. My wife, Dawn, was . . . she was targeted. And killed. I think by Mars Sorros, but I don't have proof."

He couldn't go into detail. Not about that.

And Stormi didn't ask, just nodded, her eyes glossy. "I'm so sorry."

"Yeah." Now his leg really hurt.

"They asked you to testify?"

"Yeah. I refused. I thought it was the only way to keep Luna safe. Conan's trial kept getting delayed—lawyers, appeals, jurisdictional issues. Then Jago got killed in prison a few months ago, right before he was supposed to testify against his brother in exchange for a plea deal. That's when the DA reached out to me."

"Because you were the only witness left."

"Yeah. The only one still alive. Gabe Tatum OD'd a few years ago." The bitterness in his voice surprised even him. "They needed my testimony to put Conan away for life. First-degree murder of a federal agent."

"So you agreed to testify."

"Darrin deserved justice, but I couldn't take Luna with me to Juneau." He leaned back against the couch cushions, suddenly exhausted. "She'd been through enough upheaval already with losing her mom."

"So, where is she now?"

"She's with my neighbor, Vic Dalton. In hiding. I'm hoping Sloan can't find her—that's why he hasn't come looking."

"Wait—Vic, who runs the Midnight Sun?"

"Yes, that Vic. She's a former cop. She's got tactical training, weapons experience, and a cabin that's isolated but defensible. More importantly, Luna likes her." A small smile crossed his face. "Vic sort of filled in after Dawn died. They made cookies and she read Luna stories and just, you know, helped keep life normal while I . . ." He looked away, shook his head.

"Grieved," Stormi said.

He sighed. "Luna barely remembers her mother. I try to keep her memory alive by spending time with Dawn's family. They live off the grid on a compound south of Copper Mountain. But it's not the same." He dropped a hand onto Rome's head. "I love Luna. But I can't seem to take the place of her mom."

"Not that you should." She touched his arm. "You're her dad. And that's all you can be."

"Yeah, well, I've spent the past three years hiding or being jumpy or just waiting for the nightmare to find us."

"I thought you said the Sorros boys were in jail."

"Not Sloan Sorros."

She leaned back, folded her arms. "Who's he again?"

"He's a cousin of the Sorros brothers. Ex-military. More dangerous than all three of the others, put together. He's smart. Slick. The rumor is that he's in charge now. I saw him around the FBO occasionally, and I think he worked for North Face Construction. After Conan and Jago were arrested and Mars took off for Anchorage, Sloan sort of disappeared. But . . . I think I saw him at the airport the day I got on Mack's plane."

"Mack?"

"Mack Maverick, from Maverick Air. He saved our lives, trying to fight off Thornwood—I mean, Conan. I should have recognized him as the third passenger. Stupid. I think maybe that's why Sloan was there—so I wouldn't see the danger in the seat behind me." He shook his head. "There was this other woman on the flight. I think she got away, but my fear is that Conan went after her, thinking it was me."

Oh.

"I should have never agreed to testify." He shook his head. "I thought if I did, if Conan went away for life, maybe Luna and I could heal. Maybe . . . figure out how to be happy again. Safe."

"How did Conan get on your plane?"

"I don't know. Before I got on the plane, last I knew was that Conan was in custody. I didn't recognize him until we were ten thousand feet up and he stabbed Mack." Wilder's jaw clenched. "I should have been smarter."

"But you survived. You fought back."

"I tried to help Mack land the plane. Managed to keep us from hitting head-on, but"—he gestured to his bandaged leg—"Conan put a bullet in me before we went down. I managed to get away . . . but . . ."

"You think he's still hunting you."

"According to Orion, Conan and Mars are behind bars. But I'm sure Sloan's still hunting me." He met her eyes, letting her see the full weight of what she'd stepped into. "That's why anyone who helps me becomes a target."

The bacon had gone cold, grease congealing on the plate she'd prepared for him. His stomach turned.

"I need to check on Luna. I called to let them know I was alive, but . . ." He shook his head. "The sooner this is over, the sooner, well, Vic can't hide her forever."

Stormi drew in a long breath.

Him too. "I should have never agreed to testify," he said again, softly.

Her mouth tightened around the edges. But she didn't disagree.

"Stormi, by saving my life, you've made yourself a target. They don't leave witnesses. They don't leave loose ends."

She just met his gaze. "But . . . how do they even know you're alive?"

He blinked at her.

In the yard, the kennel erupted—frantic barking that cut through the wind, urgent and alarmed.

"That's not normal." She rose to check the window.

"Stormi." He caught her hand as she passed, registering how cold her fingers were despite the warm cabin. "I never meant for this to happen. If I could take it back—"

"You're alive. Don't forget that." She squeezed his hand once before pulling away, warmth lingering on his palm. "And we'll figure out what to do next."

The barking grew more frantic—multiple barks raised in alarm. Rome lifted his head, ears perked, but something was different. His tail didn't wag. Instead, a low growl rumbled in his chest.

"Something's wrong." She peered through frost-edged glass. "The dogs are going wild, but I don't see any headlights."

Ice shot through Wilder's veins. "Stormi, get away from the window."

She was reaching for her coat. "I need to check on them. They could be hurt or—"

"Or someone's out there who shouldn't be." His voice went hard, urgent. "Someone who knows how to approach without being seen."

The barking reached a crescendo.

He wanted to get up, but his leg turned to fire. "Stormi, please. Stay inside. Lock the doors."

But she was already grabbing her boots. "Those are my dogs. I can't let someone hurt them."

"If someone's out there, walking into their trap won't help the dogs." He moved to get up, wincing, and she gave him a dark look.

"Sit down!"

"Wait for backup. Wait for Deke."

She paused, then frowned. "I called for help hours ago. Where is everyone?"

The question hung in the air, cold and cutting as the wind outside.

Where was everyone?

"Stormi." His words carried weight in the sudden stillness. "I've been watching you during those vet calls."

Her eyes widened.

"Not in a creepy way, just . . . I noticed you. How you handled difficult animals, how you never gave up on the hard cases. You were the best part of those visits."

Color rose in her cheeks, pink against pale skin, but she held his gaze steady. "Why are you telling me this now?"

"Because I don't want anything to happen to you. Please don't go out there."

"I'll be fine." She zipped her jacket, grabbed her fur hat. "I have to check on the dogs."

"Stormi."

And then she was gone, stepping outside and shutting the door behind her.

Rome stood up and whined.

Yeah, buddy, him too.

Outside, the storm picked up and started to howl.

3

OKAY, this might be stupid.

The cacophony hit Stormi the moment she stepped outside—six voices raised in frantic alarm.

She should have stayed inside, like Wilder had nearly begged. His declaration that he'd noticed her hadn't helped because it had her feeling weird, her entire body buzzing. *Stop. It didn't mean anything.*

Maybe she'd blame her stubbornness on the desire to be fearless in front of him, to impress him.

Although clearly running into danger wasn't exactly impressive.

No, this was about her dogs. And the fact that . . . well, no bad guys were going to find her little outfit tucked into the woods. Which meant it might be that bear she feared. Last thing she needed was the dogs getting hurt. And the poor team was clearly panicked.

Arctic air sliced through her heavy Carhartt coat. The kennel's galvanized chain-link rattled as the dogs jumped up on it. Although the sun barely lipped the east, she flicked on her LED headlamp and swept it across the pups.

Something had spooked them.

"Easy, guys." White clouds puffed from her mouth. The digital thermometer on the kennel post glowed red numbers. "What's got you all worked up?"

Koda, her lead dog, pressed against the fence nearest her. A whine emitted low in his throat. Behind him, the others paced—Yukon and Denali, her reliable wheel dogs. Sitka and Juneau, the spirited swing dogs. And Lina, her backup leader.

All six wound tight. Hackles raised. Brown eyes fixed on the tree line behind the corrugated metal machine shed.

The familiar musk of their winter coats filled her nostrils as she worked the gate latch.

"Okay, let me see what's wrong." The chain-link swung open with a metallic squeal. "But I need you all to settle down first."

She stepped inside the enclosure. Her boots crunched on packed snow mixed with wood shavings from the local sawmill.

"Koda, easy boy." She ran her hands along his flanks, checking for injuries while her eyes swept the perimeter. His muscles bunched tight, trembling with adrenaline, but no wounds. No signs of whatever had him nervous. "What do you smell out there?"

The snow revealed the usual collection of paw prints. Fresh snow had filled some of the impressions, softening edges into gentle curves. Nothing that screamed predator.

But six sets of eyes stayed fixed on the darkness beyond the shed.

Wilder's words hung in her head. *"Anyone who helps me becomes a target."*

A bough creaked with snow, sending a shot through the yard. She jumped.

Aw, she was just being paranoid. Except . . . wind gusted through the black spruce, carrying the scent of snow and something else—motor oil mixed with exhaust fumes.

A snowmobile?

Every muscle in her body went tight.

"Easy, Koda." She moved toward the gate, one hand on his head while the headlamp swept shadows.

She stepped outside the enclosure. Snow squeaked under her boots. Behind her, the dogs pressed against the fence, whining. She should secure the gate, but her hands were shaking now, and her movements with the latch mechanism felt clumsy through thick gloves. The gate swung partially closed but didn't catch. Her dogs wouldn't run off in this storm. She'd come back and fix it properly once she was sure—

An arm went around her neck, pulled her tight against a strong chest. She jerked. The headlamp flew from her head, beam spinning wild across the snow and the tree line before hitting the ground.

The plastic shattered. Light died.

The stranger shook her, slammed a gun barrel against her temple.

"Stop. Don't move. Don't scream."

A male voice, rough with cold.

Koda snarled. Deep. Vicious. Her attacker spun toward the threat.

"Easy, Koda," she said. Last thing she wanted was to get her dog shot.

"Smart girl." The arm turned to steel across her ribs, restricting breath. "Where is he?"

He began dragging her backward toward the machine shed.

"I don't know what you're talking about. There's nobody here but me and my dogs."

"Yeah? Police radio chatter says otherwise." His breath warmed her ear, and she fought not to recoil. "You called for backup, sweetness. Help with an injured man. Easy math since Wilder was last seen not far from here. Funny thing about radio frequencies in Alaska—they bounce around like ping-pong balls."

Nice. She'd broadcast her location to every scanner within fifty miles. See—jumping first, thinking last. What. An. Idiot.

"So where is he?"

"I told you—"

"Don't." The gun dug into her temple, metal so cold, it burned. "I saw the blood in the snow. I know he's here."

She shook her head, but she felt his attention wander toward the cabin's glowing windows.

"Nice little place you got here," he continued. "Isolated. Quiet. Be a real shame if something happened to it."

Behind them, the dogs barked, lunging against the fence.

Stormi drove her elbow backward into the man's ribs, the same technique she used to escape panicked draft horses when they pinned her against stall walls.

Air exploded from his lungs in a harsh grunt, and his arm loosened just enough. She twisted, ducked, dropped her center of gravity, and slipped the hold.

Her shoulder hit snow, but she rolled and then scrambled away as she found her footing. Behind her, the man cursed and stumbled.

The kennel gate swung wide.

Six sled dogs poured into the open yard and chaos erupted.

Koda launched himself forward. Eighty pounds of muscle and fury bred for pulling thousand-pound sleds. He and Stormi's attacker went down together in a tangle of limbs and snarls, the man's weapon skittering across packed snow.

The other dogs circled, barking, snapping, creating a moving wall of teeth and fury that filled the air with the musk of adrenaline and pack hunting instincts.

"Get them off! Get them—"

The man's free hand found his gun. Brought it up, searching

for a target among the blur of movement and steam rising from six panting mouths.

Stormi threw herself at his arm, knocking his aim wide.

The gunshot cracked loud in the cold air. The muzzle flash illuminated snow and fangs and wild eyes. The sound disappeared into the forest.

Koda yelped. Stumbled sideways. A few of the others scattered.

Dark blood stained the snow where he'd been standing.

No.

She hit the man's gun hand again, driving it down toward the ground. "Touch my dogs and I'll feed you to them piece by piece!"

He backhanded her across the face. The blow snapped her head sideways. Stars exploded behind her eyes, and she tasted copper heat spreading across her tongue.

"Worthless mutts—" He scrambled to his feet, pointed his gun at Lina.

And then, out of the chaos came a deeper bark, no fear, all fury. And just like that, Rome launched at the man, his K9 skills kicking in, and gripped him by the arm. They tumbled back into the snow.

Stormi cleared her head. She wanted to run to the house, but her first thought was—gun.

She had a tranq gun in the clinic. And it was loaded with enough carfentanil to drop a grizzly bear—

She sprinted across the yard, Rome's snarls tearing the air behind her, the dogs barking, wild around him as the man shouted.

She reached the clinic door.

"Stormi!"

Wilder's voice, harsh, thundered into the air. She spun—there he was, silhouetted in the cabin's doorway, makeshift crutches under his arms, wearing the Carhartt clothing she'd given him and a Hudson's Bay blanket around his shoulders.

"Get back inside!"

"No way!"

He was moving. Actually moving, despite sixteen stitches and massive blood loss. Hobbling toward the fight through knee-deep snow, every step leaving dark spots where blood seeped through his bandages.

Stubborn, impossible man!

She turned back. The tranquilizer gun hung on its bracket just inside the clinic door, right where she'd left it after treating a wounded bull moose last month. She grabbed it, checked the cartridge.

Carfentanil would kill a man in minutes if she'd loaded it hot.

She hadn't. The cartridge held standard animal sedative—enough to knock out a wolf or a standard-size animal, not kill a human.

Back outside, the man was hitting Rome, but the dog refused to release his grip. Blood streamed from the man's wrist, and his jacket was torn in three places, the gun cast away in the snow. But he was fighting off the dog.

Her knees nearly buckled when a bowie knife flashed in his grip.

"Don't you touch him!" she screamed.

He pulled his hand back.

Stormi aimed and pulled the trigger. Shoot, the shot hit Rome and he yelped, then fell off the man.

Alive, but stunned.

The man turned then, his gaze on Wilder.

"Next one is yours," she said, shaking as she stalked toward the man. "Dare me."

He held up his hands, then pointed to Wilder. "Next time, you won't have your girlfriend to keep you alive."

Then he turned and took off across the yard.

"Shoot him," Wilder shouted.

Yeah, well, she'd been bluffing. No more darts. Still, she ran after him and scooped up his handgun, got a good look at him.

Tall, over six feet, wearing outdoor gear and a black wool hat. Built. He'd reached his machine—a dark snowmobile painted flat black.

She held up the handgun.

The engine roared to life, headlights throwing harsh shadows across churned snow.

Stormi pulled the trigger.

The shot went wide—as intended—and thudded into a pine tree over his head.

But close enough to make him duck. At least he'd know they were serious.

The snowmobile launched forward, tracks spitting snow and gravel as it disappeared into the forest. The engine noise faded, leaving only wind and her dogs' panting and the wild hammering of her heart against her ribs.

Silence settled over the compound, broken only by the distant whisper of wind through pine needles and the soft whimpers of her injured lead dog.

She ran over to Rome, asleep in the snow, and checked his vitals. Alive.

I'm sorry. She put her hand on him, and her knees just gave out. She sat in the snow, breathing hard, shaking. Koda came over to her, still whining.

She ran her hand over him and found where he'd been shot. A flesh wound, and it didn't look like it needed stitches.

"Stormi."

Wilder, halfway across the yard, crutches digging into snow, face gray with pain and effort.

"You should be inside!"

His mouth opened. "Seriously? You shouldn't have come out here."

"He would have killed my dogs to get me to come out." She kept her hands on Koda, Rome.

He reached her, breathing hard. Steam rose from his skin despite the cold. "Are you hurt?"

"I'm fine." She touched her split lip, then ran her tongue over it and tasted salt. "It's stopped bleeding. Nothing major."

"Nothing major." His eyes blazed—fury and fear warring in his expression. "He had a gun to your head, Stormi. I watched from the window. Watched him—" His voice cracked.

"But he didn't pull the trigger." She got up. "I'm okay. The dogs are okay. That's what matters."

His mouth made a dark, grim line, and his gaze went to her cheek. She awkwardly put her hand there, the skin hot, a bruise probably forming. "You should see the other guy."

"That's not funny. Sheesh." He shook his head. "I knew this would happen."

She had no words for that.

"Did you get a good look at him?"

Before she could respond, the sound of an engine thundered down the road. An SUV appeared in her driveway, the sheriff's emblem on the door.

She let out a breath. "Took them long enough."

The SUV pulled into her yard, engine cutting out. Three doors slammed shut as figures emerged, wearing winter hats and adjusting heavy coats, breath steaming in the frigid air.

"Sorry we're late." Sheriff Starr approached, taking in the scene—blood in the snow, scattered equipment, her split lip, Wilder on crutches looking ready to collapse. "What did we miss?"

AND THAT'S WHY he shouldn't have come here.

Wilder's entire body shook, his mind replaying the horror of watching Stormi wrestle for her life even as Deke came closer. "Wilder?"

"Hey, Deke."

His mouth opened a little and Wilder made a face. So, this was fun. "I'm not dead."

"Clearly. What on earth—where have you been?" Deke held out his hand. Wilder leaned on a crutch and took it.

"Long story."

Deke eyed his leg.

"Wilder Frost." Jericho Bowie's voice carried shock and something that might have been relief. "I haven't seen you in years." The man had put on weight and girth since Wilder had last seen him, maybe seven years ago, when his parents were killed.

"Jericho," Wilder said, shaking his hand too. "When did you get back? Last I heard you were in the military. Afghanistan?"

"Another long story."

He glanced over at the blond beside Jericho. "Harley Tatum. I haven't seen you since your brother's funeral."

She lifted an eyebrow. "Right. Um . . . about that . . ." She sighed, looked at Stormi. "You okay?"

"Not even a little. You just missed an attack," Wilder said as Deke helped Stormi round her dogs up and usher them back into the enclosure.

"By who?"

That was the thing. His hands turned white on his crutches. "I don't know. But let's get inside."

Stormi had gathered her dogs and now walked over to Rome. Deke bent down and picked the dog up and followed Stormi into the house.

"What happened to your leg?" Jericho asked as they, too, headed into the cabin.

"I got shot," Wilder said, and didn't elaborate, the effort of climbing the porch stairs taking all his breath.

Inside, after Deke set her dog on the floor, Stormi checked his pulse. The animal roused, whining, and she got an ice pack, put it on his wound. "Sorry, buddy."

"What happened?" Deke asked.

"The man was going to kill Rome," Stormi said.

Deke frowned. "What man?"

Stormi looked at Wilder. The split on her lip had stopped bleeding, leaving only a thin red line.

His fault.

All of it.

His presence had put a gun to her head, his stupid choices had brought danger to her doorstep. His entire body ached. "Stormi needs medical attention." The words came out rougher than intended. "That cut should be cleaned properly, and—"

"I'm fine." She touched the corner of her mouth. Winced slightly.

"You're not supposed to treat yourself."

"Says the man who tried to pry out a bullet with his hunting knife."

"That was Jenny's handiwork—"

"Hold up," Deke said, turning to Wilder. "Let's start with where you have been. We had search teams combing the wilderness for days."

"Hiding. And then more hiding." Wilder moved to the kitchen, needing distance from Stormi's bruised face. "There's an old mining tunnel system in the mountains. Shelter, fresh water, enough supplies to wait out the worst of the blizzard."

"For three weeks?" Jericho asked.

Wilder poured Jericho a cup of coffee, then handed it to him. He filled another, passed it to Harley.

"Just for forty-eight hours. Then I went looking for help. I didn't get far. I was in bad shape by then. Orion found me—brought me back to his cabin. Jenny tried to doctor me. They hid me."

"Orion and Jenny?" Harley asked. She glanced at Deke. "You didn't know this?"

Deke shook his head.

"I called Vic and Luna—they know I'm alive. But I swore them to silence. I was better off dead . . . until now."

Wilder glanced at Stormi, caught her watching him. "I should have stayed dead, probably, but I heard about the car accident Stormi was checking out yesterday and got worried. I thought it might be Luna and Vic. By the time I realized it wasn't, I was already in trouble. My injury had turned red, swelled up—"

"Infected," Stormi said from the sofa.

"Yeah, well." He shifted his weight against the crutches. "I found a body first though."

The room went silent.

"Where?" Deke asked.

"A couple clicks from here. Our best guess is the driver of the car. Actually, Rome found him, I think. I followed the dog's tracks back to the cabin."

Deke nodded. "Okay. And then . . . someone showed up this morning?"

"He caught my call to you," Stormi said, rubbing Rome's ears. The dog's tail thumped on the wood floor.

"Did you get a good look at him?" Deke asked.

Wilder's mouth pinched, and he nodded. "It looked like . . . Tommy Reid."

Deke frowned at him. "Tommy Reid? The old deputy sheriff? He hasn't been around Copper Mountain for years. Not since his wife died."

"He's working as a PI in the Juneau area," Harley said.

"Why would Tommy Reid be trying to find you?" Deke asked.

"No, why would he be trying to kill Wilder?" Stormi added.

"I know why." Harley took her phone from her pocket. "Because of this." She pulled up a photo and handed her phone to Wilder.

Surveillance photos. Airport scenes. North Face Construction trucks parked on the tarmac. And there—Pete Barrow talking with a man in a Copper Mountain Sheriff's Department uniform. The deputy's badge caught the camera flash, and his face was clear enough to be confirmed in a courtroom. Sloan Sorros was in yet another photo, the North Face Construction truck in the background.

Wilder knew these photos. He'd taken them. "Where did you get these?"

"My dad hid a file at the house. We found it—these were inside. I think Dad was building a case against Tommy and possibly North Face Construction."

"Before he died."

She nodded. "Before my parents and the Bowies were killed in a crash that we think was sabotage." She held his gaze. "And I'm wondering if you know something about that."

He blew out a breath. "Yeah. I might."

Silence.

Harley took a sip of her coffee, her gaze not leaving his face.

"I worked part-time at the FBO before . . . well, before your parents were killed." He lowered himself onto the sofa. "Tommy's wife, Heidi, worked there, so he was there a lot. Worked security shifts there himself, off and on. Sometimes he came out to talk to me. Always had questions."

Jericho's face went stone-cold. "What kind of questions?"

"Who was flying where. When planes were being fueled." Wilder's leg had started to burn. Yeah, he could use some meds. "I saw him with Sloan Sorros more than once."

"Do you remember anything about the crash that killed our parents?" Jericho asked.

Wilder glanced at Jericho. "Some, yes. I remember that Senator

Bowie's plane was scheduled for an early departure. Weather was marginal but flyable for someone with his experience. I got to the FBO around six a.m. to prep for the day."

"Did you fuel their plane?"

"No."

Jericho frowned. "Are you sure?"

"It was already fueled. Tank was full, all systems checked, prop cover removed. I remember thinking it was odd—usually I handled the morning prep work. Someone had been there ahead of me, done everything except file the flight plan. And then, a few hours later, their plane went down, and all I could think was something wasn't right."

Silence settled over the room. Outside, wind whistled through the forest, rattling the cabin's metal roof.

"You think Sloan was involved," Stormi said.

Not a question.

Wilder met her eyes. Found his own certainty reflected there. "Yeah. I think he tampered with the fuel. And I think Tommy Reid helped him."

"But you can't prove it," Deke said.

"I can connect Sloan to the airport. To Tommy. To the North Face Construction trucks, but that's all I have. I'm not sure that's enough to open the investigation into both crashes."

"But it could be. Which is why he wants you dead." Harley pocketed her phone. "You're not just a witness to Darrin Wheeler's murder anymore. You're the key to proving Sloan or Tommy killed four people."

Four people.

Five, including Dawn. The thought slammed into Wilder, stealing his breath. Then, "Maybe Dawn's death wasn't about my seeing the shooting." He didn't know why that came out.

Deke looked at him, his mouth a tight line. "Tommy's wife died just a few days before Dawn did, if I remember right. Single vehicle rollover. She died on the way to the hospital." Then he frowned. "Dawn also died in a wreck, right? Her car went through the guardrail, rolled down the embankment. They found her thrown from the vehicle?"

That's how it had seemed. Wilder said nothing. Maybe Deke hadn't read the coroner's report. Or maybe he had and was playing it close to the vest.

"Or she—they—were murdered," Harley said with a wisp of a voice.

"Why would Tommy murder his wife?" Jericho asked.

Wilder looked at him. "Not Tommy. Sloan. Tommy's wife worked at the airport. Maybe she . . . she knew something?"

Deke was staring at him.

"What?"

"Dawn. She was the first on the scene, if I remember."

He stilled, everything turning hollow inside. "Right. I forgot that."

"She might have talked to Heidi before she died."

"Wilder," Stormi said, "are you okay?"

He just stared at her.

"You're white as a sheet."

Wilder shook his head. "She never said anything about it." Or maybe he just hadn't paid attention.

"I'm getting you some pain meds." Stormi got up, then headed into the kitchen.

Jericho stood, moved to the window overlooking the dog yard where churned snow still showed dark patches from the morning's violence.

Wilder looked at Deke. "You think whoever killed Dawn was after what Heidi knew."

"I don't know."

"So what's the plan?" Jericho asked. "We can't exactly post a guard here. We don't have the manpower."

"We don't need to," Deke said. "Weather service is predicting a major ice storm moving in soon. Freezing rain, followed by snow, followed by subzero temperatures. Nobody's going to be moving around for at least a couple days. That gives us time to coordinate with state authorities, maybe even federal resources."

"What about Luna?" The question tore from Wilder's throat.

"She's safe." Deke folded his arms. "I just talked with Vic. They're fine. Your best bet is to sit tight. Reid won't be coming back."

"Let him," Stormi said as she walked over and held out a couple ibuprofen to Wilder. She had a glass of water in the other hand.

Deke gave her a look.

Wilder did too, and he caught the slight flush climbing Stormi's neck, above the collar of that wool sweater. Even exhausted and bruised, with her hair escaping its ponytail and worry lines creasing her forehead, she was beautiful.

And brave.

And again, he shouldn't have dragged her into this.

"We need to get back on the road." Harley stood, shouldering her jacket. "The storm's supposed to hit hard and fast."

"No. I have my dogs. I need to stay," Stormi said.

Jericho moved away from the window. "Tommy knows where you live now. He'll be back with reinforcements."

"No, he won't. He'll expect us to leave. And the weather is our shield."

Deke nodded. "You stay put, keep your head down. We'll put a BOLO out for Tommy."

"And Sloan Sorros," Wilder said. "Sloan is still out there. He's in all this. I know it."

"I'm still not sold on you two staying out here," Harley said. "Stay at the Copper Mountain Lodge. Jericho can keep an eye on you."

Color had drained from Stormi's face, but her chin came up. "Listen. This is my home. My clinic. My dogs that got shot at. I've never run from bullies, and I'm not starting now."

Wilder found himself close enough to catch the scent of her shampoo. Close enough to see the flecks of gold in her hazel eyes and the way her pulse fluttered at the base of her throat.

Close enough for his own pulse to hike up, for pain to net his chest. "You could have been killed."

"But I wasn't."

"Next time—"

"There won't be a next time." She met his gaze. "Because we're going to find him first."

We?

Something shifted in his chest. Loosened and tightened at the same time.

Harley nodded slowly. "She's right. Sitting around waiting for Sloan to make the next move isn't exactly a winning strategy."

Deke cleared his throat. "Ice storm, remember? Nobody's finding anybody for the next few days. Besides, you leave the finding to us, okay?"

Stormi's mouth firmed at the edges, and Wilder didn't like the look of it. He glanced at Deke. "You sure Luna and Vic are safe?"

"I'll send a patrol out, keep watch on them," Deke said. "In the meantime, we'll figure out how to find Sloan. And Tommy."

"I don't like it," Jericho said.

"You don't have to like it." Stormi moved to the kitchen, began clearing coffee mugs. Loudly. "But Wilder's not leaving, and neither am I."

She met his eyes. "Listen. Sometimes the bravest thing you can do is trust that you're not facing it alone."

And with her words, he actually felt something shift, hard, inside him. A wall maybe, being punched.

Hope, like a light, bursting through.

He nearly gasped, put a hand to his chest.

"We'll find him, Wilder," Harley said.

Jericho nodded.

Stormi had walked back into the room, and now her hand found his shoulder, warmth seeping through the flannel shirt she'd given him, straight into the cold places in his chest. "Everything's going to be okay."

And despite everything—the pain, the danger, the ice storm bearing down on them with the weight of an Alaskan winter—Wilder found himself believing her.

4

STORMI TRIED TO FOCUS on chopping carrots for the stew she was making, but her hands trembled every time Wilder shifted on the couch behind her. Twelve years of hero worship collided with the reality that her childhood idol was now bleeding and broken in her living room. She had no idea how to be anything other than completely, hopelessly undone.

Especially as her words replayed in her head. *"Because we're going to find him first."*

What*ever.* Her mouth speaking before her brain could engage.

She'd dug out the Remington 12-gauge and now it leaned against the doorframe, shells loaded. Ice pelted the windows, and the emergency weather radio crackled with updates about wind speeds and temperature drops that could kill the unprepared.

Maybe Tommy was still out there.

But he wasn't getting in here.

Inside her cabin, warmth radiated from the fireplace where Rome sprawled across worn pine floorboards, thankfully recovered from the tranq shot. Maybe she shouldn't have tried to shoot Tommy, but all she saw was him killing her dog.

Thankfully, Rome hadn't been killed—frankly, the entire thing had been panic-inducing.

Rome had recovered, and now his tail thumped, as if he knew she might be thinking of him. Sweet dog. Clearly still possessed some of his early training, because he'd taken down Tommy like the old K9 blood still flowed inside him.

The scent of simmering meat filled the kitchen—beef and chicken scraps cooking down with rice and vegetables. Her propane stove hissed under the big aluminum pot, and lamps cast golden light across her timber-framed home.

"That smells incredible." Wilder's voice carried from the living room. "I didn't realize how hungry I was."

Stormi glanced over her shoulder. He sat propped against couch cushions, wrapped in a Hudson's Bay blanket. The red flannel shirt she'd given him hung loose on his frame—but he still possessed the presence of the indomitable legendary musher.

In her home.

On her sofa.

Oh my.

Dark stubble shadowed his jaw, and those blue eyes that had stared at her from her bedroom wall in Minnesota now carried the weight of too much loss.

Still beautiful. Still dangerous to her peace of mind.

Yeah, she might be in over her head.

"Dinner will be ready in about twenty minutes." She turned back to the stove, stirring the mixture with a wooden spoon. "Hope you don't mind basic camp food."

"After three weeks of Jenny's attempts at cooking, anything that doesn't taste like charcoal sounds perfect."

She laughed despite her nerves. "Aw, her cooking can't be that bad."

"Maybe I just have destroyed taste buds from years of field

rations." The couch creaked as he shifted position. "How do you know Jenny?"

"Anuk introduced me to the Starrs before I bought the practice." Stormi added salt to the pot, tasted the broth. "Plus, I treated a couple of their dogs for worms last summer. Jenny insisted on helping, which mostly involved her talking nonstop while I worked."

"Sounds about right."

The comfortable rhythm of conversation loosened something in Stormi's chest. The trauma of this morning's attack.

The surgery last night on Wilder's leg.

The fact that she was suddenly up to her neck in his danger. And really, she didn't care. Her words rounded back to her again. *"We're going to find him first."*

She was all tough talk, impulse and bravado. And hadn't a clue what she might be doing.

But yeah, if she could, she'd help him figure out how to get free of this nightmare. Her heart broke hearing about his memory of his wife's death. Felt like there might be more to that story, but the last thing she would do was pry.

She ladled the mixture into a large ceramic bowl, then moved toward the living room. "Here you go." She set the bowl on the floor near Rome.

Wilder picked it up, inhaling the rich aroma. "This smells amazing. What kind of herbs did you use?"

"Oh, um, that's not for you." Stormi blinked. "That's dog food. I was cooking it down for the team since they'll be confined during the storm. I'm making our dinner next."

Dead silence.

Wilder stared at the bowl in his hands, then up at her face, then back at the bowl. A slow grin spread across his features, the first genuine smile she'd seen from him.

"Well, it does smell better than most of what I've eaten lately."

"Don't you dare. That's for Rome." She lunged forward, grabbing the bowl before he could take a bite. "Wait for your real food."

"I was kidding." His eyes crinkled with humor. "Mostly."

Heat climbed her neck. "Right. Of course. I just . . . I'm not used to having people over."

"Really?" He gestured toward the kitchen where dog leashes hung from hooks, vaccination schedules covered the refrigerator, and medical supplies filled every available shelf. "This place screams bachelorette veterinarian."

"Is that an insult?"

"It's an observation." His voice gentled. "Why did you move out here? This is pretty remote, even for Alaska. And you're all by yourself."

Was that a question? Probing?

Stop!

Stormi set the food down for Rome, who dug in. Through the frost-covered window, she could see her sled dogs huddled in their insulated houses, riding out the storm.

She headed back to the kitchen. "When I heard that Anuk wanted to sell her place, it felt perfect. I wanted space to work my team." She opened a cabinet, pulled out ingredients for human dinner—eggs and bread for toasting. "In town, you're limited to short runs, neighbors complaining about barking, ordinances about how many dogs you can keep."

"How's it working out?"

Stormi cracked eggs into a bowl with more force than necessary. "Not great."

Silence stretched between them, filled only by the storm's howling and the soft pop of burning wood.

"They don't work together," she continued. "Seven dogs, seven different personalities, zero teamwork. It's like trying to herd cats."

"What about Rome?"

She glanced toward the living room where the Malador mix had finished gulping down his food and now lay sprawled by the fireplace again, completely relaxed despite the chaos outside. "Rome's the biggest troublemaker of them all."

"He seems pretty mellow right now."

"That's because he's not trying to be a sled dog." Stormi poured the eggs into a hot skillet, where they hissed and bubbled. "He's got the right breeding—Malamute—but the Labrador in him wants to track. He can't focus."

"Then why keep trying?"

The question stopped her mid-stir. Because she loved him. Because giving up felt wrong. Because admitting failure hurt worse than continuing to fail.

"Because he's . . . he's not done yet." She turned. "I got him from the police department about two years ago. Former search and rescue dog, specialized in trailing. His handler got sick—COVID—and somehow he caught it too."

"Dogs can get COVID?"

"Some can. It's rare, but . . ." She turned back to the stove and flipped the eggs, watched the edges turn golden. "It destroyed his sense of smell completely. A scent dog who can't smell is a pilot who can't see."

"That's rough."

"His handler couldn't keep him after that. No job, no purpose. They brought him to a shelter, hoping someone would adopt him, but he just got depressed, wouldn't eat, barely moved." The memory tightened her throat. "I saw him on an adoption website, took one look at those sad amber eyes, and knew I had to try something."

"So you thought mushing?"

"I thought exercise, fresh air, a reason to run." She slid the eggs onto a plate, added buttered toast and crispy bacon she'd fried earlier in a separate pan. "Turns out there's a difference between running for joy and running in harness. Rome's got too much independence, too much intelligence. He thinks for himself instead of following the team."

"Sounds familiar."

Something in his tone made her glance up. Wilder was watching her with an expression she couldn't read.

"What's that supposed to mean?"

"Nothing. Just that some of the best dogs I've known were super smart, thought for themselves. Knew how to sense trouble and stay away from it."

So, she wouldn't fall into that category.

Stormi carried his dinner to the living room, set it on the coffee table within easy reach. The domestic gesture felt strange, intimate in a way that had nothing to do with romance and everything to do with caring for someone in her own space.

"How did you get into mushing?" he asked, cutting into the eggs. "It's not exactly common in Minnesota."

"More common than you'd think. We have a number of mushers who live in northern Minnesota, and my dad knows them all." She settled into the chair across from him, cradling her own plate. "He's a veterinarian, has a practice in Brainerd, but he specializes in sled dogs. He took care of Nick Dahlquist's team when he competed. Went to all his races."

Wilder paused mid-bite. "Nick Dahlquist the musher?"

"You know him?"

"Know of him. Mid-distance specialist, won the Beargrease Sled Dog Marathon three times running." He took another bite, chewed thoughtfully. "Good reputation, ethical. Seems like a good guy."

"Dad took me to a lot of the races, and later, I spent the summer helping Nick train his dogs." Warmth spread through her chest at the memory. "When I got older, Dad let me help take care of his team on one of his races."

"So, why Alaska?"

Stormi pushed food around her plate. "Nick always said the best mushers came from Alaska. The Iditarod, the Yukon Quest, the really challenging races. Minnesota's got good dogs, good training, and a couple good races, but Alaska's got the real wilderness."

"And?"

"And I wanted to prove I could do it." Actually, "Dad always wanted to be a musher. I felt like maybe I could pick up that dream. Hard to invest when you are also working full time . . ."

"For sure. It's expensive and dangerous, and the best mushers focus only on training and caring for their dogs."

She sighed. "I probably need to face the fact that it's never going to happen."

He looked at her and she put her fork down. "Truth is," she went on, "a part of me is okay with that. I sort of wonder if I followed that dream because . . . well, it was the only time I really got my dad to myself. It was our thing."

"Your thing?"

She drew in a breath. Considered him. Okay, why not? "I saw you run the Iditarod twelve years ago." The words tumbled out before she could stop them. "Dad took me to Alaska for my birthday, flew us up to Anchorage to watch the start. You were the youngest competitor that year."

"Twenty-two." His voice went quiet. "And stupid enough to think age didn't matter."

"You came in third."

"I came in lucky." He shifted against the couch cushions, and she caught the wince he tried to hide. "That race nearly killed me. Weather was brutal, my lead dog got injured, I made every rookie mistake in the book."

"But you finished."

"Barely."

"You inspired a lot of people." Including her. *Especially* her. "The way you handled the storm in the middle section, when half the field was scratching. The comeback after your sled broke. The media called it one of the best rookie performances in Iditarod history."

"The media loves a good story." His voice carried something dark. "Reality's usually messier."

"Is that why you stopped racing?"

Silence stretched between them. The wind howled around the cabin's eaves, and ice continued its assault on the windows. The dogs would be restless, no doubt sensing the storm's power.

"I met Dawn that summer." Wilder's voice came out soft, distant. "She was working as a nurse practitioner with her dad at their remote clinic. I was up there training, using the wilderness trails to condition my team for the Quest."

Stormi gave him her full attention.

"I'd been dealing with sponsorship issues, media pressure, everyone wanting to know if the kid who came in third was going to be the next big thing." He rubbed his temples. "I was exhausted, overwhelmed, starting to hate something I'd loved my whole life." He drew in a breath. "And then I crashed my sled crossing a creek. Nothing serious, just pilot error, but I was soaked and hypothermic by the time I made it to their clinic." A ghost of a smile crossed his face. "Dawn took one look at me and said, 'Let me guess. Another adrenaline junkie who thinks he's tougher than Alaska.'"

Despite everything, Stormi smiled. "Harsh but probably accurate."

"That's what I told her. And she said, 'Good. At least you're honest about it.'" He pulled the blanket higher around his shoulders. "Most people saw the race results, the magazine covers, the sponsorship deals. Dawn saw a kid who was scared he was losing himself in other people's expectations."

"She sounds smart."

"She was." The warmth in his voice made Stormi's chest ache. "We spent that whole summer talking about everything except mushing. She wanted to know about my family, my dreams, the person I was before anyone knew my name."

"And she saw past all the glory to the guy inside."

"Yeah." He met her eyes. "How did you know that?"

The thought hit her clearly. *Because that's what I've been trying to do since I was fourteen years old. Because I've been watching you from a distance for years, wondering what it would be like to really know you.*

"Lucky guess," she said instead.

He grunted. "Dawn understood that mushing was part of me, but it wasn't all of me."

Huh. But his words nudged something inside her.

"We got married, moved to a cabin outside Talkeetna. Dawn continued her nursing work, I focused on breeding and training instead of racing. Luna was born three years later."

"She must barely remember her mother."

Pain flashed across his face. "That's what kills me. Luna was four when Dawn died. She has fragments—the sound of Dawn's voice singing lullabies, a blanket Dawn made for her with her smell on it. But the details are fading."

"That's why you take her to see her family."

"Una, her grandmother, tells Luna stories about Dawn, shows her pictures, keeps those memories alive." He sighed. "I try, but I'm not . . . I can't replace what she lost."

"You're her father. That's irreplaceable."

"Is it?" The question came out raw. "Sometimes I think Luna would be better off with someone more stable. Someone who isn't constantly looking over his shoulder. A mom *and* a dad."

"Wilder—"

"She deserves better than wondering if her dad's going to come home."

Stormi set her plate aside, leaned forward in her chair. "Does she know what happened to her mother?"

"She knows it was an accident. A car wreck." His voice went flat. "She doesn't know it was murder. Doesn't know her father's testimony got her mother killed."

"That's not your fault."

"Isn't it?" Blue eyes met hers, blazing with guilt and grief. "I'm the one who witnessed Darrin's murder. I'm the one who agreed to testify. I'm the one who put a target on our family."

"You're the one who tried to do the right thing."

"The right thing got Dawn tortured and killed."

She stilled, ice running through her. "Tortured?"

He looked stricken, suddenly, his mouth opening. "Oh. I uh . . . shoot. That just slipped out."

"Oh, Wilder. What happened? Are you sure? Deke said she was thrown from the car."

"Deke was new to the job then. Dawn's dad, Dr. Caius Matthews, asked the coroner down in Anchorage for an autopsy. I don't know if Deke ever read it."

She said nothing, her body a knot. *Tortured?*

He looked away from her, out the windows where the snow billowed. "She didn't die in the car crash. She was taken and beaten and her body was placed near the car—they staged her death. But I knew. She was beaten because of me."

The words hung between them, stark and brutal. Stormi's throat turned raw. "And you're sure?"

"The Sorros family made Dawn suffer before they killed her," he said softly.

"Wilder." Her voice came out barely a whisper. "I'm so sorry." She reached out to him.

He flinched, then drew in a breath. "Sorry. I . . . I shouldn't have told you that."

"Yes, you should have." She had pulled back her hand, but now moved to the window overlooking the dog yard. "You can't carry that alone."

"I've been carrying it alone for three years."

"And how's that working out?"

Silence stretched between them. The wind shifted direction, sending ice pellets against a different section of window. The sound was insistent, demanding attention.

"You ever feel like, no matter what you do, you just can't win?"

She looked over at him. Swallowed. "More than you know."

He considered her a moment.

"What do you do with that?"

"I . . . I pray."

He raised an eyebrow.

"I remind myself that God is on my side."

He said nothing, listening.

"Just because we think we're not doing anything doesn't mean that's the truth. The devil would like nothing more than for us to believe that we're failures and to give up. That we're in over our heads, without rescue."

A small smile lifted. "You sound like Dawn."

Oh. Um . . .

"Not in a weird way, but . . . Dawn had this way of believing in good, that God was with her. She loved hymns—she grew up on a remote homestead, and her parents taught her hymns. She'd hum them. 'Great Is Thy Faithfulness.' 'Blessed Assurance.' I know all the words because of her."

"Even if you don't believe?" Oh, why had she said *that*?

"I believe that God is real. And once upon a time, I trusted Jesus to save me. And then . . . I grew up."

Oh. "Wilder."

"Some beds you make, and you have to lie in them. God isn't coming to my rescue."

Right. Well, given his last few years, she got that. "But you do know that's a lie, right? That God doesn't work that way. If he did, then he would have never sent Jesus to save us."

And suddenly, this felt a little like a Billy Graham crusade. All she needed was an altar call.

"Sorry. I don't mean to preach. I just . . . well, I believe God is all about rescue."

Wilder nodded, his mouth grim.

"Ho-kay, then. Have you ever played The Farming Game?"

Before he could respond, Rome lifted his head from his spot by the stove, ears twitching toward the window. But after a moment, he settled back down with a contented sigh—just the wind shifting through the trees.

"Something's out there," Wilder said, following her gaze.

"Just the storm." Stormi moved back to her chair, set the shotgun within easy reach. "The dogs would be going wild outside if it were anything serious."

The woodstove popped and hissed.

"Thank you," Wilder said.

"For what?"

"Dinner. The stories. Making this feel"—he gestured around the warm cabin—"normal."

"Normal's overrated." But her chest warmed at the compliment.

"Is it?" He leaned back against the pillows. "Sometimes I think Luna's forgotten what normal feels like."

"She's seven. Kids are resilient."

"Maybe." His voice carried doubt. "But three years is a long time to live in fear. Three years of jumping every time someone knocks on the door."

"Trouble doesn't usually knock," Stormi said.

He grunted, but she got a smile out of him.

"Is that why you haven't . . ." Stormi stopped herself before the question could escape completely. *C'mon, Stormi!*

"Haven't what?"

Heat climbed her neck. "Nothing. It's not my business."

"Go ahead. After everything I've told you tonight, I think we're past polite boundaries."

"I just wondered if you'd ever thought about . . . moving on. Finding someone else." The words tumbled out in a rush. "For Luna's sake, I mean. You said yourself she needs—"

"A mother figure." His voice went flat. "Yeah, I've thought about it."

"But?"

"But every woman I've cared about has ended up hurt or dead." The words came out stark, brutal. "My girlfriend in high school fell through ice and nearly died because of me. Dawn was tortured and murdered because she was married to me."

"That may not be true—"

"I'm just sayin', I'm not exactly a good risk."

"That's not fair to yourself."

"Isn't it?" Blue eyes met hers across the coffee table. "Pattern recognition is a survival skill, Stormi. Smart women stay away from men who are trouble."

Translation: Don't get attached. Don't start caring. Don't think the fact that her childhood hero was sitting on her sofa, sharing a meal and smiling at her meant anything beyond temporary shelter and friendship.

Message received.

Except, um, too late.

"Right." She stood, began collecting the dishes. "Of course."

"Stormi—"

"It's fine." She carried their plates to the kitchen. "You're probably tired. Long day. And I'm sure you're in pain. You should rest."

"What did I say wrong?"

Everything. Nothing.

Oh, she was an idiot.

"Nothing." She ran the water in the sink with more force than necessary. "You're just being realistic."

"About what?"

About the fact that her childhood crush had evolved into something deeper and even more ridiculous.

Good grief. Maybe she had blizzard fever.

"About keeping appropriate boundaries." She set the plates in the soapy water, reached for the coffee mugs. "You're injured. And hurting. I'm glad I can help."

Silence stretched between them, filled with the sound of running water and her increasingly aggressive dish washing.

Silence. She finished the dishes, stacked them, then dried her hands.

When she turned back around, the man had fallen asleep on the sofa, the stress lines around his eyes loosening, his face a sort of peace.

Okay, so maybe she'd run too hard and too fast into the idea of . . . well, that she had her hero trapped on her sofa. Like she could compel the man to choose her. Fall for her.

But here he was, Wilder Frost in her home. And with a blizzard in front of them . . . anything could happen.

ANOTHER DAY in paradise.

Wilder sat up from his perch on the sofa and tested his range of motion. Stormi stood in the kitchen, going through her medical kit.

Oh goody, another wound check on the horizon. And him without his whiskey.

She glanced over at him. "You're awake."

"Sorry. It's the storm. Wind makes me sleepy."

She laughed. "There is something magical about a blizzard, if you're not caught out in it. I used to love storms in Minnesota. We'd skip school and my mom would make us hot cocoa."

"You have siblings?" He rolled his shoulder, then flexed his leg. The wound pulled—still tender, but manageable. The kind of manageable that meant he could move when he needed to. When the time came.

Probably not for another day, however. He sighed, leaned back against the cushions.

"Yeah," she said, pouring a cup of coffee. "I have a brother, Ridge—he's a lawyer down in Anchorage, and a sister, Aspen, who is a life coach with a podcast and a bestselling book and celebrity clients. I'm the youngest. Just me and the dogs, hiding in the woods."

"Hey, I'm here too." He took the coffee she proffered.

"Yes, you are." She returned to the kitchen, but she wore a smile.

And it settled all the raging inside him.

He'd thought the storm might be winding down when he woke. The howling wind had dropped to intermittent gusts. And then, with the advent of dawn, the storm had riled up again.

Now, ice coated the windows in sheets and snow kept sliding off the corrugated metal roof.

Thump.

Another avalanche from the eaves.

Maybe they'd be trapped here until spring. Which, okay, wasn't a terrible thought. If he were honest, he didn't want to leave. Somehow, two days of being cooped up with Stormi had reached into his soul, balmed it, even unearthed . . . well, a terrible unnamed longing.

The kind of longing that had him wanting to take back his stupid words. *"Smart women stay away from men who are trouble."*

Wow, that was . . . epically pitiful.

And worse, he'd hurt her. Because he didn't have to have a high emotional IQ to figure out that *"You're just being realistic"* meant "Ouch."

And, yes, it had taken a whole day and another night's sleep for him to fully catch up to her story, but . . . she'd gone to his race when she was fourteen.

Fourteen.

Which put him a good eight years older than her. Made her twenty-six. Sheesh, no wonder she had so much energy. So many big dreams.

Life hadn't punched them out of her yet. No wonder she still felt God was on her side—and yes, that sat with him too. Her faith.

Reminded him a little about how bereft he was of his.

"I'm going to take a shower," he said and then pushed himself up from the sofa with a grunt.

She had poured herself coffee. "You saw my medical supplies and are making a run for the hills."

"Ha ha. But yes, something like that." He limped over to the only bathroom in the small cabin. Off the main room sat two bedrooms, one turned into an office. Hence his stay on the sofa.

Maybe he was out of practice a little but was astute enough to realize that she still harbored some feelings of hero worship. Or she had.

Clearly, the last day or so had ground those into appropriate dust. She'd beat him soundly in three hands of gin rummy, criticized the chili he'd made last night, and in the middle of the night, after waking him to check his wound, told him to stop snoring.

Shoot, he liked her. She was funny and smart and capable and . . .

He needed to leave. Before he let his stupid, lonely heart make decisions for him.

"I thought you might clean up today," Stormi told him, "so I left a fresh flannel shirt and a pair of flannel jammie pants on the hook in the bathroom."

"You just happen to have some men's clothing hanging around?" Oh, for the—why had he said *that*?

"My brother left some of his clothing here when he helped me move. I laundered them, but you might as well get some use out of them."

Her brother. Of course.

Then why did his breath release the weird coil in his chest?

Pull yourself together, Frost. Except, he'd be lying if her question hadn't settled inside him. *"I just wondered if you'd ever thought about . . . moving on. Finding someone else."*

Not until he landed here, on her porch.

Okay, maybe before, but he didn't have to admit that.

He closed the door behind him, then turned on the shower to heat up the water. Oy, he looked rough. The red-and-black flannel shirt she'd given him fit better now that blood loss was no longer stealing the strength from his body. His beard had thickened since last time he shaved it at Orion's place.

But he looked and felt like Sasquatch, or some lumbering bear from the woods. Probably he should be thankful she hadn't kicked him out into the snow.

Stripping down, he got into the shower and tried to turn into some semblance of a human, then he got back out and pulled on the fresh clothes she'd left for him.

He emerged to a weather update. "The storm should blow out over the day," Stormi said. She was standing next to the sofa. "Sit down." She patted the couch cushion, medical scissors and fresh gauze arranged on the pine coffee table beside the scattered remnants of their marathon Monopoly game. "Let me check that leg."

"It's fine." But he moved toward the couch anyway. Couldn't seem to stop himself from giving her what she wanted.

"Humor me," she said now, arms folded, not a hint of spark in her pretty eyes. "Drop 'em."

Maybe he preferred the hero worship.

He wore shorts under his flannel pants and now peeled down the pants to reveal the dressing. He stayed standing as Stormi checked the gauze for drainage, before easing himself onto the sofa.

From his angle, the stitches looked perfect, even after Tommy's attack. No redness, no swelling. She'd cleaned him up well, the edges of his wound knitting together with the clean precision of healthy tissue repair.

"You heal fast." She probed gently around the entry site, and he tried to ignore the way his pulse kicked up when she leaned closer. *Stop!*

"Clean living."

"Right." She applied more antibiotic ointment, then secured fresh gauze with medical tape, smoothing the edges with more care than necessary.

Or that could be his imagination.

Icicles hung from the eaves outside her kitchen window—some as thick as his arm and long enough to reach the ground.

"How's the pain level?" Stormi asked.

"Manageable."

"Scale of one to ten?"

"Two. Maybe three when I push it."

"Don't push it."

"I need to know my limits."

She went still. "Why?"

Aw. He pulled away from her. "You know why."

"Because you're planning something stupid?"

"Because I'm planning to end this." He stood and pulled up his pants, covering the bandage. "As soon as this storm clears, I'm going after Sloan."

Color drained from her face. Through the window, he could see the weather vane on her barn spinning in the shifting wind—north to south, then back again, as if the storm couldn't decide whether to release its grip on the Copper River Valley.

"Alone."

"Yes."

"You'd be walking into a death trap."

"Maybe." He moved to the window overlooking the dog yard where her team huddled in their insulated houses. Snow had begun sliding off their roofs, too, revealing the bright blue plastic underneath. "But it's my choice."

"What about Luna?"

He drew in a breath. "Luna needs to live in peace. It's my job as her father to protect her."

"That's so selfish."

He turned, his eyes wide. "Seriously?"

"Your daughter needs you. And you have help."

"Tell me how you really feel."

"I will." She moved closer, close enough that he could catch her scent—soap and winter air and something uniquely her that made his chest tighten. "You've bought into the lie that you don't get to have a happy ending."

His jaw tightened. "Excuse me?"

"You heard me. You said it the other day—you made your bed. Now you have to lie in it. Because you think you cause disasters."

"I do."

"No. You're a good guy who had a terrible thing happen to *him*."

He looked away. "I'm protecting—"

"Nobody. You're protecting nobody by getting yourself killed."

Yeah, whatever hero worship she'd possessed had clearly been ground to ash.

But she wasn't wrong.

"And if you ask me, going after Sloan alone is just you taking the easy way out."

He gaped at her.

"Don't look at me that way," she said. "It's easier to go it alone than to trust someone. Let someone help you. It's easier than admitting you might need a partner."

A partner?

The word landed and sort of rang in his head. She wanted to be his partner?

For a second, the word brought back memories of Dawn, of what it felt like to have someone who stood beside him, regardless of his mistakes, his faults.

And then Dawn vanished and it was simply Stormi before him, her hazel eyes on his.

They stared at each other across the small space.

The thermometer mounted outside the kitchen window read two degrees Fahrenheit. Above freezing by tomorrow. Warm enough for travel.

"I had a dog once," she said suddenly. The fire popped in the woodstove, sending sparks up the chimney and the scent of burning birch through the room. "When I was twelve. He was a big, tough old mutt named Cooper. He got into it with a bull moose out behind our place, came home with his shoulder torn open. Dad stitched him up in our kitchen—forty-three stitches. I counted while holding the surgical light. Dad gave me strict instructions to keep Cooper quiet while he healed, confined to the mudroom where he couldn't tear out his sutures. But ole

Coop was stubborn. Independent. Thought he knew better than the people trying to help him."

His mouth twitched. "Are you comparing me to a dog?"

"Cooper wouldn't stay still. He tore out his stitches twice and kept trying to patrol our forty acres despite his injuries. I found him cold and gone one morning near the old deer stand in the woods behind our house, where he used to wait for Dad during hunting season . . ." She swallowed.

"So I am the dog."

"If the collar fits." But her voice had lost its edge.

The silence stretched between them.

Wilder moved to the kitchen, poured himself more coffee from the aluminum pot that had been simmering on the propane stove since morning. Steam rose from the chipped ceramic mug. The rich scent of dark roast filled the air. "I don't want anyone else to get hurt."

"I know," she finally said, her voice soft.

He closed his eyes. Sighed. Then opened them to stare out the window. "How did you become a veterinarian?"

"My dad." She settled into the chair across from where he leaned against the kitchen counter. "I started bringing him hurt animals when I was six. Squirrels with broken legs, birds with damaged wings, anything I could catch that needed fixing."

He turned to look at her. "Did he mind?"

"He encouraged it. Said most kids were afraid of injured animals, but I had steady hands and a calm voice. He started letting me assist with simple procedures when I was ten. By high school, I was helping with surgeries on everything from farm cats to prize-winning retrievers."

"Specializing in anything particular?"

"Well, like I said, Dad was really into sled dogs, but we treated everything. Farm animals, wildlife, the occasional exotic pet that someone imported from heaven knows where." She leaned back, folded her arms. "I loved the puzzle of it. Figuring out what was wrong, how to fix it, watching something broken become whole again. Dad used to say I had the touch—animals would calm down the minute I put my hands on them."

"Is that what you see when you look at me? Something broken that needs fixing?" And he didn't know why he said that either. But maybe . . . maybe he needed to know if he might be more to her still.

She frowned. "No. I see a survivor. A fighter. But maybe someone who's been going it alone for so long, he's forgotten that's not the only way."

He set the mug down with a clunk against the granite countertop. "Some things can't be fixed."

"Like what?"

"Like me."

She shook her head. "You know what your problem is?"

"I'm sure you're going to tell me."

"You think being broken makes you dangerous to others. But being broken just makes you . . . broken. The dangerous part is refusing to let anyone help."

"And you think I should—what?—let you help me face Sloan?"

"I think you should stop thinking of it as 'letting' me do anything." She stood, closed the gap to arm's length, no further—close enough that the only thing between them was air and stubborn pride. "I'm not asking for permission, Wilder. I'm telling you I'm going with you."

"No."

"Why not?"

"Because I won't be responsible for getting you killed."

"You won't be responsible. I will. My choice, my risk, my life."

"You don't know what you're saying."

She recoiled. Her mouth tight. "Okay, maybe not. But you're

going to get killed going alone. I mean, look at you. You can barely stand up."

A beat and then, oh shoot, he couldn't stop himself. "Wow. Again with the bedside manner."

"Hey, my dogs don't seem to complain. What—you want me to rub your ears?"

He held up a hand but couldn't help a small smile.

She smiled back. They stared at each other across the narrow kitchen. Overhead, the cabin's metal roof creaked as expanding ice shifted and cracked.

"You want to know why I can't have a partner? Why I can't drag someone else in?"

"Because of Dawn?"

"Dawn was just confirmation of the truth I didn't want to tell myself."

She frowned.

"I'm not kidding when I say people get hurt when they're with me." The words came out barely above a whisper. "I told you my old girlfriend nearly died because of me."

"I have a hard time believing that."

"Regardless, it's true. I was sixteen. Her name was Laura McKenzie. She was beautiful, smart, completely infatuated with the idea of dating the local mushing prodigy. She wanted me to take her out, but there was a storm coming, not unlike this one. Against my better judgment, I did."

He sighed. "I should have said no. Should have waited for better conditions. But I was brash and stupid and convinced I could handle anything Alaska threw at me." He moved to the window, stared out at the storm's aftermath. Condensation fogged the glass where his breath hit the cold surface. "We went out and I read the ice wrong and . . . we went in. She went in. I got my dogs across and then went back for her."

"I got her out, but she'd been under too long. Hypothermia,

near drowning, three days in the Anchorage hospital before they were sure she'd live. All because I wanted to impress her."

"That wasn't your fault."

"Wasn't it? I knew the ice was unstable. Knew the storm was coming. But I wanted to be cool, so I convinced myself it would be fine. I wanted to show off."

"You were sixteen—"

"Old enough to know better. Old enough to put someone else's safety first." He shook his head. "And Dawn is just more proof of the fact that I make terrible decisions that get people hurt. My choices affect other people. Being reckless with my own life means being reckless with theirs."

"And now you're planning to be reckless again."

"Now I'm planning to face the consequences of my choices. Alone."

She moved around the kitchen table. "You know what I think?"

"Here we go again. No. Enlighten me."

"I think you're scared of the wrong thing."

"How's that?"

"You're scared of hurting people you care about. But the thing that's really terrifying you is the possibility that someone might care about you enough to choose the risk."

A beat, and his throat tightened. But he managed a, "You don't know what you're talking about."

"Don't I? Because it looks to me like you'd rather die alone than live with the possibility of losing someone you love."

He stared at her. Then he nodded. "Yes."

She shook her head, her eyes glossy. Then she turned away from him, wiping her cheeks.

Aw, and now he'd hurt her again. But better hurt than dead.

"By the way, I think I know why you're having trouble with your dog team," he said.

She looked up at him, frowned. "What?"

"They don't respect you."

"Excuse me?"

"I've been watching through the window when you go out to feed them. Every time you open that kennel gate, they jump all over you. No discipline, no boundaries."

She crossed her arms in front of her. "They're excited to see me."

"They're establishing dominance. And you're letting them."

"I'm not—"

"You are. You're too soft with them. They need a pack leader, not a friend."

"I don't want to be mean to them."

"There's a difference between mean and firm. Between cruel and authoritative." He offered a soft smile. "You want to know why your team doesn't work together?"

"Sure." She folded her arms, clearly angry. "Why not?"

He ignored her tone. "Because they don't trust you. They're looking for an alpha, someone who'll take charge."

She stared at him. "So what are you saying?"

"I'm saying you need to be the lead dog, Stormi. Stop wondering if you're doing it right and start taking charge."

She met his gaze, and something sparked in her eyes. "Fine. You're right."

He frowned.

"I have been too soft. Too careful. Too afraid of making the wrong choice. But that changes now."

"Stormi—"

"No. You had your turn to talk. Now it's mine. You're going after Sloan. Fine. I understand why, and I respect your choice. But you're not going alone."

"That's not your choice—"

"I'm not Laura, Wilder. I'm not a sixteen-year-old girl who doesn't understand the risks. I'm a grown woman who's spent her career making life-and-death decisions. Trust me to know what I'm choosing."

"Why? Why does it matter to you?"

"Because I care, okay?"

Oh. He stilled. "Stormi, I don't know what . . . listen, just because you saw me mush doesn't mean—"

"I took a picture with you. And you told me that the secret to surviving was to do the next right thing."

He blinked at her. "What?"

"Yeah. I was there with my dad, like I said, and after the race, at the party, he found you. And you saw me and you sat down and talked to me. Told me that if I wanted to be a real musher, then I needed to never give up. To follow my instincts and to do the next right thing."

He had? Oh no . . . "I was . . . Stormi, I—"

"I had your picture on my wall for years. And I kept thinking of your words every time . . . well, every time I wanted to crumple into a ball and cry."

"Why did you want to crumple in a ball—"

"Doesn't matter. What matters is that this is the next right thing. To help you stay alive and get back to Luna."

He sat, stripped. "I—"

"And trust me, I can be an alpha dog when I need to be."

Now she was getting a little scary. "I'm sure you can," he said. "But just so we're clear, I'm not the guy you met all those years ago. I'm . . ."

"Broken? Sad? Beat-up?"

"Let's not go overboard."

"I know. And I happen to believe that broken can be fixed. That's why I won't give up on Rome."

He glanced at the dog by the fire. He groaned and rolled over.

"And you think I'm worth fixing?"

"I think you're worth not giving up on."

Oh. Silence rose between them. In their pens, the dogs began to bark, another cacophony. Stormi looked toward the door, frowning.

Rome had gotten up, and a low growl rumbled in his chest.

"Stormi—"

A knock on the front door, three strong raps that echoed off the log walls.

He stared now too. "Expecting anyone?"

"No." She moved toward the Remington 12-gauge.

Another knock, more urgent this time. A voice followed, muffled by the heavy timber but carrying the unmistakable edge of desperation.

"Please! Someone help me! I know you're in there!"

A stranger. Female, sounded young, panicked.

Rome's growling deepened, but his body language read caution rather than aggression—ears forward, muscles tense but not yet committed to attack.

Wilder looked at her. "Stormi, let's just take a breath here—"

She checked the shotgun's chamber, her face set in grim lines. The metallic sound of shells sliding into place echoed in the sudden quiet. "Trouble doesn't knock."

5

HERE WENT NOTHING. But her gut said open the door.

So Stormi opened the door.

A girl leaned against the doorframe. Early twenties, maybe. Blond hair matted with ice, designer ski jacket torn and blood-stained. Blue lips. Waxy pale skin. Her entire body shook.

"Help me." Her words slurred, her tongue clearly thick with cold. "Tyler's hurt. We need help."

Stormi set the shotgun down and caught the girl as she collapsed on the porch. Wilder had gotten up but she knew he'd only damage his leg more if he tried to help. Stormi wrapped her arms around the girl and hiked her up, hauled her inside.

Rome's hackles rose as Stormi pulled the girl into the kitchen. He emitted a growl, so something about this stranger had him on edge. The girl's legs completely gave out as they reached one of the wooden chairs around Stormi's kitchen table.

"What's your name?" Stormi knelt beside the chair, took the girl's wrist, and checked her pulse. Weak, but steady. She needed to get her extremities warm, as well as heat her core.

"Sarah. Sarah O'Malley," the girl said between chattering

teeth. "I'm f-from Anchorage. We were snowmobiling up near Bear Creek Trail when Tyler—Tyler Collins, my boyfriend—was shot!" She put her hands to her mouth, hiccupping back sobs.

Stormi's eyes found Wilder's across the kitchen table. He had started to heat water on the stove.

"Bear Creek is rough country," he said. "No cell service." He lowered his voice. "What are city kids doing that far into the wilderness?"

Stormi got up and headed to a closet to get a thermal blanket. "What happened?"

"Two days ago," Sarah said, her breath catching, "before the storm. We stopped for lunch by this old cabin. Tyler wanted to explore, said it looked straight out of a movie."

Stormi helped Sarah unzip her jacket, then pulled a blanket around her and led her to the sofa. The electric percolator burbled on the counter.

Wilder poured the boiling water into a basin, added enough cold so it wouldn't scald the girl, and brought it over.

Rome paced between the kitchen and living room, whining softly, his nails clicking on the hardwood. Stormi added another log to her fire, then came back and took off Sarah's boots, her wool socks. Her feet were ice.

Wilder had set the water on the floor and now Stormi tested it. Then she set Sarah's feet inside. "We'll need to add hot water to keep it at the same temperature."

Wilder nodded, then, "When did the shooting start?" he asked Sarah as he walked back over to the electric pot, filled it, and set it on to boil again.

"Someone was watching us from the trees." Sarah's hands shook as she pulled the blanket tighter. "We didn't see him at first. Tyler was taking pictures of the cabin, and I was setting up our lunch."

Stormi met Wilder's gaze again, drew in a breath. *Tommy?*

"Then out of nowhere, he shot at us."

Stormi turned back to Sarah. "Tell me about the shooter."

Wilder came over and handed Sarah a mug. "It's tea, sweetened with honey. What did he look like?"

"I don't know. Mid-thirties, maybe? I think he had a beard? He wore a snowmobile jacket and pants and . . . I don't know, had a cut on his face, maybe? I don't know! I didn't get a good look." Sarah wrapped both hands around the mug, her fingernails blue-tinged. Steam fogged up from the tea. "He just stepped out from behind this massive pine and started shooting. No warning, just—boom!"

The sound of her voice echoed in the warm kitchen. Tea sloshed against the mug's rim as Sarah's hands trembled. Color was returning to her cheeks, pink spreading from her nose outward, but the tremors hadn't stopped. The fire crackled in the hearth.

"Tyler went down immediately. Blood everywhere." Her voice cracked. "I screamed, started running toward him, but the man kept shooting. Bullets hitting the snow around me, around Tyler."

"Where did Tyler get hit?" Wilder asked, his voice grim.

"In the belly. The bullet went right through. There was so much blood. I was so scared." She covered her face with one hand. "I ran. I just . . . I ran away and hid. I left him there! Just left Tyler there!"

"You survived," Stormi said. "Running kept you alive. That's not cowardice."

"Yeah, well, I hid until the man drove away on our snowmobile. And then I had to go back. I found Tyler in the snow, and I dragged him to the cabin. It was an old cabin, and the windows were broken, but at least it was somewhere to shelter and we waited out the storm there."

Stormi glanced at Wilder again, frowned. "Maybe Tommy

ran out of gas?" She glanced back at Sarah. "And then . . . you came looking for help?"

She nodded. "Tyler was acting strange. His skin got really hot, and he wanted me to help him get his clothes off, but he was hurt, too, so . . . I got scared. I saw your smoke . . ." She looked up at Stormi. "Please. You have to find him. Help him."

"How long ago did you leave him?" Wilder asked.

"I don't know. Hours ago. He was alive when I left."

"Okay." Stormi moved to the radio mounted above her kitchen counter. She tuned to the emergency frequency. "Sheriff's office, come in."

Deke Starr's voice cut through the white noise. "Copper Mountain Sheriff. Go ahead."

"Deke, it's Stormi. I've got a shooting victim a few miles north of my location, Bear Creek Trail area. Civilian down, unknown condition. I think . . ." She glanced at Wilder. "We're thinking the shooter could be Tommy Reid."

The radio crackled.

"Copy that. When was the shooting?"

Stormi looked at Sarah, who clutched her mug with both hands. "Two days ago."

Sarah nodded.

"I've got the witness here, hypothermic but stable. Requesting immediate medical response and backup."

"Okay. We're still digging out here. It'll take a minute to get there, and the roads by your place are packed in too. We'll need to get a plow out. I'd say four hours at least."

Four hours.

"Can we get an SAR chopper?"

"I'll call Moose, but the ceiling is still pretty low, and the winds are still rough. It's possible, but . . ."

And right then, the wind gusted against the cabin's log walls, rattling the windows in their frames. The sound of winter pressing in, reminding them how isolated they were out here. How far from help.

So, probably no SAR chopper. "Okay, thanks, Deke." She ended the call.

If Tyler was conscious when Sarah left . . . well, he'd survived two days. Maybe he could last until they found him.

Maybe.

She turned to Wilder. "What about Jenny and Orion? They live out that way. Probably they're the closest thing to medical backup in the area."

"We can call them. But, Stormi, if Tommy's out there, you need to stay put until we can get real help."

"Says the man who argued with me an hour ago about trying to track down a killer on his own."

Wilder's mouth turned into a grim line, his eyes sparking.

"Tyler needs help now, not in four hours. And if Tommy is still in the area, every minute of delay gives him a chance to finish what he started."

"We have to go get him." Sarah struggled to stand. Her blanket fell away. "Tyler's been out there for days. If he's not dead already, he will be soon."

"You're not going anywhere." Stormi pressed her back into the chair. "You're hypothermic, exhausted, and in shock. You'd be dead weight on a rescue mission."

"Then you go. Please." Desperation cracked Sarah's voice. "I can give you directions. It's not that far if you know where to look."

"Take your snowmobile," Wilder said.

She shook her head. "It's not working."

"Who doesn't keep their snow machine working in the middle of Alaska?"

She gave him a look and he lifted his hands. "Sorry. I burned through the spare jug on the generator last week. What about the one you came here on?"

He shook his head. "It's dry-tanked too."

Silence settled over the kitchen. No working snowmobile meant no fast transport to the Bear Creek area. No way to reach Tyler quickly across miles of rough wilderness terrain.

Unless . . .

Stormi moved to the window overlooking her dog yard, her reflection ghosted in the glass against the pale afternoon light. Six sled dogs stirred in their insulated houses, breath steaming in the cold air. Her mismatched team—rescue rejects and mushing disasters, according to every musher who'd ever seen them work.

But they were what she had.

"I'll take the sled team."

"Absolutely not," Wilder said. "You can't run an untrained team in dangerous conditions. You can barely run them in *safe* conditions."

"Thanks for that." Heat climbed Stormi's neck. "And I've been working with them. They're not completely untrained."

He cocked his head. "You getting lost or hurt out there isn't going to help Tyler."

"So what? I wait while he bleeds out?" She crossed her arms.

"While you stay alive."

"This isn't up to you."

Wilder's jaw clenched.

She turned toward the mudroom where her winter gear hung on wooden pegs. She donned a heavy parka that smelled of dog hair and pine smoke, then pulled on insulated pants still stiff with cold from this morning's feeding. Slipped on snow boots rated for forty below, with spiked treads. Hello, she might not be from Alaska, but she still knew how to dress for the cold. How to gear up and survive in a place that could kill you if you made the wrong choice.

This was not the wrong choice.

STORMI WALKED OUT of the mudroom holding her fur hat and headed toward the door.

"Fine. Go get yourself killed," Wilder said, still standing by the sink.

Stormi stopped. Hand on her parka zipper, the metal cold under her fingers. Something hued his tone . . . not anger.

Fear.

She turned back. His frame was backlit by the warm glow of the propane heater. Shoulders rigid. Hands clenched at his sides. An expression on his face that suggested it wasn't fine. Not at all.

Oh.

"You think I'm going to die out there." Not a question.

"I think . . ." His voice lowered. "We should wait."

"Maybe." She moved to the kitchen counter where her emergency supplies were stacked. First aid kit. Survival gear. GPS unit. "But Tyler doesn't have time for us to wait."

"Stormi—"

"I'm going." She picked up her shotgun, then added some shells to her pocket. "With or without your permission."

He blew out a breath. "Then I'm going with you."

The quiet words stopped her cold. She turned. Wilder was heading toward the mudroom, probably to grab his borrowed winter coat. Face set in grim determination.

"Have you lost your mind? You can barely walk! You'll slow us down."

"I'd slow you down less than you'd slow yourself down by going alone." He pulled on the heavy coat. "Besides, you might think you're the alpha, but your dogs need someone who actually knows what they're doing."

Ouch. Wow.

Stormi looked at Sarah, who was gaping at the two of them. "I know what I'm doing."

Sarah just nodded.

Wilder limped out of the mudroom, wearing his snow pants and boots. "You want to be the lead dog? Fine. Lead. But leaders don't refuse help when lives are on the line."

Her hands stilled, and she cocked her head. "Leaders don't refuse help?"

He headed to the door. "I don't want to talk about it."

Oh, they were going to talk about it. She stepped in front of him. "You'll ride the sled." Not a question. "No running, no fancy heroics. Just transportation and backup."

"Deal." He took the gun from her. "Let's go save that kid."

Sarah looked up from her mug. "What about me?"

"You stay here," Stormi said. "Get warm. If the sheriff comes here before going to Bear Creek Trail, tell him that's where I went."

"But what if that man comes back?"

"Rome will stay with you." The decision surprised even Stormi as she said it. But out there—well, Rome could hardly pull in the right direction. And Sarah's terror was real.

Rome whined from his position by the window. He wanted to go. Every line of his body said he belonged with them, not playing guard dog to a stranger.

"Stay, Rome. Guard."

The big dog's ears drooped, but he padded over to settle beside Sarah's chair. Close enough to protect. Far enough to avoid being petted by a stranger.

The afternoon air bit, carrying the scent of the fresh snow. Snow crunched under their boots as they moved toward the dog yard.

Barking filled the air—rattling chains, excited whines, the soft thump of paws against insulated house walls. The sled dogs exploded into chaos as soon as they saw the harnesses. Koda threw himself against the chain-link fence, howling with joy, the sound echoing into the gusty air. Yukon spun in tight circles, kicking up clouds of snow. Lina and Sitka nipped and growled at each other in their eagerness to reach the gangline.

"Easy." Stormi's voice carried across the yard. "Settle."

They listened at least enough to let her work. She moved through, putting booties on their feet and fitting on their harnesses. Wilder came behind her, checking her work. He murmured encouragement to the dogs like he knew them.

Finally, he headed to the sled, which was parked near the enclosure. "You get this from Anuk?"

She came over to the sled. Built from ash wood, it bore deep gouges and scars from hidden rocks and rough ice over the years. "Came with the place. She left it for me." The frame squeaked as Stormi maneuvered it out into the yard. Wilder tested the wooden slats.

"It's a sturdy sled," she said. Wilder glanced at her, his mouth a tight knot. "I'm not waiting, so save round two. Get on or stand back."

"Wow."

"You wanted an alpha. Koda, line out." She pointed toward the front of the gangline and Koda walked up. She hooked him up to the lines, then Lina. Behind her, Sitka and Juneau, and finally Denali and Yukon at the wheel.

Wilder had settled on the bed of the sled. "Koda's a good lead. Confident." He put the gun between his legs and grabbed the sides of the sled, settled his weight carefully. "Question is, are you?"

Stormi gripped the handlebow, blew out the familiar surge of nervous energy that came before any run. "Yeah, let's do this." She pulled the snow hook. The dogs surged forward against their harnesses. "Mush! Hike!"

The sled lurched into motion. Six dogs pulling in something

approaching unison. Not pretty. But functional. They swept past the cabin in a cloud of snow.

Bear Creek Trail lay four miles north through brutal terrain. But Tyler Collins was out there somewhere, hurt and freezing to death.

Good grief, her team was a circus act. Koda did his part, mushing in a straight line like the general he was, and behind him Lina tried to keep up. But swing dogs Sitka and Juneau were squirrelly, easily distracted, pulling in opposite directions as the spirit moved them. Her wheel dogs followed, which meant the sled lurched and jerked and tried to upset itself.

Wilder hung on, shouting commands at the dogs. *Good luck, pal.*

But on they went into the white, her little chaotic team of misfits, the sled runners whispering through snow.

Over an hour later, she spotted a gray building on the horizon, nestled into the snow.

"Easy!" Koda's ears pricked forward. His pace slowed as he tested the air, nostrils flaring.

The team slowed. "Whoa," Stormi said, and the dogs stopped. She set the snow brake, metal teeth biting into the packed trail.

Silence, only the panting of six dogs and the whisper of wind through the forest.

A cabin squatted in a clearing, dark timber weathered gray by decades of Alaskan winters. Roof intact, but the door hung open on rusted hinges that creaked in the wind. Snow had drifted up to the opening, but footsteps led out, then disappeared into the drifted snow.

The dogs settled as she got off the sled, Wilder too.

"That's not good." Wilder pointed to a depression.

She bent and brushed away loose snow, the powder sparkling in the sunlight.

Red.

Dark against the white. Partially frozen, crystallized around the edges. But unmistakable. Blood.

"Tyler," she said.

"Maybe." Wilder stood, scanned the area around the bloodstain.

And that's when she heard the barking. She turned and spotted the big dog bounding up through the snow.

Rome.

"What in the world?" she said but crouched to meet him.

"He probably did the same thing with Sarah that he did with me—opened the door."

She stared at Wilder. "He did not."

"Totally did. He knows how to move the latch. Probably ran out after us."

Seriously. She looked at the dog, but he didn't run up to her. He had started circling, as if tracking something. Oh, sweet boy, trying.

Except . . . maybe. Because he ran off, then stopped, turned and barked. And then took off again.

"He's tracking something," Wilder said.

"Or he's just confused." Still, she spotted the trail of old blood as she followed him. Huh. Behind her, Wilder had roused the dogs, turned them to follow. She rounded back and got on the sled.

"Mush!" The dogs trotted down the hill behind the cabin to a small clearing.

"There—the drift!" She pointed to a figure on the ground, hunched a stone's throw from the cabin door, like he'd tried to walk out of it.

The scent of death was there now, under the clean pine air. Sweet and wrong.

Rome lay down beside him, whining.

The man lay on his side, designer ski jacket dark with blood that had frozen into stiff, rust-colored patches. Face pale with the waxy stillness of death, his skin taking on the blue-white color of deep cold. Young—maybe twenty-five. The kind of soft features that spoke of a life lived indoors, away from the harsh realities of wilderness survival. His expensive sunglasses hung askew from one ear. Clearly fitting Sarah's description of her boyfriend.

An open wound on his neck suggested a recent shot. Someone had rounded back to finish the job.

Wilder had gotten off the sled and now knelt beside the body. "He's gone. Probably been dead for hours."

Stormi stared at the still form and something cold settled in her stomach.

Around them, the wilderness pressed in. Silent.

"It's not your fault." Wilder's voice cut through her spiraling thoughts. "He was probably dead before Sarah made it to your cabin."

"Sarah." The poor girl was back at the cabin. Waiting for news. Believing her boyfriend might still be alive. "We have to tell her."

"We have to get out of here first." Wilder was already moving back toward the sled. "If Tommy did this, he might still be around."

But Rome had other ideas. Instead of following them back to the sled, the dog got up and suddenly took off beyond the snowbank, toward the woods.

"Rome, come," Stormi called, but the dog ignored her. Disappeared behind a stand of white birch.

"You think he's trying to tell us something?"

Stormi shook her head. "He's not working. He's . . ."

"He looks like he's working."

Right. Maybe. "Okay, let's follow him."

He got back on the sled and she turned the team, then they followed Rome's trail through the trees. The dog had stopped beside another structure, another cabin. This one newer, more intact. Had broken windows. A door that stood slightly ajar.

Rome sat in front of it, his body vibrating with suppressed energy. Every line of his posture screaming alert.

"This is a cache cabin. For the forest service," Wilder said. He'd gotten up again, groaning, then moved past her.

"Careful." She couldn't help it.

The door swung wide open at his touch. A single room furnished with basic survival gear. Sleeping bags on wooden bunks. Canned goods stacked on makeshift shelves. A cold woodstove in the corner.

And blood.

Fresh drops leading from the door to one of the bunks, where a first aid kit lay open. Gauze and medical tape scattered across the rough blankets.

"Tommy," Stormi said. "He was here. Recently."

Wilder shook his head. "We need to go. Now." He was already moving toward the door. "If he comes back—"

Rome's bark cut through his words. Sharp. Urgent. The dog was at the cabin's single window. Hackles raised. Body rigid with warning.

Through the dirty glass, Stormi could see a figure moving through the trees. Large. Bearded. With a cut on his face that matched Sarah's description perfectly.

Tommy Reid.

"Back door?" she whispered as a shot pinged against the wood of the front door.

"No back door," Wilder said. "Window?"

Broken glass formed lethal teeth around the frame. But maybe they could break it free.

"I have an idea," she said. "The dogs can bring the sled to us."

"He'll see us."

"Not from the other side of the house, he won't. We'll call the dogs over." She pushed out the glass from the window, clearing it with her gloved hand, then leaned out of the window frame. Whistled.

Koda's head came up.

Next to her, Rome stood at the window, his body practically vibrating.

"Koda!"

The dog had gotten up, now his ears perked.

"Come!"

Koda wagged his tail, not sure.

"Koda, line out," Wilder barked, joining her. The big dog jogged ahead, straightening the lines, moving the other dogs into action.

The sled moved forward, toward Stormi.

"Line out, Koda!" Wilder called again.

The dog led the team to Stormi, obedient to his voice.

She sort of got that, truthfully. Wilder's commands emerged solid and trustworthy and sure. Full of the kind of confidence she wanted to lean into.

Instead, she turned to Wilder and grabbed his arm, put it over her shoulder. "Ready?"

"What are you going to do—push me out the window?"

"Yep."

"Oh, this is fun."

"Feel free to stay and get shot."

He leaned out the window, and she pushed him the rest of the way. He landed in the snow, struggled to get up.

The dogs had dragged the sled some twenty feet away from the house.

She lifted Rome, and he scampered out. More shooting.

"Hurry up!"

She scooted up onto the frame and pushed herself free.

Landed beside him in the snow.

Then she was up, grabbing his arm to pull it over her shoulder. "Let's go!"

SNOW EXPLODED against a tree trunk inches from Wilder's head. Splinters stung his cheek. The dogs erupted into terrified barking.

How he hated when he was right.

But Wilder knew it—just *knew* it. Trouble had found him and now Stormi was going to die.

And, of course, he was the weak link here. His stupid leg burned as he half ran, half lurched, toward the sled through the thick snow.

Maybe he should have stayed back at the house. But the thought of Stormi out here by herself—

Okay, she seemed tough enough, but her dogs were chaos, and now there was a dead body.

But three days ago he'd been bleeding out in Stormi's kitchen. His body wasn't fully healed. His reflexes weren't sharp. If something went wrong—no, *when* something went wrong—she might pay the price for his limitations.

There was no way he was letting her go alone though. What had she said—pride? Maybe . . .

Too close. Way too close.

He hopped onto the sled, even as she stepped on the runners.

"Mush!" she shouted.

He pointed at a ravine. "Down the slope! Straight ahead! Haw! Haw!"

The sled lurched, six dogs pulling in mostly the same direction, Rome bounding ahead of them, barking. They plunged down the far side of the embankment at breakneck speed, runners bouncing over hidden rocks and fallen logs.

His leg throbbed with each bump of the sled. He gritted his teeth, refusing to make a sound, but he could easily shake loose the snow from the trees with a feral shout of agony.

Behind them, more shots echoed through the forest.

Then, shouting. And more than one voice. The sound of a snowmobile revving up.

So Tommy wasn't alone.

The slope ended abruptly at the edge of what looked like a frozen lake. Or swamp. Hard to tell in the failing light, but the surface stretched smooth and white ahead of them, offering open ground and speed if the ice could hold their weight.

"Stormi, wait!" Wilder shouted over the wind and barking dogs. "Test it first!"

But Stormi was already committed, the sled's momentum carrying them onto the frozen surface before she could stop.

The sled nearly slid out from under him as they hit the ice. He braced himself, even as the dogs picked up speed.

Okay, so they might be okay. The snowpack seemed thick, and for fifty yards, the ice held solid.

Then the sound below turned high and hollow.

No, no—

"The ice is too thin," Wilder shouted. "Get off! Get off now!"

The first crack split under the dogs' feet, spiderwebbing outward with the sound of breaking. The sled passed over the sliver and dark water showed through the splits—black and deadly cold.

Stormi threw her weight backward, shouted at the dogs, trying to stop their forward momentum, but the dogs had caught scent of the danger and took off in panic. The sled skidded sideways, runners scraping against ice that groaned and shifted under their weight.

Rome had run ahead, away from the danger.

Another crack. Wider. Longer. The section under Koda's feet tilted, and dark water lapped at the edges.

Not again, Wilder thought frantically. *Please, not again.*

He turned to Stormi. "Jump!" He launched himself from the sled, landing hard on ice that immediately spiderwebbed under his impact. "Stormi, jump now!"

She threw herself sideways as the ice gave way completely under the sled. The front end dropped into black water with a splash that sent spray across the white surface. The dogs fought for purchase on solid ice, their claws scratching against the ice.

Stormi had thrown her hook out, and it clamped onto the ice, stopping the sled from plummeting deeper into the yawning hole.

Yukon went down first, yanked backward and disappearing under the black water with barely a splash.

Then Denali.

Stormi screamed and scrambled up.

The other dogs fought against their harnesses, trying to reach solid ground as the weight of the submerged sled dragged them backward.

"Yukon!" Stormi crawled toward the hole on her hands and knees, distributing her weight across the treacherous surface. "Yukon!"

The back of the sled seemed to be anchored on the edge of the ice, unmoving for now. Her dogs paddled furiously in the water, trying to find purchase on the edge.

"Don't!" Wilder grabbed her ankle as she reached toward the dark water. "The ice won't hold!"

"I'm not losing them!" She kicked free, crawling another foot toward the edge, and caught Denali's harness. She pulled him toward the edge, and Yukon with him, still struggling.

Wilder caught the edge of the lines and pulled out his bowie knife. He broke the line, letting the other dogs free.

Just Denali and Yukon in the water.

Please, please let the brake hold the sled.

Stormi had hold of Denali, and now she pulled him up onto the ice. He wiggled free, shaking off the water, now pulling Yukon.

The husky's big head appeared above the surface. Eyes wide with shock and cold. He paddled frantically, trying to reach the edge, but the sled harness dragged him down.

Wilder lunged for the dog, nearly went in.

"Save him!" Stormi, shouting, crying, holding onto the lines. She unclipped Denali and he fled away, barking.

Wilder lunged again and got his hand on the line to the sled, then tried to reach for the clips that held Yukon. Frozen.

He reached for his bowie again and sawed at the line that held the dog to the sled. "Don't let him go!"

The sled started to rock.

"Hurry," Stormi screamed.

The blade sliced through the rope and Yukon surged upward, free. But the ice he jumped onto broke, and Yukon went under again.

Stormi screamed, and they both scanned the surface beneath them.

"There!" Stormi pointed toward a dark shape moving under the ice. "He's under there!"

Wilder plunged his arm into the freezing water, feeling around until his fingers found fur. *Gotcha.* He hauled Yukon to the surface, the dog limp and barely breathing. Water streamed from the animal's coat as Wilder pulled him onto solid ice.

"Is he—?" Stormi crawled toward Yukon, her face pale with fear.

Yukon coughed, choking up lake water, then struggled to his feet. Shaky but alive. The other dogs had managed to scramble all the way to the shoreline on their own, clustering together on the snow-packed bank where the spruce thickened.

"We have to get off this lake." Wilder scanned the surrounding ice, looking for the safest route to shore. "Follow me. Crawl—we can distribute our weight." He held in a groan as he started to move, only now feeling the strain on his stitches.

He eased toward shore, Stormi behind him. Yukon was now running to shore to join the pack.

The ice groaned and shifted under them, but it held. Wilder glanced back. Behind them, the hole where the sled had gone through was already starting to skim over with new ice.

Just his breath and the crunch of the snow, no more sounds of the snowmobiles, so maybe they hadn't been followed.

Maybe Tommy knew they were headed toward their deaths, anyway.

Twenty minutes of breath-holding terror as the frozen surface complained under their weight. When they finally reached the shore and stepped onto solid ground, Wilder's legs nearly buckled.

Then he looked at Stormi.

She knelt in the snow, arms wrapped around Yukon and Denali, her whole body shaking.

And just like that, he was back on the ice, pulling Laura's body from the water.

Wilder's vision grayed at the edges. His lungs shut down. He collapsed in the snow.

"Wilder?" Stormi's voice seemed to come from far away. "Wilder, what's wrong?"

He forced air into his lungs. "I'm fine." The words came out rough, unconvincing even to his own ears.

"No, you're not."

"We need to keep moving." He turned away, unable to meet her eyes. But suddenly, the what-ifs swept over him, weight burning in his chest. He couldn't do this. Couldn't watch someone he cared about—

Wait. When did . . . okay, yes sure, he cared for Stormi. But not like . . .

Shoot. When did she become someone whose loss would tear something essential out of his chest?

Around them, the forest had gone quiet again. No pursuit sounds. No gunshots.

Except—aw. Barely audible over the natural sounds came the low rumble of snowmobile engines.

Stormi stilled. "They found us."

He met her eyes. She stood, breathing hard, a stricken expression on her face.

Rome's ears pricked forward, and he came over to the huddle of dogs, whined.

Yeah, him too.

"Wilder." Stormi's voice was steady. "Can you run?"

He met her eyes. Grimaced.

"That's what I thought."

She stared at the hole in the ice, the sled, and then, "The gun is at the bottom of the lake."

Right.

"We're in trouble," she said quietly.

Oh, how he hated when he was right.

6

STORMI WASN'T SURE why she dropped to her knees. Why, as her dogs panted around her, the urge to drop and, well, pray swept over her.

She blamed her father's voice in her head, suddenly bold and strong, louder than the sound of the snow machines echoing in the distance.

"God is our refuge and strength, a very present help in trouble."

And the thought just burst inside her, blowing apart everything else.

So, she dropped.

What other choice did she have, really? With the tree line yards away and her sled still stuck halfway into the icy water—and Wilder hurt and stalled on the shore.

She looked up to heaven. *Oh, God—*

"What are you doing?"

She glanced at Wilder, then back to heaven. *Save us!*

"Are you *praying*?"

He'd stumbled over to her, holding out his hand. She took it but got up on her own. "Yes. Of course I'm praying!"

He glanced behind him, to the noise, the dogs, back to her. "We need to run."

"Where? You can't get to the forest. We're out of options. The best thing we can do is pray."

He just stared at her. "Seriously?"

And then, two snow machines burst over the ridge.

She'd found her feet, now looked at him. "Okay, we'll run too!" She put her hand around his waist, turned, the dogs bounding around them.

He struggled through the thick snow, breaking through the icy pack on top, falling while she tried to hold him up.

Lord, protect us. Save us—

Behind them, the snow machines skirted the shore. But, no shots, no bullets flying. She turned and—

One of the drivers was waving at them.

Waving?

"Wilder, look—"

He turned too and stilled even as the machines closed in, a plume of snow flying behind them. "Are you kidding me?"

She glanced at him and now her dogs lifted their heads, ears pricked, started to bark.

"It's Orion and Jenny!"

What—?

But the machines slowed as they pulled up, the drivers wearing thick, padded snowsuits and helmets. One lifted their visor.

Orion Starr, indeed. "You guys okay?"

Wilder was swaying, so no, but—"What are you guys doing here?"

"We were on the way to the clinic, but Deke and his people got there first, so we circled toward the Bear Creek cache cabin, followed your tracks—" He glanced at the ice, back to Wilder. "Did you see anyone else?"

"We saw some tread tracks near the cabin, but we didn't follow them."

Orion glanced at her dogsled, still perched on the ice as if hoping to make a dive to the bottom, just the hook and line tethering it afloat. "We should get your sled out of the ice before it goes under." He had gotten off his machine and opened up the seat. He pulled out a coiled rope, a hook on the end.

"Careful," Jenny said as she tromped over to them. "Clearly the ice has some thin places."

"Yep." Orion glanced back at Wilder. "Sit down before you fall down."

Right? Stormi turned to Wilder and gave him a look.

He lowered himself to the snow.

"Keep your dogs off the ice," Orion said to Stormi as he and Jenny got back on the snow machines.

She watched as they rode them to the edge of the lake. Orion then got off, hooked one end of the rope to Jenny's snowmobile, then worked his way out to the ice, finally lying prone to scoot out to her sled, the back runners still gripping the edge of the ice, the front half in the water.

He hooked the rope onto the back of the sled, then crawled back to his machine.

Meanwhile Jenny began to ease the sled out of the grip of the lake with easy tugs from her machine, drawing it away from the terrible, jagged maw of blackness.

The sled broke free, slid back along its track to shore.

Just like that.

"God is our refuge and strength, a very present help in trouble."

Her throat filled. Wilder glanced at her. "You okay?"

"Barely. Yeah." She drew in a breath.

His mouth made a grim line. "Let's round up the dogs. And then we need to call Deke."

An hour later, scene tape snapped in the wind around Tyler's body, yellow plastic bright against the darkening forest. Lights turned the area bright, and the Air One Rescue chopper sat in the snow while Deke and Moose Mulligan secured Tyler's body.

Stormi caught sight of Rome, who was sitting beside where they'd found Tyler—stillness she'd never seen from him before.

"Ma'am?" The crime scene tech, a female, came over to her. Her breath steamed in the frigid air. "We're about wrapped up here."

Right. The dogs waited, curled in the snow. Wilder sat on the sled, watching her, an expression she couldn't read on his face.

She walked over to Rome. "C'mon, buddy. Time to go."

Rome's ears twitched, but he didn't move from his position. The dog's breath formed white puffs in the cold air. She scratched behind Rome's ears, feeling the warmth of his thick undercoat. "Did your nose finally come back, boy?"

The Malador leaned into her touch, tail giving a slow wag that sent snowflakes scattering from his coat.

Wind whistled through branches overhead, carrying the distant crackle of law enforcement radios and the low rumble of the chopper engines warming up. The temperature was dropping fast—she could feel it through her insulated gloves.

"Frost!" Deke's voice cut across the clearing. The sheriff crunched toward them through deep snow, his heavy boots leaving deep prints in the pristine white.

Stormi met him and Wilder at the sled. Rome had gotten up and walked over beside her.

"Listen," Deke said, "the girlfriend has been transported to the hospital, and I don't like the idea of you staying out at the clinic." He pointed at Wilder's leg. "You need a visit to town too."

Wilder's jaw clenched, the muscle jumping beneath his skin. "I told you, I'm not going to the hospital."

"And I told you that gunshot wound says otherwise." Deke's radio crackled with static and voices reporting in from various positions. He thumbed the volume down without breaking eye contact. "Besides, you seriously think you're safe given what we found today?"

Silence. Wilder looked away.

"We need to swing by my place first," Stormi said. "Get some supplies for the dogs."

"That's not a good idea," Deke said. "What if they've doubled back around and are waiting for you there?"

"It'll take fifteen minutes. The dogs need their evening medications and their food."

"Fine," Deke said. "Quick stop at your place, then straight to the hospital."

"No," Wilder said. "I check on Luna."

Deke cocked his head. Sighed, but even Stormi saw the expression on Wilder's face. She didn't blame him.

Rome jerked his head suddenly, nostrils flaring as he tested the wind. Something had shifted in his posture.

"What is it, boy?" Stormi followed his gaze toward the tree line where shadows deepened.

"Time to go," Deke said. "Pack it up."

She picked up the hook on her sled and mounted the runners. Wilder settled on the sled, his expression grim.

The dogs moved with barely a call from her. An hour later, her clinic came into view ahead—the familiar outline of the converted barn and cabin comforting. Yellow light spilled from the windows, welcoming and vulnerable against the darkening forest.

She pulled up to the house, threw the brake, and started to unhook the dogs. "We'll take them to town with us," she said and gestured to her pickup, with the kennels attached to the bed.

Wilder had gotten up and now limped to the house. "Let me get my crutches, then I'll help you load the dogs." He didn't wait for her to argue.

It seemed that something dark had settled inside him. Or rather, darker.

Maybe the fear that if these guys could find him, they could find Luna . . .

She unhooked her dogs, then set up the ramp and loaded them into the kennels. She added her homemade food mix to the supply box.

By the time Wilder emerged, she had the team packed up.

"Five minutes," she said to Wilder, heading toward the house. "Let me grab some supplies."

"Stormi." He grabbed her arm. She turned. "You don't have to go."

A beat. "We're not doing this again." She shook out of his grip. "Besides, Tommy knows you were here and he'll be back now that the storm's let up. I don't want to be here when he comes."

His mouth made a grim line, but he didn't argue.

She grabbed overnight supplies and threw them into a backpack. Made sure the fire was doused and shut off the water.

Felt a little like she might be running. But it felt like the next right thing.

When she returned, Rome had jumped into the back seat of her truck. Wilder stood outside, waiting for her. He took her backpack from her, dropped it into the seat, and shut the door. Limped to the passenger side without a word.

Fine. Whatever.

She pulled out of her place and onto the plowed road, the sides creamy white drifts, then out to the highway. "I don't know where Vic lives."

"She has the property next to mine," he said, as if that helped. After a moment, she looked over at him, raised an eyebrow.

"Sorry. Yeah. Just south of town, about a half mile. I'll show you."

They drove in silence until he pointed out the road. She turned. The gravel road to Vic's place wound through dense forest. Towering pine trees created a canopy overhead that blocked most of the fading daylight. She glanced once at Wilder's profile. Lines of stress etched deep around his eyes, his jaw tight.

"She's safe. Vic knows what she's doing."

"I know." His voice came out rougher than probably intended. "But I need to see her. Need to . . ." He trailed off, but she got it. Every moment away from Luna was another opportunity for trouble to find her.

"There." Wilder pointed as they rounded the final curve.

The trees opened up ahead, revealing a small clearing with a compact two-story cabin. Solar panels caught the last rays of sunlight on the weathered roof, and smoke rose from the chimney in a languid line.

Before the truck had fully stopped, Wilder was reaching for the door handle. His boots hit the snow-covered ground, and he yanked out a crutch before taking off hard for the house.

The cabin door burst open.

Luna appeared in the doorway, seven years old, blond braids, wearing a pink sweatshirt and jeans. It would be impossible not to notice the way the little girl's eyes lit up with pure joy at the sight of him.

"Daddy!" She launched herself across the porch, down the stairs, and straight at her father.

Wilder dropped to one knee just as she reached him, catching her small body against his chest. "Hey, baby girl."

"I missed you," Luna whispered against his shoulder, her embrace tight around his neck. "Vic said you were okay, but I was scared."

"I'm here now." His voice cracked on the words. "I'm here."

Stormi hung back near the truck, giving them space for their reunion, but something twisted in her chest as she watched them together. The way Wilder's shoulders shook as he held his daughter. The way Luna clung to him.

Everything he had to lose.

The thought slammed into her. All this time she'd been focused on what Wilder had survived—the gunshot wound, the constant threat hanging over them. But watching him with Luna, seeing the absolute devotion between father and daughter, she finally understood what he was really fighting for.

Not just his own life. But the chance to be Luna's father. To see her grow up. To protect her from a world that had already taken so much from both of them.

No wonder he wanted to go it alone, not risk getting close to anyone else.

Or not let anyone else get in his way?

Everything Wilder loved most in the world was wrapped up in that small, brave little girl who was now pulling back to examine her father's face with serious eyes.

"Are you hurt?" Luna asked, gently poking at his crutch.

"I'm okay, sweetheart. Just tired."

From the cabin's porch, a woman stepped into view—blond hair pulled back, athletic build, alert eyes that missed nothing.

"About time you showed up," Vic called, but her voice held warmth beneath the professional exterior.

Wilder stood slowly, lifting Luna with him. The little girl wrapped her legs around his waist with practiced ease, settling her weight against his hip. "Thanks for keeping her safe," he said to Vic.

"No problem." She held open the door. "The dogs helped."

Stormi glanced over into the darkness, where she heard barking. "Is that your line?" she asked Wilder.

"Yeah. Vic's been feeding them." He put Luna down, clearly struggling to walk with her in his arms. He frowned. "Although it doesn't sound like all of them."

Rome had gotten out and now trotted over to them. Luna petted him. "What's his name?"

"Rome," Stormi said. "And I'm Stormi. Remember me?"

Luna laughed. "Yes. You took care of Timber when she had her puppies."

"Good memory." They'd reached the porch, and by sheer will, she didn't reach out to help Wilder. Frankly, she might have gotten burned if she'd tried, the way he radiated a sort of fury. Probably not at her.

Probably at all he'd lost. At all he could lose.

Still, his expression said "Stay away."

And for the first time since he'd landed on her doorstep, she wondered if maybe she'd invited herself into a world where she didn't belong.

At the top of the stairs, Wilder took Luna's hand. Stormi couldn't shake the image of father and daughter clinging to each other in the snow.

And the terrible urge to pray swept over her again.

SEE, SHE WAS FINE. Everyone was fine. Just fine. So he could probably calm down.

Still, Wilder's hands trembled as he cracked open the worn copy of Balto's story, the pages soft from years of bedtime readings. Vic's place even smelled safe, with the lingering aroma of the woman's famous chili from dinner in the air.

If he could just get through one bedtime routine without Luna seeing the rage that was eating him alive, maybe he could hold on to the illusion that he'd been doing the right thing leaving her in Vic's hands for the past three weeks.

"And Balto knew he couldn't give up." His voice came out steady. Good. "Even when the snow was deep and the wind was howling, he kept going. Because sometimes being brave means taking one more step when you think you can't."

Luna melted deeper into his lap on Vic's old leather recliner, the worn brown hide creaking under their combined weight.

Her small fingers traced the colorful illustrations of the heroic sled dog. "Daddy, was Balto scared?"

"Probably." He turned the page, trying not to let his chest crack open at her sweet voice. Oh, he'd missed her. "But being brave doesn't mean you're not scared. It means you do what's right even when you are."

Rome padded over from his spot by Vic's front door. Somehow his big amber eyes won Vic over, kept him from being shooed out onto the kennel line with the other dogs. He settled beside the chair with a soft exhale, and Luna's free hand dropped down to rest on his thick fur.

Kitchen sounds filtered through the thin walls—Vic doing the dishes, a low conversation between her and Stormi. He could guess at the subject of their discussion.

Maybe he should have fought Stormi harder on not joining him.

But maybe he didn't have the strength to leave her behind either. He didn't know if that made him wise or weak. But just having her around . . .

"Of course I'm praying!" That had undone him and still did. Especially because it . . . well, worked.

"Balto never gave up, right, Daddy?"

"Never." He pressed a kiss to the top of her head, breathing in that little-girl sweetness. "And neither do we. The Frost family doesn't give up."

Luna's small body went limp and trusting against his chest by the time he reached the story's end. He sat still for several minutes, feeling the weight of her in his arms, the way her hair tickled his chin. He listened to her soft breathing mix with the pop and hiss of logs settling in Vic's stone fireplace.

"She asleep?" Stormi had appeared in the doorway, her voice barely above a whisper. Lamplight caught the auburn highlights in her brown hair. She'd changed into worn jeans and a soft sweater that brought out the green in her eyes.

Wilder nodded. He lifted Luna carefully, feeling her arms automatically circle his neck even in sleep. He limped as he carried her to her small bedroom, the floorboards creaking under his stocking feet. Moonlight through the frost-covered window cast silver patterns across the patchwork quilt.

He tucked the covers around Luna's shoulders and brushed a strand of hair from her forehead. "Everything's going to be okay, baby girl." The lie tasted bitter on his tongue.

Maybe—please let it not be a lie.

Back in the living room, Vic had poured three cups of coffee, the aroma strong enough to wake the dead. Stormi perched on the edge of the couch, Rome at her feet, hands wrapped around her mug while steam rose between her fingers. A couple pictures sat on Vic's side table—a little girl with blond hair in pigtails, that same child as a teenager, her hair long.

"So." Vic settled into her kitchen chair, which she'd dragged into the living room, the wooden legs scraping against the floor. "We need to talk."

Wilder remained standing, every muscle coiled tight. "About what?"

"Your place." Vic sighed, her voice rough. "It's . . . it was set on fire."

The coffee mug slipped from his fingers.

Ceramic exploded against Vic's hardwood floor, the crash echoing through the small house. Hot liquid splashed across his jeans, soaking through to burn his skin, but the pain barely registered past the roaring in his ears.

"Oh—sorry—sorry!"

He stared at the broken mug as Rome leaped up, barked. Stormi got up also, headed to the kitchen.

"Sit down, Wilder. It's okay." Vic had also gotten up, and

Stormi returned with the garbage can and a roll of paper towels. Frozen, he watched as she mopped up the liquid.

"Set on fire." The words finally landed. And he said, "How bad?"

Vic returned with the broom. She and Stormi cleaned up the mess and then Vic grabbed the trash can and put it into the kitchen.

Wilder had sat down on the sofa—collapsed, really. Stormi sank onto the seat beside him.

"Bad," Vic said, returning. She sat and leaned forward, elbows on her knees, her weathered hands clasped tight. "The blizzard put the fire out, but the damage . . ." She shook her head. "I'm sorry, Wilder."

The room tilted sideways.

Every photograph of Dawn—their wedding, Luna's first steps, quiet moments he'd treasured—and every memento from their life together, every memory he'd tried to create for his daughter . . .

"The dogs?" His voice sounded off, not his own.

"The pen gates were open. I saw tracks heading into the woods, but with the snow . . ."

Stormi was reaching for him, but he held up a hand. If she touched him right now, he'd shatter.

He got up. "I have to find them."

"Wilder—" Stormi started.

"Those dogs are all Luna and I have left." The heat was building now. It started in his chest, cascaded through his body, up his throat. His hands clenched into fists. "Everything else is gone. Everything. But those dogs . . ." He ran both hands through his hair, limped to the window and back, not needing his crutch for the heat inside. "I trained half of them from puppies. They don't know how to survive on their own."

The wind howled around the eaves of Vic's old house, rattling the windows in their frames. Snow pelted the glass with tiny, urgent taps.

"They're around, Wilder. I've been leaving out food. And Atlas and Timber are in my barn. They're fine."

"I'm going to the house. They'd stick around—"

"It's not safe," Stormi said. "If whoever hit your place is still watching it—"

"I'm done with this!" The words exploded out of him. "I'm tired of being careful. I'm tired of running. I'm tired of letting them take everything from me while I hide and hope they'll give up. *They're* not giving up!"

He spun toward the kitchen, needing to move, needing to do something with the energy burning through his veins. The house shrank around him, the walls pressing in.

His leg burned, but he didn't care. He pushed his way outside, into the cold, down the steps, and then—

He shouted, a feral roar that shook out of him, emptied him, sluiced the heat out of his bones. It released the coil of darkness in his soul.

But the cold swallowed his cry, and it wasn't enough.

Breathing hard, he headed for the barn behind the house, the outbuilding Vic used for storage. Threw open the door.

Two of his dogs slept in fresh straw, the bare moonlight casting over them.

Timber thumped her tail. Atlas lay beside her.

He stared at them, then his legs collapsed and he landed on the earth, crawled toward the dogs. Timber whined, licked his face, and he put his arms around her.

And then, oh he just pulled her into his lap and . . . wept. Just let it all thunder out of him, his hand over his face, his body shaking.

It wasn't fair. Wasn't right. Where was the justice, the protection—

Where was God?

A crunch in the snow made him lift his head, and he didn't care that tears raked his cheeks.

Stormi stood in the doorframe, holding a flashlight, her face pinched. "You okay?"

He stared at her a long time, then ran a hand down his face, clearing it. "No."

She swallowed, nodded. Came inside and shut the door.

"This is what I get for doing the right thing." Wilder laughed, but it came out harsh. "I told the truth. And I got on a plane to do it again, and . . . this is what I get for it? My house burned down, my dogs scattered, my daughter sleeping in a stranger's bed because nowhere is safe anymore?"

"Vic isn't a stranger," Stormi said. "And yes, this is what you get. Because doing the right thing doesn't guarantee you won't get hurt. It just guarantees you can look at yourself in the mirror afterward."

He put his hand on Atlas, the dog's tail thumping down beside him. Oh, please, let his other dogs be alive.

Stormi moved closer. "The right thing is still the right thing, Wilder. Even when it costs everything."

Something in her voice—steady, certain, unshakable—cut through the noise in his head.

He looked up at her, breathing hard. "I'm not like you, Stormi. I can't just pray my way out of this."

She frowned, then crouched and reached out, petting Timber. "Of course you can. That's the only thing you can do, really."

He frowned.

"Listen. Just because we get in over our head does not mean that God won't save us. He doesn't work on the 'You made your bed so lie in it' mentality. He says, 'I know you're in trouble. I'm here. I love you.'"

He wanted to take in her words, but, "Have you not met me? People die because of me."

"People die because bad people do bad things. And they tend to do them to people who do the right thing." She touched his arm. "You're a good man, Wilder. And God very much wants to help you get through this." She held out her hand. "C'mon. It's cold out here."

He struggled to his feet.

"I need to go to the house. Find whatever dogs I can and then . . ." He stopped. Because he didn't know what came after that. The future stretched ahead, darkness under a cloudy sky.

"Then we're leaving," Stormi said, putting her arm around him. "All of us. Tonight we go to your place, look for the dogs. Tomorrow we pack up Luna and we go somewhere the killers can't find you."

"We?" He turned to stare at her, taking in her expression, the fierce glint in her hazel eyes, the grim line of her mouth.

He hadn't a hope of turning her away. Still, he gave it a go. "This isn't your fight."

"Wow. We just keep circling that, don't we?" She pulled him close. "I'm sticking around. Get used to it."

His mouth opened, but then she looked up at him, smiled.

And if she hadn't been holding him up, yes, maybe his knees would have betrayed him. Oh, she was pretty and, shoot, now he didn't want her to leave.

But, "Stormi . . ."

"I understand that you're scared."

Oh. Um.

"I understand that losing people hurts so much you'd rather be alone than risk it again. But I also understand that Luna needs more than just survival. She needs to see that good people don't run from hard things."

Right. And her words landed in the center of his chest, a fist, with heat and truth that found his bones.

Luna did need more. She needed to see her father fight instead of flee. She needed to know that doing the right thing mattered, even when it cost everything.

"Besides." Her hand landed on his chest, right over his heart, warm, solid, even through his flannel shirt. "What are you going to do, outrun me?"

She grinned at him, and her smile was light in the terrible darkness, exploding a different kind of heat inside him.

"Come on." Stormi moved him toward the door. "Let's go find your dogs."

Right.

He let her help him back to the house, then he pulled on his winter gear and followed her back outside.

The trail between his house and Vic's hadn't been recently trod, but Vic handed Stormi a key to her Arctic Cat. He climbed on behind her and held on.

She motored through the snow to the house next door.

He froze as the headlights swept across what used to be his home, now just a skeleton of charred timbers and collapsed roof sections, black against the white snow. The metal roofing must have buckled from the heat, creating twisted sculptures that caught the light and threw grotesque shadows across the clearing. The acrid smell of burned wood and melted plastic still hung in the air, mixing with the cold, clean scent of snow.

The home he'd built for Dawn. For Luna.

Gone.

His workshop, however, still stood—a miracle maybe, given the char on the steel roof. But inside would be his sled, his tools, his mushing equipment.

Now he just needed the team. But a look at the dog yard made his chest constrict, the air suddenly too thin to breathe.

Twelve empty pens with their gates hanging open, the chain-link twisted and warped from the heat. Food and water bowls scattered across the snow, some melted into nearly unrecognizable shapes. The doghouse he'd built for Timber when she was pregnant was overturned and broken, the careful craftsmanship reduced to splinters.

"Wilder." Stormi's voice was gentle. "I'm sorry."

They sat on the rumbling Arctic Cat for a long moment. The heater continued to blow warm air, but it couldn't touch the cold spreading through Wilder's chest.

"I've given most of them their shots and checkups at one point or another. But tell me about them as a team."

Right. "Twelve total. All huskies, all proven. I keep my team tight." She got off the sled and turned to him.

He hated how he needed her hand to help him off. "Kodiak's my lead dog. Big gray male with yellow eyes and more attitude than sense. Then there's Spruce—she's smaller but twice as smart. Aurora, Rockey, and Copper—"

Barking. He stilled, then, "Kodiak!"

His voice echoed across the snow-covered clearing, swallowed by the darkness beyond their headlights. The silence stretched out, broken only by the snowmobile's idling engine and the whisper of wind through the burned timbers.

Then—

A bark, deep and familiar and definitely Kodiak.

"Spruce! Aurora!" Wilder cupped his hands around his mouth. "Come on, guys!"

More barking now, coming from the tree line behind the ruins of his house.

Six dogs emerged from the shadows between the trees, their thick coats dusted with snow. Kodiak first—massive gray frame appearing between two trees—followed by Spruce's smaller, more delicate build and Aurora's distinctive black-and-white markings. Three others behind them, all moving with the eager, bounding gait that meant pack reunion.

"Hey, boys. Hey, girls." Wilder slid off the seat of the snowmobile as they reached him. Enthusiastic huskies knocked him backward, and he let them, laughing for the first time in days. Okay, maybe years.

They nudged into his hands, tried to lick his face.

Spruce put her head on his leg, whining, while Kodiak planted both front paws on his chest and proceeded to wash his face with a tongue that felt like warm sandpaper. The others circled and yipped.

"Six." Stormi knelt beside him in the snow, letting Aurora sniff her gloved hand before the dog bumped against her leg, seeking attention. "That's half."

"Eight with Timber and Atlas. The others might show up later. I'll keep calling them." He scratched Kodiak behind the ears, feeling the thick double coat that had kept him warm through the Alaska winter. Warmth flooded through him. "These guys probably stayed close to guard the territory."

"Smart dogs."

"The smartest." He stood, brushing snow from his knees.

Eight dogs were better than no dogs. Eight dogs were enough to rebuild.

And when the horror cleared, he'd mourn the loss of the others. They'd been good dogs, his team.

He trekked over to the workshop and opened the door.

Like a miracle, both his sleds had survived—his original Iditarod sled, and the newer, faster one he'd built for mail runs. The harnesses still hung on the wall, the lines neatly coiled.

"This is quite the setup," Stormi said as she stepped inside and flashed her light around.

He nodded. "Not sure why I need all this if I'm not going to compete again, but I'll set up a line at Vic's while we figure out what to do." He grabbed the leads and then whistled to the dogs. They came, and he attached them to their leads.

They got back on the snowmobile, and he called to the team. They trotted after him as Stormi drove the Cat back to Vic's place.

Then he staked out a line, far enough from Stormi's team to keep them out of trouble, but close enough to watch them. He added Timber and Atlas to the line, and they settled down in their snow nests, curling together the way sled dogs did to conserve heat, their thick coats creating a living blanket of fur and warmth.

By the time they finished, Wilder's jacket was covered in dog hair and his gloves were soaked through, but something inside his chest had loosened. The tight band of panic that had been squeezing his ribs since Vic delivered the news began to ease.

Not everything was lost.

Not everything could be taken.

"So, what now?" Stormi asked, her voice slightly muffled by the scarf she'd wrapped around her face.

"Now we get warm. Tomorrow morning we load up Luna and head south to the Matthews compound. It's the only place left Sloan doesn't know about."

"And after that?"

Wilder glanced at his dogs. Then at the woman who had chosen to stand with him when she could have walked away, her face pale in the glow of lights from the house. "I don't know."

She turned to face him fully, close enough that he could see the snowflakes caught in her eyelashes, melting from the warmth of her skin. "We'll figure it out."

He didn't correct her. "Stormi."

"Yeah?"

"Thank you." The words felt inadequate, too small for what she'd given him. "For coming with me. For not walking away when you should have."

"I'm not going anywhere."

Something in the way she said it, fierce and final and completely uncompromising, simply broke through him. He took a breath and then blamed the quiet of the snowflakes peeling from the darkness for the fact that he reached out to her.

He pulled off his soaked glove and touched her face with his cold hand, then moved it behind her neck.

Somehow the space between them disappeared.

He met her eyes, lost in them for a moment.

And he simply led with the tugging of his heart. The kiss started gently and, frankly, he didn't know what he might be doing. Why he—

But she was soft and tasted of hope, and when her arms encircled him, holding on, he forgot about everything except the way she felt against him—solid and real and utterly unafraid.

And right then, he needed her. Oh, he needed her. And he couldn't stop himself from wrapping his arms around her, pulling her in, deepening his kiss.

She tasted of coffee. And a strange, easy sense of coming home. Her hero worship still lingered in the back of his brain, but maybe she was his hero too. Maybe this wasn't wrong, wasn't a betrayal of Dawn, or even Stormi. Maybe it was simply . . . truth. The fact that she was right after all.

He didn't want to be alone. Not anymore.

When they broke apart, he drew in his breath, breathing hard, realizing he'd kissed her harder, deeper than he intended.

Okay, he hadn't really intended on kissing her at all. He rested his forehead against hers. "I . . . uh. Sorry, I guess. I wasn't . . . I didn't mean for that to happen."

"That makes one of us. I've been wanting to do that since the moment you walked into my clinic a year ago."

And he had nothing for that. She was just so . . .

"I wish that—" he started.

"Your life wasn't complicated and dangerous and probably going to get worse before it gets better?" She pulled back enough to look him in the eyes.

Oh. "Yeah, that."

"Me too. But if it wasn't, then you would have never ended up on my doorstep, needing surgery. So yeah, life might be scary, but . . . you know."

"You know?" He lifted his head.

"You have me now. And maybe you should kiss me again. Just in case you have any lingering doubts."

His mouth opened. And she grabbed his lapels and leaned in again.

Oh. Okay, then. He kissed her again, slower this time, trying to memorize the moment before reality crashed back in. The taste of her, the way she fit against him, the incredible rightness of not being alone.

Please, please let it not get her killed.

7

STORMI STARED OUT Vic's frost-covered kitchen window at the chaos of sled preparation in the yard, her heart hammering against her ribs.

The smart move was probably driving home to her clinic, not following Wilder into the woods. But her heart said go.

That, and the kiss last night, and oh, please let her not be getting in over her head.

She was all bravado on the outside, but no, she didn't want to be killed, thank you very much.

Still, now that she had Wilder Frost, the last thing she wanted to do was let him go.

Her coffee had gone cold twenty minutes ago, leaving a bitter film on her tongue. She'd been standing here on the worn linoleum floor, watching Wilder move through the morning with the efficiency of someone who'd packed his gear in the night a thousand times. He'd gone back to his house on the snowmobile and brought his sleds over to Vic's place. Now, he used the snowmobile to load each sled onto the top of the kennels in the bed of Vic's truck, then hers. He strapped both down for transport. All while limping. Oh, the guy was tough.

Or just angry and scared. Maybe all of the above.

They were in for a long day. Apparently, they'd drive thirty miles south of town, then take the dogs and sleds cross-country to the Matthewses' place. Hopefully they'd arrive by midday.

Her stomach twisted. Not from the bitter coffee or the thick-cut bacon Vic had insisted on frying for breakfast.

No, this was the terrible, too familiar knot of someone who'd dreamed too big again.

Celebrity crush. Maybe that's all this was. She'd always been a foolish romantic.

This was sort of over the top, given the stakes.

"Just go outside and help him."

Vic appeared beside her, steam rising from her own coffee mug—this one advertising the Midnight Sun Saloon in faded red letters. The older woman wore insulated Carhartt coveralls over thermal layers, steel-toed Timberlands, and the no-nonsense expression of someone who'd been up way before dawn organizing supplies in her freezing garage.

"I dunno," Stormi said. "Feels like he needs to do this—pack up his life—alone." She pulled her merino wool thermal shirt down over her wrists, the fabric soft against her skin. Despite the layers—thermal shirt, thick fisherman's sweater, and her heavy Patagonia coat waiting by the door—it would be a cold trip. Even now, the chill seeped through Vic's single-pane windows. She fogged the glass with her breath.

"Uh-huh." Vic sipped her coffee, the sound loud in the quiet kitchen. "Looks like you're brooding."

"I don't brood."

"Honey, you've been brooding since you got out of bed. Which was what, four a.m.? I heard you pacing upstairs, those old floorboards creaking with every step."

Heat crawled up Stormi's neck, warming her skin despite the drafty kitchen. She'd tried to be quiet, but Vic's house was older than her clinic, and sleep had been impossible, anyway. Every time she'd closed her eyes, she'd felt Wilder's calloused hands in her hair. The taste of him on her lips. The way he'd looked at her in the glow of the house lights, snow swirling around them.

She could have kissed him all night.

"I'm fine."

"Sure you are." Vic moved to the stove, refilling her mug from the battered aluminum percolator that had probably been making coffee since she arrived in Copper Mountain. The liquid gurgled as it poured. "Rethinking this little adventure?"

She sighed. "No."

"You should be."

She glanced at Vic. The woman stood at the counter, her mouth tight. "I haven't told Wilder, but a couple weeks ago, Conan and Mars Sorros held . . . um, a woman . . . hostage to try to find Luna. It didn't take. Dawson Mulligan, a cop from Anchorage, tracked her down and arrested Mars. Jericho and Harley got Conan last week."

"Which means that the only Sorros left is Sloan. Jericho said he saw him last week, but he's still out there. Along with Tommy Reid."

"Right. Tommy. I always knew there was something off with that man." She took another sip of coffee. "But these boys are definitely trouble so you'd better figure out if that's what you want."

She looked out at Wilder, now gathering up his team.

"Or rather, if the man is worth it."

That's why I moved here. She didn't say it, but watching Wilder, seeing him with Luna . . . "He's worth it."

He was loading up his dogs in the back of Vic's truck, with the kennel topper over the bed. Good dogs, they obeyed him immediately, bedding down in their cubbies.

Her own dogs were a different story.

They stood, a little tangled in their lines, barking—until Wilder came over and, one by one, lifted them into the kennels in the bed of her truck. Two of them—Koda and Yukon—had gotten into a snarling match over a piece of dropped beef jerky. Rome sat calmly beside Luna, who was bundled in her puffy pink snowsuit, as she fed him pieces of crispy bacon she'd saved from their early breakfast, her mittened hands careful as Rome's gentle mouth accepted each offering.

She turned to Vic. "Truth is, I've been in love with Wilder for . . . well, years actually."

And she didn't know why she told Vic that, but frankly, she just needed to test it all out. This . . . this *thing* between them. "Since he ran the Iditarod."

"I see," Vic said. "Celebrity crush. You sure you're ready for the real thing?"

She nodded. "I just . . . I just hope he is."

And there it was, right? Maybe he'd kissed her out of fear. Or a moment of loneliness. Or . . . "He might still be grieving Dawn."

"Of course he's still grieving Dawn. He'll always grieve Dawn. The question you're really asking is, is there room for you?" Vic raised an eyebrow.

She turned back to the window. Wilder was still loading her dogs into the kennels on her truck. "What if I'm a liability?"

Silence behind her, and again, she didn't know why she had spilled this all out on Vic, but, "I'm just a veterinarian, not a superhero. What am I doing here?"

Vic said nothing.

And maybe she was right. "Look at my dogs. Look at his. I can barely manage seven animals, and he's worried about keeping his daughter safe while I fumble around pretending I belong in his world."

Vic set down her mug with a loud clunk against the Formica

counter, the sound echoing in the small kitchen. "That man kissed you last night."

Fire shot up Stormi's spine, heat flooding her cheeks. "How did you—"

"Honey, I may be old, but I'm not dumb. You came back from that house looking like you'd been struck by lightning, and he's been avoiding eye contact with you ever since. Plus, Luna keeps asking why her daddy looks sad this morning."

Stormi's chest went tight, ribs constricting around her lungs. "He looks sad?"

"Confused. Conflicted. Like a man who did something he wanted to do but thinks he shouldn't have."

Oh. "Maybe he shouldn't have." Stormi pulled her coat from the wooden hook by the door, the heavy fabric rustling as she gripped it. "This is exactly what I always do. I get carried away by some romantic notion and forget that real life doesn't work that way."

"What way?"

"The way where the gorgeous single father with the complicated past actually falls for the small-town vet who can't even control her own sled dogs."

Vic snorted. "You think you're not good enough for him?"

"I think I'm realistic." Stormi started to pull on her insulated gloves. "I think I'm someone who gets swept up in the moment and forgets that men like Wilder Frost don't end up with women like me."

"Women like you?"

"Women who dream too big. Women who fall for guys who are out of their league. Women who—"

"Women who drop everything to help a stranger? Women who risk their lives to save his daughter? Women who stand by him when anyone with sense would run the other direction?"

Stormi stopped, gloves half on.

"That man needs you," Vic said. "Not because you're perfect. Not because you've got everything figured out. But because you showed up. You stayed. And that, Stormi White, makes you a superhero."

Oh.

Outside, Wilder straightened from checking his sled runners, then looked toward the window.

Stormi stepped back instinctively, her stocking feet sliding on the smooth linoleum.

"He keeps looking this way." Vic picked her mug back up.

"Probably wondering if I'm going to bail."

"Are you?"

The question hung between them. Stormi could walk out that door, climb into her truck, and be back at her clinic in twenty minutes. Back to her world of vaccinations and wellness checks and . . . regret.

"I'm not going to bail."

"Good. Then get packed up. We need to get to the Millers' place and be on the trail so we can arrive before dark." Vic finished her coffee and set her mug in the sink. Then she picked up a duffel bag near the door and headed outside.

The kitchen fell quiet except for the steady tick of the wall clock and the distant rumble of the trucks' diesel engines warming up outside, ready for the thirty-minute drive to their departure point.

She, too, finished her cold coffee, walked to the door, put on her boots, and scooped up her backpack.

Here went nothing.

Wilder slid into the truck with Luna and Vic, but he glanced over at Stormi with a grim smile and a nod.

Maybe Vic was right. He looked conflicted.

She followed Vic's truck out of the driveway and south, toward the Millers' place, the headlights pushing back the fading night.

Thirty minutes later, the cold hit Stormi's lungs as she stepped out of her cab onto the frozen ground at the old hunting lodge. This remote property, owned by one of the Matthewses' family friends, provided the perfect staging area where they could leave their vehicles and disappear into the wilderness without anyone tracking their route.

The air carried the scent of fresh snow mixed with faint diesel exhaust and the earthy smell of eager sled dogs who'd been whining in the truck bed for the entire drive. Dawn was breaking over the Chugach Mountains, painting the sky pale gray and casting long blue shadows across the staging area where sleds and supplies waited.

Wilder looked up as Stormi crunched over to him, headlamp creating a halo of light around his black wool beanie. He'd already loaded both sleds with sleeping bags, freeze-dried food, and emergency gear, everything secured with bungee cords and the kind of packing expertise that spoke of years in the wilderness where a loose load could mean death.

Of course, his dogs waited in perfect formation beside his hand-built sled. Six Alaskan huskies arranged by size and temperament—Kodiak's massive gray frame at lead, followed by Spruce's smaller but muscular build, then the others in precise order. Their thick double coats were dusted with fresh snow, and they sat quietly. Ears alert. Yellow and brown eyes fixed on their musher with the kind of devotion that came from trust built over years.

"Ready for this?"

"Yep." She stopped beside his original birch-and-ash racing sled, taking in the tangle of nylon harnesses and the restless energy of her dogs, who whined and shifted.

He nodded. "We'll be at the compound before lunchtime if the weather holds."

If.

The word carried weight they both understood. Alaska weather could change in minutes, turning a routine journey into a survival situation where visibility dropped to zero and temperatures plummeted to lethal levels.

"Stormi!" Luna bounded over through the snow, her puffy pink snowsuit rustling with each step. "I'm happy you're going on our adventure. You're going to love Grandma Una. She makes the best hot chocolate with real marshmallows, and Grandpa Caius lets me play doctor sometimes, and there's this place where you can see the whole valley and the glaciers and—"

"Luna." Wilder's voice carried gentle warning. "Let's get you packed up."

But he glanced at Stormi, a question in his eyes.

She met it.

His jaw turned hard, stubble dark against skin reddened by the cold. He dropped his voice as Luna stood nearby, not entirely out of earshot. "Just to be clear, this isn't some adventure. This isn't—"

"A romantic fairy tale where the hero sweeps the girl off her feet and they live happily ever after?"

"I wasn't going to put it that bluntly."

"But that's what you're thinking." She moved closer to him, close enough to see the gold flecks in his blue eyes. "That I'm some starry-eyed dreamer who doesn't understand reality."

"Aren't you?"

The question was quiet. Serious. Fair, maybe.

Stormi looked at her tangled dog team, then at his perfectly organized one. At Luna now watching them with bright, hopeful eyes that reflected the growing dawn light. At the sleds loaded for a journey into wilderness where cell service didn't exist and the nearest hospital was a helicopter ride away through terrain that could kill a pilot in bad weather.

"Probably." The admission surprised her. "I've always been a dreamer. Always reached for things that were probably out of my league."

His mouth made a grim line.

She walked over to Rome, who had walked up to Luna and sat. She patted his head. "But sometimes . . . sometimes the reaching was worth it."

Wilder studied her face, the warm sunlight illuminating the planes of his cheekbones and the concern etched around his eyes. "This could get dangerous."

She nodded, let him see her eyes. *I'm in. No regrets.*

He sighed, and the careful distance he'd maintained all morning cracked for just a moment, and the smile he gave her felt real. Finally.

"Then we better get your team sorted."

He moved to her dogs, his limp a little less pronounced, and Stormi watched him work. No wasted motion. No frustration when Koda and Yukon started another scuffle, their growls harsh in the cold air. Just calm, consistent authority that had both dogs sitting within seconds, ears back in submission.

"Remember," he said to her, "the key is making sure they know you're in charge. Dogs need a leader."

"Alpha dog, I got it."

He glanced at her, a smile tipping his mouth as he clipped Yukon into position. "Let's just get there safely."

He moved to Denali next, the big wheel dog who'd been causing most of the trouble. Instead of approaching directly, Wilder stood still in the crystalline morning air. Waiting until Denali looked at him, brown eyes meeting his steadily.

Eye contact. Acknowledgment.

Only then did he step forward, his movements deliberate and calm.

"If you act like you're not sure, they won't be sure either."

He worked down the line, bringing order to chaos with

nothing more than presence and certainty. Stormi's dogs responded to him the way he responded—with immediate, unquestioning trust born from recognizing true leadership. He clipped in Sitka and Juneau, then turned to her.

"Your turn."

He stepped back and handed her the lead rope. "Confidence, remember?"

Her team looked up at her with bright eyes and eager expressions, waiting for direction.

"Line up," she said.

Nothing happened. The three remaining dogs continued to mill around.

"Louder," Wilder told her. "Like you mean it."

"Line up!" This time her voice carried across the yard, sharp and clear, echoing.

Lina and Koda moved into formation beside the sled, ears forward, bodies aligned with perfect precision. Only Rome seemed confused. He sat, and his tail brushed the snow.

Stormi blinked. "They actually listened."

"Alpha dog." He held up his fist. She bumped it, a sort of heat sluicing through her as he smiled at her. The words hung in the cold air between them.

She smiled back. "Rome, come."

The dog obeyed and she clipped him into the traces, while Wilder hooked up Lina next to him, then finally Koda.

"Ready?" Vic called from beside Wilder's sled. She'd insisted on coming with them, and Luna had cheered when Vic announced she'd be riding along in Wilder's sled. They'd packed all the gear on Stormi's. "I just called Deke. They haven't found Tommy or Sloan. Let's get going."

Wilder nodded, moving to help Luna into the sled, his boots leaving deep prints in the snow. He tucked a sleeping bag around her small form, making sure she was secure and warm, then helped Vic settle onto the sled behind Luna. The older woman had added serious winter gear over her coveralls—insulated pants, thick parka, and a furry hat.

"Ready?" Wilder asked Luna.

"Ready!" Luna said, her voice muffled by the fleece neck warmer pulled up to her nose.

Watching Wilder's expression soften as he kissed his daughter's forehead through her knit hat, seeing the absolute trust in Luna's bright eyes, maybe Stormi wasn't ready at all.

Because Vic was right. This was the real thing.

"Trail positions," Wilder called, moving to his sled, the runners scraping slightly against the hard-packed snow. "I'll take point. Stormi, you follow my line exactly. If I stop, you stop. If I turn, you turn. No improvising."

"Got it."

He paused, one gloved hand on his sled handlebow, the birch wood worn smooth from years of use. "Last chance to turn around. You sure about this?"

She looked at him.

Was she? Standing in the early morning cold with a dog team that had finally decided to behave, wearing enough layers to survive an arctic expedition, heading into wilderness that could kill them all if the weather turned—was she sure about any of it?

"Absolutely."

For the first time since last night's kiss, the texture in his eyes changed. Not the careful, cool, maybe confused expression he'd worn all morning, but something real and warm and entirely him.

And her heart just about burst.

He stepped onto his sled runners, the wood flexing slightly under his weight, and his dogs came alive. Ears forward. Muscles coiled. Ready to run. Luna waved from her nest of sleeping bags, her mitten bright against the dark fabric, while Vic adjusted her position behind her, a slight grimace on her face.

"Hike up!"

The command cracked across the yard, sharp as a gunshot, and Wilder's team lunged forward. Snow flew from their feet, the sled runners hissing against the packed surface as they settled into the ground-eating lope that could carry them for miles without rest.

Stormi waited three seconds, counting her heartbeats, then called out to her own team. "Mush!"

Her dogs exploded forward with enthusiasm that nearly jerked the handlebow from her hands, the sudden acceleration sending snow spraying behind the runners. But they followed Wilder's trail, falling into formation behind his sled without the circus act.

Huh.

The cold air burned her lungs and brought tears to her eyes, the water immediately freezing on her cheeks. Snow kicked up by the lead team stung her exposed skin. Her muscles already ached from gripping the sled, and they'd been moving for less than a minute.

But as they left the Millers' property behind, heading for the tree line where the real journey would begin and the packed trail gave way to wilderness, Stormi felt the absolute certainty that she was exactly where she belonged.

Even if it was stupid. Even if it was dangerous. Even if she was probably in way over her head again.

For once in her life, reaching for the impossible felt like the smartest thing she'd ever done.

THIS WAS a terrible idea.

Wilder gritted his teeth against the fire shooting up his leg. Two hours of mushing through mountainous terrain, and his thigh burned with every jolt over hidden roots and rocks beneath the snow.

He'd finally gotten a good look at Stormi's team and why Rome struggled. The big Malador ran second behind Koda, whose graying muzzle and slower pace spoke of years leading a team. But Rome's attention kept drifting—ears swiveling toward sounds, nose testing air currents that carried scents invisible to human senses. The dog's breath steamed in the cold air, white puffs that dispersed quickly in the mountain wind. His body language spoke of distraction, not the focused energy of a working sled dog. Rome might be half Malamute, but the Labrador inside him had no business pulling a sled in formation.

Snow flew from the paws of the dogs, catching early afternoon light that slanted through black spruce, tiny ice crystals sparkling in the air before settling back to earth. The sun had hidden behind the clouds, leaving the sky the color of tarnished pewter. Wind whispered through the boughs with the dry sound of winter settling deeper into the mountains.

The familiar scent of woodsmoke reached him first, carried on the crisp mountain air along with the distant sound of the homestead's barking dogs. Through the trees ahead, he caught the first glimpse of the Matthews compound—stone chimneys sending gray smoke into the pale sky, warm yellow light glowing from the windows.

It had been three years since Dawn's death, and this was still the only place that felt like sanctuary. Not just the log buildings scattered across the cleared meadow or the vast wilderness that surrounded them but the people who'd chosen to love him and Luna when his terrible choices had taken from them the daughter they loved.

"Daddy, look." Luna's voice carried back from his sled. "There's the workshop and the big barn and—oh, there's Uncle Everest!"

A figure emerged from one of the weathered outbuildings,

waving. Tall, broad-shouldered, wearing insulated Carhartt coveralls. Everest Matthews lived up to his name—big, bold, and unyielding. He'd loved his sister with the fierce protectiveness of a big brother.

Wilder's dogs slowed as they approached the compound proper. Multiple log cabins sat connected by covered walkways and packed snow paths. The main lodge dominated the center, a massive fieldstone chimney sending the rich scent of burning birch into the crisp air. Smaller cabins dotted the surrounding area—Sage's place, with her arctic climbing gear hanging on hooks near her door, Everest's workshop, dark and quiet now, the scent of fresh-planed cedar still carried, and the medical office where Dr. Caius and Bear treated everything from broken bones to difficult births.

Behind his sled, Stormi's team followed, their eager whines and the scrape of their claws on packed snow audible.

His chest constricted. Not from the physical pain this time but from something that felt dangerously close to hope.

"Hike!" He guided his team toward the main lodge, pain shooting through his leg as he applied pressure to the metal brake. He managed to bring the sled to a smooth stop beside the wide front porch where icicles hung from the eaves.

Everest jogged toward them through the snow, a grin splitting his bearded face. "Well, look what the trail dragged in." He reached down and helped Luna out of the sled.

She took off toward the lodge. "Grandma Una! Grandpa Caius!"

Vic climbed out of Wilder's sled and met the man's outstretched hand. "Everest Matthews, still causing trouble?"

"Never, Vic." He pushed away her hand and grabbed her in a bear hug that lifted her feet off the ground.

Two more figures appeared in the doorway, warm light spilling around them.

Una Matthews was exactly what a grandmother should be—silver hair pulled back in a practical bun, dressed in a thick wool cardigan over thermal layers, sturdy mukluks on her feet, arms already open for Luna's flying embrace.

Behind her, Dr. Caius Matthews stepped onto the porch, boots heavy on the weathered planks. Sixty-eight years old and still carrying himself like the military medic he'd been in his youth. Thick wool sweater stretched over a frame that had seen hard use. Beard more gray than brown now but eyes as keen as ever. His gaze found Wilder immediately, and something flickered across his weathered face. Concern.

"About time you brought our girl home," Una called. "Two months is too long, Wilder Frost."

Wilder started to step off his sled runners—

White-hot agony shot up his leg, stealing his breath. Black dots spiked at the edges of his vision. He gripped the handle-bow, forcing his expression to remain neutral even as his knees threatened to buckle.

"Wilder?" Dr. Caius came down the steps. "You okay?"

He managed a nod but didn't meet the man's eyes. He'd never been able to call him just by his first name. He'd always be Dr. Caius, the man who knew him when he was broken.

Everest turned to Stormi, who brought her team to a stop with a sharp command. Her team settled, thick coats steaming slightly in the cold air. "I'm Everest Matthews," he said to her. "Welcome to the compound."

Movement from the other cabins caught Wilder's attention through the haze of pain. Sage emerged from her place, auburn hair braided back. She wore practical outdoor gear—insulated pants, heavy parka, thick boots. Behind her, Bear stepped out of the clinic, surveying the new arrivals. He lifted a hand to Wilder.

Family. *Dawn's* family.

And now he was bringing Stormi into the middle of it.

Maybe he should have thought this through more.

"Hey," Sage said as she came up to Stormi. "I'm Sage." She shook her hand. Everest was unhooking her team from the sled.

Dr. Caius stepped off the porch, still fixed on Wilder. "You look like death warmed over, son."

"Good to see you too, Doc." Wilder tried for his usual grin, but it came out sort of pained and Dr. Caius was no fool, apparently.

He stopped beside the sled, close enough that his voice wouldn't carry to Luna. "Don't tell me you're fine. I recognize Frost stubbornness when I see it."

"I'm—"

"If you say fine, I'm going to have Everest carry you into my office over his shoulder." Dr. Caius's tone was mild, but he smiled, all shark teeth. "Luna's watching, so let's make this easy on everyone."

Wilder glanced toward his daughter, who was talking with her grandmother. The tension that had been constant in the girl's small shoulders since they'd been reunited was gone.

That was what mattered.

"Maybe I'm a little tired."

"Uh-huh." Dr. Caius moved closer. "Let's get everyone settled and fed, then you and I are going to have a conversation."

It wasn't a request.

"Let me get your dogs settled," Bear said and started to unhook them from the sled. Already, Everest was leading Stormi's line toward the kennels, Rome fighting the lead. Stormi stepped up and unhooked the rascal from the rest, and he ran up to the porch, tail wagging, to nudge Luna, who laughed.

"Okay," Wilder said and Bear met his gaze. He wore the same concern as his father, probably due to his own medical credentials.

"C'mon," Dr. Caius said and gestured to the lodge.

Home. He loved this place. Massive fieldstone fireplace dominating one wall where birch logs crackled and sent sparks up the chimney, hand-hewn log walls covered with decades of family photographs in mismatched frames, comfortable worn leather furniture arranged to accommodate large gatherings. The air carried the rich scent of woodsmoke and whatever Una had been cooking, probably the elk stew that had been Luna's favorite since she was old enough to eat solid food.

But it was the photographs that made his chest tighten.

Dawn was still everywhere. Wedding photos where her blond hair caught the light, candid shots from family gatherings where her laugh seemed to echo from the frames, the professional portrait Una had painted the Christmas before Luna was born. Dawn glowing with pregnancy while Wilder stood behind her with his hands on her shoulders. Three years had passed, and Una had refused to pack them away. Luna deserved to see her mother's face every day, she'd said.

Now, watching Stormi take in the room with quiet observation, he wondered what she was thinking. The photographs were impossible to miss—Dawn's bright smile, her arm around Wilder in their wedding shots, the family portrait where she held baby Luna while Wilder stood behind them with the expression of a man who'd never imagined he could be so happy. There were others, too, of the rest of the family, but Stormi's gaze lingered on the mantelpiece where the largest wedding photo sat in its carved wooden frame. Her expression remained carefully neutral. No jealousy, no discomfort. Just acknowledgment of someone who'd been loved.

"Sit," Una commanded, gesturing toward the long wooden table that dominated the dining area, its surface scarred from decades of family meals and heated discussions. "All of you. Food first, then talking." She started moving toward the kitchen. "How long are you staying?"

Wilder started to answer, but another spike of pain shot

through his leg as he limped toward the table. He gripped the back of a heavy wooden chair, fighting the wave of dizziness that followed.

"Daddy?" Luna came up to him. "Are you okay?"

"Just tired from the trail, baby girl." He forced himself to straighten, to smile through the pain. "Nothing a good meal and some rest won't fix."

But Dr. Caius was already positioning himself to catch Wilder if he fell. And Stormi—Stormi was watching with a pinched mouth, her eyes assessing.

"Sit down, Wilder." She'd already peeled off her jacket, taken off her boots, put her feet into warm slippers.

Okay. Wilder sank into the chair with more relief than he wanted to admit. The warmth of the lodge was starting to penetrate his layers, and with it came the kind of bone-deep exhaustion that he'd been fighting for days. The scent of Una's cooking filled his nostrils—rich elk stew and yeast bread and something that might have been apple pie.

He pulled off his jacket, eased out of his boots with a grimace.

Dr. Caius watched him with a grim slant to his mouth. "So you're hurt. But that's not all. What else aren't you telling me?"

"They're still . . ." He glanced around to find Luna, but she'd escaped into the kitchen with Una. "Hunting us."

Dr. Caius drew in a breath.

"They burned down my house. I . . . I needed someplace safe for Luna." He looked at Dr. Caius. "I hope it's okay I came here."

"Should have come here from the beginning of this mess," Una said from the kitchen. So, oops, his voice carried.

"I didn't want to . . ." He glanced at Vic. "Anyway, it's just for tonight." His leg throbbed with each heartbeat. "Tomorrow I'm heading back to end this."

The room went quiet except for the crackle of the fire and the soft clink of Una's cooking preparations.

"Not alone." This from Everest, who'd returned from settling the dogs, snow still clinging to his boots. "You think we're going to let you walk into a trap by yourself?"

"You think I'm going to let them hurt anyone else I care about?" Wilder retorted, his voice sharper than intended, but okay, maybe right. "This is my fight."

"No." Sage hung her coat by the door. "It stopped being just your fight the minute you brought Luna here. We're family, Wilder."

Yeah, that was the point. "I can't ask you to—"

"You're not asking," Bear said, also coming in. "We're telling you."

"Oh goody. This argument again." Stormi moved to the table, carrying a platter of warm bread with real butter melting into the crust. "Give it up, Wilder."

"One of the dogs is favoring his left rear leg," Bear said to Wilder now, changing the subject. "You might want to take a look."

"I'll do it," Stormi said.

Everest looked at her. "You know dogs?"

"I'm a veterinarian." Stormi headed back to the kitchen. "So yes."

"Interesting." Dr. Caius leaned back in his chair. "Wilder, you didn't mention you'd found yourself a medical professional."

Heat crawled up Wilder's neck despite the lodge's warmth. "She's not—we're not—"

"She patched you up pretty well," Vic interjected, spooning sugar into her coffee. "For someone who's not . . ." She raised an eyebrow.

"Vic."

"What? I'm just saying." Vic's grin was pure trouble. "A woman who can handle sled dogs and field medicine? That's a keeper in my book."

Stormi's cheeks had gone pink, but she was smiling as she returned from the kitchen. "I hardly think I land in the category of 'can handle sled dogs.'"

Vic laughed. "You did fine."

"Because my dogs followed Wilder." She glanced at him. Smiled.

Oh. It hit him like pure light, cutting through all the dark shadows inside. He had nothing for the way it scooped him out.

"And while she's looking at the dog, I'll take a look at your leg, Wilder." This from Dr. Caius.

"Just some stitches that need checking," Wilder said. "Nothing serious."

Dr. Caius made a sound that might have been agreement or skepticism. "We'll see."

Una appeared with a steaming pot of stew. "Enough with the tough guy talk. Everyone to the table."

They gathered around the long wooden table. Luna chattered about the trail, about how good Stormi was with her dogs, about how exciting it was to be back at the compound. Vic shared gossip from town, updating everyone on mutual friends and the latest drama at the Midnight Sun and how she'd repaired it after the fire last fall.

And through it all, Wilder thought of Stormi.

She fit. Not the way Dawn had—Dawn had been fire and laughter, filling every room with her presence. Stormi was quieter. Steadier. Deep water that reflected everything around it while keeping its own depths hidden.

She listened more than she spoke. Asked thoughtful questions. Made Luna feel important. Earlier, when Everest mentioned he'd been working on a woodworking project—a rocking horse for one of the neighbors' grandchildren—she asked about techniques. When Sage had talked about preparing for the upcoming climbing season on Denali, Stormi shared stories about altitude sickness in pack animals that had everyone laughing.

She belonged here.

The realization hit his bones, slid into his soul.

"More stew?" Una was beside him with the ladle, but her eyes were concerned as she took in his barely touched bowl. "You've barely eaten anything."

Wilder looked down at his bowl, surprised to find it still mostly full. The pain in his leg had been building throughout dinner, making it hard to concentrate on anything else. He shifted in his chair, trying to find a position that didn't feel like torture. The wooden seat that had been comfortable minutes ago now felt like it was made of rocks.

Stormi's gaze found his across the table.

Sage got up and started clearing plates. "I'll warm up the apple crisp. There's time for you to go take a look at the dogs," she said to Stormi.

"Good idea." Dr. Caius stood, but his attention remained on Wilder. "Son, let's take a look at those stitches."

Right. Wilder started to rise, pushing against the chair arms—

The world tilted sideways.

Pain exploded through his leg, radiating up his spine and into his skull. The room grayed at the edges, and he heard Luna's intake of breath as he gripped the table edge to keep from falling.

"Daddy!"

Strong hands caught him before he could hit the floor. Dr. Caius on one side, Everest on the other, supporting his weight as his leg collapsed under him.

"I'm okay," he managed, though the words came out through gritted teeth. "Just—"

"You're not okay," Dr. Caius snapped, the family patriarch replaced by the combat medic who'd saved countless lives under fire. "Everest, help me get him to the office. And bring my bag. Una, keep Luna here."

"Is Daddy going to be okay?" Luna's voice emerged small. Scared.

"He's going to be fine, sweetheart," Stormi said. "Your grandpa is going to fix him up, and then he'll be good as new."

Everest and Dr. Caius hauled Wilder up and he wanted to object. To insist he could walk under his own power. But as they helped him toward the door, his leg betrayed him again, sending fresh waves of agony through his body. He grunted, and the darkness edged in.

The last thing he saw before they carried him out was Stormi picking up Luna.

Taking care of his daughter while he fell apart.

He knew he was in big trouble, given Dr. Caius's tone as they walked into the clinic, which was connected to the lodge. It housed a small reception area, two big rooms, and an office. They dragged him into one of the rooms.

For a remote office, the medical setup was equipped with everything needed to handle serious trauma. The examining table was positioned under bright LEDs, and the familiar scent of antiseptic filled the air, mixing with the underlying smell of coffee and the leatherbound medical journals that lined the wooden shelves in the reception area.

"On the table." Dr. Caius patted the old wooden table. "Everest, help him with those layers."

"I can—" Wilder started.

"You can pipe down and let us work." Dr. Caius reached for his latex gloves. "What happened?"

He ground his jaw, glanced at Everest, who gave him a look, brow up.

Fine. "I was shot," Wilder told them.

Bear chose then to walk into the room. His mouth opened. "Shot?"

"It's a long story."

"I'm sure it is," Dr. Caius said. "How long since you were shot?"

Wilder grimaced. "Three weeks."

Silence. Everest and Bear stared at him.

Dr. Caius made a sound. "Pants off. Let's see what we're dealing with."

Wilder struggled out of his thermal layers with Everest's help, gritting his teeth as the movement jarred his leg. When they finally got his pants off, the damage was obvious.

Blood had soaked through the bandages Stormi had applied. Dark stains spreading across the white gauze. The skin around the wound was angry, red and swollen, radiating heat. The stitches were holding, but barely.

"You've torn a couple stitches." Dr. Caius's voice was grim as he leaned in for a closer look. "How did this happen?"

"Bullet caught the outside of my thigh, all the way through, but it left chips behind. Jenny Starr did the first cleanup, but she left some trouble behind. Stormi got in there next, a few days ago. She cleaned it out, added sixteen stitches."

"Stormi did good work. Clean stitches, proper spacing. Better than some residents I've supervised. But you've been pushing too hard, haven't you? Not resting, not keeping it elevated. It hasn't had a chance to heal."

"I haven't had a choice."

"There's always a choice. The question is whether you're smart enough to make the right one."

Sorry, but Dr. Caius didn't live in his world.

"This is going to sting," Dr. Caius said.

Fire in his leg as Dr. Caius cleaned around the wound with antiseptic. "Holy cow, Doc, you call that a sting?" Wilder grimaced. "Gimme a shot of whiskey and a piece of wood to bite down on next time."

Dr. Caius looked up, a slight smile on his face. Everest had stepped back, arms folded, wearing a smirk. Bear, who had donned gloves for the assist, also smiled.

Dr. Caius glanced at Wilder. "Don't be a baby."

His mouth gaped, and he gripped the sides of the examining table, fighting the urge to be sick.

"I think he's really in pain, Dad," Everest said. His hand landed on Wilder's shoulder. "Just breathe through it."

"Bear, grab some Novocain," Dr. Caius said.

"Here you go, Dad," Bear said, handing him a syringe from the glass-fronted cabinet. He glanced at Wilder. "Sorry. Dad forgets that we're not at war sometimes."

Dr. Caius gave him the shot, and the wound slowly numbed. Wilder leaned back, breathing.

Within minutes, the edge came off the pain. Wilder's death grip on the examining table loosened, and he could breathe without feeling like someone was driving railroad spikes through his thigh.

"Better?" Dr. Caius was already preparing fresh bandages.

"Yeah." Wilder's voice came out hoarse. "Thanks."

"Don't thank me yet. You're looking at a week of bed rest, minimum. Maybe two if this infection doesn't respond to treatment."

"I can't—"

"You can't what? Fight off a murderer with a leg that won't hold your weight? Protect Luna when you can barely stand up?" Dr. Caius's voice was sharp. "Son, I've met a lot of men who thought they were bulletproof. Most of them ended up dead." He paused, hands gentle as he secured the fresh bandages. "At some point you're going to have to trust God to protect you."

"Sloan Sorros and his men are after me. He's not going to stop until—"

"Until we stop him." This from Sage, who appeared in the doorway carrying a fresh cup of coffee. "All of us. Together."

"I won't put this family at risk."

"Too late." Sage moved into the office, settling into the wooden chair beside the examining table. "Loving others is always a risk. Besides," Sage continued, a smile playing at the corners of her mouth, "looks like you brought reinforcements."

"Stormi's not—"

"Stormi's out in the barn, looking after your dogs. She's impressive." Sage gestured toward the window. "And she's got Luna helping, teaching her about canine anatomy while keeping her distracted from worrying about you."

Through the office window, Wilder could see the barn where warm light spilled from the open doors onto the snow. He could barely make out Stormi kneeling beside one of the dogs while Luna held a flashlight.

"She's good for you," Sage said.

The words settled into Wilder's chest. Warm. Unexpected.

Oh. And the memory of their kiss just lifted, settled in his head, his heart. Yeah, she was good for him.

But maybe he wasn't so good for her.

"It's complicated."

"Love usually is." Sage stood, moving toward the door. "But sometimes the complicated things are worth figuring out."

Love? Um . . .

But she winked, then left. Through the window, Wilder could see his daughter's face—bright with interest, smiling.

It sent a little jolt through him. Maybe Stormi was good for her too.

Maybe Dr. Caius was right. Maybe there was always a choice.

Maybe it was time to start choosing the complicated things that were worth figuring out. Like what it meant to let Stormi White into his world.

What it meant to love someone again.

Even if it scared him more than facing Sloan ever could.

8

COFFEE. WOODSMOKE. The scents pulled Stormi from sleep. She blinked at unfamiliar log beams overhead, their rough-hewn surfaces showing they'd outlasted decades of Alaska winters. The cabin walls creaked as wood contracted in the morning cold, and outside, dogs barked their greeting to the dawn.

Sage's cabin. The Matthews compound. Wilder's in-laws. *Dawn's family.*

Stormi's stomach knotted. Okay, this might have been a bridge too far. Her enthusiasm, her wild impulsiveness, getting her in over her head, again.

A soft knock rattled the bedroom door. "You decent in there?"

Stormi sat up, her thermal shirt wrinkled beyond salvation. The wool blanket scratched against her arms. "Come in."

Sage poked her head around the door. Already dressed in cargo pants and a hand-knitted sheep's wool cream sweater that carried the faint smell of lanolin. Her hair hung in a sleek ponytail, not a strand out of place despite the early hour and dry cabin air.

"You sleep okay?" Sage's eyes took inventory of Stormi's rumpled state. "You look like you wrestled a bear."

She'd wrestled something—maybe her choice to say yes to landing in the middle of Wilder's guarded past.

Sage leaned against the doorframe. “Mom’s making her famous sourdough pancakes, and Luna’s been asking for you since she woke up.”

Stormi’s chest filled with something warm. “She has?”

“Every five minutes. ‘Where’s Miss Stormi? Is she staying for breakfast? Can she help me feed the dogs?’” Sage’s mouth quirked. “Kid’s got it bad.”

Heat crept up Stormi’s neck. The cabin suddenly felt too warm despite the morning chill seeping through single-pane windows. “I should probably—”

“Get dressed and come eat.” Sage straightened. “Fair warning though. I’ve got questions.”

“Questions?”

“About your intentions with Wilder.” Light tone, but steel underneath. “Dawn was my sister. Luna’s my niece. I take protecting them seriously.”

Stormi’s mouth went dry. “Protecting them from me?”

“From getting hurt.” Sage stepped into the room. “Look, I can see how you look at him. How he looks at you. But that little girl’s been through enough heartbreak for ten lifetimes.”

The knot in her stomach pulled tighter. “I would never—”

“I know. That’s why we’re having this conversation. Get dressed. We’ll walk to the main house and talk.”

Talk?

The door closed behind her with a soft click, leaving Stormi staring at her reflection in the small mirror above the dresser.

Twenty minutes later, she followed Sage down the worn path between cabins. The morning air bit her cheeks and made her nose tingle.

The main house loomed ahead—a massive log structure with smoke curling from its stone chimney. Warm golden light spilled from the windows. The scent of bacon drifted on the morning breeze, making her stomach growl.

"This place is magical."

Sage glanced at her, let out a low chuckle. "Say that when you want to order a takeout pizza."

Stormi laughed. "Right."

They passed the dog yard, where a dozen huskies stretched and yawned in their individual kennels. Several whined at their approach. "I need to feed the dogs."

"Everest already did. Is Wilder's dog going to be okay?"

Oh. She stared at the dogs. Okay then. "Yes. Just a pad abrasion. He'll be okay with some booties."

"So," Sage said, continuing their walk to the lodge. "Tell me about yourself."

"I'm a veterinarian. I live outside Copper Mountain. I have a dog named Rome who—"

"Not your résumé." Sage glanced sideways. "Tell me who you are."

Um . . . "I don't understand."

"Sure you do." She cocked her head. "Listen. Dawn knew exactly who she was from the time she could walk. Determined, stubborn as a mule, wanted to save the world one patient at a time." Affection and pain wove through Sage's voice.

"She and Wilder met during a medical emergency. He'd crashed his sled in a creek and ended up hypothermic."

Stormi nodded. "He told me the story."

"Did he include the part where a kid that had been watching also went in the water and that he pulled him out and nearly died in the process?"

Oh. "No."

They reached the main house steps, wood worn smooth by countless boots. Sage stopped, turned to face her.

"Dawn took one look at Wilder—soaking wet, half frozen, holding this unconscious boy—and she said, 'Well, aren't you a sight.'" Sage's mouth curved. "Not exactly romantic, but that was Dawn. Direct. Fearless. She loved him from that first moment."

"They were both alphas," Stormi said.

"Exactly. Two forces of nature, constantly challenging each other, making each other stronger." Sage climbed the first step. "But that's not what he needs now."

"Then what—"

"C'mon. Let's get some coffee in you before the real interrogation continues."

The main house kitchen enveloped them in warmth and noise and the rich scents of a family breakfast. Una Matthews stood at the massive gas range, silver-streaked hair caught in a loose bun with wisps escaping to frame her face. Flour dusted her burgundy cardigan and the wooden counter beside her. The air hung thick with vanilla and cinnamon, mixing with the rich aroma of coffee and the underlying smell of woodsmoke from the stone fireplace.

Cast iron pans sizzled on the stovetop. The ancient refrigerator hummed in the corner, its surface covered with photos held in place by magnets from every tourist trap in Alaska. The wood floors creaked pleasantly under their boots.

"There she is!" Una beamed, face flushed from cooking. "How did you sleep, honey?"

"Fine, thank you." Stormi's voice came out smaller than intended.

"Liar." Sage nudged her toward the kitchen island, where someone had set out mismatched coffee mugs—ceramic, enamel camping cups, all bearing the scars of constant use. "She looks like she spent the night planning her escape route."

"Well, that's rude but probably accurate after meeting our crew." Una poured coffee into a blue ceramic mug, steam carrying the rich scent of grounds that had been brewing strong since before dawn. "Drink this. Everything looks better with caffeine."

Stormi wrapped her hands around the warm mug. The coffee was strong enough to wake the dead, with undertones of something that might have been cinnamon. "Thank you."

"Don't thank me yet. Wait until you taste my pancakes." Una winked. "Family recipe. Secret ingredient is love, but don't tell anyone."

Despite her nerves, Stormi smiled. The kitchen's warmth was seeping into her bones. "Your secret's safe."

"Good. Now, Sage, stop hovering and help me carry these plates. Everyone's waiting."

They loaded their arms with platters of golden pancakes that steamed in the cool air, their surfaces dotted with wild blueberries. Crispy bacon and venison sausage arranged on a platter that had seen better decades. A pitcher of syrup smelled like pure maple heaven.

Stormi followed them through an archway into the spacious dining room where morning light streamed through tall windows, illuminating dust motes dancing in the air. The windows looked out over the dog yard and the lake beyond, where morning sun painted the ice in shades of gold and pink. The long wooden table dominated the room, surrounded by mismatched chairs that creaked when anyone shifted.

And there, at the far end, sat Wilder.

Her breath caught.

He looked completely different. The rigidity that usually held his shoulders had melted away. His dark hair was still damp from a shower, curling slightly at the edges where water drops caught the morning light. He'd traded his usual guarded expression for something that resembled actual contentment. When their eyes met, his mouth curved in a smile that made her stomach flutter and nearly caused her to drop the bacon platter.

Oh. This could be dangerous.

"Morning." His voice carried warmth she'd never heard before. "Sleep okay?"

"Like a baby." She set the platter on the table with exaggerated care, painfully aware of the lure of his morning shower smell and something distinctly male that made her want to lean closer.

Sage raised an eyebrow.

"Good," he said. "Sage talks in her sleep most of the time. Usually stuff about climbing routes and protein bars."

"I do not!" Sage swatted his shoulder as she passed. "And you're one to talk, Mr. I-mutter-weather-forecasts-in-my-sleep."

"That was one time. And I was sick."

"Five times. And you were perfectly healthy." She glanced at Stormi. "We all camped out in the lodge during a blizzard a few years back."

Luna bounced in her chair, the wooden seat creaking under her enthusiasm. Syrup already decorated her mismatched pajamas—pink bottoms with puppies, blue top with snowflakes. Her hair stuck up in impossible directions. "Miss Stormi, do you like pancakes? Grandma Una makes the best pancakes. She'll make you a bear or a turtle or even a tree cake!"

"That sounds fun." She glanced at Una, who winked at her.

"Sit by me!" Luna patted the chair beside her.

Stormi settled into the offered chair, its wooden seat slightly warmed by the nearby fireplace. Wilder sat directly across the table, close enough that she could see the flecks of gold in his blue eyes. Close enough to notice the small scar above his left eyebrow that she'd somehow missed during all those medical examinations. When they reached for bacon at the same moment, their hands nearly brushed, and she jerked back as if his skin might burn her.

Good grief. What was wrong with her? She'd *kissed* the man, after all.

Dr. Caius Matthews appeared in the doorway, medical bag

in one hand and his other already reaching for the coat hanging on a peg by the door. "Sorry, folks. Emergency call in Willow Creek. Mrs. Henderson's having chest pains again."

"Snow machine or dogs?" Una asked, already moving to wrap bacon in a clean dishrag. The movement was practiced, automatic—the wife of a bush doctor who'd seen thousands of interrupted meals over the years.

"Snow machine. That way I'll be back sooner." He kissed her cheek and grabbed the makeshift breakfast. Cold air swirled into the warm kitchen as he opened the door, bringing the scent of snow and pine and the distant smell of wood fires from other cabins. The door slammed behind him.

"Thirty-seven years of marriage," Una murmured, settling into her chair with a soft sigh. "You'd think he'd remember to eat breakfast before emergencies."

"Some things never change." Sage reached for the syrup pitcher. "Speaking of which, Vic should be here any minute. She is on the SAT phone with someone."

Wilder's fork paused halfway to his mouth, a piece of pancake dripping syrup back onto his plate. "Everything okay?"

Sage lifted a shoulder. "I think so."

"Who wants more pancakes?" Una said.

"Me!" Luna's hand shot up, nearly knocking over her glass, orange juice sloshing dangerously close to the rim.

"I hope you're still not thinking of leaving today," Sage said, giving Wilder a look.

He sighed, his mouth tight.

"Does that mean that Miss Stormi is staying too?" Luna clapped even as Grandma Una brought over a plate of fresh bear-shaped pancakes.

Heat crawled up Stormi's neck. The dining room suddenly felt too warm. Every adult at the table suddenly became very interested in their breakfast, studying their plates as if the pattern of syrup might reveal the secrets of the universe. Except Wilder, who watched her with an unreadable expression, his bite of pancake still frozen halfway to his lips.

"I . . ." Words jumbled together, refusing to form coherent sentences.

"Miss Stormi has her own life, sweetheart." His voice carried the careful tone parents used when trying to let children down gently. "Her own home and job and responsibilities. But, yes, I think she's planning on staying."

And he met her eyes. Held her gaze.

Her throat tightened.

Then she turned to Luna. "I'll stay as long as your dad needs me."

She thought the little girl might smile, reached for the pancakes.

Except, no. The light in Luna's expression dimmed, and the child's fork clattered against her plate.

What—?

"Daddy says we don't need anybody," Luna said, frowning.

Oh.

And the room went very quiet.

"Luna," Wilder started, but his daughter held up one small, syrup-sticky hand.

"It's okay." Luna's voice went very small, barely audible over the crackling fire. "Daddy says it's just us. And that's all we need."

Oh. She glanced at Wilder now, who made a point of staring at his coffee.

Right.

The only sounds were the fire snapping in the hearth and the distant barking of dogs outside.

"Well," Sage said brightly, "for now, we're all here, and it's the perfect day for a puzzle. Why don't you go into Grandma's study and find one for us, Luna."

"Sage." Una frowned at her.

Luna got down and ran into the next room.

Sage waited until she left, then she turned to Una. "What? I'm just saying. We're sitting here eating pancakes in paradise, the sun's shining"—she gestured with her fork, syrup dripping onto the table—"and we're all acting like someone died."

"Someone did die." Wilder's voice went flat, all the morning warmth leaching away. His knuckles went white around his coffee cup. "People I love have a tendency to—"

"Stop." Sage's fork clattered against her plate. "Just stop. Dawn died because evil people made evil choices. Not because you loved her. Not because she loved you. Because monsters exist, and sometimes they win a round."

She leaned forward, dark eyes fierce, hands pressed flat against the table's scarred surface.

"But they don't get to win the war. And they sure as heck don't get to steal your happiness forever. And all this malarkey you've fed Luna about not needing anyone is a lie and you know it."

Wilder's jaw tensed. "Sage—"

"No. Dawn would be furious if she could see you now. Furious. She'd probably throw something at your head and then drag you outside for a reality check." Sage's voice softened, but her eyes remained intense. "She loved you, Wilder. All of you. Your protectiveness, your strength, even your stubborn refusal to believe you deserved good things. But she also knew you needed someone to call you on your nonsense."

"And you think that's Stormi's job?"

And Stormi really just wanted to slide under the table, crawl away, help Luna find that puzzle. She stared at her pancakes.

"I think," Sage said carefully, "that she's not Dawn. And that's okay."

Oh, now that hurt. She drew in a breath, but Sage wasn't finished.

She turned toward Stormi. "Dawn was a force of nature—brilliant, stubborn, strong enough to go toe-to-toe with this guy and make him better for it." Sage gestured toward Wilder. "They clashed beautifully, constantly challenging each other and creating something bigger than either of them could alone."

"And Stormi is what, a gentle breeze? A light drizzle?" Wilder said.

"She's exactly what Wilder needs." The new voice came from the doorway, where Vic stood silhouetted against the morning light. Tall, steady. She walked into the room. "There are seasons of life. Not every season is the same. And God knows what we need in each one."

Vic settled into a chair next to Una.

Una turned to her. "How did it go?"

"About as well as expected."

Silence, then Vic sighed. "I recently was reunited with my daughter, Keely. She's . . . well, she has a daughter she also got reunited with and she just needed some advice." She picked up a napkin. "Not that I'm a great source of mom advice, but I'm who she has." She reached for the pancakes. "These look delicious."

"I didn't know you had a daughter," Wilder said.

"Yep. Fact is, I should have called her months ago. Should have reached out when I first heard about the trouble she was in. Instead, I let pride and fear keep me quiet, and she suffered for it."

"Fear of what?" Sage asked gently, pouring coffee into the mug Una set in front of Vic.

"That she wouldn't want to hear from me. That I'd make things worse. That I'd say the wrong thing and push her further away." Vic accepted the coffee with both hands, wrapping her fingers around the ceramic as if drawing strength from its warmth. "Turns out, staying silent hurt her more than anything I could have said."

Her eyes found Stormi's across the table. "Sometimes we get so afraid of not being enough that we forget being present is what matters most."

It seemed an echo of what Vic had told her at the house. *"That man needs you. Not because you're perfect. Not because you've got everything figured out. But because you showed up. You stayed. And that, Stormi White, makes you a superhero."*

Maybe.

"And while I don't think any of this conversation is any of our business," Vic continued, "I did know Dawn, and I know that she'd want Wilder to be happy. She'd want Luna to have a mother who loved her. She'd want this family to heal and grow and find joy again." Her gaze stayed fixed on Stormi, steady and unblinking. "She wouldn't care if that person was exactly like her. She'd care that they showed up. That they stayed when things got hard. That they chose love over fear."

Right.

Wilder sighed and got up, slowly limping toward the kitchen with his plate.

So, that was awkward.

Stormi set down her fork, glanced at Vic. "Okay, so now that we're full on into an episode of *The Jerry Springer Show*, what if . . ." She sighed. "What if I can't be what they need? What if I'm not strong enough?"

"Honey," Una said softly, reaching across the table to pat Stormi's hand with fingers that smelled of vanilla and flour, "strength isn't about being the loudest person in the room or the one who can bench-press a moose. It's about getting up every morning and choosing to try again. It's about showing love even when you're scared. Even when you feel inadequate."

She always felt inadequate, thank you.

"Dawn was strong, but you know what else is strong?" Sage leaned back in her chair. "A different kind of dawn, the first light that comes every morning, consistent and gentle and absolutely essential."

She smiled, her face brightening.

"Maybe that's what this family needs now. Not another wildfire, but steady dawn light that never goes out," Vic said.

"You just have to be a light." Una's voice held warmth. "That's all any of us can do. Show up and shine and trust that it's enough."

Something shifted in Stormi's chest. The room felt warmer, the coffee tasted better, the morning light streaming through the windows seemed brighter.

Maybe she didn't need to be spectacular. Maybe she just had to show up. Stay.

"I found a puzzle!" Luna came running back with a large box with a scene of a unicorn on the front.

Sage took it. "Oh, I love this one. Three hundred pieces. Let's do it in front of the fire." She got up and led Luna to the family room, then turned. "You coming, Stormi?"

Really?

She hadn't seen Wilder return, so who knew if he'd heard the pep talk, so that was swell, but now she caught him watching her over his coffee cup, his expression soft in a way that made her breath catch. When their eyes met, he smiled.

And light just shot straight through her, to her soul, his own brand of light and heat and . . . hope.

Yep, dangerous.

And sweet.

And maybe Luna was right.

Maybe she'd never leave.

THREE DAYS of cabin fever was about two days too many.

Wilder touched his leg, then extended it out, back in, testing.

No sharp pain. No ache that spoke of infection. Stormi's veterinary skills, his father-in-law's medical skills, and Una's relentless mothering had done their work, but sitting still had never been his strength. Every instinct screamed at him to move, to do something productive instead of lounging around.

"Now, Luna, we need to measure the flour carefully." Una's voice carried the patient tone of someone who'd raised four children. "Baking is science."

"But I like lots of flour!" Luna's giggle bubbled up from the kitchen island. "More flour means bigger cookies!"

"More flour means hockey pucks." Stormi's voice, warm with amusement, made something in his chest loosen. "Trust your Grandma Una. She knows what she's doing."

Wilder turned from the window. He had to see this.

Una hummed while presiding over an impressive array of bowls and measuring cups. Luna perched on a step stool, flour dusting her nose and the front of her purple sweater. And Stormi . . .

She leaned against the counter like she'd been part of this kitchen's rhythm for years instead of days. She had braided Luna's hair this morning—something his daughter had specifically requested.

"Like this, sweetheart." Stormi's hands covered Luna's, demonstrating with infinite patience how to crack an egg. "Tap it gently, then use your thumbs to pull it apart."

The egg cracked perfectly. Luna beamed. "I did it!"

"You absolutely did." Stormi tweaked one of the girl's braids, and Wilder's throat thickened at how natural the gesture looked.

This was what his daughter had been missing.

And, of course, the conversation from a few days ago, Sage's sudden inquisition of poor Stormi, rushed back at him.

"What if I can't be what they need?"

He'd heard her question as he walked away, his heart squeezing, not sure of the answer. Not until he came back in, stood at the doorway, and heard Vic say, *"Maybe that's what this family needs now. Not another wildfire, but steady dawn light that never goes out."*

Yes, Dawn had been a blaze of fire. But Stormi was . . . well, just as Vic said, a light in their dark world.

The thought hit him sideways. He'd convinced himself Luna didn't need another mom because he was enough, had to be enough. But watching his daughter glow under Stormi's attention, soaking up every bit of maternal warmth . . .

Maybe he'd been wrong about a lot of things.

"Daddy!" Luna spotted him lurking by the window. "Come see! We're making snickerdoodles and Miss Stormi says I'm a natural baker!"

"Are you now?" He crossed to the kitchen island, inhaling cinnamon and vanilla that had already begun to perfume the air. "What's my job?"

"Quality control," Una said, winking. "Very important position."

"The most important," Stormi said, laughing.

Her laughter seeded his soul with joy. Their eyes met across the floury chaos, and something electric passed between them. Awareness. Interest. The same tension that had been building for days, getting harder to ignore.

Dangerous territory, Frost. Because maybe he had no right to bring Stormi here—something he hadn't thought about until they showed up. But now that she was here . . .

She belonged.

Luna chattered on about proper cookie formation while Una guided her through rolling dough in cinnamon sugar. Stormi listened with the kind of focused attention she usually reserved for injured animals, asking questions that delighted his daughter.

He could tell she wasn't just being polite. She was actually enjoying herself.

"Where is everyone else?" Stormi asked, glancing around.

"Everest is on a mail run to town," Una said, sliding the first batch of cookies into the oven. "Won't be back until this evening. And Caius took Bear to check on the Henderson place again. Mrs. Henderson's been having more of those chest pains."

"So it's just us girls," Luna announced with satisfaction. "And Daddy, but he doesn't count because he's not helping."

"Hey." Wilder pretended offense. "I'm supervising."

"That's not helping, that's watching." Seven-year-old logic.

"She's got you there." Stormi's mouth curved in a smile that made him want to do something impulsive.

Like what? Kiss her in front of Luna and Una? Smart plan.

But the restless energy that had been building all morning suddenly found focus. He wanted out of this house, away from the domestic warmth that made him think dangerous thoughts about hope and happy endings. Wanted time alone with Stormi where he could figure out what was happening between them without an audience.

"Want to get out of here?" he asked her.

The words escaped before he could second-guess them.

Stormi looked up from where she'd been helping Luna arrange cookies on the cooling rack. "What did you have in mind?"

"Training session. You've been asking about advanced mushing techniques." He gestured toward the window where fresh snow was still falling. "Perfect conditions."

Her eyes lit up. "Really? What about your leg? You feel up to it?"

"I feel up to getting some fresh air before I go stir-crazy." He looked at Luna, who was already covered in enough flour and cinnamon sugar to qualify as a baking casualty. "Think you can handle cookie duty without Miss Stormi, kiddo?"

"I'm an expert," Luna said with the solemnity of someone entrusted with state secrets. "Grandma Una said so."

"That's right." Una shooed them toward the door. "Go on, you two. Work off some of that restless energy before you start pacing holes in my floors."

Wilder caught Stormi's amused glance. "That obvious?" he asked.

"You've been standing at that window for twenty minutes watching snow fall." She pulled on her boots, movements easy despite the bulky gear. "Either you're planning a weather report or you need to move."

"Definitely the second one."

Wilder pressed a kiss to Luna's forehead. "Save some cookies for us."

"Bring Miss Stormi back safe." Luna's instruction carried the seriousness of someone who'd learned too young that people didn't always come home.

His chest squeezed. "I promise."

Stormi patted her leg and instantly Rome was up from his perch by the fireplace. He bounded outside where the world was crystalline and perfect.

Fresh snow crunched under their boots as they made their way to the kennels. The air was cold enough to make their breath visible but not so bitter that it would interfere with the dogs' performance.

This was better. Space to breathe.

"This is nice." Stormi tilted her face up, catching a few snowflakes on her cheeks. "I love Una and Luna, but—"

"But you needed space too?"

"Is that terrible?" Guilt flickered across her face. "They're wonderful, it's just—"

He got it. "I've been feeling like a caged wolf for the past two days."

"Exactly." Relief colored her voice. "I'm not used to being around people all the time. My clinic's pretty isolated."

"By choice?"

She was quiet for a moment. "Maybe. It's easier to focus on work when you don't have distractions."

"And now?"

"Now I'm starting to think maybe I was focusing on the wrong things." She opened the massive kennels and called to her dogs. She affixed their harnesses and then led them out to Wilder's sled. She clipped them into the traces and Wilder got on as she mushed them to the area that Everest used to train his dogs.

"Rome's looking less restless," Wilder said as they pulled up to the area.

"He seems to have calmed down a little since we've been here. Not sure why."

"Maybe he feels safe." Wilder got off, surveyed the blue sky, the clean air. "I love it out here. Everest made this course, and I used to come out here and run the trails for hours." He turned to her. "There's something about it being just you and your dogs, surviving. Taking on nature, figuring it out on your own."

"You're such a lone wolf," she said.

Her words hit him. Yes, maybe he was.

"I didn't mean that in a bad way. You're smart and brave and capable and that's why I had your picture on my wall." She made a face. "It inspired me."

He didn't know what to do with the thunder inside him, the way she looked at him like he wasn't damaged, wasn't trouble.

She walked out past him then and looked over the course. "Truth is, I'm not sure I really want to run the Iditarod. It was an impulsive move—but I think maybe God used it to bring me here." She looked at him. "And all those memories bring me back to that winter, right before everything went south, when Dad and I didn't have pain between us."

He frowned at that, but she didn't elaborate, just stood, looking out at the horizon.

Ho-kay, maybe it wasn't any of his business. So he stepped up to her and pointed at the sled trail. "Let's get started," he said. "You'll run this course. It has some sharp turns as it works down to the lake."

She gave him a look.

"You can do this."

She made another face. "I used to think so. But watching the way you are with the dogs . . ."

"Listen. The way you read animals—understanding what they need—that translates to mushing better than most people realize." He gestured toward her team. "Dogs don't lie. If they trust you completely, it's because you've earned it."

Pink touched her cheeks. "You really think so?"

"I know so." The words came out more intense than he'd intended. Her eyes widened slightly in response.

And yeah, his gaze fell to her lips. To the memory of pulling her into his arms.

Calm *down.*

"Ready?"

She blew out a breath. "Yep."

He climbed aboard and she yelled, "Hike."

She worked her team with a new voice, a new confidence. Maybe the ride to the compound, following his trail, had helped. Sometimes people, like dogs, just needed an example. And she had a feel for the sport. Not the technical perfection of a champion musher but something deeper. As if she might be part of the team, moving with them, even as she guided them.

She eased the team to a halt just before the turn, and he stepped off the runners.

"Time to learn the Gee-Haw Oversteer Technique," he said.

The dogs stood taut and quivering, a hum of energy running up the gangline and into his hands. Funny, his leg hadn't ached all morning.

"The what?" Her hazel eyes lifted to his. Nervous, sure, but there was steel there. It struck a spark in him—light and something more. Life. She made him feel strong.

"It's how you make the team hold a wider arc, keep the sled from cutting a corner or hitting trees, posts, or even a soft shoulder," he said, nodding toward the bend. "A slight oversteer can also keep the sled from sliding straight and pushing into the team on hardpack or ice. You're going to over-cue the turn—'gee, gee!'—early and firm, lean to the outside, and feather the brake so the sled doesn't push. Then release and let them finish clean. Ready?"

"I think so," she said.

"Thinking won't cut it out here," he said. "You need to know. I'm telling you—you're ready."

She drew another breath, squared her shoulders, and smiled.

Oh, she had a beautiful smile.

Focus!

Don't. Kiss. Her.

"Let's ride it out together. First thing, spot your turn early. See that bend?" He pointed down the trail where it hooked hard to the right. "That's your target. You're going to cue 'gee' before you get there so the whole team sets the arc. But here's the catch"—he met her eyes—"they won't commit if you sound like you're asking."

"Gee," she tried, the word lifting at the end.

"Come on, Stormi. You're their leader. Act like it."

She squared her shoulders, planted her feet on the runners. "GEE!"

The sled started to move, and he held on, arms around her.

Koda's ears snapped forward, the line tightened, and something unclenched in Wilder's chest. "There you go. Early and firm. Now lean to the outside—that's what I'm talking about.

"Once you give that command, the leads will start the turn.

Your job is to help the sled follow. Lean into it—'gee' for right, 'haw' for left. Not too much, just enough to guide her through."

She nodded, focused now in that way that reminded him why he loved mushing, the feel of the sled under him, moving with the dogs.

"Next—the drag brake. Light touch, about two seconds." He watched her try it, felt the sled resist. "Perfect. Feel that? That's control."

"Now for the tricky part." He moved closer and caught a whiff of her shampoo. Something fruity that had no business smelling that good on a dog trail. *Focus, Frost!* "Oversteering. As the sled follows the dogs through the turn, you counter-steer slightly. For a right turn, pull the handlebow a little left. Keeps you from fishtailing."

She glanced back at him, listening intently, that little line forming between her brows that showed up when she was really concentrating.

"Think you can handle it?"

"I've got this." The confidence impressed him more than it should have.

She executed the turn and brought the sled around.

"Let me off and then we'll run it again."

She slowed the sled and he hopped off. Stood in the snow.

"Alright then. Get them moving. Use 'hike' and focus on the turn."

She gripped the handlebars, and for a second he wanted to reach out, adjust her grip, maybe just touch her hands to steady them. Instead, he held back and watched her take control.

She nodded once, eyes on the bend, breath steadying in the cold.

"On my call," he said. "You take it wide and keep that line tight."

Her smile flickered again. "Ready."

"Go."

"Hike!"

The dogs lunged forward, snow flying, and the sled began to glide. Wilder kept his eyes on her form, her face, the way she held herself.

"Here comes your turn," he called. "Now—'gee!'"

"GEE!" Her voice carried strong and clear this time.

Koda responded instantly, banking right, and Wilder's heart kicked up a notch.

"Lean into it! That's it!"

She shifted her weight smoothly, and the sled curved behind the dogs like it was meant to be.

"Drag brake—light touch!"

She found that perfect balance, not too much, not too little, and something warm spread through his chest.

"Counter-steer now! Wide arc. Don't let the sled push the team!"

Her hands moved on the handlebars, precise and controlled, and the sled glided through the turn like she'd been doing this for years.

"Beautiful!" The word burst out of him before he could stop it. "Straighten them out—'On by.'"

"On by!"

The dogs straightened and picked up speed, pulling the sled smoothly down the trail. Wilder watched her disappear around the next bend and realized he was grinning, probably like an idiot.

"How was that?" she called as she drew close.

When she brought the team to a stop next to him, her cheeks were flushed red, and her smile could have lit up the entire trail.

He gave her a thumbs-up, trying to ignore the way her smile knotted up his insides. "That was—" He stopped himself before he said something stupid like "amazing" or "perfect" or "the most beautiful thing I've ever seen."

Instead, he settled for, "Not bad for a beginner."

Her smile widened and, oh, he was just done for.

He hadn't believed he'd find anyone again and here she was, in his world. No, not just in it.

Embedded into it.

"Same thing on the next turn," he said, hoping his voice sounded steadier than it felt. "And the one after that. By the time we're done, you'll be ready for anything."

She nodded, that spark of determination back in her eyes. Wilder felt something shift inside him.

She looked at him with so much joy in her expression, he couldn't move.

Then Stormi bent down and packed a handful of snow, mischief dancing in her eyes.

Oh no.

"What are you doing?"

"Nothing." The innocent tone didn't match the impish grin on her face.

"Stormi—"

The snowball caught him square in the chest, exploding in a shower of powder. Her laughter rang across the frozen landscape, bright and infectious.

"Did you just—"

"Maybe." She was already backing away, hands up in mock surrender. "You looked entirely too serious."

"I'll show you serious."

He bent and scooped up his own ammunition.

She shrieked and turned to run, but her boot caught a patch of hidden ice.

Instinctively, he lunged forward to catch her. They went down together in a tangle of limbs and winter gear, landing in a drift deep enough to cushion their fall.

For a moment, neither moved.

Then Stormi started laughing—deep, genuine laughter that made her whole body shake.

"Graceful," he managed to say, though his own laughter took any sting out of the words.

They were lying face-to-face in the snow. Close enough that he could see the gold in her hazel eyes. Close enough to notice how her lips were slightly parted as her laughter faded into something softer.

"Wilder," she whispered.

He should move. Should put distance between them before he crossed a line they couldn't uncross. This wasn't before, a moment of comfort, of gratitude.

This was . . .

This was desire. Longing.

Hope.

"Yeah?" He couldn't stop himself from reaching up to brush snow from her cheek, his gloved thumb lingering against her skin.

"I'm really glad you asked me to get out here today."

"Even though I just tackled you into a snowbank?"

"Especially because of that." Her eyes were serious now. "I was getting tired of pretending I don't feel this too."

Oh yes. He hadn't a hope of untangling himself now. Still, he leaned in slowly, giving her every chance to pull away. But her eyes fluttered closed, and her breath hitched in a way that made his pulse stutter.

Soft. She was so soft.

He kissed her. Her lips parted under his, tentative at first, like she was afraid she might shatter this moment if she moved too quickly. He understood that fear. Had lived with it for years—

the terror that anything good in his life would disappear the moment he reached for it.

But Stormi wasn't disappearing. She was here, real and warm beneath him, her mittened hands coming up to frame his face as she kissed him back with growing confidence.

The taste of her flooded his senses—snow and cinnamon mixed with something clean and bright that was purely her. Her lips were cold from the winter air but warmed under his touch, sending heat spiraling through his chest despite the cold seeping through his jacket.

Stormi. She made a small sound in the back of her throat, and he deepened the kiss, pouring a year of watching her from a distance into this one perfect moment. A year of admiring her competence, her gentleness with animals, the way she never gave up even when everything seemed hopeless.

Her arms encircled his neck, pulled him closer, and he obliged gladly, moving his arm around her, pulling her against him.

And every thought, every pain, left him as light poured into him, a fire that touched his heart, his bones, his soul, and swept him out of the darkness that was his life.

Stormi.

He lifted his head, met her eyes, so very beautiful, holding his. She was breathing as hard as he was, maybe caught in the sense of him too.

He liked it—the idea that maybe he could still dazzle her.

He touched his forehead to hers.

They said nothing, his gaze roaming her face, back to her lips.

"Please don't say this is a mistake or too complicated," she said softly.

Oh. "Are you sure this is what you want, Stormi?"

She rolled her eyes. "Seriously—"

He didn't let her finish, his mouth catching her words, losing himself again in her response—

"Hey, you guys!"

He looked up, his heart slamming against his ribs.

Everest stood on the hill overlooking the ravine.

"What's going on?" Wilder called to him.

If Everest saw them kissing, he said nothing. Instead, he grimaced. "We just heard back from the Hendersons. Mom called over there—said the trip was running long. They told her Dad and Bear left their place hours ago. They should've been back by now."

Wilder stared at him, glanced at Stormi, back to Everest. "What do you mean?"

"I mean, they're lost. Or hurt. Or something terrible has happened. And we need to find them."

9

NO ONE SAID IT, but it was there, right there, in the room with them.

Had someone attacked the family? Did Sloan Sorros find Dr. Caius and Bear and . . .

Stormi read the look on Wilder's face as he sat in a chair and stared out the window.

His jaw was set in a line that screamed of barely controlled panic.

"Daddy." Luna's voice was small from her perch on the couch. She was wrapped in one of Una's quilts. "Are they going to find Grandpa?"

Wilder got up and went over to her, pulling his daughter into a hug. Stormi didn't hear his response as she stepped into the kitchen, drawn by the need to do something besides stand in the doorway feeling useless. Una was plating cookies, as if that might be the thing that brought her son and husband home. Then again, by the smell of them . . . maybe. "Can I help with anything?"

Una looked up from the cookies and her expression softened. "Of course. Would you mind making some coffee? It's going to be a long night."

A long night. Yes. Dr. Caius and Bear had been gone for seven hours on what should have been a four-hour call. Max. Worse, the cold had turned bitter, the wind howling, and night would soon fall like a shroud in a moonless sky.

Stormi moved to the coffee maker. The rich scent filled the air, mixing with the lingering sweetness of cinnamon from this morning's cookies and the woodsmoke that always seemed to permeate the log walls.

"Where did Sage and Everest go to look for them?" she asked.

"They took the trail to the Hendersons and then I think they were going to check the old mining trail. Sometimes the guys take that route if they don't want to cross the creek."

The coffee finished brewing with a soft gurgle. Stormi poured mugs for everyone except Luna, who got hot chocolate from the pot Una kept simmering on the stove. Stormi carried two steaming mugs back into the living room, set one on the side table near Wilder. The little girl accepted the mug with both hands, her dark eyes too serious for her age.

Vic chose that moment to come in from the darkness, stamping her feet. She carried a load of wood and now headed over to the fire.

She glanced at Wilder as she set the logs into the firewood cradle. "They'll find them."

Wilder nodded. "Yes, Dr. Caius has been in these mountains longer than any of us. He knows every trail, every shelter."

"Then why aren't they back?" Luna's question hung in the air.

Silence, then Wilder reached for her again and drew her onto the couch beside him.

"MISS STORMI?" Luna's voice was barely above a whisper. "Are Grandpa and Uncle Bear going to die?"

"Luna—" Wilder started, but Stormi held up a hand.

"I don't know, sweetheart." She settled on the couch beside Luna. "But I know your grandpa is really smart about mountains, and your Uncle Bear is strong and tough. They know how to take care of themselves."

"That's what everyone said about Mama."

Wilder's coffee cup stopped halfway to his lips.

"Oh, baby," Una whispered.

"Mama was smart too. And strong. But she still died." Luna's voice trembled. "So maybe being smart and strong doesn't matter."

Stormi's throat closed.

She turned to face Wilder. His mouth made a grim line, and he looked away.

Okay then. "You're right," Stormi said finally. "Sometimes bad things happen to good people, even when they're smart and strong. But that doesn't mean we stop hoping or stop fighting or stop believing that most of the time, people do come home."

Luna's eyes held hers. "Do you really believe that?"

"Yes." She put her arm around Luna. "I do." She met Wilder's eyes.

Luna seemed to accept this, snuggling deeper into her quilt. "I'm glad you're here."

"Me too."

The radio crackled to life and everyone jumped.

"Base, this is Sage. Come in, Base."

Vic picked up the handset. "Sage, this is Base. What's your status?"

"We made it to Hendersons'. No sign of Dad or Bear."

"Copy that. What's your next move?"

"We're going to check the old mining road, see if they had mechanical trouble. But . . . it's getting dark up here, and the temperature's dropping fast."

"Understood. Check in every thirty minutes."

"Will do. Sage out."

Silence. Deafening silence.

"Well," Una said, her voice too bright. "That's one place we know they're not. That narrows it down."

Wilder made a sound that might have been agreement, but his knuckles whitened around his coffee mug.

"Luna," Una said, "time for bed, sweetheart."

"I don't want to go to bed." Luna's voice took on a stubborn edge. "I want to wait for Grandpa."

"You can wait better after a good night's sleep."

"That doesn't make sense. How can I wait if I'm sleeping?"

"Because when you wake up, it'll be morning, and they'll probably be back."

"What if they're not?"

"Then we'll keep looking," Wilder said, his voice rough. "But right now, you need to get some rest."

"I won't be able to sleep."

"You can try," Una said.

Luna's lower lip trembled. "I don't like when people are gone. What if they don't come back while I'm sleeping? What if I never see them again?"

And right then, Wilder looked up, met Stormi's eyes.

And she got it, this fear of letting people inside his life. Because even if evil wasn't hunting him, life was dangerous, right?

"You know what?" Stormi said. "I'll stay up and keep watch."

Luna turned, looked up at her. "Really?"

"Really. I'll be right here in the living room, and if the radio makes any noise at all, I'll hear it."

"And you'll wake me up if they come back?"

"The minute they walk through that door."

Luna narrowed her eyes. "Promise?" She held up a pinkie.

"Promise." Stormi looped hers through.

"Okay." Luna shook them, then got off the sofa. "Will you help me get ready for bed?"

The request unmoored her. She glanced at Una, then Vic. Certainly one of them . . .

But both women just smiled at her.

"I . . . sure. If you want."

"I want." Luna took her hand.

Luna slept in a small room off the back of the lodge. She had a twin bed with a fluffy sheepskin blanket on top and star glow lights plastered to the ceiling. A stuffed husky that had seen better days sat on the bed, and a photo of Dawn holding baby Luna rested on the bedside table. A collection of stones were lined up on the windowsill.

Stormi sat on the edge of Luna's small bed, smoothing the blanket that smelled like lavender.

"Miss Stormi," Luna said, staring at the ceiling.

"Yeah?"

"Do you think Daddy's mad at me for asking about dying?"

Stormi's throat filled. "No, sweetheart. I think he's scared, just like you are."

She looked at Stormi, eyes wide. "Grown-ups get scared?"

"All the time."

"What do they do when they're scared?"

Stormi considered this. "Different things. Some people get really quiet. Some people get really busy. Some people try to fix everything so they don't have to think about being scared."

"What do you do?"

Oh. "I pray."

"Like Grandma Una does?"

Huh. "Yes." She grabbed the little girl's braid and tickled her nose with the end. Luna laughed. "See, God commands us not to be afraid because he is with us. And if God is with us, we are strong and brave, and even if bad things happen, he will help us."

"How?"

She propped an arm on the other side of Luna. "By sending

us people—like your dad or your grandpa—to help us. Or by giving us the right thoughts and actions. Or sometimes, just by filling our hearts with peace, even though it seems things are out of control."

Luna bit her lip as if taking that in.

But the words found soil inside Stormi. Peace, even though it seemed things were out of control.

"God is our refuge and strength, a very present help in trouble."

"Luna, can I pray for you?" she asked.

Luna nodded. Stormi took her little hands, held them. "Lord, I pray for Luna tonight, that you would help her have sweet, God-given dreams, peace in her heart, and the knowledge of your love and care every day. And bring Grandpa Caius and Uncle Bear home safely. Amen." She leaned in and kissed Luna's forehead.

Luna smiled up at her, then wiped her sleeve across her eyes. "Will you stay until I fall asleep?"

Oh. Her throat tightened. "Yes."

"I'm glad you're here," Luna said, closing her eyes.

"Me too."

Stormi stayed until Luna's breathing evened out, then she crept back to the living room where the adults maintained their vigil. Wilder had claimed the chair closest to the radio, his elbows on his knees, head in his hands. Una and Vic sat at the kitchen table, their conversation low.

"She asleep?" Wilder asked without looking up.

"Yep." Stormi settled on the couch, pulling one of Una's quilts around her shoulders. "She's so sweet."

Wilder smiled, and the warmth in his gaze simply poured through her. Then he sighed. "She's been asking about dying a lot lately." His voice was barely above a whisper. "Ever since we got here, actually. I think being around family again reminds her of what she lost."

"Or what she could lose again."

"Yeah." He met her eyes, said nothing.

"Wilder, you can't live your whole life bracing yourself for the worst thing to happen."

He frowned.

She drew in a breath. "Remember before, when you said I couldn't pray myself into rescue? I can, actually. In fact, I'm already rescued. And nothing can happen to me on earth that will keep me from that rescue. Nothing—not even evil—can separate me from God's love. Even when my heart breaks and evil thinks it's won, God always has the last word."

Wilder's gaze never left her face.

"The Bible says that perfect love casts out fear. We forget that it's *God's* perfect love for us that casts out our fear."

He looked away then. "Hard to believe that when we're sitting here waiting for tragedy."

Oh. But, "That's exactly when we have to believe."

The radio crackled to life.

"Base, this is Sage."

Wilder grabbed the handset. "Go ahead, Sage."

"We've covered the mining road. No sign of them. We're going to check Bear Creek Ravine, but . . ." Exhaustion and growing desperation colored her tone. "It's been over eight hours. If they had mechanical trouble with the sleds, they would have walked somewhere and contacted us by now."

Eight hours. The number hung in the air.

"Copy that. How long before you're back to base?"

"We'll be back soon."

"Understood. Be careful out there."

"Yep. Sage out."

Silence settled over the room again. Heavier this time.

"I should go out there," Wilder said suddenly. "I know these mountains better than anyone except Dr. Caius. I could—"

"You could get lost in the dark and give us three people to

worry about instead of two," Una said. "And your leg puts you in no shape to search. Sage and Everest know what they're doing, and they know these mountains too. Your job is to stay here with Luna."

"My job is to protect my family. All of it."

"You can't protect everyone from everything," Stormi said.

The words slipped out without permission, carrying weight she hadn't intended to share.

Wilder looked at her with a frown. "What do you mean?"

"I mean, I know what it feels like to think everything is your responsibility." She pulled the quilt tighter around her shoulders. "I used to think that if I could just do everything right, make all the right choices, then bad things wouldn't happen to the people I loved."

"Did it work?"

"No." She made a face. "It just meant I never learned how to make any choices at all."

"What do you mean?"

She lifted a shoulder. "When I was fifteen, my mom was pregnant with my little brother. She really wanted to have a home birth, but Dad was against it. Mom's water broke, and she was having contractions, but she told me to wait to call him. That she was fine. But I knew she wasn't."

Stormi still revisited that day in her nightmares sometimes, the memory too vivid, sweeping through her. The way her mother had gripped the kitchen counter, breathing through contractions while insisting everything was fine. The way Stormi had stood there, phone in hand, paralyzed by the fear of making the wrong choice.

"So I didn't call him. I just . . . waited. Brought her water, timed the contractions. She kept saying everything would be okay, that this was what she wanted. But it wasn't okay. She passed out and I ran to the clinic."

Wilder's eyes were on her.

"My dad put her in the car and drove to the hospital."

The room had gone quiet.

"The baby was breech. The placenta tore. Mom lost too much blood."

Wilder was still staring at her, something of horror in his eyes. "Stormi."

"She and my little brother died." Stormi had lived with this pain for over a decade, so she didn't know why her throat filled, her chest webbed. "It was . . . well, anyway . . . I shouldn't have waited. I should have called my father."

He stared at her. "You were fifteen years old and dealing with a medical emergency while trying to respect your mother's wishes. That's an impossible decision."

"Yeah, well. Ever since then, I second-guess every decision. What if I'm wrong? What if I make things worse?" She looked at him directly. "I don't want to live with regrets. So . . . I follow my heart. But then I end up in over my head." She shrugged. "I just don't want to hesitate and miss something I should be doing."

Wilder frowned.

"And that's why I pray and ask God for help." She made a face. "I know it's bad theology. I know I should pray *before* I leap . . . It just . . . well, it's the only way I know to live with the what-ifs."

He drew in a breath, then nodded. "I get it now."

What?

Before she could respond, the front door burst open, bringing in a rush of cold air and the sound of stamping feet. Sage and Everest appeared in the entryway, their faces grim with exhaustion and defeat.

"Any word?" Sage asked, though the tone in her voice suggested she already knew the answer.

"Nothing," Vic replied. "You?"

"We covered every trail between here and Willow Creek."

Everest's voice was flat with fatigue. "Bear Creek Ravine, the old mining roads, even the hunting shacks. Nothing. It's like they just . . . disappeared."

The last word hung in the air, carrying implications nobody wanted to voice.

"We'll start again at first light," Sage said, but her voice lacked conviction. "Maybe we missed something in the dark."

"Or maybe—" Everest started, then stopped himself.

"Maybe what?"

"Maybe we need to consider that they're not just lost."

The temperature in the room dropped.

"What are you saying?" Una's voice emerged barely above a whisper.

"I'm saying Dad wouldn't just get lost. He's been in these mountains for thirty years. He knows every trail, every shelter, every possible hazard. If he's not back by now . . ."

"Then something happened to them," Wilder finished.

Just then, Rome bolted upright from his place by the fire. Ears pricked forward. Body rigid with attention. A low whine escaped his throat as he padded to the front door, then back to Stormi, then to the door again.

"What's wrong with him?" Sage asked.

"I don't know." Except . . . Alert posture, focused attention, the whine? "I think he's picked up something," she said slowly.

Rome whined again. More urgently this time. Ran back and pawed at the door.

"What kind of something?" Everest asked even as Sage reached for the doorknob.

"Don't—" Stormi started, but she was too late.

Rome bolted through the open door.

"Rome," Stormi called and ran to the doorway. He was already gone, vanished into the darkness.

And sure, maybe it was impulse, maybe following her heart,

maybe just a feeling, deep inside, but she turned and looked at Wilder. "I'm getting my gear. And I'm going after him."

YEAH, WELL, not without him. And he didn't even need to say it. He simply got up and headed out into the darkness after her.

He joined her in the barn, where she was suiting up in one of the snowmobile suits hanging on the hook. She'd already pulled on her boots and layered up and now reached for a helmet.

"If you're going with me, you'll need to keep up," she said.

He raised an eyebrow. "Um, I'm riding with you."

She considered him a moment, then nodded and headed out to the snow machines.

He'd sort of meant he was driving, but apparently not because she was waiting for him at the helm when he stalked out of the barn.

The snow had kicked up, of course, because it had to be the perfect storm when his family disappeared.

Now Stormi drove them deeper into the night, the light of her headlamp swallowed by swirling snow.

Trusting the woman he was falling for to lead them into a blizzard because she believed in a dog's nose more than common sense was either the bravest thing he'd ever done or the stupidest.

Maybe he should have stayed back at the lodge. That tidbit of truth gnawed at him too, but he couldn't stop himself.

Impulsive. Following his heart. Yeah, he understood that feeling more than he wanted to admit.

The cold bit through his expedition gear—brutal despite the layers. Snow stung the exposed skin above his balaclava. The wind howled through the trees with a sound that spoke of death.

Occasionally, her headlights would skim over Rome's dark form as he led them through the wilderness.

Please let them not be running after a dog chasing a rabbit. Or a moose.

For twenty minutes they drove through terrain that grew rougher. Fallen logs blocked their path, forcing them to drive around, or sometimes over, the obstacles. They nearly got stuck more than once. Wilder's breath burned in his lungs.

"There." Stormi stopped, raising her voice above the din of the motor. "Rome's found something."

The dog stood thirty feet ahead, barely visible in the swirling snow, his head lowered, tail still.

"What is it?" Wilder asked.

"Dunno." Stormi was already climbing off the sled. Wilder followed, his thigh burning as they trekked through the deep snow. But he followed her over to—

His flashlight glanced over the grizzly.

Eight hundred pounds of apex predator sprawled across the trail, its dark fur matted with snow and gore. Deep gashes marked its flanks.

"Whoa," Stormi said. "That's a big grizzly."

"Dead grizzly." Wilder let out a heavy breath. At least they wouldn't have to deal with an injured bear protecting its territory.

Rome whined softly. Trotted around the carcass, then took off toward a cluster of rocks that formed a natural shelter.

Wilder flicked his light over to follow and nearly crumpled.

Dr. Caius and Bear sat in the protection of the stone outcropping. Dr. Caius was propped against the largest boulder, his left leg extended at an awkward angle. Blood seeped through an improvised bandage made from what looked like a strip of his torn shirt. Bear lay unconscious beside him, wrapped in an emergency blanket. His arm bent wrong. A makeshift head bandage covered what looked like claw marks.

"Dr. Caius!" Wilder rushed forward.

"About time," Dr. Caius managed, his voice thin. "I was starting to think we'd have to walk home."

Stormi was already kneeling beside Bear, her headlamp illuminating his pale face as she checked his pulse. "How long has he been unconscious?"

"About an hour. He was awake for a while, but the head injury . . ." Dr. Caius winced as Wilder examined his leg. "Grizzly got him with a backhand swipe. Knocked him ten feet into those rocks."

"What about you?"

"Leg's torn up pretty good, but I'll live. Bear took the worst of it." Dr. Caius gestured toward the massive carcass. "Took both of us, lots of bear spray, all my bullets, and a hunting knife to bring that thing down. Not sure why she was up and roaming around, but my guess is her cubs are near here. She wasn't in a negotiating mood."

Stormi worked over Bear, pressing her fingers to his neck. "Pulse is steady, breathing's regular. Pupils are equal and reactive, so that's good news."

The unspoken concern in her voice made Wilder's gut clench. "But?"

"But head injuries are unpredictable. And this arm's obviously broken." She looked up at Dr. Caius. "How bad is your leg?"

"Bad enough that I can't walk on it. The bleeding's mostly stopped, but I need help, and soon."

Wilder keyed his radio. Static filled the cold air. "Base, this is Wilder. We found them."

"Wilder!" Sage's voice crackled through the speaker. "Thank the Lord. What's their condition?"

"Dr. Caius has a severe leg laceration. Bear's unconscious with a head injury and broken arm. Both stable but need immediate medical evacuation."

"Okay. I'll call Deke. Maybe he can send out the Air One Rescue team. Can you give me your exact location?"

"It's too dense here to land. We'll need to bring them back to the house."

"Got it. How's the weather out there?"

Wilder looked up at the swirling snow, the wind a frenzy. "Still rough, but visibility's better than it was."

"Copy. I'll have Air One meet us here."

"Tell Sage we're going to need the snowmobile sled to transport Dr. Caius back to the compound." Stormi's voice carried loud enough for the radio to pick up. "I don't want to risk moving him on foot with that leg wound."

"Smart thinking," Sage said. "Everest can bring the sled out."

"Negative." Wilder shook his head. "I'll go back and get it. Faster than waiting for Everest to gear up and find us."

"Wilder—" Stormi started.

"It's a forty-minute round trip, and I know where we are." He looked her in the eye. "You okay to stay here and keep them stable?"

She gave him a grim nod. "Hurry."

And oh, he just wanted to lean in, to kiss her, hard. To tell her—what?

That she was a good partner?

No. That she was exactly what Sage said—a light.

"Be careful," she said as he got up.

"Pray," he said in return and then headed for the sled.

Cold was his friend, turning his body numb as he pushed back to the compound. He drove the snow machine harder than was probably safe, driven by the image of Bear's pale face and the growing pool of blood beneath Dr. Caius.

He spotted Everest in the yard, attaching the snowmobile to one of the utility sleds they used for supply runs. "Let's go," he said and turned around.

Sage stood at the open door to the lodge. "I called Deke. He's sending Air One to the compound."

"We'll be back before they get here."

The return trip was slower. The sled made the machine harder to maneuver through the trees. But he found them exactly where he'd left them—Stormi checking their vitals while Rome provided warmth by lying against Bear's side.

He shut down the machine and followed Everest over to them. "How are they?"

"Stable. I've got Dr. Caius's bleeding under control, and Bear's vitals are holding steady." Stormi looked up from where she was adjusting a makeshift splint on Bear's arm. "But we need to move fast."

Loading the patients onto the sled required all three of them. Dr. Caius gritted his teeth but didn't make a sound as they lifted him. Bear remained unconscious throughout the transfer. Stormi rode on the sled with them, monitoring their condition while Wilder and Everest drove back.

The compound had never looked so welcoming. Warm light spilled from every window as it appeared through the trees. Una met them at the door. "Air One's en route. ETA ten minutes."

"Good." Stormi was checking Bear's pupils again, her face grave in the lights that flooded the compound. "His responses are getting sluggish."

"Increasing intracranial pressure?" Una asked.

"Possible. We need to get him to a neurosurgeon."

The sound of rotors thundered, growing louder until the helicopter appeared above the compound, cutting through the snow. The aircraft settled onto the flat area in the yard. Two figures emerged from the cabin.

Wilder recognized the pilot immediately—Moose Mulligan, Air One Rescue team leader and one of the best bush flyers in Alaska. His brother, Axel, hopped out of the chopper too. And with them, someone Wilder didn't recognize, a woman. She flung a medical duffel over her shoulder.

Blond, with braids and a grim look, she appeared capable. Probably a flight medic.

"What've we got?" the woman asked, ducking under the still-spinning rotors as she approached the house.

"Two patients." Stormi shouted over the engine noise. "Male, mid-sixties, severe leg laceration, stable. Male, late twenties, head trauma with possible increased intracranial pressure, broken arm, unconscious."

The woman nodded. "I'm Phoebe, flight paramedic. You the doctor?" she asked Stormi.

"Veterinarian, but I've been providing field care."

Phoebe knelt beside Bear, checked his vitals. "Good work on the splint. How long has he been unconscious?"

"About two hours total, maybe less."

"We need to get him to Copper Mountain fast." Phoebe looked up at Moose, who nodded. "Load them both."

They worked together to transfer the patients to the helicopter's medical bay.

Una appeared in the helicopter doorway, her face set with determination. "I'm riding with them to the hospital."

"Mom—" Sage started.

"That is my husband and my son. I'm going."

Moose came up beside them, checking his watch. "We need to go. Weather window's closing fast."

"We'll follow in the morning," Wilder said. "Once the weather clears."

Una nodded, turned, and gave Wilder a hug. "Thank you, Wilder." He didn't know why those words slid inside, held on.

Maybe because the last thing he really deserved was a thank-you after he'd taken so much from them.

The helicopter lifted off in a whirlwind of snow and noise. Its lights disappeared into the storm. Wilder stood, watched until the sound of the rotors faded completely.

"They'll be okay," Sage said softly.

Stormi moved to stand beside Wilder. "The leg looked worse than it is. Muscle damage, but no major arteries or nerves affected."

"And Bear?" He looked at her.

"He's young and strong, and we got him help as soon as we could." She paused. "Thanks to Rome."

Rome. He glanced at the dog. "Clearly he's not a sled dog."

She nodded. "That's the second time he's tracked something . . . something not alive."

"Third time. First was the man from the car wreck," Wilder said. "Then Tyler. Then . . . the grizzly? You sure his sense of smell hasn't come back?"

She crouched, rubbed the dog's ears. "What's going on with you?"

Rome leaned hard into her touch and she laughed.

"Thanks for . . ." He trailed off.

She looked up at him. "For what?"

"For being exactly who you are when it matters most."

She stood up. "And that is?"

"Brave."

"Or just impulsive."

"Either way, tonight it saved a life."

She stilled. "No. Tonight God saved a life. Lives."

"Yeah." His voice came out gentle. "He did."

Behind them, the compound settled into quiet. Sage had gone inside.

"Wilder?" Stormi said gently. "You okay?"

"Just thinking."

"About?"

"About how fragile everything is. How fast it can all disappear." He looked at her—really looked. Taking in the exhaustion lines around her eyes. The way she was fighting to stay upright after hours of adrenaline and fear. "About how much I could lose."

"Hey." She caught his hand, her grip warm despite the cold. "We're all okay. Everyone's going to be fine."

"Are they? Because tonight could have gone very differently. If Rome hadn't picked up that scent, if we hadn't found them in time, if the weather had been worse . . ." He shook his head. "There are so many variables. So many things that could go wrong."

"But they didn't go wrong. We found them. They're getting help. Everyone's safe."

"I know. It's just . . ." The knot inside his chest cinched. "I'm not good at this. At caring about people and not being able to control what happens to them."

"None of us are good at that. It's terrifying to love people."

"Then why do we do it?"

She was quiet for a long moment. "Because the alternative is worse. Because connecting with people, even when it's scary, is what makes life worth living."

Right. *Oh*, she was right. The fear of losing people had kept him isolated. Safe. But it had also kept him from really living.

"Come on." She tugged his hand toward the house. "Let's get inside before we freeze. Also, I promised Luna I'd wake her when we found them."

They walked toward the warm light spilling from the windows. Toward the family waiting inside. Toward the life he suddenly wanted to build despite all the reasons it was dangerous and complicated and likely to end in heartbreak.

Inside, Luna was already awake and curled up on the couch with one of Una's quilts.

"Are Grandpa and Uncle Bear okay?" The question came the moment they walked through the door.

"They're going to be fine." Stormi settled beside her on the couch. "The doctors at the hospital will take good care of them."

"And Grandma Una?"

"She's with them, making sure they get everything they need."

Luna nodded solemnly, then she looked at Wilder. "Are you okay, Daddy? You look sad."

"I'm not sad, sweetheart. Just tired."

"And worried?"

"Maybe a little." He sat down on Luna's other side. Let her lean against him.

Luna yawned. Her eyelids heavy, despite the excitement. "I'm glad Rome is so smart."

"Me too."

"And I'm glad Miss Stormi knew what to do."

"Me too." He glanced at her. Stormi had taken off her outerwear and gone to the kitchen.

He pulled Luna into his arms, warming them both up by the fire. Stormi came out of the kitchen holding a hot cocoa. Sat down in the overstuffed chair, stared at the fire.

Luna fell asleep in his arms.

Wilder found himself studying Stormi's profile in the firelight.

She looked exactly like what she was—someone who'd spent the night saving lives in impossible conditions. Someone worth trusting. Someone worth loving. Someone worth the risk.

The thought should have terrified him. Instead, it filled him with a quiet certainty that had been missing from his life for three years.

"Tomorrow we'll mush back to Copper Mountain," she said. "Check on Dr. Caius and Bear."

She looked at him and he nodded.

We. The word landed, and warmth flooded his chest.

He just might be able to embrace *we*.

10

PREDAWN AIR SLICED through Stormi's parka. Sharp. Clean.

A new day. A new hope.

"Easy, Koda." She clipped her lead dog's tugline. The aging husky mix danced with nervous energy. Behind him, the rest of the line was set, the dogs barking, ready.

The cabin door banged open and Wilder emerged, holding hands with Luna, who was bundled up in pink snow gear, Vic behind them.

Sage and Everest walked out onto the porch. They'd stay behind to keep watch over the homestead.

"Weather's turning." Vic shouldered her duffel, gaze scanning the steel-gray sky. "Radio says maybe four hours before this front hits."

"We'll make it," Wilder said as he brought Luna over to his sled. His dogs stood, ready, obedient.

He zipped Luna's jacket higher. "You'll need to hang on tight. This isn't a fun run, little bear. We need to get to Copper Mountain to check on Grandpa and Uncle Bear."

So far, according to the call from Una on the SAT phone, both had survived the night, and Bear had regained consciousness.

Stormi checked the gangline, ignored Sitka's attempt to tangle with Juneau.

Wilder helped Luna into the sled basket where Vic waited. His team stood perfect—six matching huskies worth more than her vet school loans.

"Ready?" he asked and she waved.

His voice rang out into the beautiful morning. "Hike up!" His team took off.

"Mush!" Stormi's team lunged forward with chaotic enthusiasm. Rome moved with them, in sync.

Snow swished under their runners. Dawn crept across the sky, painting the trees with light that did nothing for the chill building in her bones.

Wilder ran his sled twenty feet ahead—close enough to help if her team staged a mutiny but far enough to avoid her disasters.

The trail curved through birch, bare branches reaching out like skeleton fingers. They crossed the creek single file, ice crackling under combined weight. The trail climbed through dense timber and Stormi's shoulders relaxed as they settled into a rhythm.

Luna's laughter drifted from the sled basket—some counting game with passing trees. The sound should have warmed the morning air.

But Wilder's continued silence cast shadows over everything.

"You're quiet today." She tried casual conversation during a brief rest. "Everything okay?"

He checked his team's harnesses with unnecessary attention. "Just thinking."

"About?"

"Things."

The nonanswer stung. Certainly after the past twenty-four hours—from the kiss to their rescue of Dr. Caius and Bear—they'd moved past polite small talk.

This retreat into careful distance felt like losing him.

Before she could ask another question, he called his team up.

So . . . that was weird.

The frost-covered trucks sat where they'd left them. While Wilder loaded the dogs into the back of Vic's truck, Stormi helped hers into their kennels. Then they strapped the sleds onto the tops of the kennels in the back of each truck.

"Hospital first?" She started the engine, grateful for reliable heat.

"Yeah." Wilder climbed into his driver's seat, his jaw still tight. Vic and Luna climbed in with him.

She had forty minutes of quiet to rewind the morning and try to figure out what might be eating at Wilder.

Nothing. He'd been on the radio. Then he'd packed his gear and harnessed the dogs.

And last night everything had been fine.

At the hospital, they left the dogs and headed inside. Vic mentioned something about checking on her restaurant and left them. As soon as the glass doors of the clinic whispered shut behind them, the hospital smells hit them—industrial cleaner mixed with human anxiety.

"Excuse me," Stormi said.

The desk nurse looked up as they approached. Middle-aged with kind eyes, graying hair pulled back, practical.

"Can you tell us what room Dr. Matthews is in?"

The woman directed them to the second floor.

They got off the elevator and Wilder approached the nurses' station.

"I'm here for Dr. Caius and Bear Matthews?"

The nurse's smile brightened. "You must be Wilder. Your father-in-law's been asking about you. And little Luna too."

For the first time, his face relaxed. So maybe it was simply the tension of getting here. "Can we see them?"

"Of course. Room 204, down the hall." The nurse frowned. "I should mention—there was a bit of confusion earlier when he was brought in. Dr. Caius was asking about someone named Dawn? He seemed quite concerned about her medical supplies."

Stormi went cold.

Wilder went perfectly still. "Dawn?"

"Yes. He kept saying he needed to make sure Dawn was safe, that she had everything she needed." The nurse's brow furrowed with concern. "Sometimes patients get disoriented after trauma, especially older folks. They mix up past and present."

"Dawn was my wife," Wilder said softly. "She died three years ago."

"Oh." The nurse's face softened. "I'm so sorry. Clearly he was just confused. Sometimes trauma can trigger memories in unexpected ways."

He turned away, his jaw tight.

"What do you think that's about?" Stormi asked.

"I don't know." He glanced at her. "But I'm going to find out."

WILDER TRIED not to recoil at the sight of Dr. Caius in the hospital bed. He seemed terribly smaller than he should be. Gray hair mussed against white pillows, the bear of a man who'd raised a family in the wilderness had been diminished by medications and beeping machines.

He'd been running this scenario through his head all morning, trying to clamp down on suddenly fresh memories of showing up at the hospital so many years ago to find Dawn had passed away.

Not again. The thought, however, had turned him quiet. Pensive.

Luna climbed up on a chair and nearly flung herself into her grandpa's arms before Wilder caught her around the waist. "Not yet, sweetheart."

But he did help her lean over and kiss her grandfather's leathery cheek.

"How are you feeling?" Wilder asked him as he set Luna down.

"Like I got mauled by a bear." A weak smile. "Oh wait, I did."

"Very funny." Wilder shook his head. He glanced over at the other bed. Bear slept, his left arm casted and in a sling. "How's he?"

"Okay. Concussion, but no brain swelling."

Una sat beside the other bed, holding Bear's hand. She looked up and gave Stormi a bare smile that Wilder caught from the corner of his eye.

Wilder sat down in the chair by his father-in-law's bed. "Dr. Caius, the nurse said you were asking about Dawn? About her medical supplies?"

The change was immediate. Dr. Caius's eyes cleared, became sharp with alertness that cut through whatever fog the medications had created.

"Not asking about." His voice dropped low. "Remembering."

"Remembering what?"

Dr. Caius glanced toward Luna, who had climbed onto her grandmother's lap. He lowered his voice further. "Dawn's bag. The one passed down from her grandmother. We gave it to her when she graduated from medical school. After she died, I helped you pack up her things, remember?"

"Yeah."

"I don't remember packing that bag, and it occurred to me that maybe she'd left it here. Maybe they didn't realize it was hers and put it in lost and found."

Wilder frowned. "The bag was in her belongings, Dr. Caius. I got it when the police returned everything to me. Do you want it back?"

"So, she had it with her when she was taken."

Wilder nodded. "It was in her car. Why?"

Dr. Caius's mouth thinned. "When we arrived at the hospital last night, the nurse on duty was a woman named Alicia Dunkin. She's been here for years—knew Dawn, of course. We started reminiscing and she told me about the last time she saw Dawn."

Wilder said nothing.

"It was when Dawn brought Heidi Reid in after her car accident."

"Tommy Reid's wife," Wilder said solemnly. "I forgot that she'd been the one to find her."

"It was traumatic. She came upon her crash and tried to administer first aid. Heidi died on the way to the hospital."

"What does that have to do with Dawn's medical bag?" Stormi asked.

Dr. Caius glanced at her. "I happened to be in town that day and I saw my daughter. She told me what happened with Heidi and that Heidi had told her that she had files that needed to get to Deke. Dawn had taken them and put them in her bag. That was a few days before her own accident."

Wilder froze, punched. What? If Heidi Reid had been gathering evidence about her husband's corruption, if she'd hidden it in Dawn's bag . . .

His voice emerged on a rasp. "Dawn died because she knew something. Or *had* something."

"What do you think Heidi gave her?" Dr. Caius asked.

Wilder looked at him, pieces clicking together in his mind. "I don't know. I worked with Heidi at the airport. She had access to video footage and flight schedules and . . . well, we talked about the crash that killed Sheriff Tatum and Senator Bowie. She said she knew something wasn't right—and I did too. But maybe . . . maybe she had the evidence to prove it."

"She did."

The voice came from the other bed. Bear had woken, and Wilder turned toward his brother-in-law.

"Hey, buddy," Wilder said. "You okay?"

"My head feels like it's been used as a kickball, but . . . I heard what you were saying and . . . you should know that I was doing my residency here when Heidi Reid died. I wasn't on shift, but I came in later that day, and Tommy Reid came in. He was looking for Heidi's belongings."

Oh no.

"I told him"—Bear's voice cracked—"I told him that Dawn had been with Heidi when she died. I didn't think . . ."

Wilder couldn't breathe as it all crashed over him. Tommy Reid at the airport. Tommy Reid in the surveillance photos with Sloan. Tommy Reid disappearing from Copper Mountain right around the time Dawn died.

"He killed her." Wilder's words fell like stones in the quiet room. "He killed Dawn because she knew about Heidi's evidence."

"We can't know that for sure," Dr. Caius said, but Wilder heard the lack of conviction in his protest.

"I do." Wilder leaned forward, scrubbing his hands down his face. "Photos, documents, evidence. Everything Heidi had collected about Tommy's activities. It's in Dawn's bag."

"Hidden in plain sight," Dr. Caius whispered.

"Heidi gave her the evidence, and Dawn stored it away, intending to give it to Deke. And then . . . three days later, she was forced off the road, taken and . . ." He didn't finish, glancing over at his daughter.

But the rest echoed in his mind. Tortured. Killed.

Silence stretched in the room, broken only by the soft hiss of an oxygen machine.

"Luna, how about we get you some hot cocoa?" Una stood up,

her face white, her granddaughter's hand in her grip. She gave Wilder a crushing look that made even him want to shrink back.

"Can I have marshmallows?" Luna asked as she followed her grandma out of the room.

The door swished closed. Bear shifted in his bed, wincing. "The car accident—"

"Wasn't an accident." Wilder's voice came out flat. "Single vehicle rollover on a clear day. No skid marks. No mechanical failure. She was thrown through the windshield—or so they made it seem."

Bear's face had gone gray. "If I hadn't told him . . ."

"Stop." Wilder stood, despite his aching leg, and moved to the window. Snow gusted off snowdrifts, the sky confused as clouds blotted out the sunshine. "You couldn't have known."

He pressed his forehead against cool glass. Beautiful Dawn who was brave and strong and willing to do anything to help another soul.

"Where is her bag now?" Stormi asked, her voice cutting through his spiraling thoughts.

Wilder turned from the window. "In my shed. Along with her other belongings."

"Then we need to get it." Stormi gave him a "don't argue with me" look.

And it hit him. Dawn had been a spark, something that ignited him. But Stormi was becoming something different—a partner who made him stronger, who could handle the storm instead of just weathering it.

Echoing footsteps in the hallway mixed with Luna's excited chatter. Una appeared in the doorway, Luna bouncing in beside her with a paper cup of hot chocolate topped with an impressive mountain of marshmallows.

"The cafeteria lady gave me extra because I said please," Luna announced proudly.

Wilder patted her head sweetly. "That's awesome, honey. Good girl." Then he turned to Una. "Can I leave Luna with you for a bit?"

"Why, Daddy? Where are you going?" Her eyes widened.

Aw. Wilder cleared his throat. "Luna, sweetheart, I need to go take care of some things."

"What kind of things?"

He knelt beside her, eye level with his daughter. "Remember that special teddy bear you wanted? The one from the house?"

Luna's face lit up. "Mr. Buttons!"

"Right." He smiled. "I thought maybe I'd go get him for you."

"He's in Mama's bag."

Silence, and his heart thumped. "What did you say?" he asked.

"Mama's bag. I found it in the shed while Vic was feeding our dogs. Mr. Buttons lives in it. I brought him to Vic's house."

Wilder just stared at her. And then, he reached out and pulled her tight.

"Daddy, you're squeezing me."

He buried his face in her hair, drew in the sweet smell of her. Then he let her go and kissed her cheek. "I'll be back, sweetie. I promise."

She nodded.

He looked at Una. "Are you going to be okay here?"

"We're fine." Dr. Caius waved to the call button clipped to his bed rail. "Plenty of staff, good security."

He moved toward the door.

"Wilder." Bear's voice stopped him. "I'm sorry. About . . . well, telling Tommy that Dawn had been with Heidi—"

"Don't." Wilder turned back to look at his brother-in-law, pale and guilt-stricken. "You did what any good man would do. You had no way of knowing what Tommy really was up to. It's not your fault."

He walked out of the room.

Footsteps. Of course Stormi followed him. "You okay?"

He shook his head, glanced over at her. "I suppose the words 'don't follow me' don't matter to you, huh?"

"Not even a little." She got on the elevator with him.

And he couldn't stop himself from grabbing her hand, folding his fingers through hers. "You know, if Tommy is after that evidence in Dawn's bag . . ."

"It gives him even more reason for coming back and haunting you."

He nodded.

"It also means that maybe you're not even a little to blame for her death."

The elevator doors opened and she squeezed his hand as they walked out, glancing at him as they crossed the lobby.

"What you said to Bear," she started, "about it not being his fault. It wasn't yours either. Maybe her death had nothing to do with you testifying. Maybe it had everything to do with what she discovered." They walked out into a block of parking lot, the afternoon already gone gray with thickening snow.

She headed for Vic's truck. "Let's go find Dawn's bag."

11

STORMI HAD NO IDEA how to light up the darkness that seemed to permeate Wilder. He drove, staring out the window, his jaw tight.

Please God, help him. And help me help him.

Maybe he was churning through her words about Dawn's death not being his fault.

Maybe he'd lived with that assumption so long, he didn't know how to let it go.

They had stopped at her truck to retrieve Rome from the cab. She checked on her dogs—they'd all be snug until she returned from Vic's place.

Then she loaded Rome into Vic's truck, and Wilder drove out of town, passing Main Street, the airport, and heading south to Vic's house. Snow peeled from the clouds in big chunks, turning the windshield into a white kaleidoscope. The truck's heater worked overtime against the cold seeping in through their windows.

"Tell me about Dawn," Stormi said.

Wilder glanced at her. "What do you want to know?"

"What was she like? Really like, not just the saint everyone talks about."

A ghost of a smile. "She wasn't a saint. She was stubborn and opinionated and she had absolutely no patience for people who wouldn't help themselves."

"Sounds familiar."

"She would have liked you." The words emerged on a roughed voice. "She would have said you had spine."

"I take that as praise."

"You should." He offered a slim smile.

Vic's house appeared through the trees. Compact two-story cabin, solar panels glinting under the porch light.

"Home sweet home," Wilder muttered. "I should have offered Vic a ride home."

"She went back to the Midnight Sun," Stormi said. "Said something about checking on the bar." Funny that he hadn't remembered that.

He glanced at her. "Right." He got out and together they let his dogs out of the kennels, securing them in the barn, then he unhooked his sled and they set it on the ground.

They finally climbed the porch steps. He grabbed the key from the top of the lintel.

Warmth hit them despite their absence, the furnace keeping the place livable. It smelled of Vic, coffee, and woodsmoke. Luna's drawings covered the refrigerator.

Rome nosed past her and into the house, sniffing.

Wilder moved toward the stairs. "Dawn's bag should be in Luna's room."

"I'll check it. You sit down." Stormi touched his shoulder. He made a face but nodded.

She climbed up to the second floor and found Luna's room—small but comfortable. Quilt-covered bed, pine furniture that looked handmade, a few stuffed animals on the bed. She looked under the bed but no bag. Opening the closet door, she also rooted around, found extra winter clothing, a few of Luna's clothes, and there, on the floor, a worn leather medical bag. Brass clasps tarnished with age. Leather showing years of use.

She pulled it out and put it on the bed. Inside sat a worn teddy bear that was missing an eye, the mouth stitching fraying, one arm dangling. Clearly loved.

She carried the bear and the bag downstairs to where Wilder sat in the living room. No, not sat. Perched on an arm of the sofa.

"Found it, I think." She handed the things to Wilder.

"It was her grandmother's. Dawn inherited it when she started her nurse practitioner program." His thumb traced the initials embossed in the leather. "She said it made her feel connected to all the women who came before her."

He set it on the coffee table and searched the belly of the bag. "Nothing."

"Try the outer pocket."

He turned the bag around and the clasps opened with soft clicks.

He reached into the pocket. "Wow. Papers, photographs, a manila folder."

Stormi sat next to him.

"Look at this." He pulled out a photograph. Two men shaking hands beside a fuel truck. "That's Sloan."

"And that's Tommy Reid," Stormi said, a stone landing on her chest.

They spread the contents of the folder across the table. Fuel receipts, flight logs, photographs of late-night meetings at the FBO. Emergency dispatch records with discrepancies highlighted in Heidi's neat handwriting.

"She built a complete case." Stormi picked up a folder marked "Thornton Shipping." "Look at this." Inside they found shipping manifests, truck routes, a jump drive, and a photograph that stole her breath. Sloan shaking hands with a man in an expensive suit. Government building in the background.

"That's Senator Bill Thornton," Wilder said. "She connected it all the way to the top."

"And this." Stormi pulled out a shipping manifest. "Thornton Shipping has been moving product through half the state, in conjunction with North Face Construction—or rather Summit Construction, as they're calling it now. Thornton Shipping could be the head of the snake that the Sorros family is working for. The head of the entire drug trafficking operation in Alaska."

"Maybe beyond Alaska." He stared at the evidence spread across the table. "Dawn died for this."

"We can finish what she started." Stormi began gathering papers. "This is enough to put Sloan away. And open an investigation into Senator Thornton too."

"And get us both killed in the process."

"Maybe. Or maybe we can finally end this nightmare." She looked up at him. "What do you want to do?"

Quiet. He stared at the photograph of Sloan and Thornton. "I want to stop running."

The words hung between them.

"I want to stop looking over my shoulder every five minutes. I want Luna to have a normal childhood with friends and school and sleepovers." His eyes met hers. "I want a life."

A beat, and her heart banged hard in her chest.

"With you."

Oh.

Something shifted in his expression and he swallowed, hard. Then, softly, "I can't lose you, Stormi."

Her throat thickened. "You won't."

"You can't promise that."

"I can." She leaned closer. Close enough to see the layers in his blue eyes. "I'm not going anywhere, Wilder. I'll fight for what we have here."

"What do we have here?"

Her heart hammered against her ribs. "I think you know."

He reached up and cupped her face in his hands. Palms warm against her skin. "I haven't felt this way since Dawn. Except, this is different."

"Good." She covered his hands with hers. "Dawn would want you to be happy."

He sighed. "Yes. Yes, she would." He shook his head as if in disbelief.

Then he kissed her. Soft and tentative at first, sweetly, and oh, of course she kissed him back, following her heart right into his embrace. His arms came around her then, pulling her close, kissing her with a surety, a focus, the kind of confidence she'd seen in him years ago, when he'd run the Iditarod.

The sense that he wasn't afraid.

And, frankly, neither was she.

When they broke apart, she was breathing hard.

"That was—"

"Right," he finished. "It's been right since I showed up on your doorstep, Stormi. I just didn't want to admit it."

"Until now."

He nodded. "Until now." He rested his forehead against hers.

Rome barked, stood, the ruff of his neck raised.

Both froze.

"Rome?" Stormi said.

He barked again.

Wilder was up instantly, moving to the window. "I think someone's out there."

"Vic coming back?"

"Vic wouldn't skulk around her own property." He grabbed his coat. "Stay here."

"Oh, please—"

"Stay here." Oh, he was using his alpha voice. "If something happens, grab the bag and run."

He slipped out the back door, but not before Rome could run past him. Good dog.

Stormi's hands shook as she grabbed the papers. Dawn had died for this information. The least she could do was make sure it saw daylight.

She shoved everything into the pocket of the medical bag, and her hand brushed another envelope buried at the bottom. She pulled it out. A manila envelope marked "Insurance."

She opened it. Of course. A life insurance policy, taken out by Tommy a month before Heidi's death.

The back door clicked open. Wilder stepped inside, face pale. Eyes wide.

"What did you find?" Stormi asked.

"Footprints. Fresh ones, leading away from the house." He locked the door behind him, moved to check the front windows. "Someone was watching us."

"How long?"

"Hard to tell. But they were definitely here at some point today." He turned from the window, ran a hand through his hair. "We need to go. To get this evidence to Deke."

The snow had continued falling. Covering their tracks and the tracks of whoever had been watching.

But for the first time in three years, maybe Wilder Frost wasn't hiding from the future.

Maybe he was running toward it. And Stormi was running hard with him.

THE COPPER MOUNTAIN Sheriff's Department buzzed with fluorescent overhead lighting. Coffee, stale from sitting too long on the hot plate, burned in his nose as Wilder pushed through glass doors, Dawn's medical bag heavy in his hand.

"Wilder." Relief flickered across Deke's face as he came out of his office. "How are Dr. Caius and Bear?"

"They're going to be okay. But we found something you need to see."

Deke opened the door to the conference room. "We've got everyone here. What do you have?"

As they walked in, Jericho glanced up from where he stood at a map board, coffee mug in hand, examining pushpin locations, wearing a wool tuque over his dark hair. Behind him stood Harley, wearing a grim look.

Another man stepped forward, his hand out to Wilder. "Rio Parker, FBI." Dark hair, a leather jacket, jeans, and all-weather hiking boots. He looked like someone who knew his way around Copper Mountain.

Wilder shook it. "Wilder Frost."

"You're a hard man to track down." He gave him a wry look. "Glad to see you're okay."

"That's debatable, but thanks."

Stormi came into the room, Rome padding beside her. The dog's attention shifted to a Bernedoodle sitting near Jericho's chair—ears up, tail wagging.

"That's Orlando," Jericho said, following Wilder's gaze. "He's friendly."

Rome approached with careful canine diplomacy, the two dogs touching noses, circling, sniffing. Orlando's tail swept the air.

A moment later Rome settled onto the floor, head in his paws.

"Where's your daughter?" Deke asked, heading into the conference room.

"Hospital. With Una." Wilder set Dawn's medical bag on the conference table.

Deke moved closer, eyeing the bag. "That it?"

Wilder nodded. "Everything Heidi Reid collected before she died." Wilder's fingers found the clasps, opened the outside pocket. "She must have told Dawn and given her the evidence when Dawn found her after the crash."

Wilder handed him the file folder.

Deke had put on latex gloves. *Oops.*

"Sorry."

"It's okay. We'll print you so we can add that to the database, sort out the different fingerprints."

Harley stepped up, holding a cup of coffee. "Walk me through what we've got."

Deke opened the file folder. Photographs spilled across the metal table—surveillance shots of the airport, men shaking hands by fuel pumps, North Face Construction trucks parked on the tarmac. But the close-up made everyone lean forward.

Tommy Reid in his sheriff's deputy uniform, badge catching the camera flash, as he handed something to Sloan Sorros.

"When was this taken?" Harley's voice came out tight.

"Seven years ago." Wilder studied the photo. "Right around the time your parents died. I worked at the airport. I saw Sloan talking with Pete Barrow numerous times."

Silence settled over the room, broken only by fluorescent humming and forced air through heating vents.

Deke picked up the jump drive. "What's on here?"

"Everything, according to Heidi's notes." Wilder pulled out a small notebook, pages covered in careful handwriting. "Financial records, shipping manifests, delivery schedules. Maybe even video footage from the airport security cameras."

"The cameras that were supposedly malfunctioning the day our parents died." Jericho's voice carried a dangerous tone.

"Yep," Wilder said. "It's possible that Heidi downloaded the footage. Maybe she accidentally wiped it from the airport database." Wilder met his eyes. "Or maybe it was wiped after she grabbed it. Tommy sometimes worked security at the airport, which meant he had access to security protocols."

"Access to destroy evidence." Harley moved toward a laptop, inserted the drive. The screen flickered, then populated with file directories organized by date. She clicked on one labeled "October 15" and hit play.

Grainy security footage. The timestamp showed 5:47 a.m., the hangar still dark except for work lights. A figure moved through the frame—tall, broad-shouldered, wearing a sheriff's department jacket.

Tommy Reid.

He worked with purpose, opening the fuel cap on a Cessna, pouring something from a small container into the tank, his face clearly visible as he checked his watch and sealed the cap.

"Holy cow," Deke said. "How did he get away with this? Especially under my watch?"

Wilder glanced at Deke. "Under Sheriff Tatum's watch. You didn't take over until after this."

Deke's mouth made a grim line. "I was a deputy at the time."

"My dad had been surveilling Tommy and North Face Construction for a while," Harley said. "We found his investigative notes. This isn't on you."

Deke shook his head.

Harley scrolled through more files. "North Face Construction had legitimate contracts for airport renovations, and with Tommy working security, he had access to fuel systems, security protocols, flight schedules."

Deke moved closer to the screen. "Show me the manifest files."

Shipping records filled the screen.

"They used Thornton Shipping to deliver the fuel," Harley said. She looked at Jericho. "I'll bet your dad, as a senator, was onto Thornton. Maybe even investigating him."

"You know about Thornton?" Deke glanced at her.

"The state prosecutor's office has been investigating his campaign finances. Lots of money flowing from sources that don't quite add up." She took a sip of coffee. "Senator William Thornton owns the biggest shipping company in Alaska. We've been working with local police on following the supply chain for a number of local drug operations."

Wilder stared at her. "Not just local corruption. Not just a deputy gone bad. A conspiracy at the state, maybe federal level."

She nodded. "And maybe, with this, the police can start trading in deals."

"Did Tommy kill his own wife?" Jericho asked.

"No. Tommy was with me when Heidi's car went off the road," Deke said. "But we have the forensic evidence of the crash in our storage."

"What do you bet you find paint from one of the North Face Construction vehicles in the scrapes on Heidi's car?" Harley said.

Silence, a beat.

Wilder spoke next. "The Sorros men—probably Sloan, although it could have been Mars since Conan and Jago were in jail—took out Tommy's wife."

"And tortured yours," Deke said.

Stormi took his hand—probably because Wilder had put his other on the table, his knees wanting to buckle.

"I thought our parents were killed because of what my dad was investigating," Harley said. "But what if . . . what if it is all connected to Thornton?"

"And what my dad was investigating?" Jericho put a hand on her shoulder. "What if they're all involved?"

Wilder barely heard him, Stormi's words from the hospital whooshing inside him. *"Maybe her death had nothing to do with you testifying. Maybe it had everything to do with what she discovered."*

Not his fault.

Dawn had died because she'd tried to help a dying woman seek justice.

Everything inside Wilder seemed to congeal, to heat.

He looked at Deke. "Someone was out by Vic's place today. Followed us from the hospital, is my bet."

"How do you know?" Deke asked.

"Rome. He started barking."

Rome's tail thumped on the floor, as if he might be agreeing.

"The question is," Jericho said, "how long has Tommy been tracking you?"

"Since Wilder showed up at my place," Stormi said. "I'm sure he was monitoring law enforcement communications. He said as much."

"He could have been listening to everything." Jericho moved to the window as if he might catch Tommy outside, lurking. "Scanner frequencies, radio chatter, even cell phone calls if he's got the right equipment."

"Which means he knows we're here," Wilder said.

Harley looked at Deke. "We should call Lydia. Tell her what we found." She looked at Wilder. "Recently, there was a big drug bust in Juneau. They're questioning everyone, but there's evidence of drug trafficking not only through North Face but across state lines."

"Thornton Shipping."

"Yep. Which means federal jurisdiction."

She looked at Wilder. "And we need your testimony."

He stilled.

Harley moved closer, her voice only for him. "You're the only one who can testify about Sloan at the airport, connect him to the fuel tampering. Without you, the photos are just circumstantial evidence."

The weight settled on his shoulders. Three years of hiding,

three years of looking over his shoulder. It could all end here. But ending it meant stepping into the light.

"If I testify," he said slowly, "Sloan Sorros won't stop trying to kill me."

"You're already on his terminal list." Rio's voice was matter-of-fact. "The question is whether you want to keep running or start fighting back."

Stormi's hand tightened in his. He glanced at her, found those hazel eyes on him, steady. *"I'm not going anywhere, Wilder. I'll fight for what we have here."*

"You should see this." Deke pulled a manila folder from beneath the evidence pile, opened it to reveal a police sketch. "We got this from the woman who survived the snowmobile attack and showed up at your clinic, Stormi. She was able to give our artist a description."

The sketch showed a man in his mid-thirties, handsome, intense eyes, strong jaw. Slight beard, wearing hunting gear. A faint scar crossed his cheekbone.

"That's Sloan Sorros," Harley said.

Beside her, Jericho nodded.

"What? I thought Tommy attacked them," Stormi added.

"The cache cabin." Wilder's voice hitched. "That's where he'd been hiding. And Sarah and Tyler were about to stumble right into him. That's why Tyler was shot. Twice." He blew out a breath. "Tommy must have been hiding with him. Maybe waiting for the storm to clear before they . . ." He glanced at Stormi.

Her mouth made a tight line. "Before they circled back to the clinic." She took a breath. "We need to end this. And you need to testify to what you saw at the FBO."

"I can have the state prosecutor on video call in ten minutes," Harley said. "I just need a computer."

"Do it." Wilder blew out a breath. Squeezed Stormi's hand. "Time to bring Sloan—and Tommy—to justice."

Outside, snow continued falling over Copper Mountain, covering tracks, turning the world clean. Peaceful.

As if maybe . . . maybe this could really be over.

12

IT WAS THE RIGHT THING to do. *Of course* it was the right thing to do. But Wilder's words just wouldn't leave Stormi. *"Sloan Sorros won't stop trying to kill me."*

She stood, arms folded as she watched Wilder and state prosecutor Lydia Harper finish up their video call. "Thank you, Mr. Frost," Lydia said. "Your testimony is exactly what we need to move forward with charges against the Sorros family and open an investigation into Senator Thornton and his shipping network."

Wilder leaned back, ran a hand through his dark hair. Nodded.

"The federal case is solid," Rio added from his position near the door. "We've got financial records, shipping manifests, and now eyewitness testimony linking Sloan Sorros to the plane crash, not to mention enough to link Thornton to the Sorros drug operation."

Sheriff Deke Starr leaned on the long conference table, nursing a cup of coffee. "I always knew there was something wrong about the Bowie crash. Now to find Sloan and put away these guys for good."

"I need to get my daughter and lie low until then." Wilder glanced at Stormi, although she didn't know why.

Or maybe . . . yes, she did. They were still in this together.

"We'll start with taking Thornton in," Lydia said onscreen. "We'll see if he knows where Sloan is hiding. You guys hunt down Tommy Reid."

The video call ended and Deke got up, shook Wilder's hand. Stormi couldn't take her gaze off Wilder.

The tension lines around his eyes had softened. His jaw no longer carried that constant clench of hypervigilance. For the first time since she'd known him, Wilder Frost looked like a man who believed he might actually have a future.

"I should get back to Luna," he said, pushing back from the table.

"Actually," Deke said, "I need your statement and description on the body you found near Stormi's house a week or so ago. I know it's been a minute, but we need it for our records."

"I'll get Luna. Jericho can drive me over to the hospital—my truck's still in the lot." Stormi said. The grateful look he gave her warmed her to her bones.

Still, old habits died hard. "You sure?" he asked. "I know you've got your clinic to run, and—"

"Wilder." She stood, gathering her jacket from the back of her chair. "I want to spend time with Luna. Stop looking for reasons why I shouldn't."

Jericho chuckled from his position near the window where he'd been silently observing the proceedings. "Tell him, Doc."

He moved toward the door and Stormi followed. Rome had gotten up, padded beside Stormi, the big Malador's tail wagging after an afternoon of being petted by everyone in the room.

The hallway was quieter, insulated from the ongoing discussions. Late afternoon light filtered through the front windows, casting everything in that golden glow that made even the sheriff's office look welcoming.

They headed out to Jericho's truck.

"How's the work going with Rome?" Jericho asked, no preamble.

Oh. "Um. I . . . I'm not sure. He won't respond to any of my tracking exercises, but he seems to have tracked the man from the car that Wilder found, and he tracked Dr. Caius and Bear Matthews . . ." She opened the cab door, and Rome jumped inside. "He's been training to run, but . . ." She frowned. "Poor guy isn't sure what he is—a sled dog or a tracker."

"Maybe he's both." Jericho set his hand on the dog's head a moment before he turned the key. The truck fired up.

She nodded, sighed. "Truth is, I'm not sure I'm the one qualified for real SAR work."

"Why not?"

"Because . . . sure, I like doing everything, but I don't do any of it well."

Jericho pulled out of the lot. "Stormi, from what I've heard, you're not struggling because you lack ability. You're struggling because you think you need to choose one thing and be fantastic at it. But really, what if you're called to simply . . . join. To offer up your talents and see what God will do with them? Say yes and ask God to use your talents as he wants. You might be surprised."

Rome's tail thumped against the seat, as if he agreed with Jericho's assessment.

They headed down the street, toward the hospital.

"What if I fail?" Oh, she made a face, hating the question in her words. Some alpha dog.

"What if you succeed?" Jericho glanced at her, and his smile held a warmth that transformed his entire face. "Here's what I've learned—just show up and do your best. That's enough."

Rome turned and lay his head on her lap. The simple gesture of comfort made her throat tight with unexpected emotion.

"I've been afraid of disappointing people," she said. "Of not being enough. Of choosing something and failing at it."

"Get in line." He smiled wider.

She laughed. "Right."

"You miss all the shots you don't take," he said.

"Thank you, Wayne."

He grinned. They pulled onto the hospital drive. "Stormi," Jericho said, "I know Moose is trying to get you to join Air One Rescue. Whatever you decide, don't make the decision out of fear or from what you think others expect. Decide based on what tugs at you when you're quiet enough to listen. Some might even call it the gentle voice of God."

Hmm. Maybe she should stop to listen first.

The hospital parking lot sat under the pool of lights, brilliance glistening on the piles of snow as Jericho pulled up beside her truck and let her out. She crossed to her own rig, the dogs in the bed lifting their heads in greeting. She glanced at Rome after loading him into the cab. "Stay."

He lifted an eyebrow. Right. She was getting as bad as Wilder.

Still, she cracked the windows, then headed inside. The lobby held a handful of visitors checking in at the reception desk, their voices echoing off the polished floors.

She took the elevator up to the second floor and headed down the hallway. Knocked on Dr. Caius's door, then eased it open.

Una sat in the recliner, watching a televised hockey game with Dr. Caius and Bear. She glanced around the room. Dr. Caius seemed to have dozed off.

"The Blue Ox?" Stormi asked, coming inside.

"We never get to watch them out at the compound," Una said. "They're saying it's Wyatt Marshall's last year as goaltender, but after the game he's having today, they'd be stupid to trade him. Or let him retire."

She sort of followed hockey, and she'd gathered that the Minnesota Blue Ox was a local favorite.

And then it hit her—"Where's Luna?"

"She went with Vic over to the Midnight Sun to grab dinner," Una said. "Vic said she'd bring her back with takeout."

Yum. She'd smelled the woodsmoke of the hickory-style ribs coming from the Midnight Sun's smoker when she left the sheriff's office.

"I'll pick her up. Wilder should be done at Deke's any minute."

Una glanced at her, in between watching the game. Bear was also half sleeping. Stormi didn't have to wonder who the real fan was here. "Great. Thank you, Stormi."

Then she drove over to the Midnight Sun and parked in the lot.

She got out and noticed the closed sign hung on the door.

Weird.

She tried the front door. Locked.

The windows revealed an empty dining room, chairs stacked on tables as if Vic had been preparing for a thorough cleaning. But the coffee machine was still on, its red light glowing like a beacon in the dimness.

Stormi walked around the building's perimeter.

The side entrance was unlocked. She walked inside, past the bathrooms, to the dance floor, and then into the dining room, with the long bar and booths. The place had gotten a makeover since last summer when a fire had caused damages, but it still contained its charm—flat-screen televisions, red vinyl booths, a jukebox against the far wall, a pool table at the front. But it was . . . quiet. Too quiet, no patrons, despite the early dinner hour.

"Vic?" Stormi called. "Are you here?"

A muffled sound came from the direction of the kitchen. The

door hung open, revealing industrial equipment and stainless steel surfaces that gleamed under fluorescent lights.

"Help!"

A voice from the walk-in refrigerator. What? Stormi ran over, opened the door.

Inside, Vic sat on the floor, holding a gash on her forehead. Bruising had formed around her left eye, but nothing that appeared immediately life-threatening. Except she was shivering, almost violently.

"Holy cow—Vic, what happened?"

She helped the woman out into the warmth, grabbed a towel for the head wound. Vic shook, clearly freezing. "My jacket—it's in the office."

Stormi found Vic's small office and the wool jacket hanging from a coatrack. She grabbed it and headed back to Vic, who pulled it on.

Yeah, the former cop might be freezing, but a fire blazed in her eyes. "They took Luna."

"What—?"

"Two men. Tommy Reid. And I think the other was Sloan Sorros. I tried to stop them—" Her jaw clenched. "I shouldn't have taken her from the hospital."

"When?" Stormi was already reaching for her phone.

"Maybe a half hour ago. They just came in on us." Vic touched the gash on her forehead, wincing as her fingers came away bloody. "I didn't see them come in—they just scooped up Luna, and when I turned around, Tommy clubbed me."

"We have to call Deke," Stormi said. "Get search teams organized."

"No." Vic grabbed her wrist. "They said if anyone followed them, if any law enforcement got involved, Luna would disappear permanently."

Stormi froze. No. "They're going to ransom her for Wilder."

Vic's mouth made a grim line. "My guess too."

Which meant, probably, they'd be in touch with Wilder. Soon. If not already.

"Let's get you to the doctor."

"Not until I talk to Wilder, warn him. He's going to freak out."

Right. Stormi helped Vic to her feet, supporting the older woman as they made their way back through the restaurant and out to her truck.

Rome sat up and whined as Vic got in.

Yeah, her too.

And then, as she got in, Rome scrambled past her, out into the parking lot, barking.

She stared at him, her heart thudding.

Vic leaned on her. "Stormi?"

"I think he's alerted on something." She reached for his lead, her heart hammering. She snapped it on before the dog could run. He whined, sat, immovable.

And then it all clicked into place. The alert at the crash site, the alert at the snowmobile accident, even the alert on the bear who'd attacked Dr. Caius and Bear. They weren't on the living . . . they were on a different smell. She drew in a breath and glanced at Vic. "And it's not good. I think Rome is a cadaver dog." She swallowed hard. "Which means whatever he's scented on . . . is dead."

OF COURSE it would end this way. With his daughter dead.

There was no justice, Wilder should have figured that out by now.

He hadn't needed Stormi's realization and Vic's harrowing tale to know that something terrible had happened to Luna.

He felt it in his soul. Even before he got the text from . . . Sloan? Probably.

He stared at his phone. A photo filled the screen. Luna in her pink coat, her eyes wide with terror, but alive.

Below the image.

Old rail yard. One hour. Come alone or she dies.

Wilder knew the place. The old rail yard outside of town, just east of the current depot.

He needed to get away, right now, before Deke and his team decided to follow him.

Vic sat in a metal chair beside Deke's desk, looking like she'd survived a war. Blood matted her hair despite fresh bandages, and her left eye had swollen shut. But her good eye had blazed with fury when she came in with the news.

"They took her right out of my hands, Wilder." Her voice cracked, and she seemed near tears. "I fought—"

"I know." The words scraped his throat raw. "I know you did."

And that's when Deke came up and led her away.

And Wilder hid his phone message.

Yes, he was going alone, just as the text had instructed. But . . . yeah, getting out of here might take a little finagling.

Stormi seemed as antsy as he did. She crouched next to Rome, running her hands over him, her jaw tight. "You think they knew you testified?" she asked.

His gut clenched. "I don't know."

Deke came out of his office. "All right, Jericho, do you think Orlando is up to tracking Luna?"

Jericho cast a glance at Stormi, back to Deke. "We can try. He's an air sniffing dog, so it's possible he could pick up her scent—"

"No." Wilder's voice cut through the room like a blade. "No units. No backup. They said come alone."

The sheriff's office went silent except for radio chatter.

"Who said?" Deke asked.

Aw, he was just . . . stupid. *Really, Frost?* He got up. "I need some air."

Deke stepped in front of him. "They contacted you."

He pocketed his phone, met Deke's gaze.

"That's not how this works," Rio said, stepping up behind Deke.

"They killed my wife," Wilder snapped. "You think they won't do the same to my daughter?"

"Wilder," Stormi said, "you can't just walk into a trap."

"Watch me." And he didn't even bother to hide his exit as he turned toward the door and pushed out into the cold. The setting sun painted the mountains blood red as he made his way toward his truck.

"Wilder, wait!"

Stormi's voice stopped him cold. He turned to find her running down the sidewalk, winter coat unzipped, hair escaping from her wool hat. "I'm coming with you."

"No." He resumed walking. "This time, absolutely not."

"Listen." She fell into step beside him. "Rome found the trail. Let's see what he's found."

He stopped. "Stormi—"

"C'mon, you know he can do this."

"Rome's a failed sled dog with attention problems."

She stared at him, her mouth open. "He's more than that. I think Rome's a cadaver dog."

He drew in a breath and probably wore a stricken look because she added, "I mean—he can smell blood. Maybe Vic's blood—I dunno, but—" Her mouth pinched. "Right now, he's the best chance Luna has."

"I need to do this on my own." He turned, stalked toward Vic's truck, fumbled for the keys.

"And that's it? You're going to turn yourself over to them?"

"I'm going to do whatever it takes to get Luna back."

Stormi slid between him and the driver's door. He glared at her.

"Including trading your life for hers?"

"Of course. I have no other choice. Please get out of my way."

"And then what?" Her eyes blazed. "Luna grows up an orphan? Spends the rest of her life knowing her father died because she was taken?"

"Luna grows up." He tried to step around her, but she shifted to block him. "That's all that matters."

"That's not all that matters, and you know it." Her voice rose. "She needs you, Wilder. Not a martyr—you."

"She needs to be safe. Please don't make me push you out of the way."

Something shifted in her expression. Hurt flickered across her features before she masked it with anger. "I think you already have."

The accusation hung between them like a loaded weapon. Wilder's chest knotted. "Okay, then."

She stared at him and he hated how her eyes filled.

"Don't, Stormi." He looked away. "You know I have no choice."

"There's always a choice."

"That's enough."

"Is it?" She was close enough that he could see the gold in her beautiful eyes. "Because I think it feels better to believe you have no choice. To believe that you have to sacrifice yourself."

Her words dropped through him like a stone. "This is my daughter's *life*. I will do anything to save her. *Anything.* And if you were smart, you'd pay attention and run from me as fast and far as you can."

She stared at him, a pulse throbbing in her neck, her eyes filling. "Yeah, well, I may not be smart but I'm not a coward."

The word hit him like a bullet. Clean. Precise. Devastating. "What did you say?"

"You heard me." Her chin lifted.

He shook his head, his words a growl. "Get out of my way."

Her voice shook. "You're trying to save yourself from having to trust."

He blinked at her. "Excuse me?"

"If you go it alone, you don't have to trust anyone—"

"Who am I supposed to trust?"

"Besides me and Deke and everyone in there? How about *God*?"

What? "God isn't on my side."

"God is the only one who is *always* on your side."

He drew in a hard breath. "What do you expect me to do?"

"You could pray."

He stared at her. "What?"

"Pray. You could pray."

And for the tiniest moment, the words landed, sunk in, took root. Heated him.

And then—no. Prayer meant hope. And he was fresh out. "*You* pray." Then he pushed past her and got into Vic's truck. Met her eyes before closing the door. "Stormi, go home. You've gotten yourself too far into this. Go home and forget about me." His throat closed, even as he said it, but he slammed the door, then started the truck and pulled out.

And forced himself to ignore her, standing there on the sidewalk.

His phone buzzed again. Same unknown number.

Forty-five minutes.

The rail yard was twenty minutes away if he drove fast. Which left him twenty-five minutes to figure out how to trade his life for Luna's in a way that actually saved her instead of just getting them both killed.

He was nearly out of the parking lot when movement caught his eye. Rio jogged toward him, one hand on his radio, the other waving him down. Behind him, Crew, one of the local deputies, and Deke emerged from the building.

Wilder hit the gas.

The truck fishtailed slightly on the icy pavement before the tires found traction. In his rearview mirror, he watched Rio's mouth move, shouting.

By the time they coordinated backup, by the time they figured out where Wilder was going, it would be over. One way or another.

The road unwound before him, asphalt dark with melted snow and lined with towering evergreen trees. His headlights carved through the growing shadows as the sun dropped behind the peaks, painting the sky purple and gold.

Forty minutes to save Luna.

Forty minutes to end this.

But even as the fist formed in his gut, he glanced up at the bleeding sky and wished he could pray.

13

COLD SEEPED through Stormi's jacket as she stood on the sidewalk outside the Copper Mountain Sheriff's Department, Wilder's words still echoing in her head.

"Stormi, go home. You've gotten yourself too far into this. Go home and forget about me."

The sun cast long shadows across the snowpacked street, but the chill hit her bones.

Home? Where was that, anyway? The clinic in Anchorage? Even Minnesota felt like something from another person's existence.

Her home was here. It was doctoring Wilder in her kitchen and eating pancakes at the Matthewses' lodge. Tucking Luna into bed . . .

And kissing Wilder Frost under the northern lights.

Home was where she'd gotten her heart shredded in a parking lot.

Her hands shook as she fumbled for her truck keys.

Maybe she *didn't* belong here. Clearly she'd flung herself headlong into a dream, following her heart all the way to the bitter edge of heartbreak.

"Stormi!"

The voice cut through the winter air. Female, breathless, familiar in a way that made her chest constrict.

What?

She spun around.

Her sister sprinted down the sidewalk, her long blond hair streaming out of a wool hat, her breath clouding the air. Aspen was slipping on the icy pavement in thick designer Uggs. Behind her, a tall figure in a dark wool coat jogged to keep up—*What is Ridge doing here?*

Sheesh, a gal goes off the grid for a few days and—

No! "Dad?"

Dr. Marcus White got out of the back seat of a pickup and waved, his silver-streaked hair catching the last rays of sun. He wore a canvas work jacket, jeans, boots.

And she had nothing. Just . . . "What are you guys doing here?"

Aspen reached her first, nearly tackling her. "Thank goodness you're okay. We've been looking everywhere."

"I don't under—"

"We stopped at your place, but when you weren't home, we came here." Ridge wrapped both of them in his arms, his familiar warmth cutting through the shock.

"Didn't you get my calls?" Aspen released her, met her eyes.

Stormi's mouth opened. Closed. "Um. Probably. I was out of service for a few days, and then . . ." Oh, there was too much, really. She'd have to sum up. "I just got back. Sorry."

"Aspen's been nearly frantic," Ridge said. His voice carried the steady calm that had made him a successful lawyer. "When we couldn't reach you for a few days—"

"A *week*," Aspen corrected, pulling back to examine Stormi's face with the intensity she usually reserved for analyzing her clients' life choices. "Not a single call returned. Radio silence."

"Aspen's imagination got the worse of her." Her father stepped up and pulled her in, and Stormi had nothing for that. The scent of his aftershave—something woodsy and familiar—brought back a rush of memories. Late nights in the clinic, him teaching her to suture, the patient way he'd explained anatomy while she held flashlights over injured animals.

She didn't want to lean in, the ache hard in her chest. But . . .

"We flew in last night and drove up from Anchorage this morning." Dad touched her shoulder, the gesture gentle. "We got scared, sweetheart."

Sweetheart? The word cracked open something in her chest. "You flew all the way out here?"

"You think I'd let my baby sister disappear in the Alaskan wilderness without a search party?" Ridge's mouth quirked upward. "We may not understand your life choices, but we're not letting you face them alone."

Tears burned her throat. She blinked them back. "I'm fine. I mean, I *was* fine. I am—"

"You don't look fine," Aspen said, again surveying her. "You look like someone who's been through a trauma. Multiple traumas."

Stormi's mouth opened, then she shook her head, met Aspen's eyes. "Something like that."

"What's going on, Storm?" Dad's use of her childhood nickname unraveled another thread of her composure. "The truth."

She drew in a shaky breath, the cold air burning her lungs. Where did she even start? She glanced at Aspen. "I was right."

Aspen frowned at her, shook her head.

"Wilder Frost was—*is*—alive." And she wouldn't think about . . . well, all of it.

Or the fact that he might not stay that way if his plan worked.

Silence. Complete, absolute silence from her family. Well, she'd felt that way too when she found him on her doorstep, so . . .

A car drove past, its tires crunching on the snowpacked road. Someone's dog barked in the distance. The flag in front of the post office snapped in the wind.

"Wilder Frost," Ridge repeated slowly. "The musher."

"The one who—" Dad stopped, his eyes widening with recognition. "The Iditarod runner. The one from that poster in your room. I remember him."

Heat climbed her neck. "It wasn't a poster. It was a signed photo."

"Right. The signed photo." Ridge's lawyer brain was clearly processing. "The one you kept on your wall through high school—"

"I took it down a long time ago." The defensive edge in her voice made her wince.

"Storm." Dad's voice held the same gentle patience he'd used when she'd brought home injured animals as a child. "Help us understand."

She looked toward the sheriff's office, its windows glowing warm yellow against the gathering dusk. Inside, Deke and his team were probably coordinating search efforts. Trying to find Luna. Trying to save the little girl who'd probably become way too important to her in such a short time.

"He was shot," she said finally. "Four and a half weeks ago. He ended up on my doorstep during a blizzard a week back, bleeding and hypothermic. I performed field surgery."

"You *what*?" Aspen's voice pitched higher.

"I saved his life." The words came out stronger than she felt. "And then . . . things got complicated."

"Complicated *how*?" Clearly Ridge's cross-examination mode had engaged.

"People were trying to kill him. *Are* trying to kill him. There's this whole conspiracy involving drug trafficking and corruption and"—she gestured helplessly—"his seven-year-old daughter was just kidnapped."

Another beat of silence.

"His daughter was *kidnapped*," Dad repeated carefully, "and you're standing on a street corner instead of . . . ?"

"He told me to go home." The admission tasted bitter. "He said I should forget about them. Us." She looked away. Aw, she didn't know why she'd told them all that. Maybe because they were here, standing in Copper Mountain, just . . .

"Ah." Understanding flickered across Dad's features. "And that's why you look like someone ripped your heart out."

Aspen's expression softened. "Oh, honey."

"I thought . . ." Stormi's voice cracked. "I thought we had something real. But maybe he was right. Maybe I was just chasing some childhood fantasy."

"Were you?" Dad asked.

She looked at him now, the softness in his voice pinging inside her, smarting. He'd taken her to that Iditarod race, stood beside her in the crowd as Wilder crossed the finish line. He'd seen the hero worship in her teenage eyes.

But that was before everything shattered, wasn't it?

So yes, maybe she was clinging to a dream, a time when things felt . . . well, when her body, her very cells didn't ache inside her.

"I don't know. Maybe." She took a breath. "Probably." She looked at Aspen. "I thought I was helping him. Thought I was . . . needed."

"And now?"

"Now I don't know anything."

The scent of pizza drifted from the restaurant across the street, rich with garlic and oregano. Her stomach reminded her she hadn't eaten since this morning. Since before the world tilted sideways.

"Anyone else starving?" Ridge asked, clearly reading the same aromatic cues.

"Food sounds perfect," Aspen agreed. "We can talk somewhere warm."

But Dad's gaze remained fixed on Stormi's face. "Give us a minute."

Ridge and Aspen exchanged a look. "We'll grab a table," Ridge said. "You still a pepperoni and mushroom gal, Storm?"

Stormi nodded, not trusting her voice.

As her siblings headed toward Starlight Pizza, Dad stepped closer.

She folded her arms against a terrible rush of memory, the scent of his cologne, the gaping hole that suddenly burned inside her.

"I know you blame yourself for your mother's death."

Oh. She stepped backward, her heel catching slightly on an uneven patch of sidewalk. "Dad—"

"It's not a question, sweetheart. And it's my fault."

She frowned.

"I've watched you carry that weight for eleven years." His voice softened, and then he swallowed, a hint of guilt on his face. "And I . . . I was too absorbed in my own grief to fix it."

"I should have called you sooner." And of course, she was right back there, in the moment, the horror rushing through her. "I knew something was wrong, but she kept saying she was fine, that this was what she wanted, and I—"

"It was what she wanted, honey." Dad's hands settled on her shoulders, warm and steady through her jacket. "Your mother had you and Aspen and Ridge at home. She wanted our last child to be born at home too. She had no reason to believe it wouldn't be just fine. Sure, she was older, but . . ."

"But if I'd acted faster—"

"No. The placenta ruptured before we left for the hospital." He made a face, shook his head. "The doctor told me later. Even if we'd gotten there immediately, even if she'd been there from the start . . ." His voice grew thick. "Sometimes there's nothing anyone can do."

The street blurred. "You never told me that."

"I should have. I'm so sorry. I wasn't thinking clearly about what you needed to hear."

He reached up and touched her face, and she nearly jerked away. But his thumb brushed away a tear from her cheek, the gesture achingly familiar. "I'm sorry for that. For letting you carry blame that was never yours."

She looked away then. "I stopped trusting myself that night," she said quietly. "And since then, I started second-guessing everything. So, I just leap first . . . and get in over my head." She drew in a breath. "I know I should stop and pray, but . . ."

"That's where grace comes in."

She frowned, looked at him.

"Prevenient grace, the divine grace that God offers us because we're his children. Yes, wisdom comes from praying, asking, being obedient, but that doesn't mean that you walk away from God's favor if you make a quick decision. Being in over your head is not evidence of God's punishment or even his disfavor. God's unmerited favor doesn't depend on us getting everything right."

A gust of wind sent snow swirling around their feet. She shivered.

"His grace covers our mistakes, our hesitations, our imperfect choices," Dad continued. "But we don't stop trying to make good decisions or ignore wisdom. But it does mean we're not condemned by our failures."

"Even when people die because of them?"

"Especially then." His hands gripped her shoulders again. "Your mother made a choice that night. So did I, when I decided to respect her wishes. So did you, when you tried to honor both our positions. We all did the best we could with love as our motivation."

"I don't know how to live without the fear of getting it wrong."

"You lean into God's perfect, complete, unwavering love for you."

Oh. She wiped her face with her mittens.

And then, without asking—and maybe that was okay—her dad pulled her into a hug. Fierce, solid. It quelled the shaking inside her. "I love you, Storm. I'm proud of the woman you've become. The healer, the risk-taker, the one who runs toward trouble instead of away from it."

She closed her eyes. Maybe she *should* go home.

He pulled back to meet her gaze. "By the way, being in over your head isn't a terrible place to be when you know God has you in his hands."

Huh. Didn't sound so different from what she'd said to Wilder.

"So, Wilder Frost, huh?" He smiled.

"Don't get excited, Dad. I don't think he wants to be with me. He thinks loving me puts me in danger."

"Does it?"

Oh. Um. "Probably."

"And that matters to you?"

She stared at him. Did it matter? The explosions, the gunfights, the constant threat of violence—should that change how she felt?

"No," she said. "It doesn't change anything."

"That's love."

Beside her, Rome had gotten up, the fur on the back of his neck rising. He barked, then sat, looking up at her. Then barked again.

"I should probably tell you," Dad said with a shrug, "I came prepared to offer you a partnership."

"What?" His offer drew her attention away from Rome.

"The practice. I'm getting older, Storm. I could use someone with your skills and your passion." He smiled. "Full partner.

Your name on the building. Complete autonomy over the canine division."

Everything she'd thought she wanted. Financial security. Professional respect. A chance to work beside the man who'd taught her everything about veterinary medicine.

A chance to go home.

"Do you want to come back to Minnesota?"

The question hung in the evening air between them. Behind them, warm light spilled from the windows of Starlight.

Another bark, and now Rome stood up again, nose lifted.

He was alerting to something.

"I think I belong here," she said.

Dad followed her gaze to the dog. "Because of him? Wilder?"

"Because of me." The certainty surprised her. "Because this is who I am when I trust God's grace to cover my mistakes."

Rome barked again and pulled on the lead, toward the Midnight Sun parking lot across from the sheriff's office. He stopped, looking back at her as if to say, *Are you coming or not?*

"I have to go," she said, tugging on Rome's lead, moving them toward the sheriff's office.

"Stormi—"

"Rome's found something. Or someone." She turned back to her dad. "Thank you. For coming here. For . . . for everything you said."

Her dad nodded. "Okay. Be careful, sweetheart."

"I will." She started toward the building, then stopped. "Dad? I forgive you too. For the grief. For the distance. For letting me think I was responsible."

His breath caught, and he blinked. "Thank you."

She pushed through the glass doors of the sheriff's office.

Jericho looked up from a map spread across Deke's desk. Harley stood beside him, her finger tracing routes on the paper.

"Stormi," Deke said, looking up, "I thought you'd gone home."

"I think I know how to find Luna," she said. "Rome's alerting to something behind the Midnight Sun. If he's picked up her scent . . ."

Deke glanced at Jericho, back to Stormi. "You think he can track Luna?"

"I think he can track whoever took her. And that's where we'll find Wilder."

OKAY, maybe this was stupid, but he had nothing else.

The truck's engine roared as Wilder pressed the accelerator harder, the speedometer climbing past safe limits for traveling down the icy mountain roads. Pine trees blurred past his windows, their snow-laden branches creating dark tunnels in his headlights. The heater blasted hot air, but nothing could warm the ice that had settled in his chest.

Sloan would kill his daughter. Wilder knew it in his soul.

His knuckles ached from gripping the steering wheel.

He couldn't believe he'd pushed Stormi away. Told her to forget about them. The look on her face when he'd said those words—her recoil—burned behind his eyes every time he blinked.

What an idiot. But what choice did he have? Death followed him like a shadow, claiming anyone foolish enough to get close.

The truck hit a patch of black ice and fishtailed slightly before the tires found purchase again. Wilder's heart hammered as he corrected the steering, forcing himself to ease off the gas. Luna needed him alive and functional, not wrapped around a tree on some back road.

The train yard could work to Wilder's advantage. Remote, lots of places to hide, multiple escape routes. But it also meant Sloan had the advantage of choosing the terrain, the timing, everything.

He should pray. Stormi's advice, of course, rounding back to him. But the words wouldn't come. How could he ask for help from a God who'd allowed his wife to be murdered? Who'd let evil men tear his family apart?

Who was now letting those same evil men threaten his daughter?

He just didn't know which way God would play it. And he needed guarantees.

A melody surfaced in his mind, unbidden.

"Blessed assurance, Jesus is mine . . ."

Dawn's voice, clear and sweet, rising from memory. The hymn she'd loved. The one she'd hummed while working in their garden, while cooking dinner, while rocking Luna to sleep as a baby.

Wilder's throat closed.

"Oh, what a foretaste of glory divine! Heir of salvation, purchase of God, born of his Spirit, washed in his blood."

He could see her so clearly—standing in their cabin outside Talkeetna, three-year-old Luna asleep in the next room. He'd just come back from meeting with the federal prosecutor, his hands still shaking from everything he'd agreed to do. Testify. Point a finger at the Sorros family and put a target on his own back.

Dawn had been at the stove, stirring soup, but she'd taken one look at his face and turned off the burner.

"You're terrified."

Not a question. She'd always been able to read him.

"I saw a man die, Dawn. Shot in the back of the head." He'd sunk into a kitchen chair, pressed his palms against his eyes. "And now I'm supposed to stand in a courtroom and tell the world what I saw? These people—they don't leave witnesses alive."

She crossed to him, put her hands on his shoulders. "So you want to stay silent? Let them get away with murder?"

"I want to keep you and Luna safe."

"By living the rest of your life looking over your shoulder? Knowing you could have stopped them and didn't?"

He looked up at her then, desperate for her to understand. "What if they come after us? What if testifying is the thing that brings them to our door?"

Dawn knelt beside his chair, took his face in her hands. Her eyes—those steady green eyes—held nothing but certainty.

"His love supersedes the evil in this world, Wilder. Evil exists. Wicked men do wicked things. But that doesn't mean we hide from doing what's right."

"Easy to say when you're not the one who watched Darrin die," he said.

She hadn't flinched at the bitterness in his voice. "You think staying quiet will keep us safe? These men know you saw what happened. Silence won't protect us. It just means they won twice. Once when they killed that agent, and again when they silenced the man brave enough to witness it."

He gripped the steering wheel now, knuckles white against the memory.

"You're working so hard to figure out how to protect us on your own," she'd said. "But you're not trusting the Lord to help you through this."

"How can I trust him when he let me see that? When he put me in that place at that moment?"

"Maybe he put you there because you're the one brave enough to tell the truth."

He wanted to argue, to explain that it wasn't bravery but necessity, that he was just a musher who'd stumbled into something terrible. But she continued before he could form the words. "You think accepting help means weakness. You think you have to figure this out alone—protect me, protect Luna, handle everything yourself." Her thumb had traced his cheekbone. "But that's your pride talking, love. Not wisdom."

Another memory surfaced as he drove down the icy road—one from later that same night. They'd been lying in bed, Luna's soft breathing audible through the baby monitor. Dawn had been quiet for so long he'd thought she was asleep.

Then her voice in the darkness. "Don't let your fears keep you from embracing the grace God has for you."

"What if I lose you?" The question had scraped out of him, raw and honest in the dark.

"What if instead of trying to control everything, you trust him to work through this? Through the prosecutor, through the Marshals, through whatever protection they can offer?"

He'd pulled her close, breathing in the scent of her hair. "I don't know how to stop being afraid."

"You don't have to stop being afraid." Her hand had found his in the darkness. "You just have to do the right thing in spite of the fear."

So he had. He'd testified. He'd trusted her words, trusted her faith, trusted that doing the right thing would matter.

And people had died because of it.

Now, hurtling through the darkness toward a confrontation with the men who'd murdered her, the bitter irony nearly choked him. She'd told him to trust God. She'd told him fear didn't have to win. And her faith had gotten her tortured and killed.

But even as the old rage surfaced, so did her stubborn faith. Dawn would have had something to say about that rage. She always did.

"Evil tried to steal me, tried to destroy our family. But it didn't win, Wilder. The Lord has the victory."

That's what she'd say. He could almost hear the certainty in her voice.

But how? How could the Lord have the victory when Dawn was dead? When Luna had grown up without a mother? When he'd spent three years running and hiding and pushing away anyone who tried to help?

She'd probably point to Luna and remind him that their daughter was alive, was strong, was braver than both of them combined.

His vision blurred. He blinked hard and focused on the road ahead, wiped his face with his sleeve.

And now there was Stormi.

"I told her to leave," he said to the empty cab. To Dawn, maybe. To himself.

He knew what his wife would say to that. She'd said it that night in their kitchen, when he'd tried to handle everything alone.

"Because you're afraid."

"Because I'm realistic." The argument came automatically, even though no one was there to hear it. "Look what happened to you."

But Dawn wouldn't accept that excuse. She never had. She'd say what happened to her was evil, yes. What was happening now was also evil. But that didn't mean he should reject the grace God was offering.

"Don't let your fears keep you from embracing the grace God has for you."

He could picture her face as she'd said those words—serious, her hand pressed over his heart.

"What if I lose her too?"

The question scraped out of him, aimed at a woman who couldn't answer. But he didn't need her answer. He already knew what she'd say. She'd said it their first year of marriage, when he'd been terrified of fatherhood, of failure, of loving something so much it could destroy him. And she'd said it again that night in Talkeetna, when the weight of what he'd witnessed had nearly crushed him.

"What if instead of trying to control everything, you trust him to work through this?"

The truck crested a hill and his headlights cast over the rail yard below. A sprawling cluster of railroad tracks, abandoned freight cars, and old buildings. And at the end, a warehouse, dim light pressing into the darkness.

"I don't know how to stop being afraid," he said quietly.

Silence answered. Of course it did. Dawn was gone, had been for three years. But her voice lived in his memory. And he knew exactly what she'd tell him.

"You don't have to stop being afraid. You just have to trust him in spite of the fear."

The hymn drifted through his mind again.

> Perfect submission, all is at rest;
> I in my Savior am happy and blest,
> watching and waiting, looking above,
> filled with his goodness, lost in his love.

Something shifted in his chest, something solid settling where the ice had been.

He pulled over, hands shaking as he put the truck in park. In the yard, freight cars arranged in long lines, creating dozens of hiding spots. Somewhere down there, Sloan waited with Luna.

Somewhere down there, his daughter needed him to be smarter and stronger than he'd ever been.

"You could pray." Stormi's words.

Yes, yes, he could.

"I'm sorry, Lord." The words came easier than he'd expected, flowing from a place that had been locked tight for three years. "I'm sorry I've been trying to do this myself. I do want to trust you, but I'm afraid it won't be enough."

The wind picked up and rattled the truck slightly. In the distance, a train whistle echoed across the valley, lonesome and haunting.

Then Stormi's words from those first days in her clinic came back to him, as clear as if she were sitting beside him. "*Sometimes the bravest thing you can do is trust that you're not facing it alone.*"

She'd been talking about his injuries, about letting her help him heal. But the truth landed, seeded his heart. He'd been facing *everything* alone since Dawn died.

But he wasn't alone.

And he didn't have to be enough. Because . . . "Oh God, I want to trust you—help me trust you!" He shouted the words, forcing them out. "Please forgive me for not trusting you sooner. For thinking I had to carry this alone."

He hung onto the steering wheel and looked up at the dark sky. "You are enough."

Yes. The words echoed in his chest, then sank into him.

"Make me smart and courageous for whatever it takes to save my little girl." He breathed out, his words soft. "And if you're willing . . . bring Stormi back to us safely too."

The clutter in his chest cleared, and with it, light seemed to spear through him, rush into the hollow places, fill his limbs.

And in that moment, it was enough.

Wilder reached over and switched off the headlights, plunging the truck into darkness. The rail yard below disappeared. He'd approach on foot and use the shadows and his knowledge of the terrain to his advantage.

Sloan might have chosen the location, but Wilder had spent years running these mountains. Years learning to survive and move through the lethal Alaskan wilderness.

He turned off the engine, opened the truck door, and stepped into the night air. The scent of pine and snow filled his lungs. Familiar smells that reminded him of dawn training runs with his dogs, of early morning races when the world was still and perfect.

Time to go get his daughter.

14

PLEASE, ROME, *don't let me down.*

"You sure he alerted?" This from Jericho, who held Orlando on lead, as he watched Rome circle the parking lot behind the Midnight Sun.

Behind her, Deke and Rio sat on snow machines, all their hopes pinned on her belief that Rome could find Luna.

And save both her and Wilder.

The wind sliced through her winter gear. Rome circled the lot for the third time.

"The tracks are clear as day heading to the road." Rio gestured toward a snowmobile trail, his voice carrying the patience of someone explaining obvious facts to a child. "Two snow machines, heading to the road."

Jericho nodded. "It looks like they're headed toward the highway—"

"Wait," Stormi said. "I know he's onto something."

Deke stepped up, holding a flashlight. "Stormi, I know this is hard, but we need to move fast. Those snowmobile tracks are fresh, and—"

"Rome disagrees."

Her dog's nose was working the air with intensity she'd dismissed as distraction during months of failed training sessions.

"Dogs make mistakes," Deke said. "Especially dogs that aren't proven SAR material."

And she didn't know why, but she rounded on the sheriff. "Listen. Rome is right—I know it."

"How?"

Her heart? She looked upward, toward the dark sky, and there it was . . . peace. She wasn't following her heart . . . she was following peace.

"Because."

Then she heard it. His whine started low, urgent, building to something that raised the hair on the back of her neck. Rome dropped to his haunches and released a sound she'd never heard before—part howl, part bark, all urgency. His amber eyes fixed on hers.

"I believe you, bud," she said.

Rome whined again, adding a scratch against the snow that revealed dark earth beneath. His tail stayed low, body language screaming alert in every line. The behavior she'd mistaken for confusion suddenly made terrible sense.

"Stormi," Deke's voice gentled, "I know you want to trust your dog, but lives are at stake here. We can't afford—"

"To be wrong," she finished the sentence, meeting his eyes. "I know."

"Ma'am, with respect—" Rio started.

"Rio." Stormi's voice found strength she didn't know she possessed. "Sloan Sorros isn't some desperate amateur. And neither is Tommy Reid." She gestured toward the obvious snowmobile tracks. "Tommy's a former sheriff's deputy who knows how searches work. Those tracks are too convenient. Too obvious."

"Or they're exactly what they appear to be." Rio's voice carried the frustration of someone watching precious time slip away. "Kidnappers heading for the nearest road with their victim."

Rome added a sharp bark that echoed off surrounding trees. Then, he sat next to a barely visible path that led out of the parking lot and disappeared into dense wilderness.

"Look at him." Stormi's voice dropped. "That's not confusion. He's alerting."

"Alerting to what?" Jericho asked.

She made a wry face. "I'm hoping it's not what I think, but Rome isn't just a tracking dog. He's a cadaver dog."

Silence.

"You're sure about this?" This from Deke.

She drew in a breath. "No. But it feels like the right thing."

He cocked his head.

"Let me rephrase. My bones, my soul, tell me this is the right thing." She knelt beside Rome. Her dog's eyes met hers with trust so complete, it made her chest ache.

Deke shook his head, looking at the tangle of forest beyond the lot.

"The snow machines can't go in there, Stormi," he said. "It's too narrow, too dense."

"Wait." Her dad's voice cut through the debate. He'd been standing nearby with Ridge and Aspen, who'd given up on them at Starlight Pizza and returned to watch the search teams organize. Now her dad stepped forward. "What about the sled dogs? The ones in your truck?"

Stormi blinked. She'd been so focused on Rome's alert that she'd forgotten about her team, still harnessed and waiting in her truck.

"Dad, that's"—she looked toward her truck, then back at the narrow wilderness trail—"that's brilliant."

Ridge frowned. "You're talking about going into the forest. At night. In subzero temperatures."

"With a dog team that's . . . well, not trained," Aspen added.

"They're trained," Stormi said. "They can do this."

Her dad was already moving toward the truck. "If Rome's right about the trail . . ." He met Stormi's eyes. "This could be our only chance to reach them before it's too late."

She headed over to her truck and opened the doors. "Get the racing sled off the truck!"

The dogs jumped out of the truck bed kennels, shook out their muscles, barking. She grabbed their leads while her dad unhooked the sled from the kennel top. Together they snapped off the bungees securing the narrow sprint sled.

"This is wild," Aspen said, but she was helping too, holding the sled steady as they slid it down off the truck. Light as breath. Dad pushed it across the packed snow to her team, lines still coiled on the sled bed.

Deke had done nothing to help. "Stormi—"

"For the love. I know what I'm doing."

The dogs were already in their harnesses, trembling with pent-up drive. "Hang tight, kids."

Her dad and Ridge pushed the sled over. She dropped the snow hook, ran the gangline, clipped tuglines and necklines, checked carabiners with numb fingers. Dad checked on her work.

Stormi rose and shouldered her pack, turned on her radio, her GPS, then clipped the emergency flare gun to her belt.

"Stormi." Deke's breath smoked in the cold. "We should take the machines the long way around."

"And lose the trail? No way." She met his eyes. "I need weight on the runners—you're with me."

Dad brushed snow from his gloves. "The sled's ready. You're right, Stormi, these dogs know what they're doing."

Jericho and Rio stood by their snow machines, engines idling low, staring into the black tangle of trees. Jericho grimaced. "No way we fit in there."

"Then follow the other track," Stormi said, nodding to the broad snowmobile cut angling east toward the highway. "We'll keep in touch."

"Copy," Rio said. "Be safe."

Aspen stepped forward, her expression mixing fear and fierce love. "Don't die out there."

Stormi met her sister's eyes, seeing her own worry reflected back. "Pray."

Ridge pulled her into a quick, hard hug. "You've got this, Storm."

Dad's hand settled on her shoulder, warm and steadying. "Trust your instincts. Trust your dog. And trust the Lord to guide you."

She nodded, her throat thick. Then she crouched by Rome, hand on his collar, the wind tugging at her words. "Find," she said low and certain. "Find, Rome."

Rome surged upright, indecision gone. He punched for the mouth of the wilderness trail, a dark arrow in the thin light. The rest of the team lunged with him, lines thrumming, but the brake held them in place.

"I hope this isn't a mistake," Deke muttered as he climbed onto the back runners.

"Just hold on." She yanked the hook, dragged the brake up, and called, "Mush!"

They slid into the piney tunnel, the world closing around them. Snow hissed under the runners as cold bit her lungs and her headlamp carved a narrow cone of white into the darkness.

Rome ran just ahead of Koda, his nose working with bloodhound intensity, his silhouette ghosting at the edge of light. Every few strides he glanced back at her, amber eyes catching the headlamp beam.

The trail pinched and twisted through trees so thick, their branches formed a ceiling overhead. Black trees pressed close on both sides, their heavy branches snapping, snow breaking off and powdering the air. The only sounds were the rhythmic panting of the team, the whisper of runners on snow, and the gentle jingle of hardware.

Ten minutes of mushing passed. The dogs worked together like a true team, Koda leading with confidence, the wheel dogs driving hard behind.

See, she did know what she was doing.

Then the world dropped away ahead.

The river! Her stomach clenched. A glint of moving black showed where the river had chewed through the ice. The trail took a hard right along the bank—

But the dogs were running straight toward the thin ice.

"Stormi!" Deke's voice cracked with alarm as he braced himself, seeing it the same heartbeat she did.

"Oversteer!" Wilder's words rushed at her, his voice as clear as if he were standing beside the sled. *"Wide arc. Don't let the sled push the team."*

"Gee! Gee!" she called to Koda, her voice cutting through the night air.

Her heart hammered against her ribs as she leaned hard to the inside. She feathered the brake with the delicate touch Wilder had taught her, just enough pressure to keep the sled from shoving into the team. The gangline stretched like a drawn bow.

Koda hesitated a fraction—she could see the way his head turned slightly toward the easier path. Her breath caught. If he didn't commit to the turn . . .

Then he swung inward, along the bank, his powerful shoulders driving into the harness. He led the team in a tight arc that followed the safer ground. "Hold—good! Easy." She tapped the brake twice, quick touches that helped the sled track cleanly through the curve. She held the line, completed the oversteer, then released.

They slid past the black mouth of the river on their left, close enough to taste the cold rising from the water. The team sailed along the safe edge, leaving the danger behind them in a wash of moonlit ice.

Deke huffed out a sound that might have been a prayer. "Okay. That was—okay."

"I have good dogs," she said, the words more breath than voice.

Deke's radio crackled. Jericho's voice came over the line. "We're on the east track along the creek. The tracks cut into the forest."

"Copy," Deke said.

Rome drove on, and his confidence surged through the team, Koda fighting to keep up. The trees thinned, and the trail opened into a pale clearing under a rag of moon, blotted by thick clouds. Rome slowed, casting her a look, then slowed more, stance rigid, nose sampling the breeze. He gave that low, certain whine that had started to live in Stormi's bones.

"Whoa." The dogs slowed too, and she dropped the hook. She stepped off the runners and moved forward, palm out. "Easy. Good boy."

A shape lay half covered in drifted snow. Parka. Boots. Fur hat.

For one jagged heartbeat, one terrible moment, her brain went to—*Please, no, don't let it be Wilder!*—but the build was wrong. Broader.

The blunt snout of an Arctic Cat sat half hidden near the tree line.

Deke had also gotten off, and now swept his light, crouched, and checked for a pulse, pulling back a glove. "It's Tommy Reid," he said, voice tight.

The fist inside her released, but even as she looked at Tommy, her heart sank.

Rome had found Tommy.

Luna was still out there with Sloan.

"We have snowmobile tracks," Deke said, his beam washing

over churned runner lines. "Sloan must have come through here."

Deke keyed his radio. "Jericho, Rio—we located Tommy Reid's body in a clearing off the creek line. Deceased. We're continuing east."

"The tracks head into the woods," Jericho said. "Toward your position."

Deke looked at Stormi, and then, into his radio, "We're just west of the rail yard, near the south end. Head there. We'll secure the scene after we link up. Keep moving."

Stormi pulled up the hook, swung onto the runners. "Line out!"

Koda pulled the line taut, looked back at her, waiting.

Yeah, she was the alpha. And for a second, she got it, the deep aloneness, the feeling of surviving that Wilder loved when he mushed.

Please, God, let him survive tonight.

"Mush!"

Rome ran ahead, and Koda followed, the team stretching into a ground-eating lope.

They climbed steadily through dense timber, winding between massive pines that blocked most of the moonlight. Air chapped her face. The woods gave way by degrees—fewer spruce, more scrub willow—then the bite of wind that held the taste of steel.

The trees opened up into another clearing.

The air changed—cold metal, diesel, creosote. A long string of dark shapes shouldered up against the sky—the train yard, sleeping under snow. It sprawled across several acres of cleared land. A tangle of tracks, old railroad cars, and a large warehouse.

"The old Denali line," Deke said. "We used to play here as kids. There are a couple old engines inside the warehouse."

He pointed, and Stormi's gaze fell on a flicker of light, small and fleeting, against the warehouse windows.

She eased the team to a trot along the fence. "Easy. Slow." They slid through a service gap and onto a plowed lane between hulking boxcars. Sound changed—snow deadened under the runners.

Rome trotted between the cars, nose working the narrow seam between two parked cars. He let out that same low, certain rumble.

"Stop," Deke said, stepping off to sweep his light. He lifted his radio. "We're at the rail yard, south service lane, row C."

The sound of engines grew in the distance. Jericho and Rio must have been approaching along the outside track corridor.

Stormi got off her sled, knelt by Rome, hand warm on his ruff. "Good boy. Hold." Her heart hammered, but her voice stayed steady. She glanced at Deke.

"I'll bet Wilder parked at the road and hiked in," Deke said. He held up binoculars and scanned the area.

But she didn't need them to see a figure moving along the tracks, hunched over, limping.

Heading toward the warehouse.

Wilder!

Even at this distance, in the moonlight, she knew his walk, the way he favored his healing leg. He was exactly the hero she'd always known him to be.

The lone ranger.

Lord, protect him!

She heard Rio through the mic, calling back to the sheriff's office. "Harley, we've got a visual on a large facility. Old rail yard. And we have a civilian approaching from the north. Repeat, civilian on site."

So Rio had spotted him too.

"Copy that," Harley said. "Can you identify the civilian?"

"It's Wilder Frost. He's walking into the facility."

So much for secrecy.

Static filled the frequency. Then Harley's voice. "Wait. Did you say the Copper Mountain Rail Yard? Does it look recently renovated?"

A pause, then, Rio again. "Affirmative. There are a couple of new buildings. Looks like recent construction work."

"According to Summit Construction, they were renovating it for Thornton Shipping."

"Why would Sloan pick this place?" Jericho asked.

"Maybe he knew we'd trace it back to Thornton," Deke said. "Maybe he's so desperate, he's trying to take down Thornton with him, possibly planning on a deal?"

"And with Wilder gone, there is no evidence to tie him to the previous murders," Jericho added.

"Except the murder of Wilder Frost." She stared at Deke. "We need to get down there."

But even as she tracked Wilder in the darkness, he vanished behind a boxcar . . . heading straight for the warehouse.

And into the hands of Sloan Sorros.

WILDER CROUCHED behind a rusted freight car.

The yard's warehouse loomed ahead, industrial windows glowing with fluorescent light against the darkness. Wind whistled through the maze of freight cars.

Lord, I'm trusting you. Make me smart and brave for whatever's waiting in there.

His injured leg sent fire up his thigh with each step across frozen gravel.

Help me see what I'm missing. Help me think like you would think.

The heavy steel door stood open, yellow light spilling onto the loading dock. The door's hinges groaned as it shifted in the wind.

Wilder stepped inside.

Old diesel fuel and the scent of rusted metal tinged the air. The cavernous room stretched up into shadow, white fluorescent light illuminating the stained concrete. A steel table held a laptop, a radio. And Luna, pushed up to it, not tied—*thank you, God*—but impossibly small in a battered office chair as she bent over the table. Her bright pink coat flared against all that gray concrete. Blond hair escaped her knit hat, curling around her flushed cheeks. She colored in a coloring book with focused intensity, her tongue poking out slightly in concentration, as if she was in a small bubble where none of this existed.

She saw him and her face lit up. "Daddy!"

She launched herself from the chair, flung herself toward him and crashed into his legs. Small arms wrapped around his waist. He breathed in the scent of her strawberry shampoo, sweet against the industrial air.

"Hey, princess." His voice was gravelly.

"I knew you'd come." She looked up at him with Dawn's beautiful green eyes. "Mr. Sloan said you would."

Mr. Sloan? "Did he now?"

"Welcome to the party, Frost."

Wilder steeled himself even as Sloan stepped out from behind a concrete support beam. The man looked exactly like Wilder remembered him from years ago—medium height, brown hair. He held the same cold calculation in his eyes and a sort of lingering military bearing that made him dangerous. He held a black handgun, almost casually. "You're late."

"Let her go." Wilder kept his voice level, one hand gripping Luna's shoulder. "This is between us."

"Oh, I don't think so." Sloan gestured toward a laptop on the steel desk. "See, this stopped being between us the moment you brought the cavalry."

Sloan walked over and turned the computer screen toward Wilder. Even from ten feet away, Wilder could see that it showed multiple camera angles throughout the depot complex—rail yard, loading docks, perimeter roads. The infrared images revealed heat signatures moving through the maze of freight cars.

His chest knotted, but that solid peace from God remained underneath. *You knew this would happen. Help me see the way through.* "What do you want?"

"What I've always wanted." Sloan gestured with his handgun toward the table. "To clean up the mess you made."

"I didn't kill anyone."

"Really? Remember Heidi Reid? Worked at the FBO, always asking questions?"

Wilder's gut clenched.

"Sweet girl. You two worked together, right? Are you the reason she started investigating that plane crash that killed Senator Bowie and Sheriff Tatum? Did you tell her to look into it?"

Not really—she'd already suspected her husband of something. But yes, he'd mentioned his suspicions about Pete Barrow and Sloan Sorros and . . .

His throat dried. Maybe her death *was* his fault. But again, Stormi's voice thundered in his head. *"Nothing—not even evil—can separate me from God's love. Even when my heart breaks and evil thinks it's won, God always has the last word."*

"You won't get away with this, Sloan."

"Yes. Yes, I will." He smiled. "Because I'm not the big dog in this fight."

Wilder stared at him. "You're going to broker a deal?"

"We'll have a big family reunion in Spring Creek Prison." He lifted a shoulder. "And then, when we're out . . ."

Wilder stilled. Luna's hand found his.

"Or maybe they won't have enough to pin me to anything," Sloan continued. "Amazing how evidence can disappear when the right person has an accident."

He pushed Luna behind him.

"Like a car that loses control on icy roads, especially when the brake lines have been compromised."

The words landed, but something solid remained underneath it. *You've got this, Lord. Show me what to do.* He kept his voice tight. "You can't win this. Too many agencies involved."

"Win?" Sloan's laugh bounced off the concrete walls. "Frost, I already won. The moment you walked through that door, I won."

He frowned.

"You didn't think I only wanted you, did you?"

What?

Sloan tipped his chin toward the screen. "You brought the whole family."

And right on cue—there was Stormi moving through the rail yard, her small frame distinctive even in the grainy infrared feed. His heart thundered, but underneath the spike of terror was something unshakable. *You're not alone.*

"This whole thing was never about you. You were just the predictable piece that would draw out everyone else and finish this chess game."

Show me what to do, Lord.

"The yard has some very interesting modifications that weren't in the original renovation plans." Sloan gestured around the cavernous space. "Pressure-sensitive charges in the loading dock. Explosive devices positioned throughout the rail yard." He picked up a black trigger box from the table, its red LED blinking. "One wrong move and this whole complex becomes a very large grave."

Then he reached over and turned up the volume on a radio.

Wilder caught Deke's voice. "In position at loading dock. Awaiting go signal."

"Sloan, don't."

Luna tugged on Wilder's jacket. "Daddy, I'm scared."

"It's going to be okay, baby girl." He met her eyes, put the truth in it. Yes, it would be. *You've got her, Lord. You've got all of us.* "Just stay close to me."

Through the large windows, the rail yard was engulfed in the darkness, illuminated occasionally by tall lights. Massive freight cars sat on rusted tracks. Overhead cranes hung at awkward angles, their cables swaying in the wind.

"This whole facility is a death trap waiting to happen." Sloan sat on the edge of the desk. "Amazing how winter weather and aging infrastructure can cause tragic accidents."

"The explosives will show evidence."

"Will it matter? You'll be gone. The evidence tied up in conjecture. And finally, people—the law—will think twice about tangling with the Sorros family."

The rescue teams were walking into a minefield. Wilder glanced at the door. If he could just get Luna to run, maybe . . .

"Here's what's going to happen." Sloan pulled out a satellite phone. "You're going to call Lydia Harper and recant. All of it. And that will buy you the lives of your friends." He cocked his head. "And I'll let her go."

Wilder stared at him, then down at Luna. Now Sloan was just talking nonsense. Lydia would know Wilder's confession was coerced. But desperate men did desperate things.

How he knew that.

Luna looked up at him, her eyes wide. "Daddy, can we go home now?"

"Soon, princess—"

"I want to go now!" Her eyes filled with tears. She yanked free.

"Luna!"

But she pivoted and sprinted for the door.

Out of the corner of his eye, he spotted Sloan lifting the gun. "Well." Sloan's voice carried cold amusement. "That simplifies things."

Wilder launched at him. "No!" They smashed to the concrete, and the pistol skittered across the dirty floor.

An elbow drilled into Wilder's ribs and fire exploded through him, but he didn't care. He rolled and scrambled for his feet. "Luna! Hide in the freight cars! Don't come out until you hear Stormi's voice!"

Her small form vanished into the dark rail yard.

Sloan got to his feet with the weapon, pointed it at Wilder. Finger on the trigger. "Touching. Pointless. The charges are still live. The second those teams get close to her . . ." He shook his head. "Your daughter just turned herself into bait, Frost. And there's nothing you can do to save her."

Or the woman he'd pushed away to keep her safe. The familiar darkness tried to rise, but a thrumming rose in his chest. *You're not doing this alone. Trust God. There's a way through this.*

Voices sounded on the radio—garbled words cutting through static. He couldn't make them out clearly.

But all of the people who came to help him were walking into Sloan's trap.

Lord, I need wisdom. I need to see what he doesn't want me to see. There's something here—

Sloan's mouth flattened. "Should've taken the deal, Frost." His kick found Wilder's thigh, white-hot lightning burning through the old injury.

Wilder roared, even as he rolled over, even as Sloan said, somewhere outside the roar of pain . . .

"Game over."

15

SORROS WAS GOING to kill Wilder—Stormi spotted the showdown through the open door of the warehouse. Sloan, holding a gun on Wilder.

God, please*!*

And yet, Luna was screaming, terrified and—shoot, what choice did Stormi have?

And right then, yes, she got it. Why Wilder had shoved her out of the way to do what his heart demanded. And that was the fight, right? Trusting her heart versus trusting God.

Right now, she'd do both.

"Luna, I'm coming!" She lifted her radio as she sprinted toward the rail yard. "Deke, I'm going after Luna."

"Negative. We don't know the layout—"

She pocketed the radio and hit the rail yard running. Winter air burned her lungs as she dodged between massive freight cars. Moonlight cast upon the tracks, turning them silver.

"Luna!" Her voice echoed off steel and concrete. "Where are you, sweetheart?"

"Here! I'm up here!"

The voice came from somewhere ahead and above, and Rome

barked somewhere in the distance. Stormi ran between the rail cars. "Keep talking, Luna. We're coming."

Rome, still barking.

"I'm scared! I can't get down!"

The terror in that small voice made Stormi's chest clench. Behind her, the sounds of fighting from the building had gone quiet. Either Wilder had won, or . . .

Focus. Luna first.

Stormi stopped at the base of a freight car that stretched up into shadows. "Luna?"

"I'm on top! I'm stuck!"

Her blood chilled. The freight car had to be fifteen feet high, the metal roof slick with evening frost, no railings, nothing to keep a child from sliding off.

"How'd you get up there?" Stormi asked, her neck craned back to see the little girl.

"The ladder—"

Then Stormi spotted it, a long ladder down the back, a crate fallen next to it, just tall enough for a seven-year-old to climb on and reach for the ladder.

"Okay, sweetheart, stay very still. Don't try to come down on your own."

"There's a bad man down there! He has Daddy!"

Yes. She caught her breath. "Everything is going to be okay." *Please, please, God.*

A shot sounded, ricocheted into the night, pinging through the yard.

Rio's voice came over the radio, garbled from her pocket. "Stormi, where are you?"

She couldn't answer without giving away her position.

Frost coated the ladder rungs, treacherous for climbing, but Luna had managed it somehow—probably driven by pure terror.

"Luna, I'm coming up to help you."

"Daddy said you'd find me!" Relief flooded that small voice.

Stormi didn't know what to think of that—refused to consider it might be because he knew that he wouldn't. "Stay right where you are, sweetheart."

Stormi grabbed the first rung, tested its stability. Her gloves froze to the metal, but she wrenched them free and pulled herself up, rung by rung. The rail yard spread out below.

Her radio crackled. "We're at the warehouse. It's empty."

She drew in a breath and pulled herself onto the freight car roof. Ice covered the slick surface, with the sides sloping slightly toward the edges.

But there, huddled in the center in her bright pink coat, sat Luna.

"Hey there, brave girl." Stormi kept her voice calm. "That was some impressive climbing."

"I was running from Mr. Sloan and got scared and just kept going up." Tears streaked her face, but she wasn't hysterical.

"Very brave. Can you scoot toward me? Very carefully?"

Luna started moving across the icy metal. Stormi's heart hammered against her ribs. One slip and Luna would slide right off the edge.

"That's perfect. Nice and slow."

The crack of another shot split the night air.

It pinged off the freight car. Luna screamed, slipped—

Stormi grabbed her jacket just as she started to slide. She yanked the girl to herself, pressing her body over her.

"All units, shots fired in the rail yard!" Deke, on the radio.

"Luna, we need to move. Right now."

"I'm scared!"

Stormi leaned up. "I know, but staying here isn't safe. You're going to have to be brave."

Another shot sparked off the metal roof inches from Luna. She whimpered but didn't move.

Then suddenly, Stormi heard a bark—a warning, a growl. She spotted Rome below, barking, snarling—

Then her dog launched himself at someone running hard down the tracks.

Shouts, then Rome's growls, and she looked away, wincing.

"Luna, we're going down. I need you to trust me completely."

"What if I fall?"

"You won't fall. I've got you."

Stormi held on to Luna's jacket and scooted them toward the end. "I'm going down first, then I'll help you down one rung at a time."

"What about the bad man?"

"Um . . ." She glanced into the shadows where she spotted someone who was shouting. "I think we're safe. But we still need to get off this roof."

Luna nodded. "Okay. But don't leave me."

"Never. I promised your daddy I'd keep you safe." Maybe not in words but in heart.

She slid over the edge, then helped Luna, and covered her with her body as they climbed down. Stormi's feet finally landed on the cold earth, and she pulled Luna into her arms.

And that's when she heard the yelp. She stilled, looked down the yard, and couldn't help herself. "Rome!"

Deke came over the radio. "All units, suspect has fled the immediate area. Continuing pursuit to the north perimeter."

And . . . what about Wilder . . . ?

Rome came running up, barking, pushing into Stormi's embrace.

"Rome!" Luna threw her arms around the dog's neck. "I knew you'd find me!"

What?

She bent and looked over Rome. He seemed unhurt, but a wetness on his fur had her pulling her hand away.

Blood.

She stood. *Wilder, where are you?* "Luna, we need to get you somewhere safe."

"Where's my daddy?"

Before Stormi could answer, shouts erupted from the darkness. "Stormi! Get down! The yard is wired to blow!"

Wilder's voice, raw with panic, as he half sprinted, half fell toward them. Blood smeared his face, but he was alive.

"Explosives! The whole yard!" He held out his hand to her as he ran.

She grabbed it, even as she took Luna's hand.

"Go!"

Rome sprinted ahead of them. Wilder ran as if he'd never been shot, hadn't gone round with Sloan, was exactly the man she remembered from so many years ago, fighting to survive the last leg of the Iditarod, all out, headed for safety.

So she just hung on and followed.

They had just made it past the final freight car and out of the yard when the first explosion lit up the night sky. The blast threw them to the snow, and she caught up Luna, clutched her to herself, rolled over to protect her.

And wouldn't you know it, Wilder did the same, pulling them both into his arms, his back to the explosion, cocooning them.

Another explosion, and then Luna looked up, her eyes wide. "Wow."

Stormi lifted her head. "Yeah. Wow." The warehouse plumed with fire, many of the freight cars burning, the entire yard aglow.

Wilder rolled off them and lay in the snow, breathing hard, his breath raspy. Luna launched herself at him, and he caught her, sitting up, pulling her tight.

"Thank you. Thank you." His words were muffled by her jacket, the way he pressed his face into her collar.

But the blast illuminated his expression—the fear, the relief, the fury. He looked over at Stormi.

"Sloan rigged the entire yard to blow. And he was about to shoot me when Rome just . . . showed up." He looked over at the dog. "Good boy."

"Maybe the old K9 training in him."

"Yeah, well, he attacked Sloan. I got ahold of the explosives trigger and then"—he drew in a breath—"Sloan took a shot at Rome."

"He's okay. What about you?"

"I got a kick in, but the shot nicked me." He reached over to a tear in his sleeve. "I'm so tired of getting shot by this family."

Was that a joke? Now? She gave him a look that was purposely horrified.

"I went down. Lost the trigger. And Sloan took off."

"Rome chased him down," Stormi said. "Caught him in the yard. Probably slowed him down."

"He didn't want to set off the explosives on himself. Probably waited until he got clear." He kissed Luna's forehead. "Are you okay? Are you hurt?"

"Stormi saved me! She climbed up on the train and got me down!"

Wilder's eyes found Stormi's again over Luna's head. Gratitude and something deeper flickered before he looked away. "Thank you."

Before Stormi could respond, Rome's head came up, nose working the air.

"Rome, don't you dare—"

His entire body tensed. "Rome, no!"

But he was already gone, streaking into the wilderness.

"Sloan," Wilder said grimly, passing Luna back to her. "He's tracking Sloan."

"You're not going after them." Stormi took Luna. "Wilder. You're injured, and—"

But Wilder had already stood up, a force against the moonlight. "He killed my wife. He kidnapped my daughter." Wilder's voice carried deadly calm. "And he nearly blew up the woman I love. This ends tonight."

She had nothing, his words stripping her. Love?

"Take care of Luna."

Her throat filled. "Wilder—"

"And, Stormi—pray. Pray hard."

Her mouth opened, but he took off into the darkness.

OKAY, that was a rash and impulsive decision.

But he couldn't let Sloan just . . . *disappear*, right? Not again. Not anymore.

Although it did seem that the wilderness swallowed the man whole.

Undergrowth whipped at Wilder's face as he pushed deeper into the forest beyond the rail yard. Behind him, distant shouts of Deke and Rio and the rest of the team faded into winter silence. Ahead, somewhere in the darkness, Sloan was running.

Blood from the fight had dried sticky on Wilder's face, and his injured leg sent fire into every step. But adrenaline and three years of rage kept him moving. This ended *tonight*.

He'd spent a lifetime learning how to survive in the frozen winter tundra. He could outlast and outsurvive Sloan Sorros.

Rome's prints in the snow were easy to follow—four paws cutting deep into fresh powder, lit by the glow of the yard fire. Smart, loyal, brilliant Rome.

The forest opened ahead, revealing a frozen lake stretching into shadow.

He stopped at the edge, scanning the icy surface. There—two

dark figures moving across the white expanse. Rome, sprinting toward a lone man fighting through snow toward the other side.

Sloan.

Finally.

Wilder stepped onto the ice without a pause. The surface felt solid under his boots, thick enough to support his weight. He struggled across the lake, following Rome's path.

And all Wilder could think was . . . *Help. Help me, God. Help me finish this.* And no, he wasn't going to kill the man—he had no doubt that Deke wasn't far behind. He just had to stop him.

And somehow, his leg felt stronger, the ache subsiding, the heat in his chest expanding as he hiked up his pace.

Ahead, Rome had cornered Sloan against a dense stand of cattails protruding through the ice at the lake's far edge. Probably the ice also thinned there. Or maybe Sloan had just decided to fight back because he raised his handgun, the barrel reflecting moonlight.

The crack of the gun split the winter air.

Rome yelped as he fell into the snow.

No. *No!* Heat exploded through his chest.

Another shot, this one aimed at Wilder.

The bullet sparked off ice and snow inches from his feet, sending up a spray of frozen chips.

Shouting lifted in the breeze. Deke. And Rio. Wilder looked up, searching for them and . . . no, *no*!

Stormi was running hard out of the forest, heading toward her dog.

Wilder dove sideways, rolling across the slick surface as another shot whizzed overhead.

In that second, all he heard was Stormi's voice, resounding in his head. *"We're out of options. The best thing we can do is pray."*

Yeah, okay, he got that. *Please, God! Please!*

Wilder pushed to his feet. He sprinted directly at Sloan,

moving awkwardly through the thick snow—the bullets popped up snow by his feet. The wind roared around him, working in his favor to sidetrack the shots. Ice cracked under his boots as he hit a thin section, but he kept moving.

Twenty yards. Fifteen. Ten.

Sloan braced his hands on the gun. Backed up.

More shouts, these from Deke and Rio, but Sloan had a bead on him.

"The ice!" Stormi screamed. "Wilder, the ice!"

He glanced at her, back to Sloan.

The man stood right in front of a dark pool of thin ice.

Wilder stopped his charge, backpedaling just as the ice beneath his own feet began to crack—the sound of fracture spreading across the frozen surface.

Behind him, Stormi was still moving across the lake, but she was following a completely different path, zigzagging toward her downed dog.

Doing everything to save her dog because that's who she was. Fierce. Light in his dark world, despite his attempts to keep her out.

"Sloan," Wilder called out, no longer charging, moving over to Stormi. "You're standing on thin ice!"

"Stay back," Sloan shouted.

Stormi landed next to her dog, but the animal was already up, already growling at Sloan.

"I'm serious. You need to move slowly toward—"

Sloan took another step back. "Stay where you are."

Rome launched himself from solid ground, hitting Sloan center mass. Eighty pounds of perfectly trained law enforcement canine. Sloan left his feet, and his gun went flying.

They landed with a whuff in the mess of cattails, Rome pinning Sloan, jaws locked around the man's wrist.

"Good boy, Rome," Stormi said, scrambling to her feet. "Hold!"

And that's when Deke arrived, plowing through the cattails to the tussle. Rio grabbed hold of Rome's harness. "Release."

Rome obeyed, just like that. Sat back, still growling.

"Sloan Sorros," Deke said. "You're under arrest for the murders of Dawn Frost, Heidi and Tommy Reid, and Pete Barrow."

"Keep the mutt away from me," Sloan gasped, backing away from Rome.

"Stop moving or I'll let him go," Rio said.

Sloan froze.

Deke reached Sloan and turned him over, cuffing him.

"He's a little scary," Wilder said, glancing over at Stormi, who ran up to him.

"He's a K9 professional," she said, then she walked over to Rio. She knelt and examined her dog. "He's got a flesh wound across his flank. Nothing a few stitches won't fix." She caught up his mug, met his eyes. "You're such a brave boy." She kissed his snout.

Deke and Rio hauled Sloan to his feet. *Wait—*

"Luna—" He turned to Stormi.

"She's with Vic. She came out to the train yard when they got Deke's call. Luna's fine." She gave him a grim smile. "I didn't want to leave her, but I didn't . . . well . . ."

"Rome."

She nodded, her eyes glistening. She wiped her cheek. "You two are a pair. Trouble."

Rome wagged his tail. He looked down at the dog, ruffled his head.

Deke was reading Sloan his rights as they walked to the snow machines. Rio was on the radio.

"It's over," Stormi said softly.

He stilled, the wind in the trees, the sense of it cascading through him. *Over.*

"Yeah." He turned to face her. Oh, she was beautiful. Her

brown hair escaped from her wool hat, cheeks pink from cold, eyes bright with exhaustion and relief. Beautiful and brave.

He met her gaze.

She met his.

"Thank you," he said.

"Somebody has to patch you up."

His mouth opened. "Stormi." Her name came out rough, uncertain.

"What?"

"I love you." The words escaped before he could second-guess them, stark and honest in the winter air. "I know it's complicated and probably terrible timing—"

"Wilder."

"—but I love you. And not in some protective, distant way that means I have to leave to keep you safe. I love you in the way that means I want to build a life with you."

She smiled, soft and sweet. "Are you done?"

"Am I done what?"

"Talking." She stepped closer, her hands on his jacket, eliminating the inches between them. "Because I love you too. And not in a rabid fan kind of way, but in the way that I want to be your partner. Your best friend. And maybe your mushing buddy."

"Mushing buddy?"

"Okay, that might be the fan part."

He laughed, and with it, a brilliant light encompassed his entire body, chased the darkness out of the corridors of his heart. "I'm okay with that."

Then he bent down and kissed her. Sweetly at first, but then she firmed up her hold on his jacket. He attributed her ardor to the last few hours, the fear, the adrenaline, the running . . .

The hope that lay in front of them.

She tasted of joy. Of possibility. Of a fresh start and grace.

And of the kind of love that didn't make you weak—but stronger than you could ever be alone.

Behind them, Rome barked once—approval, maybe, or just announcing that the rest of the rescue team had arrived. A chopper hovered over the scene, then set down beyond the trees in the rail yard.

Wilder pulled away, his gaze in hers. "I have to tell you something."

She raised an eyebrow.

"My leg really hurts. And I think I broke open some stitches."

A slow smile. "I know a really good doctor."

"No more vet medicine."

"Don't knock the vet medicine. It saved your life."

He looked down at her, leaning on her. "I think *you* saved my life, Stormi."

Her eyes shone. "Yeah, well, what can I say? A dead guy shows up on my doorstep, what's a girl gonna do?"

He laughed, then winced as he took a step. She put her arm around his waist.

"C'mon, Wilder Frost, you can lean on me."

And he did.

EPILOGUE

ONE MONTH AFTER Sloan's arrest, Stormi White stood outside the federal building in Juneau with Wilder, watching Rome work the crowd like the celebrity he'd become.

Celebrity K9. Who would have thought?

Three different news crews wanted interviews about "the dog who broke Alaska's biggest conspiracy," and Rome was eating up the attention. Tail wagging, head high, he posed for cameras like he'd been born for this moment.

"You ready for this?" Stormi asked Wilder.

He cleared his throat. Nodded.

"So, no."

He looked away, shrugged. "I'll be okay."

"You will." She put her hands on his suit, smoothed it. "I've been watching you prepare for weeks. Endless depositions. Evidence reviews. Going over strategy sessions with federal prosecutors until your eyes turned glassy."

"I'm fine."

"Yeah. The man who'd once preferred hiding in the wilderness to avoid human contact is about to testify in front of national media about the most personal tragedy of his life."

"When you put it that way . . ."

"You've been ready for years." She straightened his tie. "Time to finally put the Sorros boys away for good."

"Not just the Sorros boys. Thornton is implicated in the testimony." He blew out a breath. "They have him in custody, but who knows—"

"Stop." She took his hand and closed her eyes. "Lord, give us peace. Help us not to look at trouble tomorrow but at your provision today. And give Wilder presence of mind as he testifies."

She opened her eyes and looked up. He still had his head bowed, his lips moving. Then, "Amen."

She smiled at him, and he winked. "If God is for us, who can be against us."

"Exactly."

Her phone buzzed.

Jericho Bowie
Harley and I just testified about my dad's evidence against Tommy and Sloan.

"You're up."

He kept hold of her hand and led her through the building's glass doors, Rome following, the words "Working K9" on a patch on his harness.

She hated the idea of giving him up to the Copper Mountain Sheriff's Department. But he had sort of come alive, his old training kicking in, and . . .

He deserved to live the life he was trained for.

She showed Wilder the message from Jericho.

His jaw tensed. "How many victims of Tommy and Sloan's violence does that make in total?" The weight in his voice made her throat close.

"Ten confirmed murders." The number sat like lead in her chest. "Senator Bowie and Margaret. Sheriff Tatum and his wife, Cora. Mack Maverick. Pete Barrow. Heidi Reid. Dawn." She paused, throat burning. "Plus Tyler Collins, an innocent bystander. And even Tommy Reid."

The courtroom doors opened. Prosecutor Lydia Harper emerged—steel-gray hair pulled back in a bun, her expression focused and landing on Wilder.

"Mr. Frost." She extended her hand. "Ready to finish what you started so many years ago?"

"More than ready."

"How's their defense looking?" Stormi asked.

"Desperate." Lydia's smile held edges. "Sloan's team is trying to claim he had no knowledge of Reid's methods or the scope of the drug trafficking operation. Pitiful. But we're putting together a plea in exchange for his testimony against Thornton."

"And the brothers? Conan and Mars?" Wilder asked.

"The judge will rule on their actions after Sloan's trial wraps up." Lydia glanced down at Rome. "Your dog brought down one of the largest fentanyl trafficking organizations in Alaska's history."

The doors opened again. Rio stepped into the hallway wearing a suit. "Showtime." His dark eyes sparked. "And I just got word from our team down in Washington state. Thornton's shipping partners are in custody in Vancouver, and the construction company raids yielded enough evidence to expose the entire distribution network in the Lower 48."

Stormi's breath caught. She looked at Wilder.

He met her eyes. Nodded. Even smiled.

Through the courthouse windows, they could see news vans lined up like carrion birds. Satellite dishes pointed toward a pewter sky.

"Wilder, you're the star witness. Everything hinges on your testimony about the conspiracy and the murders." Lydia turned to him. "Ready?"

"Let's do this."

The packed courtroom gallery hummed with tension. Federal prosecutors. FBI agents. Families of victims who'd been waiting years for this moment.

Stormi found a seat at the end, behind the prosecution table, close enough to see Wilder's profile as he prepared to take the witness stand.

At the defense table, Sloan Sorros sat with his team, all slick suits and money.

"The prosecution calls Wilder Frost to the stand."

Stormi's chest filled as Wilder rose. No hesitation. No backward glances. Just a breath in, the smoothing of his suit, and a few steps toward the witness box.

For the next hour, Stormi watched the man she loved systematically dismantle Thornton's—and the Sorroses'—criminal empire. Wilder looked Sloan in the eye, his voice solid as he connected the man to Thornton and the massive fentanyl-trafficking conspiracy.

And he put to bed the source of the plane crash that had killed the Bowies and the Tatums.

Justice.

For the Bowie family. For the Tatum family. For the Matthews family. And so many who were touched by the horror of drugs.

Wilder stepped down from the witness stand, his gaze landing on Stormi, a small smile on his handsome face.

Oh, she loved him. And if he thought she was a fan before . . .

Two hours later, Prosecutor Lydia Harper stood on the courthouse steps and announced the news of coordinated arrests across three countries to the chaos of reporters shouting questions, families of victims crying with relief, and law enforcement coordinating the final phases of what the media was calling "Alaska's most significant organized crime takedown."

"Twenty-three arrests total," Lydia announced. "Assets

worth over fifty million dollars seized. We've disrupted the largest cross-border fentanyl-trafficking operation in Alaska's history."

Stormi pushed through the crowd, after walking Rome, looking for Wilder.

She found him near the fountain, surrounded by the Matthews family. Una and Bear had brought Luna to meet them. Dr. Caius had Rio's ear, gesticulating something with vibrant gestures while Wilder held Luna's hand.

Finally safe.

"Hey." Wilder caught sight of her pushing through the crowd, Luna bouncing with excitement in her bright blue dress. "The woman who made all this possible."

"How?" She frowned at him. "I didn't testify."

"You stitched me up. Kept me alive. And . . ." His voice lowered. "You shined a light into my dark world."

Oh. She stepped up to him. "And you, you are my hero. I love you, Wilder Frost."

His eyes darkened, his gaze in hers, then it fell to her lips.

"Miss Stormi," Luna said, tugging on her jacket with small hands that carried the sticky residue of courthouse vending machine candy, "Daddy says you're going to marry him now."

Stormi's eyes widened. *Really?*

Wilder gave her a look. "Luna! That was a secret between you and me."

He glanced at Stormi. "Sorry."

"Oh no, I'm very interested in this conversation. You can bet we'll talk about this later." Then she reached down to hug the little girl who was well on her way to becoming her daughter.

She held Luna, glanced up at Wilder, and listened to another impulse of her heart.

No, listened to the answer to a prayer she'd lifted long ago.

FOR THE FIRST TIME in three years, Wilder didn't check his rearview mirror as he pulled onto Copper Mountain's main street.

The absence of that constant vigilance left him almost dizzy.

No . . . Hopeful. Joyful. God's perfect love made him dizzy.

Applewood smoke drifted from Vic's ever-cooking barbecue, mixing with the crisp promise of spring that hung in the lengthening daylight. Through the frost-etched windows of the Midnight Sun Saloon and Grill, warm amber light spilled across the snowpacked boardwalk.

He cut the engine. Sat for a moment in the sudden quiet.

It had been a week since he walked out of that courthouse in Juneau. Three days since the words that finally put the Sorros family away for good.

The nightmare was over.

"Can we go in now? Please?" Luna bounced in her seat, the pink dress she'd insisted on wearing rustling with each movement.

"Yeah, baby girl." The words came easier than expected. "We can go in."

Luna was already unbuckling her seat belt. "Come on, Daddy, Miss Stormi's probably wondering where we are."

Stormi. Who'd found him in the storm and saved his life. Who looked at him like he was worth the trouble. So of course he'd asked her to marry him three nights ago.

She hadn't answered him yet. He tried not to read into that. It was fast. Impulsive, even.

Luna pushed open her door, cold air rushing in.

But the scent of new life hung in the air.

He got out. Luna was already running toward the entrance, dress fluttering behind her.

The door swung open before they reached it, spilling out light and warmth and the sound of voices and laughter. Stormi appeared in the doorway, a yellow sweater bringing out the beauty in her eyes, her hair down in waves around her shoulders.

"There you are. Luna, you look beautiful."

"Miss Stormi!" Luna launched herself forward, and Stormi caught her in a hug that lifted her off the ground.

And if that wasn't enough to make his heart clench, his knees buckle . . . He put a hand to his chest just to stop his heart from bursting.

"Ready for this?" Stormi asked over Luna's head, her voice pitched low.

"No." The honesty surprised him. "But I'm here."

"That's all I need." She set Luna down. "Come on. Everyone's been waiting."

The moment they crossed the threshold, it hit him—the scent of barbecue sauce, the sounds of country music playing from the jukebox.

"Well, look what the cat dragged in." Vic's voice carried across the room. The wound over her forehead had healed, just the faintest scar remaining. She emerged from behind the bar, blond hair pulled back, wearing her standard uniform of black jeans and a Midnight Sun T-shirt. "About time you showed up, Frost."

Conversations dimmed as heads turned in their direction. The old instinct flared—step backward, grab Luna, bolt for the door. Too many eyes. Too much attention.

Don't. Run.

"Luna!" Dr. Caius appeared from the corner table, arms open wide. "There's our brave girl."

Luna released Stormi's hand and ran to him, launching herself into a hug that nearly knocked the older man backward. Una reached out. "Easy there, sweetheart. Grandpa Caius is still on the mend." She pulled Luna into her arms, her face lighting up.

"Oh, sweetheart, you've grown two inches since we saw you last week." Una's voice carried the warmth that had made the Matthewses' homestead feel like home. "And this dress! You look like a princess."

"Miss Stormi helped me pick it out," Luna announced, spinning to make the skirt twirl. "She said pink was perfect for celebrations."

"She was absolutely right." Una's eyes found Wilder's across the room, and something passed between them. Understanding. Acknowledgment of how far they'd all come.

Jericho was sitting at the bar with Harley. Deke played pool with—wait, was that Dawson Mulligan? When did he get back in town?

His gaze fell on a pretty blond sitting at a high top nearby, watching the men play. A memory stirred inside him.

"Wilder, good to see you." The voice belonged to Orion, who came up, hand out. "How's the leg?"

"It's good," he said, shaking Orion's hand. "But I think maybe Jenny should lay off the field surgery."

Orion grinned and glanced behind him, toward his wife. She stood with Kennedy Bowie, who held a baby in her arms, tucked into her shoulder.

"Wow, have I been gone that long?" Wilder asked.

"Um, that's not . . . well, I think she and Sully might be adopting, but they're fostering a baby whose parents died in a crash. Apparently, there are no other relatives."

"Wait, is that the baby I found?" Stormi asked. And maybe Kennedy heard her, because she looked over at Stormi, then smiled.

Huh.

"Wilder!" Axel Mulligan pushed through the crowd. "Man, it's good to see you. How'd the testimony go?"

"It went." He accepted Axel's handshake. "Just waiting on

sentencings, but my guess is that they'll all be locked up for a long time."

"Good," Deke Starr said, coming up behind Axel. "Mack would be pleased."

"Speaking of Mack," Winter said, joining them, "I think it's time for that toast."

But before Winter could continue, Vic raised her hand, a slight smile playing at the corners of her mouth. "Actually, before we get to that, I've got something—someone—I'd like you all to meet properly." She gestured toward the blond woman, who stood slowly, a nervous smile crossing her face. "Folks, I want you to meet my daughter, Keely."

The room went quiet.

"Your daughter?" Hudson Bowie spoke up from where he was shooting darts.

Vic's smile softened. "My biological daughter, who I gave up for adoption twenty-eight years ago. Some of you know her by another name—Bliss. But to me, she's just Keely."

Pieces clicked into place. The woman from the plane—the one who'd been so scared, so out of place in the wilderness, but who'd fought alongside them anyway. She was Vic's daughter.

"Well, howdy," Malachi Bowie said from the bar. "Vic has herself a famous daughter."

Laughter and then Winter said, "Hey, Keely! Sing us a song!"

Keely glanced at her mother, and it was sweet, like this moment here was something between them. She moved toward the small stage area where a guitar waited. "My voice isn't what it used to be," she said, her words carrying a husky quality, "but I'll give you my newest single."

She settled onto the stool, guitar cradled against her chest, and began picking out a melody. When she started singing, her voice was rough around the edges but filled with something sweet. Almost a rawness. An authenticity.

And when the years have passed, and we look back to
see,
Every step, every dream, you were right there with me.
In your eyes, I still find the place where I belong,
In our world full of love, your voice is my song.

Wilder couldn't help but look at Stormi. Who picked right then to meet his gaze.

She was light and home and, yes, the bright future ahead of him. *Please, God, make her say yes.* Selfish, he knew, but why not pray?

As the last notes faded, the room erupted in applause. Winter waited for it to die down, then climbed onto a chair.

"For those who don't know me, I'm Winter Starr—I fly for Starr Air Service. A month and a half ago, Dawson found a crashed plane while flying north to Copper Mountain with Moose." Her voice carried the authority of someone used to speaking over airplane engines. "We lost someone that day. Cade Maverick was one of the finest pilots I ever knew, and he died a hero. Stabbed and bleeding out, he still managed to land that plane safely. Then he fought Conan Sorros with his dying breath so others could escape."

The room had gone completely quiet now, even Luna was still in Una's arms.

"But tonight isn't just about mourning the lost. It's about celebrating the found." Winter's eyes found Wilder's across the room. "Wilder Frost, you've been through darkness and came out the other side, still fighting for what matters. Luna, you're proof that hope grows strongest in the hardest ground. Keely, welcome to Copper Mountain. I hope this means we'll get to see more of Dawson."

Wilder turned to her. The woman had settled into Dawson's arms, so wasn't that interesting.

"And Jericho and Harley. We never thought we'd see the day . . ." She grinned. "You two have made us all believe in second chances and true love."

Wilder glanced at the couple. Jericho had put his hand over Harley's and wore a strange smile.

"And everyone in this room"—Winter gestured broadly—"we've all learned that family isn't just blood. Sometimes it's the people wild enough to walk into danger because someone they care about needs them to."

She raised a bottle of root beer. "To Mack, who brought them home. To second chances. And to the kind of love that's stronger than fear."

"To Mack," the room echoed, voices joining in a chorus that sent warmth spreading through Wilder's chest.

"To Mack," he whispered, the words barely audible.

Conversations resumed, but even as he watched, Jericho's dog, Orlando, lifted his head from where he lay near another dog, ears pricked. He got up and barked.

"Jericho, what's your dog doing?" Harley asked, clearly seeing it too.

Jericho had gotten up, face flushed and hands fidgeting with something in his pocket. It fell out and dropped to the floor.

Orlando pounced on it, grabbed it up.

"Orlando, no. Not now." Jericho crouched in front of him, his voice low. "Drop it."

But Orlando dropped his cargo directly at Harley's feet with a proud tail wag.

The small velvet box landed with a soft thud.

Silence.

Harley stared down at the box, then up at Jericho.

He appeared a little stricken. "Is that . . . ?"

"It wasn't supposed to happen like this." Jericho ran both

hands through his hair. "I had a speech. I practiced it. There were supposed to be candles and . . . and privacy and . . ."

"Jericho Bowie." Harley cocked her head. "Are you asking me to marry you?"

Orlando sat, looking up at both of them.

Stormi slipped her hand into Wilder's.

"Yeah." The word came out as barely more than a whisper. Then, louder, with growing confidence. "Yes. I'm asking you to marry me, Harley Tatum. I'm asking you to let me love you for the rest of my life, and I'm asking you to maybe not kill me for letting my dog steal my thunder and slobber all over your ring." He looked at Orlando and glared.

Orlando lifted a paw.

And Harley laughed. Oh, wow, even Wilder wanted to cringe.

"Jericho Bowie. Get on one knee and do it right." This from Vic.

A beat. Then Jericho dropped to his knee, reaching for the box. "Harley, I know I'm doing this all wrong, but—"

"Yes."

"What?"

"Yes, I'll marry you." She grabbed the front of his shirt and hauled him up for a kiss that sent the entire room into cheers.

And it hit him. Dawn would want this—would want him standing in a room full of people who cared about them, would want Luna surrounded by love, would want him to choose hope over fear.

"You okay?" Stormi's voice was soft beside him.

"Yeah." The answer surprised him. "I think I am."

He looked at Luna, who was leaning against his leg. "Want to head home?" The word slipped out before he could catch it. *Home.* Stormi's place, where they'd been staying while he figured out where to rebuild.

But Luna was already shaking her head. "Can we stay a little longer? I want to hear Keely sing more songs."

"A few more minutes." He lifted her into his arms. She nestled against his shoulder.

"Come on." Stormi tugged gently on his free hand. "I want to show you something."

She led him toward the side door, past the bar where Vic was holding court with a story that involved dramatic gestures and something about Harley and Jericho once upon a time. The night air hit them as they stepped outside.

Above them, the aurora borealis painted the sky in ribbons of green and purple and gold, dancing across the darkness.

"Look at that." Stormi tilted her face up toward the lights.

But he was looking at her—the way the northern lights caught in her hair, the peaceful expression on her face, the way she fit perfectly under his arm when he pulled her close.

"My dad used to say the aurora was evidence of grace," he found himself saying. "He said it was proof that even in the darkest nights, there was still beauty. Still light."

"Smart man."

Stormi turned in his arms, studying his face.

"I love you, Stormi White. And I'd really appreciate it if you'd answer my question."

She grinned, something soft and sweet. Luna had her arms around his neck but now lifted her head.

"Yes. I'll marry you. I didn't want to steal Jericho's thunder, but . . . yeah." Stormi put her hand on Luna's head. "If Luna is okay with that."

Luna nodded. "Maybe you could be my new mommy."

"Sorry it took me so long. I just . . . I didn't want to jump into anything. I needed time to pray about it and . . . well, of course the answer is yes."

Oh. For a moment, he couldn't breathe. Then he cupped

Stormi's face in his free hand, thumb tracing the line of her cheekbone. "I love you, Stormi. Not just because you saved us but because of who you are. Because you are a healer. You see broken things and believe they can be whole again."

"I love you too," she said. "All of you. The careful parts and the reckless parts and the parts that think loving people is dangerous."

"It is dangerous."

"Yeah, I know. I'll take good care of you."

He laughed and kissed her then, soft and sure with Luna drowsing in his arms and the sound of laughter spilling from behind them. This was what Dawn would have wanted—not for him to stop loving but for him to love bigger, broader, with the kind of faith that believed good things could last.

When they broke apart, Stormi was smiling. "Ready to go home?"

Home. The word no longer felt foreign.

"Yeah. Let's go home."

Outside in the truck, Luna buckled safely in the back seat and already dozing off again, Stormi reached across the center console to take Wilder's hand.

He followed the ribbons of light dancing in the night sky all the way into his future.

1

BY THE TIME Dodge got to the hospital, he'd already broken his first promise.

It was a Saturday, the same day the sun turned the Copper River into blades of ice, lethal and brilliant as they shoved and jockeyed out of Denali's shadow south into the Gulf of Alaska. The dawn had broken at the respectable hour of 7:42 a.m., and with it, the sunrise not only brought a southernly gust of warm air that cracked the freezing point and turned the starting line of the Iditarod to mush and grime but also laced the air with the scent of spring.

A balmy 37 degrees in Anchorage, nearly a heat wave this time of year.

Which only brought out the crazies.

As he stalked through the waiting room of Alaska Regional and punched the elevator button, Dodge shot a look at the flat-screen where the news recapped yesterday's celebration, aka the parade through Anchorage of the fifty-seven or so mushing teams. People dancing on icy berms, high-fiving the mushers, tailgaters wearing board shorts along with fur caps and mukluks, children wanting to pet the dogs. Outsiders from the Lower 48 were trying to grab selfies with local celebrities.

The mushers would be starting on their thousand-mile journey from Willow Lake later today, and with that information from the reporter, Echo Yazzie slipped into Dodge's mind.

He wondered—

No. He shook her away, got on the elevator, and rode it to the third, med-surg floor. As he got off, he recognized the smells of a hospital, not that different from Walter Reed, and his insides clenched.

He wouldn't stay long.

Of course, the old man hadn't died in the accident, and maybe that was crass of Dodge, but if he had, maybe it would all be over, the burn in Dodge's gut finally extinguished.

He spotted his sister, Larke, standing at the end of the hall, staring through the window at the blue sky, the muddy streets. She stood with her back to him, so he only guessed it was Larke, her long blond hair in a singular braid down her back. But she also wore a Sky King Ranch flight jacket, the words emblazoned on the back, so that seemed a dead giveaway.

A man sat in a nearby molded chair, his hair cut military short. He considered Larke with worried eyes.

Probably Riley McCord, her SEAL husband. *Perfect.* With Dodge's luck, his brother Range and Riley would have met on some classified SEAL mission, become best of pals, and Riley would have gotten an earful of family dirty laundry over a post-mission debriefing.

Dodge, of course, starring as the villain of the story.

He braced himself. "Larke?"

She turned, and of course she looked older—the last time he'd seen her she'd been eighteen and joining the Army.

And he'd been sixteen and just stupid enough to think that he had his life buttoned up.

"Dodge?" She wore trauma in her eyes, probably fatigue and worry, but also residue from the years she'd served as a medic. Still, he wondered if she had been the one to find the wreckage of their father's DHC-3 Otter bush plane. His friend Moose had been sketchy on that part when he'd called to tell Dodge about the accident.

Glancing at the man in the chair, who rose, Larke put her coffee on the ledge of the window. "Wow. I didn't think . . . I mean . . . how did you find out?"

Dodge wished she'd finished her first thought. She didn't think . . . *what?* That he cared about the old man? That he'd ever return? That he didn't think about his choices nearly every day, especially recently?

"Moose Mulligan, down at Air One Rescue," Dodge answered.

Larke wore a pair of jeans, Sorels, and a wedding ring on her left hand, but he knew that, too, thanks to the *Copper Mountain Good News*'s online portal.

He just kept his subscription for the obits. And maybe the police report. Really. The fact that it listed her engagement to a Navy SEAL a couple years ago was just a bonus line item.

"Have you been in Anchorage all this time?" She seemed to be working her words, trying not to accuse.

He felt it anyway.

"How'd it happen?" He glanced at the other man—Riley—now standing. Big enough, built like a linebacker, he stepped close to Larke and put his arm around her.

Dodge met his eyes even as Larke spoke.

"Otto Smith saw him go down and called it in. Dad was low, coming in for a landing at the Copper Mountain airfield, and his wing clipped a tree. Otto wasn't sure but he thought the wing might have detached before it hit."

"A faulty wing attachment?" His gaze went back to Larke, having found some solid ground in his silent face-off with Riley.

Riley loved her—he would protect her, and Dodge appreciated that. Larke might be two years older than him, but she was still his sister.

"It's the only way we can figure it." Her gaze flitted toward the closed door that Dodge guessed was the old man's room. "He's been flying for forty-nine years. He doesn't make mistakes."

"It doesn't have to be a pilot error for accidents to happen, Larke. Weather. A wind gust. Anything can happen in the bush."

Her jaw clenched and her husband tightened his grip on her. He finally held out his hand to Dodge. "Riley McCord."

Dodge met it. "Dodge Kingston. When did you two finally hitch up?"

"Before my first tour," he said. "About a year ago."

Dodge didn't ask if he knew Ranger, figured it would come up if it needed to. "Congrats. Sorry I wasn't there."

"We eloped," Larke said. "You and the boys were too hard to track down, and Dad already gave his blessing, so . . ."

She was being kind with her words. Truth was, he hadn't a clue where Ranger, and especially Colt, had landed on the globe. And he didn't ask. Just because they were triplets didn't mean they were close. At least, not anymore.

"How bad is it?" He gestured with his head toward door number one.

"Dislocated shoulder, broken arm, a couple cracked ribs. One of them nicked his lung, though, and it collapsed. Moose and a team from Air One Rescue flew in to the crash site. Took them forever, but they did save his life." She frowned. "But you know that. What, are you flying for them now?"

Dodge wrapped a hand around the back of his neck. Not really. Maybe. "Moose has my number and he called me."

He left out the part where he'd gotten on a plane in DC and flown eight-plus hours before he'd let his brain kick in.

It wasn't like his father wanted him around. Or like Dodge

would swoop in and save the ranch, walk back into the life he'd longed for once upon a time.

Pick up where he left off with the girl he left behind.

Clearly, he needed a shower, breakfast, and coffee—although he'd given up the last one during his stint in Walter Reed, so maybe just tea. He'd promised his docs to keep his heart rate at a reasonable tick going forward.

Still, maybe he needed to offer Larke something of an explanation because she just looked at him, through him, clearly not believing him. But if he kept going with his explanation there'd be more judgment, questions, and who knew what else. He might even end up doing something he swore he'd never do.

Like return home.

Nope. His stupid impulses had done enough damage. "How long are you in town?"

"We've been here about ten days. Riley has about a week left on leave." She wrapped her arms around herself. "I should have gone with Dad."

"Larke," Riley said quietly, "he's been flying by himself for years."

Maybe he didn't mean the indictment, but Dodge's chest tightened anyway.

She glanced at Riley. "What? I know what I'm doing up there."

A muscle ticked in Riley's jaw.

Behind them, the door opened, and Dodge turned just as a doctor in her midforties walked out. She seemed no-nonsense, with short brown hair, seasoned eyes, and a lean frame. She wore a jacket over a pair of scrubs and held out her hand to Larke.

"I'm Doctor Madison. I operated on your father. He's going to be pretty sore, and we're going to keep him here for another day or two, but he's a tough one. He'll be okay."

Dodge's throat thickened with her words.

"Thanks, Doc," Larke said for them both. "Can we see him?"

Doc Madison nodded, and Larke headed for the door.

Dodge didn't move.

Larke stopped, turned. "Really?"

"It's been ten years, Larke. I know you weren't around, but . . . it was bad. He doesn't want to see me."

Her mouth tightened around the edges. "Don't be stupid. You're here. Come in with me."

He held up his hand. "He's wounded. Maybe now's not the time to—"

"See his oldest son? Confirm that you're not dead in some Taliban-occupied valley in Afghanistan? Yeah, you're probably right. He wouldn't want to know that you're okay and standing in the hallway afraid to walk in and say hi to your father."

Oh, she could light him up. He clenched his jaw.

Riley looked away and shoved his hands in his pockets.

"What are you afraid of, Dodge?"

"I'm not afraid, Larke."

She met his gaze, and in hers he saw a woman who'd been through her own trauma and survived. So not the girl who needed to be protected, not anymore.

Fine. "I left for a reason, and that reason hasn't changed."

"Hasn't it?"

A beat passed, and he still didn't move.

She opened the door and went inside.

Riley gave him a thin-lipped smile and followed.

Dodge walked to the end of the hallway and stared out the window.

With the break in the freeze, blackened snowdrifts edged the parking lot, muddy with thawing rivers of ice. Cars splashed mud, and ice floated in the Knik Arm waterway. The view looked out over Merrill Airfield and the hundred or so parked Beavers, Otters, Cessnas, and Piper Cubs that roamed the skies, then extended past the airfield to Joint Base Elmendorf–Richardson, to the north. Beyond it, the ridge back of the Alaskan range razored across the sun-soaked blue sky, bold and white and impressive. Denali and Huntington, Foraker and Russell, were tucked in there, each glacial runnel and granite ridge imprinted in him like the lines of his palm.

The mountains called to him like an old familiar song, a tune embedded in his bones.

One he was trying to forget.

Though he couldn't see it from here, Sky King Ranch was nestled in the foothills of the range, perched on a lake that hosted cabins and a lodge for the family.

They also ran thirty or so head of cattle and a handful of horses.

Barry Kingston, his father, was one of few remaining born and bred Alaskans in Copper Mountain. And his sons were supposed to carry on the legacy.

Dodge crossed his arms, glued there because, of course, Larke was right.

He *was* afraid. Afraid of the memories that still broke free sometimes. And most of all, afraid of the words that he longed to hear and never would.

He should leave. He'd made himself promises, and he'd already broken the first one by standing in this corridor. Yes, stupid impulses.

"Oh, thank God, Dodge, you're here."

The voice jolted him, made him turn.

Winter Starr. Daughter of the legendary bush pilot Sheldon Starr. Her family ran Starr Air Service, northwest of Copper Mountain. She wore her dark hair in two long braids and had on a pair of boots and a Starr Air sweatshirt. She probably ran her own plane by now.

He had no words when she walked right up to him and pulled him down in a hug. "I'm so sorry about your dad."

She'd beat him out for valedictorian by a half point and that had intrigued, if not irked, him enough to like her. But she'd also been Echo's best friend, so that was as far as his interest went.

"Thanks."

She let him go. "I was coming up to talk to Larke, but I'm so glad you're here. We can divvy up his charters, but I can't do his mail route, Dodge. I just can't."

He raised an eyebrow.

"I've already got the mail run to Paxton, plus every homestead east of the Copper River, and if I add the western mail, that fills me right up."

"You're running the mail?"

"And medical and groceries for most of the east side north of Susitna. Your dad has the western run, over the range, to Nikolai and Stony River, and even out to Russian Mission."

Of course he did. An area that would probably keep him in the air for days.

"He also checks in on the homesteads in the area—he's got a schedule."

"I know it." He'd flown that route more times than he could count.

She cut her voice down. "They're talking pilot error."

"No. Otto Smith said his wing was coming off."

"Ernie Wright just did a hundred-hour inspection on the plane. It was cleared." She sighed. "I don't know how much you know, but your dad has had a few close calls lately. Nearly clipped another plane in the Copper Mountain airfield during taxi, and I heard he spooked a recent group by flying too close to one of Huntington Mountain's spires."

"Aw, that's just Barry Kingston showing off."

"The National Air Transportation Board is coming in to do an investigation, and depending on what they find, he could be shut down. At the very least, he can't fly, not for a while, right?" She gestured to his room.

"Larke is here. She knows the routes—"

"In her condition? I'm surprised that Riley let her get in a plane with me to fly them down."

Condition? So that's what the look between them was about.

Winter's expression portrayed concern. "I get it—high-risk pregnancy and all that, but he's a little overprotective, if you ask me. But that's a SEAL for you." Her voice turned sweet. "Where've you been, anyway? Someone said Air Force."

"Something like that."

"Afghanistan?"

"Sometimes."

"I heard your brothers are big-shot military guys too. Ranger made the SEALs."

Dodge nodded.

"And Colt, some sort of special forces in the Army?"

Delta Force, according to Ranger. Dodge lifted a shoulder.

"All a bunch of overachieving heroes, aren't you?" Her eyes shone, maybe a little of their untried past in them. "Glad you're back."

"I'm not back," he said, the words just slipping out.

Winter frowned.

And what was he going to say? That not only had he vowed to never return to Sky King Ranch but he wasn't keen on getting in the cockpit again either?

He shouldn't be here, for so many reasons. But Winter was the last person who should know that. Mostly because if Winter knew, then her sister Shasta knew . . . and if Shasta knew, well it wouldn't take long for the entire town to buzz with the news.

So he found a benign smile. "Never mind. Good to see you, Winter."

"Your dad keeps that yellow Piper 14 you used to fly tuned up.

I saw him out in it a few weeks back. You flew that thing like it was a part of you. Like you had wings."

He'd forgotten that. But yes, she was right. Once upon a time, the sky felt like home. Maybe it would again—he just had to get back on the proverbial horse-slash-cockpit.

Or not.

"Well, like I said, I'm glad you're back." She looked at him, paused. Then, "She will be too."

His smile faded. "I didn't ask."

"Sure you did." She winked and walked away, and his heart slammed like a fist in his chest.

"She will be too."

The door to the room opened and Riley stepped out. "Going for more coffee. Your dad is still sleeping. Larke didn't get much sleep last night."

He didn't move down the hall, however, and again Dodge braced himself.

"Listen," Riley said. "I don't know what went down, and she doesn't talk about it, but she can't stay, Dodge." He took a breath, looked past Dodge to the window, his mouth tightening. "She lost our first baby about six months ago, so this one is higher risk. I can't have her up there, doing . . . well, I'm well aware of the perils of being a bush pilot." He shook his head. "We met the summer of the Copper Mountain fire. The one that took out your grandparents' house. She was a daredevil, even then. I can't—"

Dodge held up his hand. "Stop. I get it."

Riley turned his gaze on him. "Get this, then. If you don't fly, he loses his contracts. And if he loses his contracts—"

"He could lose the ranch. I can do the math, Riley. Once upon a time, I was planning on taking over Sky King Ranch."

Silence fell between them.

"You weren't planning on going home, were you?" Riley asked.

Maybe the guy was an interrogator, but Dodge had no secrets, not really.

The entire town knew why he'd left. He shook his head.

"Why are you in town?" Riley asked.

What could it hurt? "I have a job offer with Air One Rescue flying choppers." He'd been sitting on his answer for a while now, not sure of the wisdom of saying yes to a job that might be doomed, but what else could he do?

His answer seemed made when Moose called him.

"I see. So nearby, but not all the way home." Riley raised an eyebrow.

"You should stop right there, because you don't know anything about it."

"I know that I wish, with everything inside me, that I had a second chance to show my pop that I turned out okay. That I finally became the person he knew I could be."

"My father couldn't care less how I turned out." And that came out exactly as bitter as it felt in his chest.

"He has your picture on his mantel," Riley said.

"He probably has my brothers' pictures up there too."

Riley nodded slowly.

Dodge drew in a breath. Managed not to put his fist in the wall. Instead, he sighed and said, "Okay, here's the bottom line. Nothing has changed since the day I walked into the recruiter's office and enlisted. I'm not back. I'll fly his routes until he can take over, but you tell Larke not to mistake any of this for a happy ending. There's no sunrise of hope here." He glanced out the window at the slush and rivers of melting snow. "This winter isn't over, and everyone should just calm down. We have at least one more deadly blizzard ahead of us."

Riley gave a slow nod. "Okay. So how do you like your coffee?"

Dodge looked at him. Right. So much for promises. "Black and bracing."

DEAR READER,

Thank you for reading *Trail of the Brave*—and for walking the entire Call of the Wild series with me! I so enjoyed writing this story of Stormi, the quietly competent vet who believes she has to be everything to everyone to earn her place, and Wilder, the grieving musher who is convinced his love is a curse and isolation is the only way to keep the people he loves safe. And of course, Rome—the "failed" sled dog who wasn't failing at all. He was simply being called to a different purpose than the one she tried to force on him!

I saw more of myself in Stormi and Wilder than I expected as I wrote their story. Don't we all wrestle with the lie that if we just try harder, do more, stay in control, we can keep the people we love safe—and earn our place while we're at it? This book became an exploration of what happens when the very walls we build to protect ourselves become the thing that keeps us from the life God has for us. Peace doesn't come from doing everything, and it doesn't come from holding the world at arm's length. It comes from surrender. From trusting that God sees us, knows our true shape, and has a specific calling on each of our lives that no one else can fulfill.

That's what Wilder finally learns beneath the aurora—that running didn't save anyone, and that God doesn't lead us *around* our storms but *through* them. And Stormi discovers that her worth was never tied to her reputation or her achievements. She finds peace not in being everything to everyone, but in being exactly who God made her to be. Sometimes that means saying a beautiful "yes" to her calling, and a brave "no" to a hundred other good things.

I especially loved writing Rome—the dog everyone had written off, finally trusted to do the very thing he was created for. Isn't that just like our Father? He sees the true shape of our gifts even when we can't. And he gives us people—flawed, brave, surprising people—to walk alongside us when we finally find the courage to stop running alone.

From the beginning, the whole Call of the Wild series has been built around the old hymn "Blessed Assurance." In *Track of Courage*, we watched Keely discover her *identity*—that she was an heir of salvation, purchased by God, wanted and chosen not because of what she could do, but simply because she was his. In *Scent of Hope*, Harley and Jericho learned what it means to live in *relationship* with the God who guides us through our darkest nights. And here, in *Trail of the Brave*, Stormi and Wilder find *peace*—the peace of perfect submission, of letting go, of discovering that God is with us even in the wilderness. "*This is my story, this is my song, praising my Savior all the day long.*" That has been my prayer for each of these books—that through the experiences of these characters, you'd catch a glimpse of the God who paints auroras across the dark sky simply to remind us he is still there. He is with us in our storms. He doesn't leave us without resources—or without each other.

Though the Call of the Wild series wraps with this book, the adventure is far from over! Keep your eyes open for a brand-new series headed your way featuring the Starr family, the incomparable Bowie brothers, and the big-hearted Matthews clan. Alaska has so many more stories to tell, and I can't wait to share them with you.

My deepest thanks to the incredible team who pours into

these stories alongside me. To my sweet husband, who has patiently fielded questions like, "How infected would a bullet wound get after three days in the bush?" and "Could a vet really do emergency surgery by lamplight during an ice storm?" (Apparently yes!) Thank you for never blinking. To my writing partner, Rachel Hauck, who helps me untangle the spiritual threads and gently pulls me back to truth when I lose my way in the weeds—I love our Saturday mornings! To my remarkable VA, Rel Mollet, whose eagle eye and honest feedback make every book stronger, and who loves these characters almost as much as I do. To my editorial assistant, Sarah Erredge, who keeps all the wheels turning behind the scenes so I can stay in the story—you are a gift. To the wonderful team at Revell, especially Andrea Doering, whose wisdom shapes every book, and Karen Steele and the marketing team, whose tireless work puts these stories into readers' hands. And to Robin VanderWall, my amazing line editor, whose keen eye catches the things I miss and whose careful work polishes every page—thank you for making these stories shine. I love working with you all.

And finally—to you, my readers. Thank you for trusting me with your story time, for cheering these characters on, and for walking this whole wilderness with me. You make every story possible.

See you in the next adventure!

Susie May

Susan May Warren is the *USA Today* bestselling author of over 100 novels with more than 1.5 million books sold, including the Global Search and Rescue and Montana Rescue series. Winner of a RITA Award and multiple Christy and Carol Awards, as well as the HOLT Medallion and numerous Readers' Choice Awards, Susan makes her home in Florida. Visit her at SusanMayWarren.com.

Connect with

Susan May Warren

Visit her website and sign up for her newsletter to get a free novella, hot news, contests, sales, and sneak peeks!

SusanMayWarren.com

SusanMayWarrenFiction   SusanMayWarren